CW01261963

LONDONIA

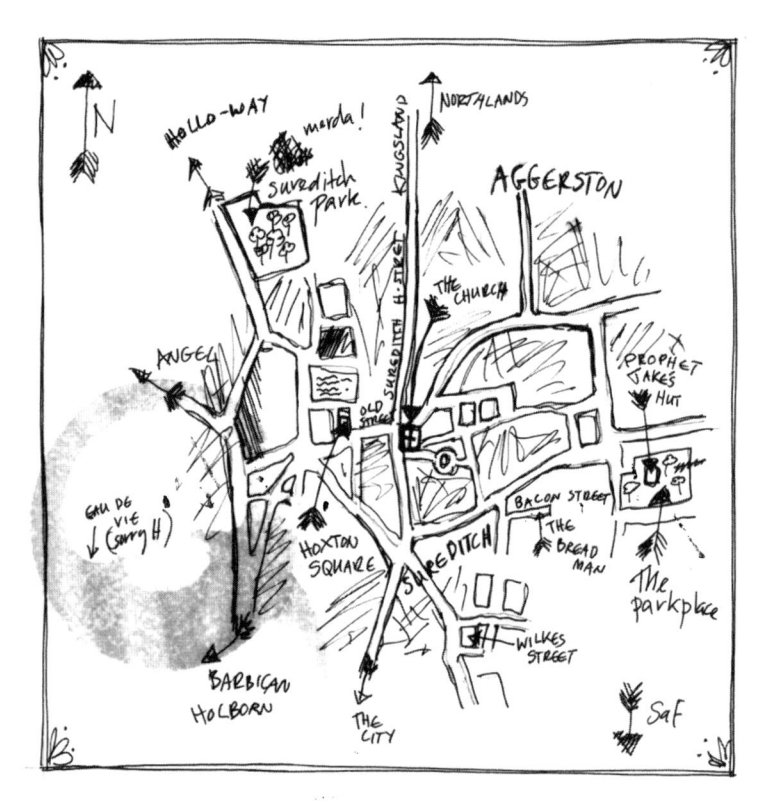

Rough map of Sureditch
Created by Spike the route-master and Jarvis
(during a night of drinking plum eau de vie)

LONDONIA

KATE A. HARDY

Kate A. Hardy

Tartarus Press

Londonia
by Kate A. Hardy
First published 2020 at Coverley House, Carlton-in-Coverdale,
Leyburn, North Yorkshire, DL8 4AY, UK

Londonia © Kate A. Hardy, 2020
Cover art © Karl Fitzgerald, 2020

ISBN 978-1-912586-19-6

Author's acknowledgments:
Many thanks to all my readers who have encouraged me
since the very first draft, and special thanks to Bob
for his goodly editing help.

The publishers would like to thank Karl Fitzgerald
(karlfitzgeraldart.com), and Jim Rockhill
for their help in the preparation of this book.

Principle places featured in this tale.
Londonia (also called the Pan)
Cincture (hyper-centre of old London Town, also called the Egg)

Important terms
wwW - the great collapse, also casually known as The Final Curtain
Unknown time/Un-time, following wwW

For a glossary of possibly unfamiliar words,
see pages 397-399

Dedication:
To my brother, Adrian

Smoke lowering down from chimney-pots, making a soft black drizzle, with flakes of soot in it as big as full-grown snow-flakes—gone into mourning, one might imagine, for the death of the sun. Dogs, undistinguishable in mire. Horses, scarcely better; splashed to their very blinkers.
Bleak House, Charles Dickens

Ouverture

Londonia
dark-quarter 2070

'Oi! Second floor. Is Tom Ov-Brixton in there?'

Tom takes a drag on the clay pipe and squints at me through the smoke. '*Scrote*. That's my hitch—gotta get to the Forrist before darking.' He abandons the pipe, rolls on top of me and kisses my forehead. 'Beauteous, you are.'

I trace a finger over his lips. 'You too.'

As we gaze at each other a brassy note sounds in the street, followed by the same voice, now more insistent. Tom leaves the bed and starts stuffing things into his kitbag.

'*Merda*! Can't find my wrist-clock.'

I hold the weathered disc out to him as he hops about, one leg trousered, the other a naked white streak in this dim room. 'Here—it was under your felty.'

He pulls on the rest of his jeans, yanks the belt's teeth into a well-used notch and takes the timepiece from me.

'Wouldn't want to go without that.'

'What's the point of wearing it?'

'Hands still move, don't they? Useful for calculating how much worktime's been done—a clockface, two, three . . . anylane, it was Dad's. Not worth nothing but it's a . . .'

'Mascot? Talisman?'

'Where d'you come from, wordsmith dame?' He grins at me, face still rosy after the activity that has made this bed so warm. I risk the icy chill, slip out from the covers and scoot to the window, a blanket about me. A makeshift carriage waits outside

LONDONIA

fronted by two horses, their breath pluming white. A man sitting behind them looks up at this window, waves his arms in a gesture of frustration and yells.

'I foitling *said, is* Tom Ov-Brixton in there?'

Heaving up the sash I call down. 'Just coming.'

Tom snorts a laugh, shoves the last item into his bag and envelops me, blanket and all into a hug.

'Sorry, I gotta go, and so sorry you can't stay here.'

I kiss his now-anxious face. 'It's fine. I'm ready to explore this . . . Londonia—find my way.'

'D'accord. They'll be here soon-time. Tell 'em thanks for the loan of the room.'

'I will.'

'Can't xacly take your address, can I?'

'Not until I get one.'

He smiles sadly. 'Write me, p'raps. Ov-Brixton, Hepping-forrist—might find me. There's a horse-letter-mec what goes in that direction—from Bethy-green.'

The brassy note shrills again and I look out to see the now furious-looking man, trumpet in hand.

'Pizzin' *come on*—got three more to pick up and Clasher territory t'get through.'

Tom shouts out a response, hugs me tight once more then he's gone, footsteps clattering on the stairs.

I consider the vast everything and nothing before me. I should perhaps layer-up and get out there to pace the streets and find . . . the next piece of this life, but the bed beckons again even with its biting population. The people that own these two rooms will return when the sun is directly overhead but as the sky is once again a sullen mass of cloud, it'll be impossible to anticipate their arrival. Tom said the merde-mec always passes late morning with his cart of shit-filled buckets, so I'll wait until then.

The bed is still warm. I burrow down into the crackling straw and sweet-stale wool covers; curl, foetus-like, try to remember—

anything from before these last few days of his kindness. A limpid blankness stares back at my mind's eye before somnolence fills my conscience.

A rattling sound from the street disturbs my slumber. Merdemec? His call affirms.

'Bring out yer merde, an' scraps. Egg for a pail.'

Least I can do for the owners of this place. Hopping out from the covers I cram on shoes and coat and go into the tiny kitchen. The bucket of peelings is full, the *other* vessel, about half, judging by its weight—no desire to lift the lid . . . I take them and join the other residents walking down the stairs with their own various wastes. The conversation is of never-ending cold, a possible arrival of some charitable and benevolent outfit and *scooptrucks*. As we reach the downstairs hall, I ask a man in front of me what these are. He looks at me beneath impressive eyebrows as if I am from a different planet—which I could be.

'Just don't be out on the street if you hear a sound like this.' He emits a wailing cry to which another resident prods him— 'Nah—more like this.' The hallway is filled with eerie moans until an old woman clangs her pail with a walking stick.

'Foitlin' shut it! Don't we fear it enough wivout you lot doin' a re-run.'

The crowd mutter apologies and the door opens to let a wave of freezing air into this slightly warmer interior. Outside, each person gives over their buckets and pots, the shit dropped into one of the larger pails, their vessels swooshed out with a watering can of water, scraps into another pail and eggs duly handed over.

The man hauling the buckets steps back at the sight of me, a half-grin on his beardy face.

'Yer not on my rounds—not be takin' advantage of the system now would yer?'

I gesture towards the house. 'I'm staying here—waiting for the owners to return.'

'So, whose crud's in de bucket, then? Yers?'

LONDONIA

'. . . Mine and someone called Tom, who was using the place . . .'

His stare softens at my obvious confusion over the *system*.

'Don't be worry'n now. Tek de yeggs and just make sure dey com t' the marsh-permafarm to do der quota.' I nod, smile with relief and take the two eggs he's handing me. His fingers trail on my skin for an instant, his smile broadening. 'If yer ever lonely fer company . . . McMurphy's de name—two, Curtain road.'

I nod, a smile surfacing at his cheek then walk back upstairs, the buckets clanging, two smooth oval shapes in my coat pocket.

Heaving the bedding off, I drape it over the windowsill for an airing, clear the ashes from the fireplace and prepare to leave this small sanctuary. Part of a loaf and hunk of cheese still sit in an earthenware pot. I make a sandwich, place the eggs on a saucer and wait, eyes scanning a book Tom had found. The words are poetic but my mind drifts away from the pages to thoughts of today and beyond today. The creak of the front door announces the arrival of someone; perhaps, the flat's owners. Argumentative voices and clumping footsteps become louder, then a rapping at the door.

'Tom? C'est nous.'

I jump up from the armchair, open the door and discover I can speak French, albeit rusty.

'Il est . . . parti.'

I explain briefly that I had stayed with him and had agreed to wait so no one would take the flat, to which the man says they have been robbed and are exhausted. The woman is hauling the bedding back in, obviously preparing to become comatose as quickly as possible. No kindly offer of chat and tea then. . . . I add a jumper Tom had given me to my clothing, haul on the coat and walk to the door.

The man turns from unpacking a knapsack.

'Sorry to 'ave been brusque, et merci . . .' He passes me a small paper bag of apples. I pocket them and briefly shake his hand.

LONDONIA

'Pas problem.'

As I reach the door, he calls out. 'Where a' you from, mademoiselle?'

I stop, a hand on the latch. '. . . I don't know.'

He smiles uncertainly. 'Fait attention—ze streets hold bad people, vous savez?'

My shoes click on the stairs, down the tiled hallway and then I'm outside thinking of his words. But the streets will also hold good people. Turning to my left, I stride out as if the very action will conjure up positive change, useful encounters and a purpose.

Daylight is rapidly vanishing as I find myself foot-sore standing in an overgrown park reflecting on an empty day and no idea where to go next. My stomach growls at too many apples, the sandwich long gone; the last drink hours ago—a mug of tea some kind soul was handing out of her window to bedraggled folks.

A pond glints here: a rough oval of pale green-blue illuminated by the last rays of a stubborn sun, only now making an appearance. A small brook trickles into the body of water. I crouch and scoop, testing the taste. It seems clean and as several rabbits are now drinking, I assume it can't be too foetid. I watch their twitchy movements and wonder about the killing of one—how to spear the body, peel off the skin, make a fire from damp sticks . . . have I done this before? No memories surface.

Next to the pond is a seat sculpted from a fallen tree. Gathering the coat about me I sit and contemplate the dusky scene. Despite the cold, I feel oddly content watching the early evening activity of various animals that have come to the pond to drink. A bird warbles a plaintive and beautiful song; another responds from a clump of trees on the other side of the water. I drift. Fitful dreams commence, interrupted as reality surfaces.

The night's bitter chill finally wakes me, the last dream still clinging: a man's face hovering above mine, his eyes as green as this pond's water.

I stand stiffly and stretch, stamp my iced feet and walk slowly from the pond. The sky is almost clear, stars shimmering in their millions, an almost full moon lighting the path before me. A squarish shape looms in the shadows to my right. Moving closer, I see it to be a hut sitting within a winter-withered garden, last summer's dead tomato vines still clinging to canes. Perhaps someone only lives here in the warmer months; maybe they wouldn't mind me borrowing their abode. The hand-written notice on the door suggests otherwise.

> Property of Jake the Prophet.
> Keep-the-fuk-out.
> Snakes inside.

Turning reluctantly, I walk from the parkland, through a twisted metal gateway and out into a different street. A distant wailing sound echoes around the silhouetted buildings. What had they said? Scoop trucks?

Within a row of black-stemmed street lamps, one is alight. I quicken my step and stand beneath the flickering flame, wondering which direction to walk. A dart of wind blows out the solitary light. A cloud passes the moon and darkness swallows the road. Two words occur to me. *Sod it.*

From the corner of another road a person appears, walking fast, so layered in clothing I can barely tell more than it is human. Dangerous? Perhaps, but too late to run. She or he stops at the sight of me.

'Oi, dame. Wot you doin' out 'ere?' The voice is gruff but not hostile.

Good question. 'I have . . . no idea.'

LONDONIA

'Eh? Well, don't 'ang about! Get away, sharpish—scoop trucks been doin' the round.'

'Scoop truck?'

He's already speeding away, glancing furtively about—flings me a question.

'You seen an 'orse 'ereabouts?'

'Sorry . . . no.'

His voice echoes in the silent street as he disappears into the shadows.

' 'Orse, you bastard—come 'ere.'

Whatever a scoop truck is, I'd like to not encounter it. Picking the coat-ends out of the puddles, I opt for a road opposite and walk as fast as my numb feet will allow, just anywhere, to any form of open-doored building. The cloud has left the moon's face; a watery light illuminates this thin street. A small pack of dogs fight over something. They scatter as a horse appears, breathing hard, pausing perhaps before re-flight. I look at his empty saddle, and dangling reins. Have I ridden a horse? The idea seems not entirely alien. I walk slowly, eyes down. He snorts as I pass, breath silver in the dim light. Searching the deep pockets of this coat I find a fragment of something soft—bread, old but perhaps tempting enough. I turn, pace back silently and hold the morsel out, hand flat as someone must have told me. He snaffles it and I carefully take the reins in a trembling hand.

'Right . . . 'orse. Let's see if you can find us somewhere to shelter.'

He's big, and this coat's a tangle around my legs. My few attempts, foot in stirrup and heave up, fail dismally. I slip the garment off, body protesting at the cold, and try once more. Success. I haul the coat back on and jab my heels into his belly—gently. He walks, swayingly, unhurried now. The heat rises from his girth up the back of my thighs. Horse-heating. Whatever and wherever, this is an improvement. Perhaps I am asleep, dreaming—this beast part of a larger reverie from which I will awake, my surroundings familiar.

LONDONIA

We reach the junction to a wider road. *Which way to go?* 'Orse decides and I drift, with the animal's steady pace; slip, and right myself time and time again as my head nods. I mustn't sleep. A word hovers just out of reach—hypo-hyperther . . . A sharp barking sound cuts through my somnambulant thoughts. The horse high-steps, hooves clopping on a different surface. I slip, finally this time, foot wrenched in the stirrup, onto something soft.

'Oi. You in the coat. Wakey-wakey.'

I sit up abruptly and peer through a thunderous headache at the voice's owner.

Dark eyes observe me beneath a dusty black homburg. As his scarred face cracks into a wide grin my muscles tense, ready for escape. I try to stand but fall back as my damaged foot decides against it. He puts out a hand in gesture of peace.

'Ça va. Wos just tickled by you an' the hounds. Anylane, I'm not *that way* inclined.'

'Hounds?' Glancing from side to side, I realise why I slept so deeply and warmly. Two enormous dogs flank me, their heads now lifted in question. 'Oh!' I start, try to move again, but the pain prevents it.

The man crouches. 'Take a squint?' I nod and he gently prises off the shoe, whistling at the sight of blue flesh. 'Merda! Wonder if The Lord 'as enyfing for that.'

'The Lord?'

He grins again and points upwards. 'Not 'im. *The Lord* wot lives 'ere—Finder par excellence. Rest. Don't mind the dogs—soft'ens they is, and I'll have a scan, see wot he's got.'

I flop back as he disappears off, shoes clacking to some other part of this . . . church. The headache has receded just enough for me to assimilate everything about *now*. I, whoever *I* really am, lie on a mass of straw, sandwiched between two huge greyhound-like dogs and a horse, in the echoing, grey-stoned interior of a church while a gangster has gone in search of drugs or a bandage, or both.

He's singing, a strong baritone: '*Champagne Charlie is me name* . . .' The song stops as he finds something. 'Gotcha.' The footsteps clatter and he's crouched again before me. ' 'E must'a been lucky with a trade—look, bandage and pills.'

He cradles my foot with great care for someone who looks as if he could wrap those meaty hands about a neck and squeeze until life ceased. The bandage applied after a slick of ointment he sits back. 'Wot about a swig 'a tea to get them tabs down then?'

'Tea?'

'Yu know—dried leaves, hot water . . .'

'That would be possible?'

'Yeah—'E's left the stove in, an' the kettle's warm.'

Questions are queueing. 'This person—*The Lord*, would he mind me being here?'

My new friend drags over a chair, sits, crosses his pin-striped legs and grins again.

'Let's see . . . nope. Mainly as I reckon 'e's dead.'

'. . . Sorry?'

'Saw a death-cart on the way here, and recognised certain *aspects* to one of the bodies on it.'

'Like?'

' 'E only had three fingers on one hand, see, and 'e always wore tweed—geezer on the cart . . . wewll, it was 'im.'

'You don't seem overly upset about his demise.'

'I'm not.'

'Oh?'

'Got a bit above 'imself, he did. Useful bastard as 'e'd got into the Cincture and could get stuff but didn't 'xactly go out 'is way to help anyone.'

'So, whose is this place now?'

He shrugs. 'Yours? Mine?'

'But, doesn't anyone own it?'

'The *real* Lord? But finders-keepers, for now, eh?'

'I can't just take over a church.'

'Got anything better to do? Dogs like ya' too. An' 'e was always cunty wiv 'em.'

'But . . . I'd have to go to, I don't know, some sort of magistrate or council, buy the place.'

He smiles. 'Which cartier you from? Bumped yer 'ead, did yer?'

I wonder where to start, but then as I can't recall anything about me, there's not much to say.

'I don't know . . . I've been staying with someone, but he had to leave.'

'D'ac. Well, first up. There's a sort 'a rule 'ere. Someone dies, or's taken away and you 'appen to stumble into their place—you can take it on. You might get challenged by some fukkaorother but if you can fend 'em off—s'yours.'

'What about you? Where do you live?'

'Ah now. Got me a barge down at Tower Bridge—wiv Parrot.'

'Parrot?'

The dark eyes soften a little. 'Been after 'im to settle down, and enfin, he's good fr'it.'

'Why a barge, not a house?'

'Parrot works the fish boats. 'E's a eel catcher most, and I likes t'be near anytruc comin' in. Load 'a citrus arrived recent. Goodly trading in the Cincture.'

'What's the Cincture.'

He gawps at this. 'You a time-traveller or sumink?'

'No . . . I've lost my memory—somehow, and Tom didn't talk about a *cincture*.'

'*The* Cincture. You did bump yer nut then?'

'I don't know why I don't know about what happened.'

LONDONIA

At the sound of a reedy whistle emanating from where the bandage was found he gets up. 'Don't go nowhere—ha.'

Even if I wanted to, I can't move and it's warm here surrounded by these huge animals. I try to reach into my mind, stir the blackness in there, find something to tell me of before those few days when I had woken as if for the first time, wandered and encountered Tom. Nothing. But, I know how to ride a horse and speak French. I know the name of a hat that sits above this man's eyes . . .

'Ow!' Something is biting me. Delving a hand down my front, I find two things: a flea, and the neck chain with its thin metal rectangle embossed with one word: Hoxton.

The hatted man has returned bearing two small bowls, one of which he hands to me as I shuffle up against the larger hound. The tea is peculiar but hot.

He nods as I sniff the brew. 'Goat milk, or p'raps donkey. Think he had one. Might be out the back . . . anystreet, you got a name?'

A recent memory flits: lying in bed with Tom, him peering at the word on the chain's tag. *'That your name, is it?'* I return to the present and answer assuredly. 'Hoxton.'

'. . . D'accord,' he says. 'Tadly atypique . . . mind, I've a cohort called Wandsworth, so not that *out the box,* s'pose.'

'And your name?'

'Jarvis. Pleased to make yor quaintince.'

'Two questions, Jarvis.'

'Yeah?'

'Why are you helping me, and what *is* the Cincture.'

His eyes widen at the second question. 'You really don't know . . . d'ac', workin' backwards—you's in Londonia wot circles the Cincture—Cincture bein' the hyper-central state of what was all once London town. An' I likes the look of yer.'

I realise with a start that, although Tom had obviously approved, I still haven't seen my reflection apart from in grubby windows.

LONDONIA

'What do I look like?'

'Reckon persons might say a tasty dame . . . very—very lot, in verity. As I said, I'm gay-way so makes no diffrence to me. You got apex teef an all, skin's right smooth—darkish, my dad would say olive . . . wewl, 'e wouldn't now as 'is mind's buggered off recent-time.'

I pass a hand over my cheek, touching the skin, trying to imagine the shape of my face.

'How old do you think I might be?'

He cocks his head, *mms* a little. 'Got a bit less cycles on yer than meself—'bout four 'n thirty? Bit less p'raps . . . wos that wound there—on yer face?'

I touch the place again; a scab crackles beneath my fingertips.

'I think a rat bit me—when I woke . . . on a bench.'

Jarvis shrinks back, just a little, his seemingly perpetual smile vanishing.

'You got mal? Aches 'n that?'

'Just the foot from falling off the horse. Why?'

'Some of 'em carry pox, crud-stream, rougefluenza, and other stuff.'

I sigh, wondering if this strange new life might be a short one.

'That's something to look forward to then.'

His grin re-appears. 'Don't just like the *look* of yer—few's got the 'umour on 'em after this rimy quarter. Too busy sneezin' and repairing their mufflements.'

'Is *rimy*, cold?'

'Yeah. Fukkin' freezin', biting, raw . . .'

'Siberian, benumbed, hyperborean?'

He raises a tangled eyebrow at my last utterance.

'Wordsmith, whatever else you is.'

'So, quarter is a season, and mufflements?'

'Foitling big wrappings—clothes, feltys 'n that.'

I stop the interrogation realising he probably has things . . . whatever he does, to do.

'Sorry. You no doubt have work to be doing.'

'T-dui? Nah. Time off, 'cept I was comin' t' see 'im—The Lord, about oranges.'

'He had some for trading?'

'Nope. I'd traded him some and 'e wos s'posed to 'ave got me something from the Cincture.'

'What was it?'

'A bit for a 'lectric thing what Bert's making.'

'You have electricity in Londonia?'

'Most don't, but there's some wot does—bods who's good with tinkering. They've got these little glassy rectangles wot goes on a roof and traps the sun—if there's any.'

'Solar panels.'

'Yeah—that. See, they got the knowledge in the Cincture but it stays there. Like most mod stuff.'

'Why?'

He shrugs and picks up his tea-bowl. 'Dunno, really. I was only a nipper when the Final Curtain happened. S'always been like this . . . 'ang on, how d'you know about them panels then?'

I wonder again about the void in my mind—a partially opened store cupboard of words and phrases.

'I really have no idea.'

Jarvis looks at me as if he's weighing up a next phrase.

'. . . Reckon you'd a make a good Finder. And not just a local one—Cincture-bound. A Grand Finder.'

I glance around me at the church walls. 'You mean like the previous owner? Why? I don't know anything about *Finding*.'

'Call it a hunch—an' mine are usually right. Or fate. But it's foitling weird why you 'appened upon the 'orse of The Lord, eh? And you speak educated—seems like you got confidence. Finders need that, and dame ones is rare. Sought after.'

'But hasn't The Lord—or didn't he—have any family who will want to take over this place?'

'Had a wife once but she died in gosse-birth, *and* it too. Probably why 'e was such a miserable fukka.'

'So . . . no one else? Brothers? Cousins?'

'Not that I ever known about.'

'You really mean I could just . . . take over from him, if I can do it—Finding.'

'I could put the word about—you's a relative or somink. End of.'

'And what would you get out of helping me?'

'A luvely warm feeling of being a vrai 'n good Londonian citizen—*and* I continue being this place's sub-finder.'

I sit up, put out a hand and he clasps it in his. I stare into those deep-set grey eyes and somehow know we will be good friends.

He squeezes my hand then gestures to where he had come from with the tea.

'Better come and see the lodgings then. 'E'd made a right chaudy place of the vestry.'

Standing stiffly, and with his help, I hop-walk over to a faded blue door to the right of the transept and enter a room which fills my confused mind with joy. The Lord had amassed a serious collection of books along with old china, clocks and some interesting pieces of furniture including a velour chaise-longue, currently occupied by a black cat. I go over and introduce myself.

Jarvis draws in a breath.

'Watchit. Zorro don't like new persons.'

The animal stretches and opens its one golden eye. I risk stroking his coat and a rusty vibration starts up.

'You got a animal gift,' observes Jarvis, poking about in various boxes on the shelves.

No images of a familiar cat or dog appear in my mind but I feel drawn to the beasts of this building.

'How would I feed them?—if I do stay here?'

Jarvis points to a rifle hung on a hook near the door. 'Tool for the job, in fact the dogs'll help yer with hare 'n rabbit.'

'I wouldn't know how to . . . kill anything.'

LONDONIA

Jarvis opens the glowering black stove, throws a chunk of wood onto the fire and looks back at me.

' 'Bout time you learned then. When yor foot's better—morrow darking p'raps.'

I reach down and feel the bruise. 'I don't think it's so bad.'

'We could get Jake t'aver look—'e's good with wounds, got herby potions and stuff. I was goin' up there anylane. You could go on the 'orse.'

The dogs have now entered the vestry, long tails snaking. I feel responsibility lurking.

'What about them? They must be expecting food by now.'

Jarvis stands up and waves them out. 'I'll go an' see what he might have 'anging in the crypt.'

As the small pack of excited dogs and whistling man move off, I peruse The Lord's eclectic book selection: Dickens, composting, tulip-growing, great French artists, a history of something called Facebook, punk rock, Mozart . . .

'Sorted.' Jarvis has returned. 'Boar's leg—nuff for a couple 'a days. So, Parkplace. First I'll show yer the graveplot and the boggost.'

'Sorry?'

'Crapper—jon, water-closet, 'cept, ain't no water, if you was used to that.'

'Where I was staying, someone collected it.'

'Oh—ver merde man. Yeah, that's usual, but you got class facilities 'ere. Bucket over there in the confessional, outside and into the boggost—crud composter.'

I follow Jarvis to the back of the church and a side door. It creaks open and we step into a large area of savage undergrowth punctuated by broken gravestones, a semi-collapsed wall encompassing it all.

Jarvis nods at the sight. 'Garden for the making. The Lord weren't that lured by growin' stuff but it'd be goodly soil—all them bodies an' that.'

LONDONIA

An excitement spreads through me. I look at my hands, turn them, feeling the smooth skin. Are these hands that could grow food, flowers, fruit?'

The dogs have appeared, stretching, licking their mouths, still bloody from their breakfast.

'Great-hounds,' assists Jarvis as I eye their stature. 'Mix-up of greyhounds, wolfhounds, maybe a bit 'a wolf, even. Lot's a stuff got chucked out from the zoo when the Final Curtain 'appened. D'ac—there's the boggost, and that there's 'orse's manure pile. Folk's 'll trade for it if it's well manked.'

I gaze at my new friend, wondering if I am going to wake from this peculiar dream any moment, a plate of something awaiting me in whatever life I had been in. My stomach grinds hopefully.

'D'you think . . . Jake might have anything to eat? I'd pay in some way.'

Jarvis grins. 'He's always got scran. Maybe if you takes The Lord's place you could find him a new hat or sumink. D'ac. Parkplace.' He pauses as if recalling something. '. . . Oh, yeah, he—The Lord, 'ad this two person saddle. Might still be about, if 'e didn't trade it. Back in a jif.'

I survey the potential garden, imagine swathes of larkspur, delphiniums and roses; lines of verdant vegetables and a chicken enclosure. The gravestones stare stolidly back at me as if refusing an idea of change—but it will happen.

'Oi, H. Found it.' Jarvis beckons me to the door where he grasps a large dust-covered mangle of leather. 'Bit mangy but it'll do for a smallish jaunt. Alors, let's saddle up.'

I wonder what the horse will think but he stands patiently enough as Jarvis wrestles with the thing, promising good grazing in the Parkplace.

Out in the front courtyard, Jarvis grinds the weighty door shut, locks it and then the gate behind us. We scramble up onto 'Orse and I look down on a very different street to the silent one of yesterday. Carts rattle, horses clop and people stride, stagger, and dazedly meander. A motorbike passes, filth belching, its rider steering edgily around holes and bushes that have pierced the road's surface.

Jarvis wraps his striped scarf about his neck, pulls the homburg down and lightly thumps the horse.

'Allez—Parkplace.'

A few streets on we approach a slightly familiar-looking stretch of wild land, its perimeters marked by rusting railings and an arched metal gateway crowned with a notice reading:

Parkplace—go about your stuff quietly and respect all

Jarvis jumps down from his seat.

'Just gotta 'ave a word with the goat-dame. You take over.'

He walks over to a woman leading a small herd of goats, and I shift into the front seat. 'Orse seems to know where he is going so I slacken the reins and observe the trees raising their winter-bare branches to this sullen sky. Names occur to me: oaks, ash, willow and the brindle-barked silver birch. Between their trunks glitters the pond I sat next to only last evening, the seat now occupied by a group of pipe-smoking women. The horse turns, walks on and within a few moments we arrive at the hut with its warning sign. Jarvis has returned, a jar of something in hand.

' 'Ere we are—chez Jake's.'

Slipping down from 'Orse, I tie him to a tree and notice the sign has gone.

'I was here, last night—before I found the horse, and was hoping to find a place to sleep.'

' 'Ad the snake-alert out, did 'e?'

'Yes.'

Jarvis smirks and raps on the peeling door. It creaks open and a weathered face topped by a darned woollen hat peers out. The bloodhound jowls crank up into a grin.

'J! Enter . . . bit worn this morn but I'll livey up soontime. Who's this dame, alors?'

LONDONIA

I step through into his wood-smoky room and hold out a hand. 'Hoxton.'

He takes it, enfolds it within his own and says nothing for a while. Jarvis looks on with a knowing smile, nods, sits in a decaying armchair and waits. At last my hand is released and Jake gestures towards another chair.

'Have a seat. Coffee?'

Jarvis produces the milk jar. 'Apex—got this too, if yer out.'

'Impec timing, my friend.'

'So, wot' d'you sense about Hoxton. Let's see if the Jake-ometer is in a goodly state, orjordui.'

Jake pours three cups of dark coffee from a pot set by the fire and hands me one emblazoned with, *I Love Southend*. He sits and stares at me again with surprisingly bright blue eyes under their heavy lids.

'A fertile grounding hidden here. Schooling, wealth . . . but you don't recall where, methinks?'

I shake my head and sip at the coffee, fingers de-icing as they absorb the china's heat.

Jarvis offers the goat's milk then adds a spoon of honey to his brew, stirring manically. 'Tell 'im wot you *do* know, Hoxton and show him yer foot.'

I do tell him the small amount I've gathered about my new life; Jarvis's *finder's-keeper's* information is verified, after which Jake duly examines my bruise and pronounces it to be well rectified. He notices me eyeing his shelves near the old china sink.

'When did you last partake of grub, Ms Hoxton?'

'Yesterday—yesty?'

'You like language and its changes, hm?'

'Oddly, I do seem to be able to speak French, and yes, language does interest me.'

'Useful for a Londonia life as our citizenry is disparate as the contents of a mixtibeast pie.'

He gets up and looks in an enamel pail.

LONDONIA

'Raisin bread, and a tadly bit of dried ham . . . will that keep bodnsoul intact for a while?'

I nod enthusiastically and he puts the small plateful together, handing it to me.

'Should have seen the feed at Fred's last darking, Jarvis.'

Jarvis looks over at me wolfing the ham.

'I had the notion to take the jaunt but found this dame at The Lord's instead.'

'So, you had business with him—before his out-snuffing?'

'How d'you nouse he'd flaked?'

'Learned of it there! Some mec had already stripped his tweed and was proposing of it to Fred.'

'Who is Fred?' I interrupt, stifling a burp.

'Someone you'll encounter muchly if you takes up the Finder profession,' grins Jarvis—'thought you was a posh dame.'

I think about this. How strange to have no memory of background or notion of character—pessimist or optimist, humorist...

'Lady by birth, but perhaps not following that river's course too closely, eh, Ms Hoxton?' divines Jake. 'A Finder's life for you now. Observations, learning the trade.'

I feel somehow that he may be completely correct.

'I'll keep you informed, Jake. Or perhaps you'll know anyway. Are you a fortune-teller?'

He smiles warmly. 'Prophet-Jake's the name, guérisseuring's my game.'

'Guéri-whating?'

'From the French—guérisseur, meaning one who can heal, and sometimes intuitively know things about a person. Father was the same—always had queues of bods wanting this 'n that checking. Witch doctor, maybe.'

'But you can't *see* where I'm from?'

'No. It's not like reading palms, or cards. I just sometimes know stuff—sort of flows through me. Maybe next time we meet I might pick up on sometruc. Or we might just have a chat about gardening—reckon you to be a green-fingered dame.'

LONDONIA

Tom slips into my thoughts and sits down looking on at this conversation. I wonder where he is in the forrist he talked of.

'Lead you to thoughts of someone, did I?' says Jake, '—a gardener too?'

I jump slightly at his words. 'Oh. Yes . . . well, he is, but mainly logging at the moment.' Jake declined the label of fortune-teller, but it is tempting to ask. So I do.

'Do you think . . .'

'He'll be back?'

'Yes.'

Jake's eyes glint within this shadowy interior. 'Wouldn't doubt it for a lizard-flicker.'

Jarvis, who's been stuffing a clay pipe with tobacco, stops and shoves it away in a pocket.

'Merde! Said I'd meet Parrot back at the barge at scrantime. You stayin' here, Hoxton? Or come and meet 'im.'

Jake decides for me.

'Better to go. A dame will be arriving sometime soon with a casserole of pheasant in exchange for a foot massage. She says I have the gift of reflexology, whatever *that* is.'

'D'ac,' says Jarvis standing up and heading to the door, 'See yer soon.'

I thank Jake for his hospitality and insight.

'Pas problem, Hoxton. Best of luck, but . . .' he pauses, a hand on my arm, 'I don't think you'll be needing luck.'

I smile at his words and leave the hut, blinking at the daylight after the musty interior.

We leave the Parkplace and head Southwards, Jarvis shouting out details of roads, buildings and Londonia landmarks.

'There—spont-market.'

I glance over at a cluster of people surrounding a couple of tables. 'What is it?'

'One bod starts up sellin' somethin' then 'fore y' know it, others join, drag tables out, sell whatever they've got spare—voila, spont. Only don't do t' get too big.'

LONDONIA

'Why?'

'Can get a bit riot-ish. Brings out the Sharks.'

'Sharks?'

'Cincturian narks—police, and then if the luck's down, scoop truck.'

A gaping hole in the road surface takes his attention and I cease questioning as he steers the horse around it. At the end of the road, beyond a cluster of semi-derelict buildings I glimpse water.

'Is that the main river of Londonia?'

'Nah, Lady Thames is beyond. That's Limehouse pool, where a lot of the barges is.'

'Including yours.'

'The black-planked one, yeah.'

The pool is frantic with movement: boats being unloaded, boats on wooden platforms being scraped free of clinging shells, nets being hauled, people yelling about fruit, wine, tobacco and lodgings; women selling fish and small birds on steaming skewers, children playing on skeletons of vessels, and everywhere small fires surrounded by locals smoking and discussing the day's events.

Jarvis turns in the saddle. 'Approve of my manor?'

As I wonder where to start, a voice cuts through the noise.

'Jaz!'

'Parrot! Said, I'd be back.' Jarvis stands in the stirrups, swings a leg over, bounces down to the cobbles and hugs his bargemate. 'Like yer to meet a new Hackrovia resi. Hoxton.'

Parrot wipes a hand on his overalls and holds it out, tawny eyes bright in a round dark brown face. 'Pleased to meet yo, girl. Sorry, I's been guttin' dem pikes 'n perch all dis morn.'

I clasp his hand, shake enthusiastically and get down from the horse. 'Pleased to meet *you*.'

'Got me one pike in a pot if you want to try a bita Creole cookery?'

'I'd love to. Where shall I tie the horse?'

Jarvis takes the reins and leads him to the barge. 'Just hold 'im a mo. Where's the sign?'

Parrot hands him a small rectangle of wood marked: DON'T Touch. We can see *you,* and Jarvis passes the two attached lengths of wire about the animal's neck, looped and clasped.

'D'ac. Scran-time.'

I step gingerly onto the gently swaying boat and Jarvis helps me down a small flight of steps into a woody, smoky interior full of a billion *things*.

' 'Scuse the derangement, and the foitling stove's a bit blocked—reckon there's a bit of a nest-remnant in the pipe after I hedgehoged it recent.'

Parrot throws a heap of clothes off a chair and invites me to sit.

'Jarvis? We got that bottle a' Elderberry still?'

Jarvis nods and opens one of the many wooden doors making up one wall. 'I'll do it. Stew ready?'

'In a tadly, man.'

Within a few moments, the table is uncovered, more chairs liberated and we sit looking hungrily at a scarred enamel pot, a chunk of bread and the uncorked dark green bottle. Jarvis unstacks three bowls and ladles out the stew.

I take the bowl handed to me. 'Sorry I had nothing to bring.'

Parrot puts a glass in front of me and pours out a generous measure.

'Hey, not a worry. You can make something 'nother time. Where you livin', girl?'

'Meet the new Lord, Parrot,' grins Jarvis.

'You taken over St Leonard's?'

'Apparently. I still don't really understand . . .'

'He dead?'

'As a coffin nail,' confirms Jarvis, 'an' she—Hoxton claimed the place.'

'Well . . . it was an accidental claiming.'

'But you was first bod after 'im.'

LONDONIA

Parrot raises a glass and clinks mine. 'Then I salut yo, Lord, or Lordess of Hackrovia.'

Capitula 1

Dark Quarter 2072
St Leonard's Church, Hackrovia, Londonia

'SHUT *UP!*'

They won't, and there's only so long you can ignore hungry, howling dogs . . . Jack the Rabbit better be doing the rounds today, or it'll be me down the Parkplace with a gun.

D'accord on a warm day, to stand waiting and watching, but these are the grey, cold short days of another long dark quarter-cycle. Dim days of persistent rain churning the detritus in the streets into grey rivers, soaked buildings and scudding clouds; days of hurrying back to warmth, least exposure possible.

My thoughts of finding wool-boots and an extra thick felty to brave the elements are interrupted by a coloured ray of light sliding across the bed and onto the floor. I can't remember the last time these pink jewels graced the stone slabs. Sun. At last.

The foot I slipped out to check the chill feels iced already. I curl back down feeling the warm straw pricking under the rough sheet; hibernation, that would be a useful thing. Bert the Swagger told me they've achieved it in the Cincture, but he's not the most reliable source of information.

The hounds start up again. Perhaps they could just hunt for rats in the front courtyard. I throw the covers back and the hovering chill hits.

'Christ in a fridge! How can it be this cold? And where in l'enfer . . .' I search desperately for my outer garments. A blanket suffices, and I scoot to the church's main door, the slabs wincing my soles, dogs bounding after me.

LONDONIA

The door creaks, and sun glances in through the narrow crack as I peer through at the scrambling scene outside.

'Hey! You little squits—Va!'

Gosses again: only ten, perhaps eleven cycles. This extra harsh weather has caused many a crop to fail, and my raised-box cabbages and leeks are prized more than gold.

'Pizzpizz yourself, Miss,' one calls and jumps up onto the wall, ripping his felty. Careful, I want to say, suddenly aware of his fragile frame.

I look up into pure blueness, broken only by a few fast-moving white clouds. It's so good to see that colour again.

The clanging bell and scrunching cartwheels of the bread man are now audible above the general street noise. A lumpy cloth bag is slapped over the wall, a shout following.

'Hoxton, you owe me!'

Merda! Three week's bread owed. I've scoured all the usual haunts looking for his request, a lead-lined document box which is proving elusive. Might have to be a trip further out—Highgate, or maybe Finchlea. There's a mec there who has an impressive collection of teak and ebony items, not that he's ever keen to part with them.

Unlocking the gate, I peer down the street. As I had hoped the water-mec is still making his deliveries; invaluable as the church roof water-collecting pipes have burst . . . another milder weather job. If the bright quarter *ever* arrives. The mec's donkey ambles towards the church, canisters and bottles rattling. I call out.

'Salut, Tig. Two bidons, please.'

He pulls the donkey to a halt, and heaves off two glass flagons.

'We still good for bacco trade?'

'Sure. Can I give it to you Wedsdy?'

'Pas problem,' he grins, looking down at my revealed undergarments.

LONDONIA

Gathering the blanket out of the mud, I grab the flagons and the bread bag, lock the gate and zip back into the church to be greeted by my horse. He stretches back his whispery lips in a grin, stamping a hoof and speaking to me in his head. I return his greeting.

'Salut, Kafka, busy day today.' I drag some more hay over and check the tin bath of water. 'Should be able to get some oats later, when we go northwards.' He answers with a snort and lifts his tail to deposit a useful load of compost onto the stone floor.

If the last congregation of St Leonard's could now see their hallowed place of worship they might have been outraged. My home of the last cycle and The Lord's before me, almost all the pews have long gone, burnt in the harsher patches of each dark-quarter; the nave, now a horse's stable; the vestry, a comfortable nest of books, bed, wood stove and detritus of the everyday struggle.

The fire is still in, just. I throw on some wood, getting it to blaze, fill the kettle and clunk it onto the stove top. A little time later, I've found my clothes and am sitting in front of the fire with a toasting fork and a bowl of tea from my diminishing supply.

The sacred brew is scarce. A fellow Finder recently came across a stash from before the unknown time but it came at a heavy enough price in trade, although there is word of a vessel coming into Red-Bridge with possible stocks.

Toast in hand, I open the agenda and check the outstanding jobs: *that* foitling lead box, Jack Russell for Bert, ham, denim, a new foot-pedal for one of Fred's Threads sewing machines, and . . . a visit to somewhere I hadn't imagined going to. My thoughts are curtailed by the sound of a key turning in the main door. I leave the fire and go to help Jarvis as he struggles in swearing, carrying a pile of boxes.

'Fuksaker, these gosses, they want to break a mec . . . and mother, she's broke her glasses, can't see a foiteling thing . . . got to take a dechet, Hoxton.'

LONDONIA

I smile at the sweating figure and point to the confessional.
'There's an empty bucket, and a new sawdust pit out back.'
'Genial. Back in five.'
I'm just studying an ancient map of North Londonia when Jarvis ambles into the vestry with a happier expression on his gnarled face. He takes off his homburg, lays it down on the table and sinks down into an ancient leather chair.
'You got it goodly in here! Right chaudy it is.'
'Toast, tea?' I offer.
'Tea,' he says. '*Proper* tea?'
'The vrai. Assam, apparently.'
'That Finder in Hollo-way got it, did she?'
'Yes . . . and don't ask what I had to part with for it! So, the glasses?'
'Yeah—really broke, like into pizzy bits. She can't see so much as a cat's arse without 'em, *and* Dad's wandering again. She found him in Commercial Road on Mundy with a curtain pole. Thought he was fishing, didn't he? Merda!'
I add a spoonful of precious leaves to the Brown Betty and look back at my friend.
'Did you find them a new lodgings?'
'Gaff in the same street as Sardi's place. It's a bit fumey of fish-smoking, but warm enuff. So, let's talk about t-dui's agenda.'
Sitting down with the teapot, I pull the book towards me and check the list.
'Did you find out about the Jack?'
'There's a litter. Only a boy-dog left but Bert'll be happy with that. I'll have to parler bit sharpish today—good ratters, everyone wants 'em.'
'What's the deal?'
'Six bales hay, haricot beans, box of vinyl 33s and Marmite.'
'Marmite! Merda . . . I haven't seen that for a grand-cycle.'
'You like it, don'tcha? Got some put by for yer!'
I could have kissed him; in fact, I do.

'Aw, you're welcome, Kitten,' he says, a wide, cheeky grin lighting up the creased cheeks. He pours out a bowl of tea and sighs.

'What?' I ask.

'Mother and her glasses . . . dunno wot t' do.'

'Take the box from here—there's bound to be something that'll work.'

'Nah . . . tried that with a load Parrot found. Trouble is she 'ad some weird prescription ones from donkey's ago—even got the bit 'a paper that says wot it is, but that's 'bout as useful as a wax saucepan.'

I smile, knowing what I am about to say will be unusual to say the least.

'Well, perhaps I can be of assistance with the problem.'

'Uh?'

'*I* have a rendezvous with a certain Mrs Caruso of Upper Grosvenor Street, Cincture Central.'

'You *wot* . . .'

'Someone called here looking for The Lord. Seemed happy that I was a dame, and happy to offload the message.'

'*Gazooks*! You're gonna move up a rung—Finder for the Cincturians . . . fuk. Could be goodly useful, H. Just don't end up like The Lord, eh?'

'Jarvis!'

He grins sheepishly and pats me on the arm. '*Relax* . . . I knows you wouldn't, ain't got it in yer. 'E was always a bastard, just hexpanded into a bigger one.'

I calm down and consider his words: *moving up a rung*. The thought of what I will see and who I might meet is both alarming and enticing.

'Did he spend a lot of time in there—The Lord?'

'Fair bit, yeah. Mouth to the ear stuff—y'know, somebod likes sumink, and then somebod else wants it and so on . . .'

He pauses, lances a piece of bread on the toasting fork and holds it to the fire.

LONDONIA

'Couldya have a go at gettin' the specs?'

'Of course. I don't suppose you've got the prescription thing with you?'

Jarvis brightens. 'As a matter 'a fact . . .' He checks through various pockets, pulls out a battered wallet and carefully removes a folded bit of paper. 'There—watch it though, bit time-knacked, it is.'

I glance at the faded writing then stow the paper safely in my carpet bag's buttoned pocket.

'So. You're going to see about the dog?'

'Yep. Then I'll bike down to the Barb. There's a whisper out on a spont market—might get some x-zotic fruit. Wot about that ham for Luigi?'

'I'll try up at the Angel exchange, and I've *got* to find the Bread-mec's box.'

'Watch it round there. Clasher territory at the mo.'

'Never travel without a gun . . . that's what you say, isn't it?'

He nods grimly and retrieves the toast, larding it with duck fat and salt. 'Two if y'got 'em, an' a cyanide dustcan.'

I grimace at the thought, but there have been times where that could have been useful: *That gosse, the two mecs.*

'What you thinkin' bout, Kitten?'

'Oh, lots of things . . . could you cut my hair?'

'Ain't done that for cycles, s'pose I still got the knack. Why d'you want t' get rid of them black locks?'

'It isn't practical, and I just felt I wanted to look a bit neater, more anonymous . . . going in *there*.'

'Cut it now?'

'We could trade it too.'

'Vrai—got scissors?'

I get up and look in the jumble of knives and cutlery in a box. 'Here, these'll do.'

'You sure, Hoxton?'

'Yes.'

LONDONIA

He hesitates: 'Well, maybe it's goodly I did that drawin' of you—on Kafka.'

'What drawing?'

'Last dark quarter, don't you remember?'

I think for a moment then recall a day of dark clouds and wind whipping hair across my face; Jarvis sitting opposite the church, his head bent over a rectangle of white.

'Yes, and I remember saying you were mad for having chosen such a time for sketching. Did you finish it? You never showed me.'

'Forgot—'til just now. I'll bring it next time—if it surfaces. Say au-revoir to the mane then.'

I sit. Jarvis limbers up his ex-barber hands, brushes and cuts. My hair falls, snakes on the flagstones, and I wonder about the parents that gave me the gift of thick, black hair and skin that stays pale brown even in the depths of a dark-quarter.

He steps back, cocks his head this way and that, looking at his work.

'Yeah . . . not bad that.'

He passes me the ivory hand mirror and I smile at my revealed features.

'More than not bad!'

He grins. 'Not my cutting wot's made you shine. Jake always says you're the most beauteous dame in Londonia. Just as well I'm gayster, eh.'

I look away from my reflection to my friend's cheery face and consider his words.

'Even in these ancient woollen layers and smelling of horses.'

'You know it, H—since you was a goss, I wouldn't wonder.' He crams a last half slice of toast into his mouth and jerks a thumb street-wards. 'Alors, better get movin'.' Then he stops, an unusually concerned look on his face.

'You sure about this jaunt into *there*?'

The tone of his voice pulls me up. Am I sure? No, probably not—at all.

LONDONIA

'It'll be fine, and hopefully I can sort out your mum's problem.'

He smiles. 'Just be careful, eh?'

I lean over and kiss his stubbly face. 'Of course.'

Perhaps this is mad—to risk a trip into the unknown world behind the walls but something more than just trades to be had excites me.

Draining the tea bowl, I reluctantly leave the cocooning armchair and pull on my felty that's been warming near the fire. My neck feels cold after the hair cropping so I select a scarf from the many hung on a hook near the door. A flash of off-white amongst the wool catches my eye. I peer at the word printed on a tattered label: *Next*. Next what? I shrug and turn to look at Jarvis as he hauls on his vast coat over blue, shiny padded trousers and sweat shirt that has the words, Keep Calm—Drink Beer, across the front.

'What are those trousers?' I ask

'Got 'em in the Spital-fields Freeforall—skiing kit the gar said.'

'Skiing?'

'You know, snow, hills, little pointy wood houses. Don't s'pose anyone does it now, apart from the buggers who might live up there, chasing elk 'n stuff.'

How do I not know about skiing?

He notices my expression. 'Check your precious books—bound to be one that has info on it.'

'Yes, maybe.'

He retrieves his hat and jams it on.

'Talking of books—Jake was wondering if y'd teach him some stuff.'

'Stuff?'

'A bit of writing 'provement . . . wants to do more than just clunk the machinery at the press.'

'Well, we owe him for that stash of scissors he gave us, so fair trade, and anyway I like teaching.'

LONDONIA

Jarvis hoists his canvas bag over his shoulder and heads towards the door.

'Be back at darking . . . want to hear about the Cincture.'

'Bring Parrot, and something to eat. I'll probably *need* a drink by then. I've got a bottle of red, St Emilion, 2018 that I traded for those sacks of windfalls.'

He smiles and strides up the aisle, his voice echoing in the musty space.

'See y', Kitten—don't forget yer shooter.'

I stand for a moment thinking about my visit to come. Perhaps I should go to the bathhouse first. A week ago was the last time; I might smell offensive. It's difficult to tell. Tom didn't complain, but then everyone seems to smell the same: damp, woolly, bitter somehow. There's a bathhouse in Angel, so maybe. If I've got the time.

I get the horse tackled up, lead him outside and do a quick check around. The great-hounds are sharing the last of a rabbit. I glance again at the leeks, considering their worth. I'll pull some later. A box to the café equals coffee, and hopefully bacon for several sittings.

I once saw a picture of Great Eastern Street, where I ride now, from the time called the 2020s. It was a very different place, congested with the vehicles that now lie rusting.

My thoughts cease as I hear a shout. My friend Sardi runs towards me, her bright robes flapping.

'Yey, Hoxton. I was legging t' see you.'

I slow Kafka and look down at the radiant dark face.

'Salut, Sardi. Sorry, I've got to get to The Exchange now.'

She nods. 'Pas problem. See you fr' Saints' day. Remember?'

LONDONIA

We clasp hands for a moment then I nudge the horse to walk on.

'I'll be there.'

I glance back at her, thinking of how we met—the day when she came to request a Finding. With the sway of Kafka's walk, my mind drifts back.

The bell on the church wall was jangling on its string. Putting down the limewash brush, I had wiped my hands, gone to the door and opened the viewing hatch. Jarvis's mirror on a pole revealed the visitor to be a dame dressed in flowing garments, her hair tied into a batik turban.

We made the deal. I was to find a blue and white china tureen in exchange for two live chickens.

Two days later I'd found the tureen in a shouting house: huge with a blue pattern of trees and bridges, and made of white china that rang like a bell when you tapped it . . .

Something breaks me from the daydream.

I swing around to see a mec sloping up to Kafka's flank. A hand springs out, yanks my coat back, grabs for the gun in its holster. *Merda!*

I've clasped his hand, pushing it away, but he's strong, fingers twisting mine. I free a foot, kick out at his head, He ducks, hand releasing. I slip the gun out just as Kafka rears and plunges. I seize the reins harder. One hand's not enough, the gun tumbles. The mec misses it, grabs a fistful of my coat instead. He's pulling at me, dragging. The saddle slips.

'Get the fuk down. Only want the horse. Won't hurt you.'

Something in his glassy eyes tells me otherwise.

Should have brought Fagin.

I kick out again, risking a yelp.

'FAGIN!'

'Said *get down*, pute.' He lunges, hauling me further out of the saddle, one hand grasping my arm, the other scrabbling in the dirt. He snatches up the gun, snaps upright and shoves the

LONDONIA

rusty barrel into my temple. I squeeze my gaze back to the church as the metal digs in.

His voice grates close to me. 'Last chance, crud-wench.'

The gate is high, but Fagin's not far off Kafka's height on hind legs; perhaps he can clear it. I risk a bluff.

'D'ac, d'ac—take the horse. Just get the fuk off me!'

The mec grins, lowers the gun a little.

'That's more like it. Allez!'

I hear the rattle of chains, barking, a howl. Fagin jumps. He's free, loping towards us. A giant, grey nightmare of a dog.

The mec hears the hound. He turns. The gathered crowd is shouting now, urging the dog on.

'Kill the Fukka! Tue le bastard!'

He swings the gun clumsily towards the beast, trips, fires— bullet lodged in grass. He runs: too late. Fagin sees me scrabbling to get upright in the saddle, sums it all up in his dog brain and leaps.

I turn away hearing bones break. A scream starts. Then it's quiet. As I walk Kafka on, the great-hound joins us, licking his lips and looking up into my face. He tells me he loves me and I'm glad he's on my side.

'Allez, home, Fagin,' I command, reaching down to stroke his velvet head.

As Kafka turns the street corner, I glance back once more. The scene is already busy with scavengers and a death-cart; clothes and belongings of an unknown man now scattered. In the sky a cluster of mutapigeons circle, waiting for the carcass.

I concentrate on the day ahead, stash the gun, now re-aware of its presence. No more day-dreaming. Jarvis always says imagine you have six pairs of eyes: snail's eyes on stalks, when you walk the streets.

We're leaving Hackrovia now and entering Isling-town where a gang war between Poles and Bretons has been raging for over a long-cycle. I hesitate and slow Kafka, thinking of a friend who lives in Wharf Road at the edge of the most troubled area. A

LONDONIA

nearby exchange of gun fire added to my own recent escape from harm decides me and I urge the horse into a gallop up Angel Hill. The terracotta dome of the exchange building comes into view and Kafka speeds ahead, knowing there will be oats and water.

Pulling Kafka to a stop, I get down and look for one of the regular horse boys.

'Hey, Henri!'

He leaves the cluster of gosses standing by the horse rails and lopes over with a grin.

'Salut, Hoxton. Ça va?'

'It's going fine, thanks.' I rummage in the large carpet bag. 'Tobacco, chocolate?'

He shrugs. 'Beh . . . Zeitporn?'

Merda! How old are you? Actually, he's probably over sixteen, but this generation of gosses are small.

'*Fifty Shades of Grey*?' I suggest, holding out a thumbed book. 'It's soft, but antique, and rare, from the 2010s.'

' 'Ave you eet in French?'

'*Come on*! It'll be good practice.'

'D'ac,' he concedes then looks at an ancient watch on a chain. 'A cycle, d'ac?'

He doesn't know what time it is but the hands still move—a calculation of how long I've got. He takes the horse's reins, ties him to the bar and fetches the food.

I stand for a moment looking out across Londonia.

Southwards the lakes glimmer like dropped coins. The Thames snakes its way into Londonia: part estuary, part river. Black dots of stilt houses line the edge; Bert the Swagger lives there with the shifting sands and mud, unearthing the past as it comes to light.

Aware that my clockface is being used up in musing, I turn and walk into the madness of The Exchange. The windows rattle with shouting and swearing; people stand on chairs, tables, even

LONDONIA

each other, holding their wares aloft, their desires scrawled on paper.

Live chicken for wine, ink for meat, teeth fixed for sex.

There's no sign of the hams.

I tour the room. At the back, a frightening looking man dressed in ancient leather trousers has a lead-lined box. I pass casually, not showing the excitement within me. It's perfect. The Bread-mec would be off my back.

I walk back, tone nonchalant. 'Locks, does it?'

'Impenetrable,' he drawls. 'See for yourself.'

I bend down and turn the silver key. The wood is beautiful, something exotic, polished by time. I'm estimating how heavy it is, when he leans forward and clamps a grimy hand onto my thigh.

'I've only one currency—don't need anything else, see.'

His grip tells me what he means. The thought is unappealing, but . . . five passes of the clock's hand and I could pay a debt.

'How long, and what?'

'You've a pretty mouth, don't suppose I'd trouble you for too long.'

A smile stretches, revealing jagged teeth, decayed as bombed buildings. I can smell the rank odour emanating from the leather trousers where a distinct bulge is now rising. Sex exchange can solve a lot of problems, but sometimes . . .

'Sorry, Bread-mec, you'll have to wait,' I mutter, and disappear back into the swirling crowd as the gar curses me.

Someone's got shoes. A huge crowd is gathering as he shouts into the dusty atmosphere.

'Italy, before the Final Curtain, all unworn, best quality!' People surge forward waving vegetables, tools, even a dog held aloft. 'D'ac, d'ac, one at a foiteling time.'

The shoes are good, stupid though, heels and bright colours, but there are good trades to be done with such things. I push forward holding a trump card.

LONDONIA

'Snash—best, for six pairs. The red, two yellow, white, green, and the black with buckles.'

He stabs a finger into the cloth bag, takes a swab and wipes it onto his gums.

'Where d'you get this?' I shake my head. 'Three pairs,' he offers.

'Four.'

'Can 'y get more stuff?'

'Maybe.'

'Tell me?'

'I'll send a pigeon when I have more. Give me your name and a message station. So, the shoes?'

He nods and bundles them up into a sack bag as he slaps ferreting hands away from his stock. We exchange, he hands me a faded card and I walk out of the crush, breathing in the wind that scurries up the hill.

I examine the moth-soft rectangle: *Suggs, Holborn*. That's easy, not too far; a reliable pigeon route from the Brick Lane station.

Kafka sees me and stamps a foot, impatient to be moving. I walk over and tie the sack bag onto the saddle.

'You 'ave found your bonheur?' Henri asks, untying the reins.

'I don't know about happiness, but, yes, it was useful. How's the book?'

He raises his shoulders in a Gallic shrug and pouts. 'Ça va . . . too soft, tu sais.'

I smile as I put a foot in the stirrup and climb up. 'A bientôt, Henri.'

Leaving the crowds, we head down Pentonville Road and join the river of humans and animals. Packs of dogs roam alongside horses, camels and scores of people; some wandering lost in drugged dreams, some striding on private missions. I pass a dame astride a camel, strung with flasks and boxes. She shouts out her trade.

LONDONIA

'Tea, blackberry ale, crepes, patties.'

I slow the horse to a walk, beside her; it's a long time since toast.

'Salut, ça va?'

'Oui, ça va. What'dya want?'

'Tea . . . and a crepe. How much?'

'Two silvers.'

'D'ac.'

'Jam or honey?'

'You've got honey?'

'Si, si, my brother, he got bees.'

'Would he trade?'

'Sure.' She hands me a stubby card. 'He's in Actonia—he got twenty hives now.'

I opt for the honey. She wraps the pancake in brown paper and hands it to me while hauling up an ancient thermos on a string. Pulling out the cork, she pours dark liquid into a terracotta cup and passes it to me then grabs a stick to beat off someone lurking at the camel's rear.

I take the rough vessel and drink; it's not bad. One more swig, and I place the cup into the basket of empties strapped to the camel's rump. She turns, grins—thumbs up. 'See you for trade in Actonia!'

Nudging Kafka back into a trot, we head towards the walls of the Cincture, the sun obscured by its towering walls. Built of shining coppery metal, no one can scale them. If they tried, they would be shot by one of the luckless people whose mindless job it is to watch from above. The cubicles built into the tops of the wall are small; just big enough for a man to stand for too much time, looking out over the mayhem below.

The buzz of The Exchange had temporarily smudged out my thoughts of the Cincture. Now, actually here, staring at these glistening walls, I am starkly aware of what I am about to do. How had I been so calm about this visit? I am going to enter this place, know what is on the other side. My stomach grinds in apprehension, hands slippy with sweat on the reins. I wonder about turning back but my curiosity is stronger than my fear.

The walls close up are smooth. I put out a hand to touch the metal, but recoil; perhaps there could be something harmful, some unannounced defence system.

As we approach the eastern access point, a rumbling armoured truck appears from the other direction, its wheels leaving a trace of white powder on the rubbled road surface. The towering metal gates of the access point swing slowly open and uniformed men appear, pushing back the crowd, one shouting through a loud-hailer.

'Move—back. NOW! Anyone with the correct papers, and reason to be here *will* be seen.'

A stubborn mec waving a banner advances. A gust of wind flattens the cloth and I catch its painted words:

Free Londonians from the tunnels!

The mec with the loudhailer produces a baton and pushes him backwards.

'You've had fair warning—now *move!*'

The Londonian starts to chant, whapping the Cincturian with his flag.

'*Free them. Free them.*' Others join in. I move Kafka back a few paces, anticipating the trouble ahead. And it happens. Fast. The scoop truck reverses. Someone aboard the vehicle unhitches the ridged metal tube at the back of the vehicle and sprays the now boisterous crowd. People collapse, are *scooped* by the crew and dumped into a side opening of the truck. It moves forwards through the gateway, just the powder and the banner left.

A voice seems to come from nowhere. 'Your name?'

I almost jump from the saddle and glance down to see another uniformed mec. 'Hoxton.'

'Your first name?'

'It's my only name.'

LONDONIA

'Reason for traversing.'

'Finder request.'

'From?'

'Madame Caruso.'

He consults a small metal tablet, presses a few buttons and waves me on.

'Walk the horse through.'

Whatever the mec who had come to see The Lord had reported back seems to have been in order. I stroke Kafka's mane, assure him everything will be *fine* . . . and dig my boots lightly into his belly. He steps reluctantly and we pass into a starkly-lit tunnel, at the end of which, I can make out an impressive yellow stoned building with two sweeping arches, and beyond that a vast, red-bricked edifice. As Kafka reaches the end of the tunnel, a mec steps forward and tells me to dismount, enter the yellow building and to leave the horse. As he is holding a large gun, I co-operate.

The first room I enter is plain, just a metal desk, a cabinet and two chairs. I am told to wait, so do so, nervously wondering what will happen to Kafka. A short time later a dame appears, dressed in the same grey uniform as the mecs.

'Sit, please.' She turns to the cabinet, opening its doors to reveal hundreds of green files. Eventually she selects one, leafs through the pages inside slowly then looks at me.

'How does Madame Caruso know you?'

'She doesn't. The request was through a worker of hers.'

'His name?'

'Benjamin Otwold.'

She shuffles more paper and stares at various sheets for a long time.

I want to leap up, smack the file from her hand and shout in her face at the slug's pace of this interview. *Allez Allez, stuff to do, busy, busy!* . . . eventually she flops the file shut. 'His journey to Londonia was recorded, and the result after visiting you.

LONDONIA

A traversement will be granted.' She passes me several pieces of paper, and gestures to a door.

'Sign these. Go through to the wash chamber, strip and you will be dealt with.'

'What about my horse?'

'It will be checked and ready for you on your return.'

She takes the papers back, stamps them all, returns the file and leaves the room. As I stare at the door, wondering if I should, and, *could* escape back to familiarity, the other door opens, and another dame leans around the door.

'Madame Hoxton, this way.'

This room is narrow. The walls hum. I have a million questions to ask, but the blank pale face in front of me is not going to supply any answers.

'Have you recently contracted any of the following maladies?'

She reels off a list while siphoning blood from my wrist with a syringe.

'Ow! No, I haven't.' Did I catch a faint smile? If I did it vanishes.

'Take your clothes off, place them in this tray and stand in the chamber. At the end of the procedure, we will have the results and if satisfactory, you will dress in a provided allinone and coat for the duration of your visit. Leave your own bag and transfer your essentials to the provided bag, or use the zipped pocket of the allinone.'

An image appears in my mind from a book I had once opened. Before the third world war, there had been another: herds of people pushed into chambers to die, poisoned by gas. There are things in the ceiling here and smells I don't recall. What to do? Mr Otwold never mentioned a wash chamber.

Well, I forgot the bathhouse, so . . .

Removing the layers, I step into the chamber under the first metal disc in the ceiling, shivering with cold and apprehension.

LONDONIA

After a buzzing sound, a spray of gelatinous liquid coats my body.

A robotic voice echoes in the room. 'Rub the cleanser into your hair and skin, then move to the next procedure point.' I comply and am rewarded with a gush of warm water, sluicing off the fluid.

As the water becomes cloudy with soap, I revel in the simple act of washing in a luxurious flow of clean water. I am rinsed; the buzzing sound starts again, and a jet of warm air chases the beads of water from my skin.

A dame stands a few paces away. She's just had the same treatment and is stepping into one of the issued garments. She stares at me as she ties a scarf around her long, blonde hair.

'What are you here for?' Her accent is unfamiliar, Russian, perhaps.

'A finder job for a Mrs Caruso. You?'

'I am mirror-dame. Some people like it here—to know their future, even though governors don't approve.'

'Governors?'

'Those who run this place.'

'Where do they govern from?'

She looks cagey suddenly. Her voice drops.

'People listen you know?' As I reach to take my allotted garment from its hanger, she continues, her voice a different tone now. 'How old is your infant?'

I step back and stare at her. 'I don't have a gosse.'

'You do, or you did—in the Cincture, and that's a truth.'

The missing cycles of my life sting my heart. What does she know about me, and how?

'But—'

'Did you never wonder about that scar, 'cross you there?' She points to the faint line running low down across my stomach. 'I can see, even without that, mind.' She nods to the door where voices can be heard. 'Time to go.'

'*Wait*! Where can I find you?'

LONDONIA

'Drinking-House. Silk Street, Barbican—I have room there.' Her frost-blue eyes penetrate me once more, then she's gone.

I stop clutching the grey fabric to me and get into the suit: cold now, freezing; not from the atmosphere of the place, more the overwhelming information. I want to turn, step back outside and bury my face in Kafka's mane, go home. Too late. The door is sliding open and I step into a place that belongs in dreams, the mirror-dame's words like billboard lettering standing in my mind.

As I stand, eyes wide, staring, I wish Jarvis was next to me, paper and pencil in hand, sketching furiously. I'm no artist and carry nothing to blemish a page with but I feel my mind filling up, recording a stock of images as I look and look at each thing, so different from everything I know. Yet somehow, like an itch, unreachable under layers of clothes, something nags at me . . . a notion of déjà-vu.

'Are you looking for a shore, Madame?'

I twist around, at this bizarre statement regarding sand? An ocean?

'Sorry?'

A young mec dressed in a bottle green uniform smiles back at me. 'Rickshaw taxi.'

'Oh . . . I see, shaw. Yes—I suppose so.'

He points towards a line of brightly-painted carriages headed by bicycles.

'Or if you wish I could call and see if a car could be available, although it may be doubtful as this is a power-save day. Are you going far?'

I take the piece of paper from the allinone zip pocket and consult the sloping script.

'Number 34, Upper Grosvenor Street.'

He places a small brass whistle between his lips and *peeps*: 'Upper Grosvenor Street.' Another youth appears from a doorway attired in a pink suit. He steps over to his matching 'shaw' and glances over to me, perhaps taking note of my grey outfit. What do the workers here think of Londonians?

He opens the door and I step up to sit within a soft, padded interior. The carriage sways off and I stare out at the passing roads. A flash of vivid red fills the window as a vehicle passes in the other direction. A London bus. Not one of the rusted hulks that adorn our streets but a gleaming, red bus; the bus of a postcard that I have pinned to the wall of the vestry.

'Hello Doris. Well, here I am in this great city with its black taxis, and red phone boxes, post boxes and buses! I do wish you were here! Love, Babs.' Summer 1965.

The vehicle continues down a wide road; a flat road without holes or weeds. No fires litter the pavements, no huddles of people dealing, fighting or staring blankly at their belongings. The few people that walk the pavements, walk calmly, as if they are assured of their safety and have pleasant things occupying their minds, not fear of possible attack, death or robbery.

I recall a fancy-dress party held by the Society of Finders in an old, wrecked hotel. Planned for weeks, everyone had rifled through their stocks to find a suitable outfit, the result being a patchwork of history: Victorians, flappers, teddy boys, pearly queens and a multitude of other faded reflections of the past.

The clothes worn in this street I look out on now appear to be copies of dress styles from around the 1900s. The women wear long dresses with nipped in waists and full, swinging skirts . . . and the hats! Fabricated, I can't imagine how—huge, statuesque, covered in lace, ribbons, bows, flowers and birds. The men's fashions similarly echo that era: beautifully tailored waistcoated suits and shining shoes.

My gaze moves away from the people walking the pavements to the buildings; preserved and perfect, each one, as if constructed yesterday. Yet, it's possible to see the link between Londonia and here; our city as it once was, now decaying and changed through people doing what they can. These buildings are cleaned and repaired, the doors and window frame colours as bright as the Cincturians' clothes. There are shops for the sake of shopping, clothes for the sake of being looked at. The carriage speeds on past windows stacked with shoes, fabrics and furniture; past people emerging from the doorways laden with bags bearing the shops' names. My mind feels hazy with a thousand images, the whirr of the shaw's wheels on the smooth roads hypnotic. I jump as the driver suddenly speaks.

'Just coming up to number thirty-four, Madame. If the lady of the house cares to call the Martindale Rickshaws when you are ready, I will return.'

I realise suddenly that I have no form of renumeration. 'How will I pay you?'

'The Carusos have an account with us.'

He nods at me, steps on a pedal and the wheels of the shaw are then zizzing on the smooth road surface as he pulls away, leaving me alone on this Cincture pavement. Londonia's rumble seems a million miles away. It is as if I have breathed in some intoxication, making all sound and colour intensified.

As I stare at the blancmange pink of the house opposite the door opens and a dame steps out resplendent in a daffodil-coloured dress and feather-covered hat. She peers up at the sky then calls back into the hallway. A dark-skinned girl wearing an apron bobs a curtsey as she hands over an umbrella. Without a word the dame takes it, walks down the steps and onto the pavement, skirts swaying.

For a moment, the door stays open and I feel the maid's eyes resting on me from the corridor. The door clacks shut: a small sound in the almost silent street.

As I turn to walk towards the Carusos' house, a mec appears from a side street pushing a green and gold-painted cart. His matching overalls bear the same crest, a circle encompassing a letter C. He stops, lifts out a brush and sweeps methodically at the dirt-free road, ceasing only to raise his cap to a couple of women who pass by in their long frock coats.

LONDONIA

As he levels with me the cap isn't lifted. I am not part of this society; obviously just someone here to perform a task.

I walk across checkerboard tiles to a door the colour and shininess of the bus we passed earlier. My finger hovers close to the bell on its brass plate. Who is Mrs Caruso . . . what will she want? Then I recall the mirror-dame's words and add them into the angsty mix in my mind. My finger meets the bell.

Bzzzzzzz. The door opens and a grave-faced man peers out, his neat black suit, greased back hair and quiet air elements of someone employed to wait on others.

'Yes?'

'I am here to see Mrs Caruso—Hoxton from Londonia.'

'Please come in. You are expected.'

I follow him into a canary-yellow hallway lined with paintings. The overpowering sweet smell of lilies almost drags a memory from me. Silky white petals and fuzzy pollen stamens, a smear of mustard colour on a white dress . . .

'Madame Hoxton?'

He is staring at me, white-gloved hand clasping the handle of a partially open door.

I stop dithering and sally forth, memory-fragment gone, gosse-dilemma pushed to one side. Whatever she wants, I'll do it, get it, make it happen.

Mrs Caruso, a weighty dame of perhaps my age sits examining a book, within a room that seems out of place within this elegant building. I suppose I had been expecting subtle striped wallpaper and walnut wood furniture, not angular shapes and gaudy textiles.

She stands up, placing the tome on a metal and glass side-table.

'Ms Hoxton. *So* ticked-up you could visit.'

I'm still confused by the sight of her in floor-length, embroidered dress within this room of steel and hard-looking furnishings, and the fact that her face appears to be almost the grey side of pink.

LONDONIA

'Mrs Caruso. Happy to be here. Thank you for entrusting me with your request after the sad demise of the Finder you had expected to be here t-dui—today . . .'

Noticing my interest in her surroundings and attire, she giggles and then whispers as if we are conspirators.

'I'm going to make the change.'

'The change?'

'Sit and I'll throw light.' She gestures to one of the uncomfortable-looking armchairs. 'Cocktail?'

'Oh . . . just a tea if possible.'

She tugs at a cord near the fireplace and the door opens almost immediately.

'Madame?'

'Tea, Gubbins, and a . . . tequila sunset.'

'Very good, Madame.'

She settles back in another chair and picks up a magazine from a pile on a side table.

'As I was saying, the *change*. Don't know about interior and clothes fashions in Londonia, but here, we've had the early 1900s for far too long—possibly even six months!'

An image of Jarvis dressed in a tuxedo, pink flares and golfing jumper enters my head.

'We don't really have fashion as such.'

Her sculpted eyebrows reach new heights. 'What do you *do* all the time?' If I had an answer she doesn't wait to hear it. 'I guessed—even before Up-Date journal suggested it—the 2020s. See, I'm *way* ahead.'

'Did The Lord find this other furniture?' I ask, beginning to feel slightly worried.

Mrs Caruso points around the room. 'The suite, that side table but what I really need is . . .' She reaches for the catalogue I now see it to be and picks through its fragile pages. Reaching a marked page, she sighs: '*This*,' and hands me the thing as if it is a holy manuscript.

The page shows a glass-doored cabinet.

LONDONIA

Designed by Olga Bengtsson, Splot is the perfect place to store your family treasures. Pine and particle board.

Depicted in the photograph is a smiling family sitting on a sofa like the one in this room. I risk a look at the cover: *Ikea, 2025*.

'Could you find it?' she says, a slight note of desperation in her voice.

'Yes,' I say, confidently, knowing it will be virtually impossible.

The beverages arrive, mine housed not in a silver pot as I had thought but a blue china vessel with gold zigzags.

'Habitat 2023,' she smiles. 'Fin-ess-*y*?'

'Tot-all-*y*.'

'We must land on your spoolies for this.'

As Jake had pointed out, I do find language fascinating but my brain is beginning to ache.

'Your fee,' she assists.

I rejoin reality and seize this opportunity.

'You must understand this is a very difficult Find.' She nods and I continue while searching for Jarvis's scrap of paper in my zipper pocket. 'This is the first thing I need. My Finder-partner's mother desperately needs glasses, and this is the prescription.'

She looks surprised as she takes the paper from me.

'Don't you have optys *out there*?'

A picture appears in my mind of Bert the Swagger showing me his latest pair of specs: a weird coagulation of wire and tortoise-shell frames held together with gluey string.

'. . . No, not as such.'

'Oh,' she shrugs carelessly. 'Shouldn't be a problem—I'm sure Caruso could get them fabried quickly enough.'

D'accord. 'If spectacles are easy to obtain, I will ask for thirty pairs of reading glasses of different strengths, and a large quantity of basic medical items—bandage, antiseptic cream—'

She cuts me short with a wave and speaks to the servant who has just appeared to offer more tea.

LONDONIA

'Gubbins. Fetch one of the medical kits, please.'

I glance around the room as we wait, wondering which of the hundred questions queueing I should ask.

'How long have you lived here, Mrs Caruso?'

'About fifteen years, I think. We moved from Portland Place after the wedding. *That* was an event! Centenary park, white peacocks, three-hundred guests . . .'

The door opens and Gubbins hands over an oblong box with a slight bow.

'Anything else, Madame?'

My employer drains the last of her cocktail and puts the glass down. 'No. I assume everything is prepped for dinner this evening?'

'Yes, Madame. You asked me to remind you of the bulletin at sixteen hours. It is nearly time.'

'Thank you, Gubbins.'

As he retires she shows me the box's contents.

'These were taken in exchange before. If that's zeny for you, how many should I ask Caruso to get?'

I wonder how far I can make this trade stretch, and what she might be expecting.

'The glasses and twenty kits. As I said, it will be a challenging Find.'

She looks slightly doubtful but recovers her buoyancy quick enough. 'And it's a def-cert you'll find what I want.'

What happens if I can't? 'It won't be a problem.'

'There might be a further Finding—clothes. As I said we're just lousy of the early twentieth C rags . . . oo, I need to eye the news. Your predecessor managed to find a television from 2020! Everyone's crazed for it. The only catsrof is the missing turn on thing . . . perhaps you could snag one while you're looking around?'

She gets up and walks over to a silver oblong on the wall I hadn't previously noticed. A button pressed, the screen jitters into life revealing an overexcited dame reeling off a list.

LONDONIA

I *have* to ask.
'How is that powered?'
She looks blank, shrugs. 'Oh, I don't know—shh.'

'Channel one for running and dance simulation
Channel two: historical: The construction of the Cincture walls
Channel three: further sexual instruction and your husband's wellbeing
Channel four: lawn maintenance
Channel five: caring for antiques
Retrofilm channel: tonight, Star Wars fifteen—The Void
Home channel—what's new in antiques—the race for Ikea
Public-cleansing channel. Executions. Live from the rectangle
The weather: cloud cover, rain expected before eight
Have a good evening.'

The screen blanks. Mrs Caruso's greyish face is flushed as she turns to me. I prepare to discuss the proposed executions, feeling terrified.
'Ikea,' she says, smiling. 'See! I knew it.'

Capitula 2

Ravel's deconstructed waltz echoes around the vestry walls as I search for the promised bottle of wine. The music warps slightly as the ancient gramophone winds down. I give the handle a few turns. I'm still feeling elated from the return to Londonia: elated, but spiky with nerves after being in that place. *Ah, the bottle, gotcha.* Of course, I hid it in the gramophone cupboard.

The dogs are barking—must be Jarvis. A few moments later the door opens and Jarvis and Parrot come in, stamping their feet.

'Putainfuker! It's froidly!' Parrot's deep voice rings out above the music. I leave the warmth of the vestry to welcome them.

'Hey, Kitten,' Jarvis greets me with a hug, snowflakes falling from his coat onto my face.

'Hey,' I'm so pleased to see them that tears start welling.

'Whatthafuk?' He stands back a little and looks at my red face.

'I'm fine. Take your coats off and I'll tell you about it.'

They unwrap. Parrot's face emerges from the parka's fur, his shock of Afro hair springing into its crazy shape. He cocks his head and listens to the music drifting.

'Coolo, classical—you one upmarket chick.' He kisses me, smiles and grabs Jarvis, whirling him into a waltz.

Jarvis dumps a cloth bag on the table. 'D'ac. We got eel stew, an' a tin v'apricots.'

'That's good as I've got potatoes ready and there's just enough milk to make custard.' I say, checking a canister.

'Where d'you get custard?'

'The café are making it, now they've got cornflour again . . . is Parrot ça va?' I ask, as we watch him dancing in the shadows.

LONDONIA

' 'E's had a bad day on the barges. Some gar killed himself with a fish-scaling knife. It was bloody—turned Lady Thames right red. 'Ad some stuff, not sure wot—it'll wear off in a bit, 'e won't miss the scran.'

'Did you get the Jack?'

'Yeah. A feisty sod, be a good ratter. I'll divi up wivyer morrow. So, wot the fukda! You been in there, right? Wot's it like then?'

'I don't know where to start really . . . just remember everything you ever heard about it and add several tea-chests of weird and ridiculous.'

'An' Kafka? D'you take him in?'

'No, they keep the horses at the wall. He seems fine though.'

'Tell me about weird then.'

I describe the day as Parrot comes back and sits next to Jarvis, head on his shoulder, calm now.

'How they got power? Where d'it come from?' he asks.

I shake my head. 'I've no idea. She wasn't exactly the Encyclopaedia Britannica. Or if she was, she kept it to herself.'

'You didn't parler then?'

'Only about what she wanted.'

'Which is wot?' asks Jarvis, a half smile playing.

'A certain piece of furniture.'

'Easy?'

'You remember that Habitat table request.'

He grimaces with the memory. 'Yeah.'

'Worse—Ikea cabinet, circa 2025.'

'Merda!'

The metal pot is hissing on the wood stove. Taking it off, I ladle the stew into three bowls, adding potatoes. I hand the bottle of wine to Parrot and he finds a corkscrew, yanking out the cork with a satisfying *toc* that echoes around the ancient stone. He takes three glasses from the cupboard and pours the deep red liquid. The wobbly recycled glass isn't worthy of the wine, but we clink them and smile in anticipation of something worth drinking.

'Holy festering dog carcass,' says Jarvis, taking another slug and letting it wash around. 'That is the real crappin' deal . . . you got any more?'

'Afraid not. Back to Bert's eau de vie, whatever he makes it out of.'

'Best not to ask. The plum'un weren't too shite though.'

The stew is thick and tastes of the river, but it's heavenly. I eat two helpings, put the bowl down for the cat and sit back sighing.

'That's better.'

Zorro slinks out from behind the stove and licks the remains, his one eye a jewel in the candlelight.

'Well, wot we really need to know,' says Jarvis, draining his glass, 'is, wot's the deal?'

'For the cabinet?'

'Yeah, for this merdic, pizzing, thing!'

'Well, to start, I've asked her for your mother's glasses.'

Jarvis beams. 'Apex! Does she think it'll be difficult?'

'No, she seemed totally confident about getting them made—and quickly.'

'Wot else then. It's a foitling difficult Find.'

'Basic medical supplies.'

'And?'

'I want her to help me.'

Jarvis sits back and runs a hand through his mad, greying hair.

'Uh?'

'Something happened in there . . . I was given information, about me.' The wine has deadened the nagging thoughts a little, but they rush back. Tears fall.

'Hey, hey,' says Parrot, handing me a vast handkerchief. 'Girl! What information?'

I wipe away the tears roughly and give them the tale.

LONDONIA

'I met a dame in the cleansing area. She told me that I had . . . have, a gosse, and it was born in the Cincture. I need to know more.'

'How the fukdaz she know?' sputters Jarvis.

'She's a mirror-dame—also she saw the scar.'

'Wot scar?'

'I have one, faint—across here.' I gesture to the layers covering my stomach.

'Just a line surely,' he says, pulling up his own numerous layers and pointing to grime incrusted folds of skin.

Seeing that he needs to know, I stand and yank up the two woollen feltys.

'There, sure as the Bread-mec is going to give me l'enfer tomorrow, a scar, see.'

He leans forward and traces the line with a stubby finger.

'. . . Could be someink else? Appendix?'

'That's higher up, man,' says Parrot. 'My gran, she had one done, 'fore the unknown time. Anyway, surely you'd have the nous about it? Yo feel anything, girl?'

'I never did before. Always assumed it was an accident or something from when I was a gosse. But now . . . feels odd, like someone is out there, thinking about me.'

'Well, if that's the deal, so be it,' sulks Jarvis, returning to the Finding matter. 'But wot could this Ikea-obsessing dame know anyhow?'

'Her husband is a doctor in there.'

'Yeah, but he might as well be the bleedin' almighty in a hat box for wot use it will do yer, info-wise.'

'I'm going to get to know her,' I say, stubbornly. 'I'll find this maudine piece of furniture, somehow. Anylane, wouldn't you want to find out a bit more about what goes on in there?'

Jarvis shakes his head. 'From wot you say, think I'll stick with chaosville, grazie.' His leathery face breaks into a grin. 'I'll help you though, Kitten. Course I will. You got the glasses and that's colossal-good! How you gonna start the Finding then?'

LONDONIA

'First, I'm going to go and see the mirror-dame, just find out what else she knows. Then, there's that new shouting-house quite near where she lives. They trade a lot of stuff from before the Curtain.'

'Vrai—might be the place to start. 'Ave you a picture of it, this cabinet?'

'No, she wouldn't rip it out of the precious book. I've got the details though, and I'll draw it for you.'

I search for an unused piece of paper. A scrap of tea-packet suffices, and I sketch the thing, adding the name and dimensions.

'Splot!' exclaims Parrot, looking at the card in Jarvis's hand. 'What? Dat the name of it?'

'All their stuff had names,' says Jarvis. 'That shelf wot you put up in the kitchen, was called Git—still had the label on it after all them cycles.'

We're quiet for a while, reflecting on the past. Then Jarvis jumps up.

'The drawing—nearly forgot, din' I.' He finds the cloth bag again and reaches inside.

'There y'go.'

He hands me a rolled-up piece of paper, and I unfurl it to find a detailed pencil drawing of the street, the church and me astride Kafka.

Parrot peers over. 'Hey, Jarvis . . . that damn good. Like the topper too, H.'

Jarvis takes the drawing back and holds it at arm's length, squinting.

'Yeah. Looks like the street—'cept someone's dragged that car off somewhere.'

'You should do more,' I suggest.

'Maybe . . . got the violin to practice too.'

Parrot sighs, his breath an exhausted whistle. 'Need to sleep, Jarvis. Gotta blot these cycles out.'

LONDONIA

'Stay,' I offer. 'Kafka's hay stack is chaudy, and I've got some warm blankets too.' The thought of the two mecs sharing the building is good. I feel the nightmares creeping already.

'D'ac,' says Jarvis, stretching. 'Want some peppermint leaves, Kitten?'

'I've got toothpowder, thanks. See you at sunrise.'

We kiss and they wander arm in arm to the straw, chewing the leaves. There's no need to flit a freezing cloth round my body as I'm still clean from the caustic shower. I burrow deep in the bedding with Zorro the hot water bottle. Sleep ebbs and then flows, soaking my mind, the first dreams disturbed by Parrot's ecstatic yelp as he climaxes away images of the crimson Thames.

Jarvis and Parrot have gone. They left early, Parrot to unload grain on a barge, Jarvis, a multitude of Findings to be done. I can't clear my head of the Cincture so decide on a walk and a mental list.

Kafka rolls in his sawdust, snorting, imagining the off. 'Sorry,' I say slapping his rump, 'bit later.' His food sorted, I sling the Winchester over my back, heave on the leather knapsack and open the door. The dogs are whirling fiends this morning; the gun means a serious walk and rabbits. I lock the door, clang the gate behind me, and scrabble with the heavy padlock as I catch a sight of the Bread-mec's cart approaching.

'Hoxton!' he yells. Too late, I'm halfway down the road, the dogs straining on their ropes.

As we reach Allan's-field. I let them off and they're away, snuffling the piles of bricks, snatching at rodents as they scatter. I cross the decayed railway lines and stand for a while looking

LONDONIA

down the tunnel of trees at the rusted bodies of trains, now homes, smoke snaking from makeshift chimneys.

Rabbits are few today. In the distance, I see the silhouette of a mec walking, a long branch across his shoulders, a few carcasses strung, dangling. *Merda!*

'Come on, Fagin, seek them out—he can't have got them all.' The dog redoubles his efforts and is rewarded as a hare dashes, zig-zag-zig, scattering grit and bark. He shares the bloody breakfast with Tilly as I wander into the Parkplace.

The thick woodland is still shiny with frost, steam rising from the piles of rotting leaves as rays of sun hit patches of light snow. The dark hulk of Prophet-Jake's hut looms in the mist. Should I go and see him? Time can become lost in that dark space but I've solved problems too in the past. He's a good trading point.

Just half a clock-face . . . I've got to see the mirror-dame. I knock on the peeling door and it creaks open a little, then wider as Jake's red-rimmed eyes take me in.

'Hoxton! Come in and give me the news.'

I decide not to embark on the Cincture information as I will be here until darking.

'Tea?' he continues, clunking a blackened pot on the wood burner.

'Vrai?'

'No, three-weed but I have got milk.'

'. . . D'ac. Lovely.'

He turns from the burner and stares at me.

'You've been somewhere very different haven't you?' I sigh internally, remembering he always knows whatever you think he won't.

'Yes, *very* different.'

'Cincture, eh? What's it like?'

'Dreadful . . . not like out here, dreadful—different.'

He hands me a tin cup. The metal's heat feels good, seeping through the wool of my gloves.

LONDONIA

'You learned some personal stuff too.'

I take my pocket-watch out; half a clock-face already gone. Jake's odd magic is enfolding me but I don't want to talk to him about the scar. The dame already knew. I need to see her.

'Another time,' he says, sensing my angst. 'So, I think you are after trade info?'

'Yes, but first—Jarvis says you want a bit of help with writing, and we still owe you for the scissors. Would that be a good deal?'

'Certainly,' he says with a beamy smile. 'Whenever you got time. It's seeing all those words appear on paper at the press.'

'How's the charcoal ink working?'

'Good and we're experimenting with pokeberry and walnuts for colour.'

'I've got more gum Arabic,' I say, remembering a recent find. 'I'll bring it over soon.'

'Marvel! So, what are you seeking?'

'I'm looking for furniture, a certain piece from the 2000s.'

He takes his patchy wool hat off and scratches his bald head. I wonder how old he is.

'2000s,' he mutters. 'Not a lot left from those times. Stuff made from real hard wood, it lasts, you know.'

I glance around his sooty room at the hunks of furniture. It's all from cycles way before the unknown times: 1800s, 1900s, perhaps. I suddenly realise that he's sitting on a wooden box.

'Is that lead-lined?' I ask, nonchalantly.

He stands, turns and stares at the box as if it's just time-travelled.

'I believe it is.' His eyes glint, an uneven smile breaking. 'You've been looking for one of these, hm?'

I sigh heavily. 'What's the deal?'

'Catch me something good with that gun, and it could be yours.'

I finish the tea and get up. No time like the present.

'D'ac. I'll see you in a while.'

LONDONIA

Something good? Rabbits won't do . . . duck perhaps.

I leave Jake's warm hut, call the dogs and walk out into the sharp air.

The swampy lake in the middle of the Parkplace is quiet, nothing breaking the surface of the water. I stand for a long time looking at the dark reflections of trees and stripes of silver as the sun escapes the clouds. It's one of those moments when the senses open up. Sounds around me magnify: squeaking bare branches, a hedgehog walking, its low body, scuffing up dead leaves, a distant shout.

A memory flickers . . . a lake, white boats. A hand is gripping my arm . . . the recollection scurries as my eyes catch a movement within a clump of bushes near the water.

The dogs are quiet, sensing my apprehension. We stalk forward ten paces or so. A boar ambles towards the water. He stops for a moment—perhaps the scent of dog on a breeze. He's going to run. I twist, pull the gun round and raise it hesitantly. *He's so beautiful . . .* The thought of bread without hassle swamps the thought and I fire, the motion knocking me backwards over a tree stump. The dogs run. I cover my ears from the squealing, and whisper a prayer to the god of pigs.

The dogs understand that this is a sacred body, something to be traded. They pace back, allowing me to root around in the knapsack for rope and straps. I attach the cords, tie a harness onto Fagin's massive back and we walk back to the hut, dragging the quarry.

Jake is standing outside, holding a clay pipe and grinning behind its twisting smoke.

'Good, good . . . think you got your box.'

A clock-face later I'm back at the church. The box has been cleaned and I've oiled the lock. The wood looks special, mahogany perhaps. I'd like to keep it. Instead I load it onto Kafka and walk him out into the street, leaving the dogs asleep, paws twitching as they continue the hunt in their dreams.

LONDONIA

No one in Londonia really knows what time it is. It's either light or dark, or shades in between. Jarvis and myself keep track as best we can—appointments kept where possible, and pocket watches set to a goodish estimate. The days and weeks, for most people, however, have remained intact. Today is Mundy and there is a purposefulness in people's striding walks: contacts to be made, debts to be sorted.

Bread-headquarters is busy. Both ovens are lit, smoke billowing from the sooted chimneys. Whatever the weather, the Bread-mec and his son, Able, are stripped to vests and jins, clanging iron doors shut, hauling logs and wielding flat metal bread-spades. I halt Kafka as we approach and, as usual, take a moment to look at the bread-compound built inside the corpse of another building, their dwelling consists of a small house, flanked on both sides by the two circular brick ovens. The rest of the yard is full of wood, fastidiously sorted into sections for size and age. Large, blackened metal bins hold grain and flour, surrounded always by a cloud of hopeful birds. Two great-hounds preside over this domain, their chains clanking ominously at anyone's approach.

Able is bent over, scraping ash from one of the ovens as I call him.

'Salut, Able. Where's the patron?'

He turns, brushes the flopping hair from his eyes and grins. 'In the bath. Come in.'

This seems odd, but I slide down from Kafka, unlash the box and follow him.

'He's in a filthy mood . . . backache,' he continues, 'but you'll cheer him up.'

He pushes open the door: an ornate slab of wood with linen fold panels, in odd contrast to the rest of the makeshift building; I wonder what once-magnificent abode it was hauled from.

We walk into a hallway littered with horse paraphernalia, boots and flour sacks. To the right is the kitchen. Able shows me in and for a moment our eyes lock. He's beautiful under the coating of white. I expect he's thinking something similar. Given another situation we might have had a liaison—layers thrown off for an animalistic tussle amongst the flour-dust and sacks.

'Pa . . . someone to see you,' he calls, then glides a hand briefly over my cheek, his smile making sweat start up under my already too-hot clothing. He returns to the oven-clearing, and me to pay a debt.

The bath sits in the middle of the kitchen. Ancient and made of copper, it glows softly like an amber jewel in the shadowy room. A fire smoulders beneath it, filling the room with wood smoke. I approach, warily. 'Salut.'

The Bread-mec is almost asleep in the water. He slides up a little and looks at me through the haze.

'Ha, it's you. Come to ask for more on the slate?'

'No, not at all. Here, look.' I hold up the box, and open it, showing him the dull grey of the lead.

'Greatly good,' he grins. I've never seen him smile before; it casts away the years, leaving a younger gar than I had thought. They must have had Able almost as gosses. They? I've never pictured a dame within the bread compound, but there must have been someone.

'What happened to your wife?' I risk, as he's looking unusually benevolent.

His eyes seem to darken at the question.

'She died . . . with Able. He was in the wrong position, you know. Sideways, or something.'

I think of the line across my skin and wonder again about an infant. 'Sorry. Not my business.'

'Not a problem.' He heaves himself up from the greasy water and snaps a cloth from a chair-back, rubbing himself all over furiously. 'That's better, nothing like a good soak to ease away the pain . . . other than a good fuk, eh?'

He's staring into my face, his smile and eyes just like his son. I step back and notice an impressive bulge under the worn cloth, now casually tied about his waist.

LONDONIA

I'm not shy when it comes to sex, but a threesome with the Bread-mec and his son could be complicated, however pleasurable for a short while. And then there's the question of Tom . . .

'Sorry—got t'go.'

He smiles sleepily and strokes the bulge. 'Maybe another time? Maybe more. I've a good business, you know that, Hoxton.'

Merda! A proposal of sorts, even before the morning has started. After a momentary image of me as a permanent filling in a Bread-mec's sandwich, I thank him, take a proffered loaf and go back out to Kafka, patiently waiting in the yard. The bread stowed, I climb onto Kafka, steer him out of Bacon Street and towards Liverpool Street.

This area that was known as *The City* has become a zone to cross with care; its once-gleaming buildings of monetary power, unstable after violent storms from over the cycles. A few, perhaps designed with nature's fury in mind, still stand intact, their original contents piled in the streets: computers, drifts of pulpy paper and rotting furniture, all picked over uncountable times for their possible use.

Some bods risk living in these glass constructions. I went to see a friend once when he was lodging high up in the top of one. I had climbed the many flights of stairs and looked in at the different floors littered with makeshift beds and hurricane lamps. The wind sighed through broken windows, the building creaking and groaning as if it would soon lie down to die in a mighty, curving thump of glass and debris.

My church is cold and busy with ghosts. Most people can't understand why I live there, but it feels as solid as a Parkplace oak tree, its roots firmly imbedded in the Londonian soil.

I stir Kafka into a gallop away from the city zone, through Finsbury Circus: a forest of poplar and plane trees where wild pigs sometimes doze in the mud, watchful of people with guns. Now we approach Barbican, where somewhere on Silk Street, is the mirror-dame's abode. I slow the horse to a walk as we pass through the decaying buildings of the Barbican centre. If I had time, I would stop at the wooden shed at the side of the lake and barter a pike butty. The fish-girl is there, hauling her latest catch from the murky depths. I greet her on passing.

'How's business?'

She shrugs. 'Been better, long dark-quarter and all. Still, got some trout here now, when the herons leave any. Hungry?'

'Later,' I call, and steer Kafka onwards into Silk Street where we walk past semi-crumbled buildings until I spy the drinking house, still standing strangely intact.

Someone has nailed a long board on top of the original name.

'Time and tide wait for no man,' I read out loud, intrigued.

' 'Twas de Jugged Hare, before,' says a wiry mec busy sweeping up piles of white dust. He stops and rests his hands on the top of the broom. 'Ye be searching for somebody?'

'Yes, I don't know her name, but she's a mirror-dame.'

He points to a window. 'Marina . . . she's on der second floor. I'll find ye a horse-boy, or ye'll be having no transport when y' comes out—just finish this.'

I notice patches of what looks like dried blood as he uncovers more pavement.

'What happened?' I ask.

'Sharks came last darking,' he says as he sweeps. 'Dey were doing a spot check in the area and just happened to turn up when a minor brawl was going aff in the street—really nuttin' but they decided to set one of dere *examples,* and they used dat bleedin' waster smoke—leaves dust everywhere.'

'Were many taken?' I ask, a screw of fear in my stomach.

'Don't know. I was too busy trying to calm folks in the Time and Tide, and now all dis merde to clean up. Just got us straight after dat last hailstorm too.'

Picking up a dustpan, he sweeps the dust up and into a box filled with bloodied clothing then goes muttering into the drinking-house.

LONDONIA

After a short while, a youth appears, nods at my offer of bacco and ties Kafka to a lamppost.

'Good for a clock-face.'

'More, if I need it?' I ask, having no idea how long this might take, if she's even there.

'Yep.'

I dismount and unstrap the carpet-bag of possible exchange goods, heart fluttering now. The interior of the drinking-house is warm of velvet and flames that dance in the fireplace. The idea of sitting with a mug of ale and a book suddenly seems enticing . . .

The landlady, a crow-like young dame with black hair and beady eyes recites me her ales.

'Nettle, dandelion root, wild oat . . . we 'ave got hop too, but it'll cost y' good.'

Deciding on nettle, I take the china mug, and wander, looking at old advertisements and newspaper cuttings covering the walls. The largest framed picture is of a sleek, silver car in front of an illuminated city: *BMW, prepare to master the road ahead.* I'm transfixed by the image: the lights in the buildings, the car and the man in dark glasses.

'Difficult to imagine, innit,' says the dame. 'It was made just down the road from here.'

I think of the decaying fences, piles of rubble and the dark of the dark at night; the spots of candlelight and stars.

'Yes, impossible.'

The newspaper pages describe ferocious weather and the solar storm precursors to wwW, now only remembered by a few like Jarvis's sage-dame mother. I stop my wandering and take the mug back to the bar.

'Another, love?' suggests the landlady.

Thinking of my meeting to come but ignoring my internal warning of the headache that will probably emerge later, I nod. As she pours, the room's only other client stands up, shuffles on a large tweed coat and heads for the door.

LONDONIA

'Quiet today,' I remark. 'Because of the Sharks?'

'Didn't help—Merde-heads! But before that we'd got quieter anyway after the Rat-flu. Foiteling big outbreak—got a lot of my clients. I was ill for I dunno how long.'

'We didn't have that. Muto-pox was the last big haul. I thought I was for it during that one.'

She smiles grimly as she wipes down the bar. 'We ain't had that here—yet.'

After warming myself at the stove for a time, I ask if Marina might be in.

The landlady jerks her head towards the stairs. 'Second floor, black door.'

Draining the last of the beer, I hand the mug back and walk up the creaking stairs. I peer down the dark corridor. Marina's room is at the end.

I pad across cracked linoleum, knock tentatively and wait, studying the inscriptions carved into its black paint. *The wheel is come full circle. Time and tide wait for no man.* The door opens suddenly and I'm looking into the cold blue eyes again.

'Thought I'd be seeing you sometime,' she says, her expression unreadable. 'You're lucky. I had someone to come this morn, but he died in night.'

'Oh, sorry.'

'Don't be. He was bastard, and had it coming. I was to tell him as much.' She notices my eyes wandering over her person. 'Yes, I'm not what most people think to expect, you know—youngish, fattish, not grey hair, not dark mysterious eyes.' But her eyes are mysterious, glacial pools, unfathomable.

'So, what can I trade you?' I ask, the anxiety wavering into panic.

'Nothing . . . yet. I keep in bank, so to speak?'

'Yes, if you like.'

'Calm down. I can't read you if thoughts are like pot of spaghetti. Come, sit here.'

LONDONIA

I haven't looked at the room yet . . . too busy wondering about her. My eyes flit around its walls as I sit down in a scarred, leather chair. The walls are black like the door, also covered with scratched inscriptions. Photographs and more newsprint, half-imbedded like fossils, break the oily surface. A large wooden bed lurks in one corner with many small dogs asleep amongst blankets and furs.

'Heating,' she explains. 'The Italian greyhound—bred originally to warm the bed.'

The other heating seems to be a small, pot-bellied wood stove, effective, as I find myself removing layers; or it could just be apprehension.

'Did you rename this place,' I ask, now wanting to delay.

'Yes. She doesn't like beasts, and I like that quotation.'

'That's good enough reason.'

'I thought so.'

I sigh deeply and shift in the chair, nerves pricking.

'I'm going to give you drink,' Marina continues. 'Something to unravel your mind, to lay threads out.' She goes over to a small cupboard, takes out a decanter and pours a measure of something into a shot glass. 'Knock back in one.'

I do, and a brimming warmth floods my veins. I splay in the chair like a contented starfish and am ready for whatever transpires.

She pulls up another chair and takes my hand. No crystal ball, no star-spotted cloths; just her odd goat-like eyes fixed on mine. The room is silent apart from a few clicks from the stove and the occasional snuffle from the dog pile. After what seems like fifty cycles, she sits back, her eyes wet, cheeks flushed.

'You have quite a history, Lady.'

'Can you see it all?'

'No. There are blocks. Your mind, it has been partly cleared at some point.'

'Cleared?'

'It happens. You have been in Cincture. They can do that.'

LONDONIA

I feel my bladder contract, its contents pressing to escape. I feel sick too, but strangely excited.

'What did you see?'

She ignores my question, but asks her own. 'What do you first remember?'

I recall hard slats and biting cold. 'I was lying down, on a wooden bench. The sky was half blue-half black with points of light. My hands felt wetness covering a long, wool coat wrapped around my body. I was aware that I was me, but I didn't know who me was.'

'Then?'

'I sat up and tried to remember something, but it was like trying to recall a dream that's just out of reach, shrinking away. There was a rectangle of metal on a string around my neck. I took it over my head and looked at it. There was only one word, Hoxton.'

'You thought it was your name?'

'Yes, well it is. I don't have another.'

'You never consider this to be . . . odd name?'

A word is just a word . . . but she's right. I never did make a connection—too busy scraping a life together with whatever name I thought I had.

I leave these wonderings as Marina continues.

'The park where you woke, where is it?'

'I don't know. I never did remember.'

'But you do. Is written in your memory—Hoxton Square. You saw sign, but never recalled name. I think perhaps you were left there and someone forgot to remove delivery note.'

I am silent for a long time, wondering if I had a name before and how I lost so many cycles. Could I ever recall them? Was there a way? A tear escapes and wends its way to my lips. I taste the salt, strange against the lingering sweetness of the drink. I expect her to comfort me, but she just sits as if in a trance.

'You dream often?' she asks, abruptly.

'Yes.'

'Of the same places, people?'

'Sometimes.'

'You are led to a lake, by someone . . . a mec.'

'Yes.'

I remember with a start, the real reason that I am sitting in this room. *The gosse* . . . 'You said I have an infant.'

Marina's brow furrows slightly. 'Yes, you do. Fair hair, and eyes of green water.'

I want to scream out all the questions piling up. 'Where was he born?'

'There was long room, other women lying down.' Her voice is very quiet now, eyes shut and head bowed. I fear the end of this session is coming. She looks up.

'You have to leave now. I will sleep.'

'Can I come again?'

'Maybe. I don't know if I find something else.'

'What about the exchange?'

'I let you know. I see where you live.'

Hauling myself from the depths of the chair, I feel frozen despite the warm room. I pull on my discarded layers and walk towards the door. Marina climbs onto the bed, scattering dogs as she covers herself. She pulls the blankets over her head and the pack re-group. As I leave the room, she calls out, voice muffled. 'Cincture dame's request—you will have luck.'

Back downstairs, the landlady stares at me and re-fills my mug from earlier.

'This one's on the house, love.' She signals to the horse boy just coming in. 'Give 'er a bit more time, eh?'

I sink down into a chair by the fire wondering if I will ever feel warm again.

Capitula 3

By the time I had got home and dealt with Kafka, nothing else was in my mind apart from sleep. Ignoring the dogs, I had crawled into bed and knew no more.

Now, lying awake again, the scar on my stomach itches as if it itself had learned things from those cycles spent in Marina's room. Stretching, I listen for a moment to the darking sounds: a first owl, the squeaking wheels and clopping hooves of the last-water round. In the front yard the dogs are howling; they and I need a meander amongst plants and wildlife. I recover my discarded shoes in the semi-darkness, find a thicker felty and walk out to the front of the church. The dogs whirl and jump as I lock up.

'Allez, let's go.'

We streak along the quiet streets to the Parkplace, the darkness punctuated by small fires where people camp in huddles, their weary faces momentarily animated by the sight of a dame running behind two thundering dogs.

The familiar park grounds are a vast plain tonight, full of mysterious rustlings. I let the dogs off and they scarper, noses to the ground, jaws snapping at fleeing rodents. Prophet-Jake's hut is a dim, frayed square in the moonlight. Sounds of a violin drift into the quietude. I sit on a tree stump listening to the melody and wonder if my gosse might also be outside somewhere looking up at the ragged clouds passing the moon.

A cric-crac of dry twigs takes my attention and I stand abruptly, cursing myself for still being within this curious daze. The Winchester is on its hook in the vestry and the dogs are now on the other side of the pond.

LONDONIA

As I inch silently away from the noise a familiar voice calls out.

'Hey, Hoxton. It's me, Tom. Your face! Such terror in the moonlight.' He walks out from the shadows and over to me, eyes wide in surprise. 'You cut your hair. I like it!'

I breathe out, relieved *and* amazed to see him. 'Jarvis's doing . . . but, how are you here?'

'I was coming to see you.'

'I thought you had a job on in the forrist.'

'Time off. Someone's nobbled the horses . . . so, thought I'd come back into Londonia while they sort it out.'

'How did you know where I was? My letter reached you?'

He shakes his head. 'Sadly, nope, but I spoke to Jake. Course he knowed about you—et voila.'

He smiles his broad lop-sided smile, half closes his eyes and sneaks a wandering hand under my coat.

'It's a magical night,' he says, drawing me close to him. A rosy flush spreads from my accelerating heartbeat. I slip my hands under his jacket and cup the cheeks of his muscular arse, causing him to groan and whisper gentle obscenities.

This is heading into dangerous territory. To be caught entangled and semi-naked by a roaming gang would be careless.

'Shall we go back?' I suggest, pulling away slightly.

'What, no spontaneous outdoor stuff?'

'It's too cold, and the dogs will stray.'

'D'ac. Got any wine?'

'Elderberry.'

He takes my hand. 'Allez . . . race you.'

I whistle for the hounds and we zip back through the streets, a human and canine blur.

I unlock the church door and we stagger in, hounds heading for their blanket pile.

'Oof, s'froidy in here,' shivers Tom, dragging off clothing all the same.

'It should be warm in the vestry.'

LONDONIA

'Foiteling hope so!'

I push him forwards in the dark, light the oil lamp and open the bottle of wine. Tom is stealthily removing my layers.

'Wash,' I say, sternly, 'I don't know where you've been!'

Moaning at the thought of cold water he complies; empties a jug into the bowl and gasps as the damp cloth makes contact. Afterwards he dives for the bed and I brave the water. He props himself up on the bolster, watching me.

'You are so very beauteous,' he says, eyes bright, hands straying to the raised area of blanket. 'Marry me?'

'What?' My voice echoes around the church. 'That's the second proposal today!'

He stares. 'Who was the first?'

'The Bread-mec.'

'Did you accept?'

'No.'

'Why?'

'I don't want to marry anyone.'

Tom grins and pulls me under the covers. 'I'll have a go at changing your mind.'

The questions and confusions of the day recede as he turns me over and massages my back, his hands rough from tree-work but gloriously sensual. He leans forward and bites my neck gently. I giggle.

'What?' he murmurs.

'I just remembered a picture of lions in the wildlife encyclopaedia.'

'Lions doing what?'

'This.'

'Fukking,' he says in such a lascivious way that I really forget everything, and being cold, and my past, and it's so absolutely, incredibly beautiful—this little piece of time.

At some point in the night I'm woken by a fox's bark. I lie curled in Tom's embrace, thinking about his offer. Why don't I just make my life with him? Do I want to be with anyone though? Does he? Sex seems to have become less heralded in these times of survival. It's just something people do, because they feel like it, or to add another gosse to their brood, for security I suppose. When I have flipped through the shiny world of magazines from before the unknown time, it seems as if it had ruled everything.

Daylight fills the vestry. Sparrows flutter in and out through a broken windowpane where a patch of blue sky is visible. Sounds of carts and street chatter fill my ears. This day I must start the search for the furniture.

I stretch luxuriously and Tom's eyes open, the laugh lines creasing. He runs a hand down my back and squeezes a cheek.

'Salut, my ecclesiastical one.'

'What?'

'You live in a church, yes?'

'But perhaps I'm not so saintly . . . last eve?'

'God gave us these bits, lust, and the desire for climax, so what can be wrong with it?'

'You have a point.'

'I'm getting one, feel.'

I laugh, pull back the blankets, and step out of our nest to check the fire. 'Do you believe then,' I wonder out loud. He's never mentioned God before.

'Nah . . . do you know anybody that does?'

I think of Sardi and her open house to all religions.

'Not necessarily *a* God. Gods, or spirits maybe.'

'There's loads 'a beliefs, gods, magic systems, mediums. I believe all of it and none of it.'

'You possess an open mind, then?'

'Don't you have to, in these times of knowing nothing?'

LONDONIA

'Yes, you do,' I murmur, thinking of the mirror-dame's words.

I wash quickly then shiver into underclothing. Tom watches me pulling on a ragged felty.

'Shall we get dressed up one darking?' he suggests. 'Just for the pleasure, and go out.'

'Go out where?'

'I've heard good talk of a scoffery run by Brazilians on the river bank? It's supposed to be good.'

The idea of putting on some of my collected pre-cycles stuff is enticing.

'That would be wonderful. Maybe when it's not so cold. Perhaps as a celebration?'

'What's to celebrate?'

'I've got to find something, which will then lead me to discover . . . something.'

'All sounds fukly vague.'

He's looking peeved so I tell him.

It takes over a clockface by which time the dogs are barking and Kafka is kicking the planks of his stall.

'Think you need to sort out the menagerie,' Tom says, scowling a little. It's the mention of Marina's last words that have caused his smile to disappear.

'Maybe it's best not to know about the past,' he mutters, cramming on his shoes. 'If it's true, what she said, could be dangerous.'

His dismissal of my lost years angers me.

'Tom! This isn't just about a wayward horse or something—my gosse, my offspring!'

He shrugs on his long coat and lopes to the door, turning briefly.

'Maybe you should foitling stay happy with what you got here. See ya.'

I'm sure he's not been exactly faithful to me, and I'm not averse to the odd liaison, but we potentially share something powerful. Have I just smashed that? So be it. I can't just bury this news within me and carry on as before. Placing the Tom-angst to one side I sort the animals out and plan the day.

By late aft the sky is almost as dark as the interior of the confessional. I've sorted clothes, china, pots of jam and bottles of fruit; trading boxes are labelled and the vestry is as clean as it ever gets. I sit gloomily in the half-light while the kettle sighs on the stove. I need real tea but an inspection of the various boxes and caddies revealed only sage and chamomile. The church door creaks again and I jump up imagining a reappearance of Tom—flowers in hand, protestations of love . . .

Heavier footsteps announce the arrival of Jarvis. I sink back into the chair feeling irritable. The door opens and his black-coated benevolence fills the room. The room where I want to be alone and sulk for a while.

'Oi-oi,' he says, tossing his hat to the table and surveying my miserable expression. 'Tea withdrawal, eh? I've Just the thing!'

Delving into a pocket he brings out a paper bag and shows me the contents.

My spirits brighten a smidge.

'Is that Assam?'

'Sure as Bert's a pervy bedswerver.'

'Fire up the kettle, then.'

Jarvis pokes the flames back into life, throws in wood, clangs the door shut and sits down opposite me.

'Not just tea is it, Kitten?'

'I'm not *that* addicted.'

'So wot then? That gar a' yours. I heard he'd made a visit?'

'Partly.'

'And partly wot else?'

'What that dame said.'

'Who?'

'The mirror-dame I told you about. I went to see her earlier.'

He rolls his eyes. 'Ferfuksake, H. How does she really know about your past?'

LONDONIA

I think of her visions: *it is written in your mind.*
'Jarvis?'
'Yeah?'
'You know . . . I never went back to where I woke up, on that bench.'

He shrugs. 'So—s'only a bench?'

'Maybe if I went back there and lay down I'd remember something. And now I know where it is . . . Hoxton Square.'

Jarvis stands up, goes back to the stove and clunks china around muttering. He returns and places a mug of dark, strong tea before me.

'You're good 'ere, H. Look at wot we got—shelter, friends,' he scans the room, eyes resting on a box of vegetables I've cut for trading . . . 'cabbage, everything.'

I smile, knowing his words are true.

'You're right . . . but I can't forget what she said.'

He shakes his head. 'Drink that an' we'll go and look at this pizzing bench. You can lie on it and I'll keep an eye out—fukin Clashers's there now.'

'Really, you don't mind?'

'Yeah, we can drop off some stuff to Fred's Threads.'

We sit in silence appreciating the flavoursome tea while a smattering of hail scours the windows. The memory of waking on the hard bench slats surfaces briefly. I click the mug down on the table.

'D'accord. Cart or Kafka?'

He glances up at the window. 'Cart. He'll freeze in this merdic weather *and* the Clashers'll kill for horse.'

'There's the bag of jumpers I darned,' I say, thinking of our stock, 'and the box of coats.'

'Sounds sound.' Then he looks at me, eyes bright under his mat of curls. 'You still got that coat wot you woke up in—on the bench?'

'I was going to make it into a horse cover but yes it's still stashed, and full of moth.'

He grins. 'Get it out and stick it on, Hox—might help.'

Half a clockface later we're pulling the metal cart up Old Street, Jarvis swearing manically as the wheels jar into potholes formed by recent ice. The long coat flaps around my heels, tripping my feet. Any moths remaining will be truly frozen to dust. A slight smell rises from the wool; just a trace of a perfume, the molecules of which rest in the fabric: musk of roses on a hot evening. Heat. Impossible to recall in this shrivelling wind.

Fred's building comes into view: dark-bricked and glowering. We shove and twist the cart until it rests on the remains of a pavement outside the door. Jarvis hammers on the flaking wood.

'Oi. Fred! Open this bastard door!'

Dogs bark inside and I picture the troop of mangy beasts he shares the space with.

'Okee-fukin-dokey,' comes his gravelly voice. A small hatch creaks open in the wood and a wild eye surveys us. The door swings wide.

'J an' H . . . come the fuk in and 'av some haddock. Leave the chariot—I'll get the lads to bring it.'

Wading in through the cluttered entrance way and pushing aside the wolfhounds, we follow Fred's boney figure into the musty, fabric-smelling interior. I glance up at the only evidence of the building's previous use: a few cardboard signs hanging from the ceiling, their bright slogans dust-covered and water stained—

New! Voice-activated Dish Washer range! Table Top Pizza Oven—The latest essential

Fred and Mimi have made some changes. Ancient wardrobes hailing from all decades now line the walls, her bold writing splayed across each door.

LONDONIA

Jumpers—wool, Jumpers of other stuff, coats, trousers, jins; boots, shoes, sack bags, work hats, Tatler hats.

'Tatler hats?' I query, thankfully dropping my heavy coat to the back of a chair.

'Useless, decoration ones,' he clarifies. 'You know, like stuff what's in *Tatler* or any of them other magazines.'

'Cincturians like this sort a' crud.' says Jarvis, opening the cupboard's door and fingering a red velvet hat embellished with a curled feather. 'Good trading.'

'Yeah, can be. Keeps Mimi busy too. Word out from a Finder friend that the era's changin' in there.'

'It's true,' I add, and describe my meeting with Mrs Caruso. 'You'll be looking more for pretend military stuff, animal print, less of the hats . . .'

Mimi looks up from her sewing machine part hidden behind a towering pile of clothing.

'Aw, what they on w' now?'

'The 2020s according to her. She seems to imagine herself and her friends as some sort of fashion vanguard.'

'Psubratys! Just finished a load a' 1905 jackets . . .'

Going over to commiserate, I watch her frantic hands pushing a satin gown through the machine, occasionally stopping to rock a pram next to her. She stops pedalling, brushes back her tangle of sandy hair and smiles with her habitual warmth.

'Aye-aye, Hoxton. What tha brought us this time?'

'Good quality wool—cable knit and Fairisle.'

'Grand!' She puts two fingers in her mouth and whistles piercingly. 'Henry, Frank—get stuff in.'

The two sons sitting at a game table, slap their cards down and reluctantly head to the door. Mimi bends her head to the white fabric again.

'Sorry, love—got a dame coming to collect this on the morrow. Fred'll sort tha out wi' trade.'

LONDONIA

I walk over to where Jarvis and Fred now sit with glasses of cloudy fluid.

'Take a pastis, H?' says Fred picking up a bottle.

'Where did you get it?' I ask, recalling a recent request.

'Frenchy brothers down at South Wharf—they got connections over the water.'

'Just a taste, thanks.'

'Haddock?'

'Er . . . yes.'

'Did n'exchange yestdy with a mec on a bike wiv fish—load of it, needed eating sharpish. Mimi's tried smoking it. Won't be a mo.'

Fred stands up and lopes over to what must have once been a glass-walled office. The cloud of smoke inside leaks out as he opens the door and plunges inside. The smoke reaches us and Jarvis inhales.

'Mm, ain't had 'addock since I was a scrap—Dad used to get it down the chippy with peas and curry sauce.'

Thoughts of crouching, cramped over the china wash bowl flit across my thoughts. *Mec on a bike wiv fish*. Still it's freezing and my stomach clamours, so I take the plate Fred is handing me and fork a chunk of white flesh to my mouth. Wonderful—sweet, slight taste of leather and old wool but so good. I wash it down with a glug of pastis and smile.

'Thanks, Fred.'

'You're welcome. Right, let's see what my best Finders 'ave got us.'

He beckons the lads bring over the cart and we unload the boxes.

I shake out the stack of cream cable-knit sweaters.

'Pure wool, and I've done the darns myself—they'll not pull.'

He nods. 'Good, good. Like it. We'll 'ave all them. And that box?'

Jarvis unpacks the coats and jackets, displaying my prized find—a dark blue lengthy coat with gold buttons and fur collar.

LONDONIA

'Got 'ta be worth a fair bit, that, eh, Fred.'

The trade gets underway for the lot and finally we agree on two pounds of salted sardines, dandelion coffee, boots for Jarvis, a new hand-printed map of the East End (as drawn up by Wandering Spike the route-master) and a better condition carpet bag for me.

'What's that coat you was wearing?' asks Fred finding bags and stashing our goods into the cart.

I fetch it and show him. He rubs the fabric between practised finger and thumb.

'This is class. Where d'you get it?'

I think of the complicated story and decide on an off-white lie.

'I found it—in a park.'

His bushy eyebrows converge. 'Odd thing to leave, or lose—see the label—Tabitha's. That's 'bout the most bleedin' expensive shop in the whole of the Cincture.'

My reply is lost in a sound of shattering glass from above us. I look up, shoving the chair back. A grey heap lands at my feet.

'Wood pigeon,' remarks Jarvis, unperturbed, and helping himself to another shot of pastis.

Fred picks up the dead bird by the leg. 'Great. Lunch tomorrow.' He walks over to the smoke filled room and shouts back. 'Hey, Frank, get on the roof and cover the skylight—can't risk no water on the stock.'

Noting the deep grey sky through the shattered glass I think of the park.

'Better go, Jarvis. Let's leave the cart here and get it later.'

He nods, downs the drink and calls to Mimi.

'Tell Fred we'll be back to collect the stuff later, M.'

She salutes a yes and carries on pedalling. As we reach the door I hear a wail from the newest member of the family. The machine stops and Mimi's soft voice replaces the whirr.

'Aye, I knows, Jewel. Scran-time soon.'

LONDONIA

I follow Jarvis out into the darkening street and pull on the admired coat. As we walk, heads down against the scratching wind, I thrust my hands deep into the pockets, feeling the velvet lining. One of the seams is broken and my fingers curl around a folded piece of paper. Jarvis strides on. Hail dashes my face. We turn into a crowded street where flames engulf things I don't want to see. Jarvis turns sharply away as eyes look to us. We run. Sparks follow blown on trails of smoke.

Jarvis stops, clasping at the railings of Hoxton Square, bent over, coughing.

'Jesu, Satan and pizzfuk, Hox! Why we doin' this? Remind me.'

He breathes pastis fumes at me, eyes mad, hat askew.

'Sorry, Jarvis, it just seemed . . . imperative.'

He stands upright and searches for tobacco in his coat pocket. 'Ça va. I saw yor expression when you heard the nipper's cry at Fred's. Must be fukly weird knowin' there's a gosse out there somelieu wi' yor name on it.'

I pass him the cigar I had concealed earlier for just such a crisis moment.

The crows' feet snarl into place as he grins. 'Come on then— let's find this bastard bench.'

The gate squeals open and we squish onto sodden grass. Bods gripping various tools appear from a nearby subsiding corrugated shed. Jarvis puts his hands up.

'Just 'ere to look for something.'

A dame steps forward brandishing a hoe.

'Look for quoi?'

Jarvis produces a slim bottle from a pocket and holds it out.

'Let's just say it's a bit complicated, but won't involve no agro.'

She snatches the gift. 'Vous—nozing to do with zem putain Clashers?'

'Do I look like it?'

A slight smile crosses her lined face. 'Non, s'pose not.'

LONDONIA

She retreats to the front of the shack, crouches and prods a wisp of fire back to life.

The other dwellers stand huddled, watching us.

'They're going to be a bit disappointed at the lack of action,' I remark.

Jarvis glances about. 'Well, which one is it?'

I look around under the shadowy trees then I see the bench; considerably more rotted, but certainly the same one.

'That one.'

'With the Fuk the Custodian tagging?'

'Well, that wasn't on it, but it's the right one.'

We squish over to it and I lie down tentatively waiting for the slats to give way. Jarvis retrieves the cigar, lights it and looks up at the speeding clouds.

'Lucky the clouds is pizzing off—you got stars. Same isit?'

I watch the curl of blue smoke rise from his mouth then turn my gaze back to the inky sky.

'Seems similar—damp, cold and stars.'

'Shut yor eyes. Concentrate.'

I lie still for a long time. My mind wanders: grasping hands, muddled voices and unclear words.

'Thi . .. s one, h..ere..hot—scalding! . . leave . . . she wouldn't know . . . NO. Get here now!'

Horses' hooves, silence. Cold, wood, slats, stars. A void.

I sit up. Jarvis is no longer with me.

'Jarvis?'

A terrible thought slinks into my head. I have dreamt this whole world: Jarvis, the church, Kafka, Finding . . .

'Jarvis!'

A figure appears from behind a massive plane tree and ambles over, faffing with the front of his trousers.

'Just pizzing—wot, Kitten? Look like you seen one too many phantoms.'

I stumble over and wrap my trembling arms around his, thankfully, real torso.

'Let's go home. Enough.'

He hugs me back. 'Goodly idea—fukin froidly, 'tis.'

We run towards the gate, the small crowd staring. A man waves, Jarvis's bottle in hand.

'Fait attention—Clashers!'

Jarvis waves back and we're out in the street, walking fast, breath steaming.

'So wot did y' feel—or see—or wotever?'

'A few words came to me . . . voices, men arguing about roughing me over.'

'Holy dechet, H. D'y think they might 'a?'

'I don't—'

A screech from behind a clump of bushes cuts my reply. A half-clad dame streaks away from two mecs, across the street and down an alley.

The taller mec's rasping voice reaches us. 'Let her go. Not much on her anylane.'

They turn to look at us, red and white zebra paint shining in the moonlight, eyes outlined in black.

Jarvis mouths a whisper. 'Merda.'

'Yeah, crud-stick,' cuts in the shorter one. 'Your lucky night—not.'

Jarvis circles, pushing me behind him, other hand reaching for the pistol in his belt.

'Strays from the pack, eh?'

'They're just a whistle away.'

Jarvis laughs. 'I don't think so . . . went after some fresh meat di' ya. Got lost?'

Abruptly his arm swings up but only a sullen clicking sound echoes in the street.

'Piece of pute-merde!'

The short mec lunges, shoves me away hard and wrenches Jarvis to his knees, a blade to his throat. Hissed words cut the night.

'Not so putain-fukin clever now, homburg mec.'

LONDONIA

The tall gar has grabbed me, arm around my neck as I flail and kick.

'You got a bit more to you, pute-bitch. Keep him at bay, Teeth. My turn first, and he can watch.'

He shoves me roughly over to the hulk of a blackened vehicle, pushes my coat up, kicks my feet apart. He's strong, hand in my hair grasping at the roots, pulling my head back; knee in my back, other hand tugging at clothing. As I writhe, a sharp blue sound fills my ears. My attacker collapses, head between my feet. I step back crushing his nose with my boot.

Jarvis is on the ground, a dark red grinning wound in his neck. His shaking hand still holds the pistol, now aimed at his own assailant.

'Yeah, maybe I *am* so clever, fuk-crud.'

He pulls back the trigger. It jams.

The mec laughs, raises the knife to finish the job. I see Jarvis's coffin afloat in the Thames.

'NO!'

The mec's forgotten me, his back turned. I leap over and kick hard up into his scrote-bag. He howls. The knife clatters away. Jarvis bundles up, rolls, stretches out a hand and clutches the blade. The mec totters, still groaning, staggers upright. He makes to run. Jarvis hurls the knife. The mec collapses, a silver wedge glinting in his back.

Pulling off my scarf I press it to Jarvis's neck. He gestures: *Wind it good.*

The wool saturates red, redder, then stops. I kneel, holding the fabric with shaking hands.

'I got it, H. Do those fukkers—get what you can.' His voice is a scarred whistling sound. The image of a bod-box fills my mind again.

'Jarvis . . .'

'D'ac. I'll live. Scour 'em—quick before more come.'

LONDONIA

I scuttle over, drag the knife out from flesh, kick the body over and feel in pockets finding tobacco, necklaces and a bottle of sardines.

'That it,' mutters Jarvis. 'Not much for near-death. Try the other.'

I crouch over the other body.

'He's still breathing.'

'Not for long.' Jarvis staggers upright, seizes the bloodied knife and plunges the blade deep into the gar's neck. A croaking sound issues from his dying lungs, a few creaky words following.

'Get you in l'enfer, fukka.'

Jarvis snarls. 'Don't think so. See what he's worth, H.'

Grasping the gar's shoulders, I turn him. He flops onto his back, a last gasp escaping his throat. Silver spills from his pockets: coins, rings and chains. I gather the lot, bundling it into my pockets.

Footsteps and voices sound in the street. 'Rats d' l'enfer! Stop! Arret!'

'Jarvis!'

'Yeah, I hear it—go!'

We run as if Hades' own dogs have spied us.

Jarvis turns once and points the pistol. 'Fire you piece 'a —' It does. Someone shouts. Footsteps cease momentarily then start again. The street is black, the moon shrunk behind cloud.

'Hox—down 'ere.'

Jarvis pulls me sideways into a snicket between houses. We dive into rubbish and lie beneath death-stenched clothing, breathing shallow, silent. The footsteps thunder past.

'Where the pute?' shouts a mec.

'Disparu . . . la peut-être,' another.

We lie for ages waiting until the clamour becomes quieter than some scrapping dogs a street away.

I sit up, slowly remove a foul, blood-smelling blanket from my chest and retch.

'Christ in a box, Jarvis . . . good choice of hiding place.'

LONDONIA

'Did the job, din'it,' he grunts, standing up and brushing filth from his hat. Let's get the fuk back to the church.'

'What about the stuff at Fred's.'

'I'll do it first thing morrow.'

'Jarvis?'

'Yeah?'

'Your pistol—what happened?'

He scowls into the night. 'Last time I ever trade bullets from some psubraty I don't know!'

We stride, heads down into the gusting wind with no further words until I wrestle with the padlock on the church gates.

'The key's stuck.'

He grabs the chunk of metal and stares at it, rattling the key.

'Unlock, you merdic piece of merde.'

It clicks open and we stumble through the dark cavern of the church to the vestry where the fire still glows enough to re-ignite. I rake the embers and throw on dismembered chair legs while Jarvis stomps about looking in cupboards.

'Got any gnole?'

I point to the cupboard on the wall. 'Emergency wine.'

He stands on a chair, opens the doors and peers inside.

'Crafty wench! Quite a little stashette here.' He selects a bottle and reads the label. 'Bien avec viande rouge . . . fuk that. Where's the undoer?'

I pass him the corkscrew and watch him grind it home, eyebrows knitted in concentration.

He pulls out the cork and sniffs it. 'Mm, wouldn't know it from a ferret's arse but let's drink to . . . near-death.'

I find two clean glasses and pour out the almost black wine.

'Sorry, Jarvis.'

He slugs back half and wipes his mouth. 'Ça va, Kitten—we's still here, ain't we?'

I look at him and his beamy grin. 'Yes, we are.'

'Wot's that?' he asks, looking at the small rectangle of paper I'm fiddling with.

LONDONIA

'I found it in the coat pocket.' I pass it to him and he inspects the eroded gold writing and inked picture of a grand house next to a lake.

'D'you know where this is?'

'Think it's the place in my dreams.'

He grunts, takes another gulp of wine and passes the bit of paper back. Deciding on a change of subject I pull the agenda towards me and open the page.

'So, what's happening morrow.'

Jarvis flips his hat to a chair, removes his shoes and puts his feet up on the chest next to the fire.

'Need a day off with Parrot—bit too close to mort-ness, that Clasher merde an' all.'

I notice new lines on his face and nod in agreement.

'Think I second that . . . might just spend some time in the garden.'

'First up, day after, though,' he continues, 'I'll go back to Fred's and reclaim the stuff, then I'll call in at the Aggerston pigeon station—see wot's about, shouting-house wise.'

'What for?'

'Got 'a find this merdic cupboard, ain't cha?'

'. . . Oh, *that*. I'd almost forgotten.'

'Where's yer Finder spirit sloped off to, eh?'

'You know the chances against locating that *very* thing . . .'

'Anything's poss. Look at wot Bert came across in Lady Thame's squelch recentime—only a five guineas piece!'

I brighten at this thought. 'I'd forgotten that. How utterly incredible . . . what did he do with it?'

'Made a deal with the Vaux-haulers.'

'What sort of a deal?'

Jarvis grimaces. 'Didn't ask but let's just say, he won't be requesting no zeitporn for a while.'

I shift my thoughts away from Bert's proclivities and raise my glass.

LONDONIA

'Thanks for the pep. I'll try a couple of places in the morn. If anything turns up at Aggerston let me know by pigeon—I'll be at Whitechapel as I've got to take that stack of weevy cloth to the blanket makers.'

He yawns massively then nods. 'Will do . . . and now, don't know 'bout you but a quarter clock-face and I'm for the straw. Just top me up—apex.'

I pour myself another half glass and we sit companionably for a while in silence, each deep in thought as the wind scours the windows.

Capitula 4

So, I did take a day off too—after an early morn futile trip to a furniture place a Finder friend had recommended. Throwing the problem aside on my return, I had planted marigolds, mended clothing and thought about what had nearly happened the darking before. Perhaps it wasn't all bad. Sometimes, living in this place, you need a kick just to remember—re-group your wits, not get too complacent.

The Whitechapel pigeon station fizzes with activity this morning as an argument rages between two men. A lanky French man in a long leather coat is shouting at a Russian man who I recognise as a trouble-maker. He's winding the Gallic guy up, their few common words becoming louder.

'Putainfuker, you 'ave take ze sac of mine.'

'I have taken no bag, believe, my friend.'

It's going to get ugly. The patron comes over as the French guy reaches for a stubby knife.

'D'ac, d'ac you two outside.' As he has his hand on the collar of a large wildy-cat, they stop and slope off outside to continue. No one seems bothered and the scrum starts up again.

I wade my way through the crowd and the patron spots me.

'Hoxton, one for you.' He scrabbles through the scrunch of pigeons behind him and hauls out a big piebald one.

I grab the bird and hurry to a spare corner. The pigeon stops struggling as I hold it down and slip the roll of paper from under the band on its leg. *Furniture sale: IKEA, JOHN LEWIS and more, down at Chancy-Lane shouting-house, before midi. See you there, Jarvis x.*

'No reply,' I tell the patron. I pass the bird back, give him the five silvers and weave my way outside. The French guy and his annoyer have disappeared but as the patch of blood glinting on the stones suggests, perhaps one of them, permanently.

A bus still stands in the middle of the street, its remaining scraps of rusty red paint almost the same hue as the blood. The goat attached to the pole on the footplate where people once alighted stares at me. Smoke twists into the mirthless sky from a pipe stabbed through the vehicle's roof. A smell of bacon drifts and my stomach grumbles.

I scramble back onto the warm saddle, ignoring my hunger pangs. Maybe the pike-butty dame will be there.

'Allez, Kafka.'

The street outside the building is crammed with steaming horses, carts and people. I walk Kafka to a side street looking for a likely horse minder. An oldish mec sitting on a doorstep nods at me.

'You look for a minder?'

'Yes,'

'I could make him a good wash and brush too?' I glance at him, hesitating. 'Ça va, I used to work with zem in La Bretagne,' he continues, waving a hand in the direction of France.

'Trade, or silvers?'

'You are a finder?'

'I am.'

'Can you get me a book?'

I think of my valuable stock in the church and hesitate: . . . 'Possibly. Of?'

'Mon pays . . . my country, tu sais. It, I miss.'

I have the perfect tome: photographs of Brittany. I weigh up the trade value as I get off the horse. I could be a long time . . . but this is a rare book.

The mec regards me with a sad smile. 'Pas possible? I 'ave searched a long time for such a thing.'

I mentally remove the edition from my shelves, and hold out a hand.

LONDONIA

'Actually, it is possible. Deal?' He nods with a smile. We shake hands and I pass him my card, telling him to call round one darking. As he leads Kafka to a yard I feel a momentary angst . . . Kafka cut up and sold but my instinct steps in; this mec is trustworthy.

Walking up the street back to the shouting-house, I pass the rusting metal railings of the old tube station and peer down the yawning mouth of the stairway. It's the same as all of them, blocked by an impenetrable metal door, half covered by a drift of sludgy leaves and rubbish. My thoughts of what might be behind it are interrupted by a clanging bell. I turn and walk swiftly on to hear the news from the street-caller of this canton, a diminutive, red-clad dame sat astride, judging by the pale stripes, a horse/zebra cross.

The dame's size does not represent her voice. The buzzing crowd falls silent at her ringing words.

'Hear this. Hear this.

'Dwellers of Chancy Lane and Farringdown Cartier, the new schooling establishment at Smithfields will be opening its doors on Mundy. Acceptance of gosses requires at least one book on any subject from before the Un-time and a pencil. Oral history from the beginning of the cycles will also be taught as well as classes in basic paper making and plant-based inks. Volunteer teachers required, especially in English, French, Polish and Hindu. Payment in food—type not specified. And hear this, hear this. Do *not* partake of any Streepeeza from a trader calling himself Ned. Four mortalities have occurred during the last darking following consumption of his products. Reward given to anyone with information of his whereabouts.'

She raises her burgundy top hat, gives one more clang of her hand-bell then moves her ride onto the next crowd outside a drinking-house further up the street.

Appreciative calls follow her, after which the conversation turns back to prospective deals to be had this morn before ceasing again as a roaring sound echoes around the buildings. The

LONDONIA

crowd parts as a leather-clad figure appears astride a blackened motorbike. The person stops, leaps off, unearths a large chain from a bag and attaches the bike to a lamppost.

'Any fukka wot touches this is a dead one!' he shouts, waving his hat about for emphasis. The audience go back about their business except for a few gosses who stand gawping, eyes round as marbles.

Then I recognise the homburg. *Jarvis!* I run over to the machine and its grinning owner.

'Where . . . and, how?'

The grin stretches even wider. 'Innit bleedin' great! 'Ad it for ages, inna shed. Parrot found some fuel in a warehouse yestdy.'

'I like the goggles and leather stuff.'

'Aviator World War Two. Traded them for a bottle of Scotch.'

'Where have you been?'

'Heppingforrist.' His eyes glaze over a little and his voice drops to a murmur. '. . . Roast chicken, good wine and fukin in the woods all surrounded by trees, birds 'n that.'

'Sounds good,' I say, thinking of wild stretches of country, no buildings and no people. 'So where next?'

'Nowhere,' he smiles sadly. ' 'Til we next find any fuel—got enuff to get home I reckon. Just wanted to show you the gleamin' monster 'fore it gets re-stashed.' The usual smile surfaces again and he puts an arm around my shoulders. 'D'ac, let's get in there and see if fate's gonna sort you out, Kitten.'

The sign, *No smoking: pipes, fags, NOTHING!* on the back wall is obscured by a thick fug of blue-grey, the pale daylight filtering in through dirty windows, diffused. It will be almost impossible to check in advance what is in here.

'S'gona be a long wait,' mutters Jarvis, echoing my thoughts. I notice a couple of hand-written catalogues circulating, but the grabbing hands are many.

'What's the deal in this house?' I ask him, realising I haven't checked.

'Individual vendor wishes.' He takes a clay pipe from a pocket and stuffs the bowl with tobacco.

'No smoking!' I admonish. He looks at me wryly as he applies a match and sucks hard on the pipe's stem.

He closes his eyes. 'Mmm, the real stuff. Here, try.'

I take the delicate object and breathe in cautiously. He's right. It's pure and fruity, very different from the standard that's usually available.

We find a seat in the form of a large velvet sofa and relax into it, anticipating a long haul.

Each lot is time consuming: the seller obliged to state what they want, the deal then made and papers signed. I slump back into the couch, remove my boots and place my socked feet on Jarvis's legs, hoping he might try out his Jake-taught reflexology. He does.

'I'll take the first watch,' he says. 'You owe me, Hoxton.'

The lots pass: a crate of turkeys, box of metal toy cars, a rifle, a canoe, assorted tins of fruit (not guaranteed); china, a package of underwear from 2016.

'Marks and Spencer's,' mutters Jarvis, shoving off my feet and springing up. He shoots an arm up—just too late. 'Merda! Could 'a used that.'

'I didn't know Parrot was so inclined,' I remark sleepily, as he sits down again.

'Cheeky wench—nah, s' for my gnole-slate in the Horse and Bucket. Land-dame would 'a gone for that.'

I stretch my feet out again hopefully. 'Just a bit more? It's so good.'

He grins. 'Ten more lots, then it's my turn.'

I'm almost asleep when the words *John Lewis* filter into my mind. I sit up and watch as a pallet of pale wood furniture is wheeled across the floor. The shouter, coughing and signalling to his throat, is replaced by another mec; short and round with red ringlet hair and violently blue eyes. He stands on a crate and demonstrates why he has his job. The room falls silent.

LONDONIA

'D'ac. *Thank* you! Now I have your attention . . . some quality items from the mid 2010s, possibly later. Mr . . .' He looks down at the clutch of papers, 'Bees, has the information in more detail. First up, birchwood dining table and chairs. Seeking fuel, kerosene, petrol, or bio-fuel. This furniture is scarce—can I get a gallon?' Four hands go up. 'One-two-three-four-five-six . . . dining table, currently trending in the Cincture . . . Come *on*, people!' There's a murmur, but no further hands. 'Going, going—gone to Scribbins. Round the back, keep the deal please, there's a load to get through.' The noise is creeping up again. He cracks a large hammer down on a filing cabinet: 'Oi, people, SHUT UP! . . . Thank you.'

He proceeds through the list and I stand as the last John Lewis item is dealed. More furniture is being brought in. The mec pushes his unruly hair from his sweating face and raps the hammer again.

'You all no doubt know that Ikea products have pretty much vanished now. Here we have an exception. Rescued from a dry basement, these items are clean, possibly unique. First up—a bamboo wood chest of drawers from the 2020 catalogue—hyper sought after. Dealing—help with roofing, sado-sex—long term, or eight crates of millet beer.'

The items are dealed, taking a long time, as competition is strong. The last piece is lifted; it's not a cabinet, let alone the one I need. I feel crushed with disappointment and hanging around. My confidence in the mirror-dame ebbs, and I look at Jarvis. He shrugs and gestures to the door.

Just as I'm picking up my carpet bag the shouter announces a misplaced lot.

'People. Don't sit on the stuff—nearly missed this *crucial* one!' The offending persons scatter and the piece is lifted onto the stage. 'Alors. A *lot* of demand for this item. Apex condition cabinet, *Splot* by Ikea, 2025. So, what am I bid? Seeking: horse, fifteen hands, not older than four cycles, boat passage to La

LONDONIA

France, access to wood—a winter's worth, class motorbike—good working condition.'

What would my life be without Kafka? I stand, body frozen as I weigh up ridiculous possibilities. The room is full of sounds like angry insects: people figuring out ways, bartering. This item seems to have caused more excitement than anything else yet. It's going to go . . . the piece of my life-jigsaw will be lost . . . my hand is slowly rising.

Then there's a yelp next to me. 'Oi, shouter, 'ere!' Jarvis is on tiptoe, waving his hat. 'Motorbike, old but apex nick—Harley.'

The shouter takes the nod from the seller and thumps the metal.

'Gone to Anderton-Wolfe.'

I stare at Jarvis. He looks oddly happy.

'Why?' I eject.

He hugs me. 'Couldn't let y' trade Kafka, could I? Anylane, keeping that thing running—nah.'

'I don't know what to say.'

'Stay here—just gonna check it's still there!'

He scoots through the crowd and I stand for a moment listening to the shouter announcing the next lots.

'Art.'

There's a collective shrug in the room and people start leaving, the tradeable stuff gone. 'D'ac let's run through this quickly. From the 2000s, Damian Hurst. Two circular paintings—dealing ten bottles good quality red wine.' Silence. 'Eight, seven?' More people are leaving. 'Six, five? . . . Sam, put these back into the Frydy flea sale. D'ac—next. Tracy Emin's Bed—piece from 1995. Seeking, six sacks of flour. Anyone? Not a bad mattress . . .'

'Disgustin' ol ting!' scowls a wrinkly Jamaican dame standing next to me. 'Could sell mine. Looks no diffrent.'

Jarvis is back. He pulls me over to the stage.

'Come on, let's get this dealed, bike's fine.'

LONDONIA

We meet the seller, a stringy Scots mec, his freckled face rosy with excitement. Jarvis passes a last loving gaze over the machine then turns to the mec with a question. 'It's a thing of beauty, no doubt, but wot you going to do wiv' it—fuel wise, *if* you don't mind me asking.'

The mec taps his nose with a skinny forefinger.

'Ach. That'd be telling, but just to say I have certain contacts within the Egg . . . enjoy yer deal.'

We carry the cabinet out of the building where the street is busy with bods loading carts and talking over the sold items. I glance over the crowds looking for familiar transport faces.

'I think you might be looking for me.' I turn to see a turbaned young mec, his yellow and gold garments matching the tasselled cart that stands behind him. 'I assume this item is destined for the Cincture?' he continues.

I take in the colourful sight before me. 'You have rights to delivery there.'

'Indeed, Madame—for the correct exchange, of course.'

I imagine the extra excitement caused at the Caruso establishment by this *exotic* personage turning up with my super-find.

'What would be your fee to go to Cincture Central?'

'Toothbrushes and medical items, including pain-killers,' he says decidedly.

'Well, we have a deal then as I will be receiving several boxes of such things from my client. Will you trust me to get one to you after the delivery?'

Jarvis, who has been listening to this exchange, helps to clinch the deal.

'You did stuff for The Lord, didn't cha?'

The mec nods. 'A highly-respected Finder.'

'Yeah. He was, but ain't no more. 'E's dead, and Hoxton 'ere's his replacement. Equally, if not more respected.'

'In that case, Madame Hoxton. You can count on me and I will wait for the box with pleasure.'

We exchange addresses and I instruct him further.

LONDONIA

'Mrs Caruso will be there, or if she isn't, the minion, Gubbins, will be. Tell her I will be over this aft or on the morrow.'

We load up the cabinet and he carefully covers it with blankets, strapping it down to protect against the jarring motion of the cart as it rolls over the inevitable potholes. I watch the golden cart trundle off, then with a start remember Kafka.

'Jarvis! The horse . . .' We run around the corner to the side street. No Kafka, no old mec. *'Pute!'*

Jarvis pulls at my arm and points down another street. 'Cut back on the frenzy, H. There 'e is.'

'. . . Oh, thank God.' I run over to the mec as he dismounts.

'Desolé, monsieur. It was a long sale.'

'Eet is not a problem. I enjoyed our walk, and see, he shines like a chestnut now.'

I thank him effusively and tell him to call round for his book—and a bottle of wine.

He smiles and strokes Kafka's mane. 'Oui, avec plaisir, mademoiselle, and I will be 'ere eef you need encore de horse-guardage.'

'So, you goin' to the Egg now?' asks Jarvis as the mec strolls off.

'After I've got us something to eat. Eel sandwich and a glass of red at Fredi and Ness's barge? You can ride too, it's only a short way.'

The barge is permanently lodged next to Waterloo Bridge, where Fredi and his family, fish, cook and run up and down a gangplank serving portions of eel and other catches of the day in chunks of bread.

We arrive and sit at a small table overlooking the muddy bank while Kafka noses in the weeds. Ness has been busy in their yard. It now has trees planted for summer shade, a collection of furniture and plants in buckets and barrels.

'Straight out of one of those house 'n garden magazines I brought you,' I say as she comes to take our order.

LONDONIA

'Yeah, looks all d'ac for an old boatyard, don't it? What d'ya fancy? Fish, or, we've chicken today.' She points to an enclosure beyond the barge. 'Just did Old Red this morning—inna onion stew.'

I look at Jarvis. He nods, busy with his pipe.

'We'll try that, thanks . . . have you still got that red from Landsend?'

'Down to the last bottle. Two glasses coming up.'

Jarvis lights the clay bowl, draws on it and leans back into the chair, smiling.

'Look at that, H. What a beauteous place we 'ave the fortune to habit in.'

As I budge my chair a little to face the river the sun appears briefly from behind a monumental cloud. Light spills across the expanse of water, turning grey to silver. Scatterings of gulls follow the silhouettes of fishing boats, bright splashes interrupting the placid surface as the birds plummet to lance fish.

On the bank a family of Polish swaggers comb the mud, their voices just audible. A small boy is jumping with excitement as he hands his mother something. She hugs him, her face radiant.

Jarvis notices my expression.

'You really believe 'er don't you? That dame at the drinking-house.'

I nod, thinking again of her words. *Fair hair and eyes of green water.*

The chicken arrives in two elegant bowls of pale cream china with a blue-ribbon design. They seem an odd contrast to the server's rough hands as she places them on the table.

She reads my thoughts. 'Posh, aren't they? Fredi got them from his aunt. Her mother used to work at the Pointy Thing's restaurant before the Un-time.'

'S'pect it was a bit different, then.' remarks Jarvis, tackling a chicken leg. 'S'occupied by the Green Lizard people now—or at least the floors wot is still there.'

'Who?' asks Ness.

LONDONIA

'Them that believes in the end of the world—again. A space ship is going to land on the top, and their messiah is a giant green lizard.' We stare at him. 'Wot? Sounds as reasonable as anything else.'

'Suppose so,' she agrees. 'I'll get your wine.'

She returns and sets down the glasses, nodding at the sky as she does.

' 'Fraid you won't have much time to 'ppreciate it.'

She's right. Storm clouds are massing, a tinge of orange highlighting the horizon. A faint murmur of thunder thrills my skin.

Jarvis raises his glass and tastes the deep red contents.

'Jesus on wheels, that's good.'

I clink his glass. 'What you did earlier—it was the kindest thing anyone's done for me.'

'Like I say, it's sort ofa relief really—would 'a got pilched sooner or later.'

'Well, I owe you! Something big. How I could ever have thought of trading Kafka . . .'

As I gaze at my horse with fondness a louder rumble of thunder causes him to lift his head from the grass. He stops chewing, eyes a little wild.

Jarvis finishes the last of the gravy and waves his spoon at the looming cloud mass reflected in the river.

'Kafka's sensed it. S'pose we should get back. Jake said it would storm sometime soon, bad too—don't think he realised *how* soon.'

Ness appears from the barge then Fredi. He glances at the sky and gestures to the yard. They start to move furniture, piling it into a tarp-covered hut. I take the bowls over then join Jarvis in helping move the rest.

'Go,' says Ness, 'you'll need the time to get back safe.'

The wind, from its gentle breeze earlier has increased to an eerie moan threading through the fish spikes, eddying dust and debris.

LONDONIA

Kafka snorts, tossing his head as I untie him. Glancing once more at the burgeoning grey, I shove my foot into the stirrup. *No trip to the Cincture today.*

Jarvis throws on his coat, jams his hat down.

'Going back to the barge. Got to see if it's tied proper. Re-tarp the store-shed, won't cha.'

'How will you get there?' I yell through the gusts.

'Hitch—cart ride. Allez!'

Pulling the reins hard to the left, I kick the horse into a gallop; he's ready to move. We charge up Fleet Street, the wind chasing us; onto Farringdown, Barbican and back into Hackrovia. All around bods are rounding up gosses and animals, flinging shutters across windows and retreating into whatever shelter they have. By the time I reach my patch the streets are empty, just rubbish and uprooted plants twirling and dancing.

I can hardly stand as I dismount to unlock the gate. The leaning lamppost across the road groans, buckles and collapses, a burst of old tarmacadam giving way with it. Heavier debris is now winging down the street. A slice of wood hits me on the shoulder. *Merda!* The gate lock jams. I rattle it furiously, try again and it clicks open. The gates swing and grind. Kafka rears up, scared by the noise.

I slap his rump and he jumps, follows me, ears down, up the steps and into the silence of the church.

The dogs leap, breaking the quiet with their barks.

'Later!' I command. Heaving the saddle off, I brush Kafka hurriedly, give him water and scoot into the garden.

Our precious shed, built to store and ventilate crops has a yawning gap in the roof, tiles shattered on the ground, tarp flapping.

Running back into the church, I haul out our stocks of plastic sheeting, find the biggest, then a lump-hammer and nails. Hail has started on my return; giant bullets of white zinging off stonework, flattening plants. I throw the ladder against the shed, shimmy up and hurl the plastic onto the roof. It flaps back at me, stinging my face with its tattered edges.

'Putain, merdic . . . *thing*!' I clamber higher, slam the nails in, *whap, whap*. It's done, as best as I can. I slip down and stand for a moment feeling ice on my face and watching the gale torment our crops then I turn and go inside knowing there's nothing else to be done.

The vestry is still warm, red embers glowing—just. I hunt about for dry wood. We'd got complacent, feeling the worst of the cold to be over. I break a couple of wormed chairs and feed the fire, putting my deadened hands towards the flames. *Dark-quarter over—huh*.

The dogs are howling at the crashing sounds outside. I open the vestry door and call them in, find enough scraps for us all and curl up in a warm canine pile on the bed. Eventually I fall asleep, almost lulled by the swishing of ice on the window.

Capitula 5

'Hox?'

I struggle awake to find Jarvis looking down at me. The dogs yawn and shuffle, undisturbed by his familiar presence. *His familiar presence* . . . 'Jarvis what happened!'

His homburg is dented beyond recognition, coat ripped, a fresh scar running from eyebrow to cheek.

'Pizzing storm from l'enfer, that's wot. 'Aven't you looked outside yet?'

Fear dredges me from somnolence.

'Is it . . . really bad?'

'Well, let's say I'm surprised you got windows left.'

'Is the barge intact?'

'Yeah. Parrot and a friend managed to haul it under a bridge.'

I scramble out of bed, throw on clothes and push the dogs out from their blankets. Jarvis is already stomping down the aisle to the garden. I follow warily. He throws open the door and I see a scoured piece of ground, nearly everything flattened, only the two remaining gravestones drunkenly upright.

He whistles a rasping note and steps out into the mud.

'Merda and pute-fuk, H.'

I can't find words, just stand looking at the shed, now a pile of wood and plastic. The hounds are frisking about by the wall where black-feathered bodies lie.

'Crow?' I say, eventually.

Jarvis nods sharing my idea of immediate food.

'Oi—Fagin, Tilly, bring them.'

They gather up the birds, bunches of them and drop them at my feet, waggy, unconcerned.

LONDONIA

I give them one apiece and they retire to the corner of the garden to splinter bone and gnash.

'Let's get what's left in,' I say, jerking my head towards the ex-shed.

Jarvis nods. 'D'ac. I'll re-build it this aft.'

By late morn we've sorted as much as can be salvaged into dry boxes, plucked the few salvageable crops from the ground and are now sitting in the vestry surrounded by crow bodies, feathers and a corpse of a small wild pig.

Jarvis wipes his hands on a cloth and hoists up the pig.

'I'll gut this and 'ang it in the crypt—be fine for a week.'

I bag up the feathers, put two crows into a pot with a few potatoes and elderberry wine and clunk it onto the stove. It'll take ages to cook and the last of the bread will have to suffice for lunch.

When Jarvis returns, his hands are white from the freezing water in the kill-trough. I give him a basin of warm water from the kettle, and sort through the box of medical stuff for something to dress his head wound.

'You should have got Parrot to do this—looks nasty.'

He grimaces. 'We're out of all that. In fact, it's well-scarce generally.'

'Well, luckily we've still got a little stock here.'

As I'm about to cut a patch of cotton gauze the doorbell jangles.

'I'll go,' says Jarvis, pulling his pistol from a pocket and checking the chamber. 'Lot of desperados out there, I predict.'

He returns after a short while, light footsteps following his. Sardi walks into the room, her dark eyes unusually serious.

'Salut, Hoxton.'

'Sardi . . . ça va?'

'Mostly. Just calling to see if you had any of your herb poultices spare?'

'Who's hurt?'

'Saul—a beam fell and he got a gashy leg.'

LONDONIA

'Is it serious?'

'He's howly with pain but I thinks it's not bad.'

'Sit down, Sardi and I'll see what we've got.'

Jarvis puts a hand on her shoulder.

'An' I'll call round later and sort your roof.'

She smiles up at him.

'Vraiment! Grazie, J.'

The box reveals a remaining pot of my rosemary balm, a roll of bandage and some painkillers dated 2021.

'I don't have any more herbal head cure but Jake gave us these and they still seem to work.'

She stows the goods in her basket and stands up.

'Best scoot, the gosses'll worry.'

'You want me to walk back?' asks Jarvis as she heads to the door.

She turns and smiles. 'No need, I have Isaac's karate teachings in me.'

Her footsteps click and echo as she walks away from the vestry. How lonely she must feel after big, blustering Isaac had died, carried off by Mutopox—when he had seemed so invincible.

Jarvis sits down with a thump, scattering my thoughts.

'Gotta get more medico trades, Kitten.'

I nod and stand to apply the patch to his forehead.

'Just as well we found that cupboard, isn't it?'

'Eh?'

'I'll be able to get Cincture supplies!'

'Vrai. Make the most of it, eh?'

'I will, but subtly . . .'

'Subtly? Sting 'er fr as much as poss, H. Was a work of fukkin' art, that Find!'

I know my next words will cause a minor explosion but I have to say them.

'I want to make friends with her . . . she might be useful.'

'For wot? Makeup instruction?'

'Jarvis! No—for tracking my gosse!'

'Oh, yeah—I forgot about *that*.' I say nothing but feel anger rising. 'When you goin' there?' he continues.

'Now.'

'Maybe wait till things is a bit more tranki. She might be mending her own place an' that.'

'No. I've got to check the cabinet got there and we're going to need supplies to trade for food if nothing else. I don't know what you've got on the barge but there isn't a lot here.'

I stomp about rounding up vital things: gun, a couple of silver rings for emergency bartering, a flagon of water, bread. Jarvis hauls out his pipe and stuffs the bowl, watching me.

'Ruffled yr, did I?'

'You can't understand, Jarvis—somewhere in those lost cycles I was a mother.' Picking up the carpet bag and stuffing the gun into my belt, I avert my eyes from him. 'Can you deal with the dogs later?'

'Pas problem,' he says. 'Watch yorself, eh?'

Quarter of a clockface later I'm seated on Kafka, heading towards the walls. The streets are full again; carts piled with wood everywhere, ladders against buildings, people discussing repairs, food and injuries. The streepeeza vendors are doing extra well. With homes temporarily damaged and food stocks down, their evil-smelling flat breads are selling as fast as rats scurry.

I turn my gaze from the crowds of gosses surrounding each seller as thoughts of the Cincture enter my mind. What might be the damage to the Caruso house? She, now preoccupied with broken windows, a battered roof? the cabinet no longer of such importance? *A deal's a deal, however.* I nudge Kafka into a gallop and leave the chaos behind.

LONDONIA

I emerge from the cleansing procedure, and step into the Cincture street expecting debris and confusion. Everything looks the same: the yellow-bricked building intact, the gothic windows of the taller one untouched. I walk over to the shaws and select a bright red one. The dame of the vehicle stops peering at herself in a small hand-mirror and looks at me.

'Where to, Madame?'

'Upper Grosvenor Street.'

'On account?'

'Yes. The Caruso's.'

''S' that near North Auderly Street?'

'Yes, I think so.'

'Thanks. Just doing the knowledge . . . not sure of it all yet. 'Op in, then.'

I climb into the gingham interior and watch her youthful red-uniformed arse bobbing above the bicycle's saddle. I wonder about her accent; it seems more akin to Londonia. I lean forward.

'Can I ask you something?'

'Surely, lady.'

'Well, two things, actually . . . one was, are you from here?'

She glances back briefly, a spot of colour blaring on her cheek.

'Don't know what I should tell ya, but no, I'm from other side of the walls.'

'So, why are you here now?'

She pedals harder at a slight incline, the response delayed.

'. . . Scoop truck, weren't it? I was on the plantations but married a bit higher up and got this job.'

'Oh . . . I see. The other question was, did that huge storm not cause any damage here?'

'You mean it was bad in the Pan?'

'Terrible.'

'Well, don't ask me how it works, right, but here there's these things called counterveils that spread out and cover nearly everythin'. There's one of the posts there—oops.'

She nearly collides with a gleaming silver car on the opposite side of the road, and I sit back.

'Sorry. I'll let you concentrate!'

We arrive, and I see the movement of a curtain at the Caruso residence. The lady of the house is out of the door within a moment. She waves a, *thanks and off you go* to the shaw-dame then grabs my arm.

'Hoxton. You did it! It's really here! How did you find it? Such a bea-ut-iful young ethnic man brought it too . . . it's been fumigated by the housekeeper—all the neighbours have heard about it, and my friends are zipping over.'

We enter the house and living room while she continues her effusive monologue. I stare at the object in its new surroundings. A cabinet of pale wood: glass doors, round metal handles, a small chip on one corner. There once must have been thousands of them; could this be the last one? Why would anyone care?

Before I can ask about the previous day's storm, she turns to leave the room.

'Wait there . . . I have the glasses, somewhere. Gubbins? Gubbins!' The manservant appears, a small bag in hand.

'The spectacles, madam.'

She takes the bag and hands it to me.

'Hope these will be the beezes. Course, I had no idea of your friend's mother's style—20s, 60s, derig, ret . . .'

I take out a gold case marked, *Peeper's Opticians*, and open it to find a pair of jewelled, lilac glasses. I stifle a laugh at the thought of these teamed with old Kitty's bizarre woollen layers. Still, they are new and the lenses shining!

LONDONIA

'She'll be delighted—being so into the 1950s as she is. And the medical kits?'

'*Pegged*! Caruso did us proud. Gubbins has put them by the door but here's one to show you. I used the cabinet!'

She opens *Splot* takes out a neat cardboard box and passes it to me. Tears threaten to emerge as I look down on its contents: bandage, plasters, scissors, ointment and assorted drugs.

'This is . . . beautiful.'

Mrs Caruso stares at me, eyes wide. 'It is? You wouldn't rather have perfume, or some foundation? I've an amazy new product called Equable.'

'No, thank you. Really, these will be so incredibly useful. There is something else though.'

'*Tell* me. After your grand-slam, I'd be pepped to help.'

Just as I search for the right words, a flurry of activity in the street takes Mrs Caruso to the window. She looks back at me, hands flapping.

'My squad . . . in a *Jag*!'

I join her and gaze out onto the bizarre sight of three dames all dressed in cumbersome floor-length dresses descending from the vehicle which I would guess hails from the 1960s.

My client dissolves into a hissy series of giggles. '. . . 1910s to go! Hail the 2020s! Imagine . . . leather skirts, military jackets, gold thigh length boots, but it has to be done in one go—clothing accessories, the complete look, and before any other posse attempt another change. *Exciting*, isn't it!'

'Wildly—yes.'

'There's still a lot to complete. In fact, you might be busy-busy-busy.'

The door opens and a cloud of perfumed dames waft into the room. They halt as the cabinet is noted.

'Beccy! It's . . . *magnifico!*'

'*Ro-yal!*'

'Plushy, B. How did you do it?'

LONDONIA

The last superlative is issued forth, slightly jealously, from a tall, angular dame, her face shadowed by an enormous bird-covered hat.

Mrs Caruso takes my arm and propels me into the centre of the group.

'Meet my new saviour. Hoxton.'

They all murmur greetings as their six pairs of eyes glide over my figure encased in its grey wrapping.

'What happened to The Lord?' asks the one attired in green.

I assume the question is directed at me. 'He died, I'm afraid.'

'Oh.' She nods at the cabinet. 'Well, you seem to be *more* than adept.'

Mrs Caruso claps her hands. 'Introductions and cocktails. This is Miss Preen—soon to be married! Mrs Nash, and Mrs Hedgefund.'

The last dame takes my hand, and, as she looks into my eyes, I feel her fingers tense.

'Delighted, Mrs Hoxton.'

I shake my hand gently away from the grip. 'Just, Hoxton, Mrs Hedgefund.'

'. . . Hoxton. An unusual name.'

And yours isn't? 'Yes . . .'

The drinks are being ordered.

'Hoxton? For you?'

I ask for a tea and perch on a chair to observe and listen, wishing Jarvis could be here to share the spectacle. The talk, punctuated by many words I am not familiar with, is of fashion, past, current, the *change* they are going to make; entertainment events, husbands' financial achievements, and on and on . . . I wonder if any of them might wonder about how the Counterveils work, or about what happens beyond the copper walls, or *anything*.

I risk a question when a pause arrives.

'How do you all know each other?'

'Through the Meridian Club,' says Mrs Caruso.

LONDONIA

'Our husbands are all members,' adds Mrs Nash. 'We met at one of the privilege do's.'

'That was a magnificent car you all arrived in,' I continue.

Mrs Nash sits up, embroidered bust inflated with pride.

'Frank was *given* it when he made partner.'

'How wonderful . . . I'm interested to know how it runs, as petrol out in Londonia has all but disappeared.'

She looks blankly at me and shrugs. 'I couldn't say.'

Mrs Hedgefund enlightens us. 'It's possibly solar or the new trial Methanerix. The few cars that run are mostly powered by it . . . does smell rather.'

'Did wonder about the stink,' adds Miss Preen. 'Can't they do anything about it? Oh, *slues*, do you think we smell of it?' They all produce perfume bottles from their bags, spritz away and the whole room is filled with sickly odours.

Gubbins appears with the tray of drinks. I pour my tea and listen to the chat over something called the Inner-Web. Miss Preen seems to be the authority on the subject.

'Hal says we'll be able to use it soon if the right clever phones can be found or made.'

'You mean, Smart-phones,' jibes Mrs Nash. 'Frank said there aren't any left within the Cincture.'

'Why?'

'Apparently, the previous Custodian had all the devices collected up for their materials, including *gold*!'

'Oh. So where can we hitch them from?'

They all turn to me and I think of Bert the Swagger. I had visited him recently, searching for a certain cable required by someone working on radio transmission. He had shown me into his hangar of stuff, and, while escaping his *advances*, I had noted the collection of size assorted flat metal and glass *things*. He had picked one up carelessly and shown me.

'This, my seraph, was called a smart-phone—you could awaken it and research anything you wanted—*an-y-thing* . . .'

'Hoxton?'

LONDONIA

I return to the Caruso salon and four excited female faces.

'. . . I was just thinking about someone who might have such things—for a good trade, of course.'

'*Crème!*' squeaks Miss Preen. 'Oh—the magazines!' She delves into a large flowered bag and produces two copies of *Vogue* circa 2020 and 2021.

Our host looks as if she may combust. 'Where did you harvest *those?*'

'That borinary antique place on Bond Street. They don't have much in there, mostly just flaky drudge but I happened to see these—jew-el!'

They examine each page and I dutifully compile a list of shoes, bags, dresses and so on, wondering if Fred's or anywhere else will have any of their requirements. Having not anticipated any of this, I try for an open-ended agreement, with a Cincture shopping list to be going on with.

'I'd like to leave the trade open for the moment, until I know what I'll be able to find, but on account I will ask for fifty pairs of ready-made spectacles of assorted strengths, and a large quantity of ordinary underwear—various ages and sizes, and toothbrushes.'

Mrs Caruso stifles a yawn. 'Yes, all of that should be fine . . .' Then she spots something on a page of the *Vogue* she is still eyeing. 'Ah—this I *must* have . . . Victoria Beckham, tropical floral bomber jacket. Lux!'

I take the magazine and mentally stock the photograph in my weary mind.

'I'm sure that won't be a problem.' *It won't?* 'But, can I just ask. Why not have the clothes you want made here?'

'Much of it will be, once the workhouses clock what's required, but with this decade, we'll have a chance of the *actual* clothing!—precious, sought after—unattainable by others who *don't* have a talented Finder, hm?'

'I'll do my best, of course. Would I be able to take the magazines—for reference?'

LONDONIA

Miss Preen nods and with a request that I guard them with my life, hands them to me.

I place them carefully in the matching grey bag I was handed at the access point and stand up, more than ready to leave this perfumed madhouse.

'Well, it's been most interesting meeting you all, but I'd better get back—livestock to deal with. Will it be easy to find a shaw nearby?'

'Just at the end of the road,' says Mrs Caruso, 'It's a Martingdale rank so put it on my account.'

'Thank you . . . no, please don't get up. Goodbye—Mrs Nash, Miss Preen, Mrs Hedgefund . . .' As I shake her hand, she presses a small folded piece of paper into my palm. I smile, watching her expression for any clue as to what she is doing but nothing surfaces.

'When you have news,' peeps Mrs Caruso, 'you can leave a note at the access point, or ask them to call the house.'

I nod a *d'accord* and leave the room, their twitterings subsiding as the door closes. Gubbins appears and opens the door for me. I wonder if he might glance at me with a knowing wink, or roll his eyes, but of course he doesn't. I walk out into early evening, the sky already inky blue. Time seems to have sloped off somewhere within that room. At the rank, a gosse, or so he seems, comes over and suggests his shaw. I get in and sink back into velvet, head lolling with tiredness but mind busy with thoughts of trades other than just material goods, a way to find out about my past.

It's quiet at the access point, just a few people having papers examined. I go through the routine, change clothes, find my belligerent horse and cross back into Londonia. The light from the tunnel slowly disappears as the gates slide shut. Clunk: back to normality.

I wait for a moment before turning Kafka from the walls, thinking about what I and all the other inhabitants of Londonia might consider *normal*. This dark street, just a few guttering

LONDONIA

candle lamps lighting a road that is more holes than surface, or the pack of rats streaking away from our sudden presence, their leader possibly as big as Zorro. A lone drunkard sings, staggering amongst drifts of cardboard, and a little further on in the shadows, a couple copulate in the doorway of an abandoned shop, their movements shaking the plastic letters above the door. Part of the word gives way, and a giant plastic M tumbles, nearly embedding itself in the mec's arse.

Kafka backs away as the thing crunches onto the pavement. I briefly stare at the remaining letters, *onsoon,* before pulling the reins to walk him on. Happiness cloaks me as we move through the familiar streets; Londonia was never so beautiful in all its chaotic, decaying madness. We pass through Isling-town and reach Hackrovia. I see the angular smudge of St Leonard's against the charcoal sky and feel the tension leave my shoulders: home.

After unlocking and checking, I go through the darking routines: dogs, chickens, horse, and much later, a cup of soup in hand, sitting in front of the fire I recall the piece of paper pressed into my hand—which I had then carefully concealed in the zipped pocket of the allinone.

Capitula 6

The green eyes dream visited me again in the early hours, following others of Cincturian streets that had felt strangely familiar. I lie half-awake now as the visual remnants fade, wondering what words might have been written on that scrap of paper. I could go back and ask . . . *no*. Whatever she wanted to say about some foitling garment or other can be said next time.

Wishing Tom was lying next to me, I push the covers back and go to check the fire. The air feels like ice and the bed beckons again. I don't want to stay with the thoughts of the Cincture, so start the morning routines, shivering into layers of wool, hands shaking. In those dream-streets it had been the golden quarter; how long ago the last one seems now. Days when the cool of the church was welcome, the garden full of birds and flowers.

Just as I'm becoming desperate to see a friendly face, the doorbell jangles. It won't be Jarvis as he would let himself in. There are very few other people I'd want to see and I consider ignoring it. The noise persists, however, so I drape myself in a blanket and go to the door.

The mirror reveals the bright fabrics and spiral braids of Sardi.

Pushing the dogs aside I welcome her. As she slips in through the gate I remember her gosse's injury.

'How's Saul?'

'Massive better. He's small but strong as a wildy-cat. What about you? Looking mighty pale, Hox—take a shot of this.'

She hands me a bottle wrapped in a cloth bag.

I read the bottle's label as we walk into the vestry.

'Eau de vie. Made from?'

'Not sure but it needs a warning label.'

'I'll try it later, thanks . . . don't need a larger headache!'

I make tea, stoke the fire and we sit, catching up on our respective lives. It's good to talk to her, another dame making her way in this mad place.

She puts down her tea bowl, dark eyes fixed on me.

'What's sittin' in yer mind, treasure?'

I consider telling her about Marina's words but decide against it—another time.

'Oh . . . many things. Mainly just recovering from the shock of being in *there*.'

'Was it *so* different?'

'Imagine a negative image of everything we see here—the front of your building for example.'

'You mean, clean, painted woodwork, not beaten old brick and kicked-in-repaired-kicked-in front door.'

'Exactly. All of it, pristine as if just finished. And they have this incredible system that protects against extreme weather—not so much as an uprooted bush.'

Sardi grimaces, a hand fanning her heart. 'Not like out here then! How'd your garden fare? Ours is mainly covered with a collapsed outhouse—not that there was muchly space as it was always chokka of the Ukrainians' goats.'

'Come and garden here.'

Her eyes shine bright. 'Vrai? I'd like that. Bit of peace away from the brood too.'

'D'ac. Let's have a look now.'

Picking my boots up from their warming spot by the fire, I pull them on and we go out into the blustery day. The rain-soaked plane trees are skeletal dark shapes, a few round seed heads still dangling despite the wind. *Will the new quarter ever start?* As if in answer a few bright crocus heads are suddenly revealed as a gust of wind blows tattered leaves into a spiral.

'Sardi, look!'

LONDONIA

'Enfin . . .' she sighs. 'Thought we was stuck in an ever-ever dark-quarter.'

I turn the saturated earth with a boot tip and reflect on all the work still to be done. After two long-cycles this once overgrown graveyard is at last beginning to look organised. At the back stands a chicken shed surrounded by their scratching ground. I have no fear of foxes or feral dogs; the great-hounds keep everything at bay. Two vegetable patches flank the wall, at present almost empty after the storm. Spiky fruit trees lift their bald branches to the sky, waiting for the first signs of warmth.

'Good soil.' laughs Sardi, crouching and poking a finger into the loam. 'All them old corpsies.'

'And I've got a great, me and horse, compost system going too. How much land do you want?'

'How much you want t'lend?'

'Take it, whatever you want—we'll share what we grow. Anyway, it's not exactly mine is it?'

She looks at me with an unusually serious expression.

'You do believe God lives in this house?'

I think of Sardi's family traditions, the shrines at the house, the pictures of saints . . . What *do* I believe?

'You might say I am open to beliefs, a willing observer if nothing more.'

'Good. Come an' *observe* this darking, then. Saints' day remember.'

When she has left, I stay in the garden for a while. There are other jobs to be done and Finds to be found, but this morn, I can't concentrate. Planting things will be good.

I clear one of the patches of weeds and make a furrow for the broad beans I saved from last autumn. In the temporary lean-to, I move Zorro from the sack of seed potatoes and wonder if it's worth putting them in yet. A spear of sunlight from a hole in the roof decides me and I take a bucketful out.

LONDONIA

A clockface later, the potatoes are in. I stand admiring my work while Blackbirds and thrushes hop from clod to clod of dark earth, their heads cocked, listening for worms.

As I rub my aching back, I recall the Bread-mec's bath. *Deep, hot water.* Would it be possible to install such a thing in the vestry?

A shout breaks my thoughts.

'Oi, Kitten, got us a treat!' Jarvis strides towards me holding a small cardboard box.

Opening the lid reveals pale pink, white and brown squares.

'Gulab jamen and kalakand—Indian sweets,' enlightens Jarvis. 'Sex in a box. Ain't seen 'em for ages. A friend of Parrot's started up a mobile business—his gran makes the stuff and he peddles it, on a mule.'

As we walk in from the garden I remember my triumph of yestdy and clap Jarvis on the shoulder.

'Hey, I got your mum's glasses!'

His expression is worth the whole trip.

'Nah . . .vraiment? fukin' apex! Ha—the Cincture, eh?'

Back in the vestry, I find my carpet bag and hand him the case. He takes it reverently, sniggers a bit when he opens the lid but his eyes are damp as he looks up from the specs.

'These are well-daft but just the best thing I've seen for many a cycle. Grazie, Kitten.'

'A pleasure. I might call in and give her them myself as I'm going to Sardi's this darking.'

'D'ac. Number three, it is—mind the upstairs's pig in the front shed. S'a bit frisky.'

He makes tea while I scrub soil away and look for cleaner clothes.

Sitting in a relatively new felty, hair washed and skin tingly from the cold water I feel revitalised.

'Lookin' natty, Hoxton,' he grins, and passes me a bowl of tea. 'Try one of them.'

LONDONIA

I select a brown cube from the box and sigh as the crumbly texture melts on my tongue.

'Gorgeous! Does he come around here?'

'No, but I'll make sure we 'ave a sufficiency.'

I look with fondness at my friend. Today, he's lurking in a musty black suit, matching dark homburg, and pointed shiny shoes.

'Why so smart?'

'S' our anniversary today,' he grins. 'Three grand cycles, give or take a few loose moments. We're meeting up at the Brazilian place after I deliver them books to the mec in Blackfriers.'

'. . . I forgot about them. Sorry, it was a very unusual bit of time, yesterday. I'll pack them up.'

'Don't frenzy yerself. Tell me about the aft then—she got other Finds for us?'

'Just a few . . . actually, pizzing loads of stuff, and complicated.'

'Wewl, that's goodly great, innit? We can get some apex stuff out of this, yeah?'

'. . . Yes.'

'Wot? *That* complicated, is it?'

'Clothing and accessories from the 2020s, *and* a visit to see Bert for some communication stuff of that era.'

He grins lopsidedly. 'Yeah, 'e's a bit creepist on the dames but he's the mec for that sort 'a milarky.'

I think of that dark shed and imagine the negotiations that might be suggested.

'A *bit*?'

'D'ac, majorly-creepist but you'll cope. Clothing from the 2020s. Could be a challenge but Mimi'll bang some stuff up and they won't note the diffrence.'

'Vrai . . .'

'Wot is it, really, H?'

'Oh . . . nothing.'

'S' about the gosse, isn't it?' He stares at me. 'You're not really considering hunting for it, are yer?'

'*It* is a he, and yes, I can't not.'

'Look . . . if wot the mirror-dame said is vrai then maybe you did come from there—and they fukkin' booted you out *after* removing half yer brain. Best to stay clear—in 'n out with the stuff, end of.'

'There's nothing wrong with my brain! Just the memories pilched.'

He sighs, shakes his head. '. . .Yeah, sorry, Kitten, didn't mean that.'

The stubborn expression on my face remains. 'I have to find out about my gosse.'

We sit for a while in silence as he fingers the brim of his hat, lips pursed and brow furrowed. I realise how much he loves me in these moments, *and* how much he means to me.

I break the non-habitual silence with news that will blot out everything else.

'Anyway, there *is* use, other than the glasses, in knowing these people.'

Jarvis grunts a reply as I go over to the old blue cupboard and bring out the stack of medicine boxes.

'How's that for a timely trade!'

He flips off one of the lids.

'Christ inna plaster cast—these is good!'

'Told you. And there's more to come.'

His knarley face springs into a smile. 'These we can shift—keep us well in scran.' Then his eyebrows twitch up, index finger raised. 'Forgot . . . present!' He hands the box back, runs out of the vestry and returns hurriedly, bearing a plank of wood.

'There!' he says, placing it triumphantly on top of a chest, 'Parrot painted it for you . . . us.' The word *Solvation* is painted in large, white letters against dark blue dotted with stars. 'To 'ang under the *salvation* sign on the church front,' he explains.

LONDONIA

'Thought we could branch out a bit—detective work, you an' me. Not just finding trucs, solving mysteries and stuff.'

I hug him, breathing in the familiar smells of old wool and tobacco.

'That's a brilli idea.'

He pulls gently away and takes my face in his hands. 'Don't go getting yorself in deep then. Work to do.'

We locate the books and wrap them in sacking. He kisses me, adjusts his unusually formal clothing and picks up the bundles.

'Anon, H,' he calls back as he leaves the room.

I locate a prized tin of cigars and run after him, slipping them into his pocket.

'Happy anniversary, you two.'

After he has gone I sit in the pulpit listening to the ghost voices singing. The words are not possible to make out, just a vague murmur, the rise and fall of tones, and reverberation of a last note from the organ.

The warmth of the vestry calls. I return to sit and stare into the fire thinking of Jarvis's words.

Perhaps a bit of religious observation at Sardi's this darking might clarify these wonderings. I pick up Kitty's glasses again and smile as I imagine her reaction.

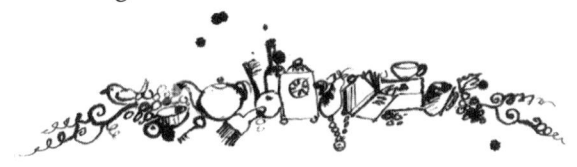

The first stars are visible in the ink-blue sky as I leave the church. It's not too far to Wilkes Street so I hurry on foot, hand on a gun tucked into the folds of my long velvet coat, a remaining dark-quarter lettuce in a string bag and the glasses hidden inside my wool vest.

The street feels different. People stand and talk, gosses kick a ball and dogs play-fight in the dust. The relief that warmth has arrived is palpable. I turn the corner and brace myself for the rush of cold wind: nothing, just a slight breeze.

In the very recesses of my mind I remember swimming in a Hampstedland pond and lying on the grass afterwards, sun drying my skin as I listened to the bees droning. I leave the bucolic memory and return to the darkness of Wilkes Street.

Number three has a clutch of makeshift outhouses attached to its wall. I avoid the lunging pig and grab the rock wrapped in wire that appears to serve as a knocker. After two hammerings the door opens a crack and Kitty peers out.

'Yes? Who is it?'

'It's me, Hoxton.'

'Jarvis's friend?'

'Yes.'

'Oh. Just a minute, my dear.'

After a series of grinding sounds the door opens wider and Kitty gazes up at me, her watery eyes struggling to focus.

'S'pect he told you I'd had an accident with my glasses—can't see a foitling thing . . . anyway, come in, come in.'

I follow her up the hallway and into a dimly lit room. The odour of fish that Jarvis mentioned is partly obliterated by a glorious smell of lavender. Bunches of the dried flowers hang from the ceiling beams and cover most surfaces.

I pick up a sprig and inhale the pale lilac fragrance. 'Mmm, wonderful. You trade it, I presume.'

Kitty feels her way to a chair and moves a pile of books from it.

'Please, sit . . . yes, I do, or did before the specs episode.'

Removing the glasses case from my undergarments, I gently place it into her hands.

'I have a solution for you.'

Her wrinkled face lights up as she takes out the glasses, feels them and puts them on. She says nothing for some time, just slips them off and on again with little exclamations of delight.

'. . . But how!'

LONDONIA

'A story for when I have more time, Kitty.'

She looks about the room.

'God's own vacuum! Look at this dump . . . I asked Gabriel to clear up but he's really lost in his own world—or asleep quite a lot of the time.' She points to a carved bedstead in the corner where a blanket-covered figure lies. She turns back to me. 'What can I *possibly* give you for these life-savers?'

'Nothing, but I would like to talk to you a little about the past—before the Final Curtain, and after, you being a sage-dame.'

'Oh, I don't know why they call me that. I just happened to have lived through those times—I'm not particularly wise or anytruc.' She looks at me curiously. 'Why do you wish to know? Jarvis never asks.'

An image of myself sprawled in Marina's chair appears in my mind. 'Something has occurred that's made me wish to know about the Unknown time, the Cincture, how the two states came about.'

'It must be something important. I can see it in your eyes,' Kitty says then smiles at her words. 'It is *so* wonderful to really see again.' She looks about her, examining closely the texture of a shawl, a cup and a blue-jacketed book. 'Things of wonder, books,' she says, picking up the tome and brushing dust from its cover. 'Strange to think they actually stopped being made, such was the draw of the screen.'

'Televisions?' I question.

'Televisions, computers, internet, hypernet. . . I think that was the start of the end, if you like, when print ceased to be.'

'So, really no books?'

'Not enough demand. And then there was a mass-pulping episode in about 2030 when the absence of paper became the norm. It's odd to see how sought-after they've become now.'

I nod in agreement, thinking of my precious stock in the vestry.

LONDONIA

'I wonder,' she continues, 'if people almost stopped thinking for themselves in the end—lost touch with what was actually real, most of them anyway. Weird people like me and Gabriel who read books and grew food . . . oddities. But we survived and many thousands of others didn't when the Whiteout came.'

I feel a thousand other questions pulsing but before I ask further the pile of bedding moves and a querulous voice starts up.

'Kitty? Feel like a walk down the beach?'

She puts down the book. 'Sorry, Hoxton. It'll have to be another time. He'll need calming now.'

I make my way over to the door as Gabriel's voice becomes strident.

'We must go now, before the storm comes.'

Kitty calls over to me. 'Thank you *so* much, Hoxton. Come over with Jarvis another darking.'

Out into the street, I almost turn to walk home, to go back and sit with a pile of books, turn pages and absorb information, but curiosity about Saints' day enfolds me and I continue to Sardi's place.

Number twenty-five is a tall house built of yellow Londonia brick, darkened by cycles of city smogs. The pavement outside the house is busy with chatting people. I push through the crowd and into the hallway which has changed considerably since my last visit.

Several bicycles in dismembered states line the walls along with rifles, bundles of goatskins and a bloody butcher's block. A cleaver stabs its surface, the blade a bright rectangle in the gloom.

'Hoxton!'

Looking up, I see Sardi at the top of the winding staircase. She observes me gazing at the chaos, and laughs as she runs down the stairs.

She nods at the butchers' block. 'The Ukrainians I told you about, but it's worth the babranina coz we get meat.'

LONDONIA

'Who's occupying the other floors now?' I ask, handing over the lettuce.

Sardi gestures upstairs. 'Crazy bird-dame and the Mummers players still on the first and Italians on the second.'

We climb the squeaking staircase to the third floor and enter their main room; a large space with a pitched ceiling of deep blue. The usual friendly clutter of effigies, flowers and furniture has been cleared away for the evening's event, and the room is bare apart from a table and a raised plank-stage area.

Other people have started to arrive bearing plates of food and bottles.

'Sorry, Love,' says one dame approaching us. 'Now't to bring—after the storm damage.'

Sardi hugs her then gestures to the table. 'No worry. Plenty here this eve. Wine? And Hoxton, a glass? Help yourselves.'

At the table Sardi's oldest lad is opening bottles. I pat him on the back.

'Salut, Mo.'

Hey, Hoxton . . . drink?'

'What have we?'

He bends to scan the various homemade labels.

'Blackcurrant, potato, leek! Elderflower and something called Edge of water.'

'I'll try that—sounds mysterious.

So, for the observations. I find a quiet corner and curl up on a pile of blankets, glass in hand. The wine is strong and tastes of mouldy blackcurrants but it's oddly soothing. I watch people arrive, chat, laugh and install themselves; scraping chairs over to sit in a semi-circle around the stage.

A group of very young gosses join me in my corner and empty out a box of ancient toys. As I listen to them organise the various dolls and animals into a game of their own devising I wonder about my own offspring's early years, and how old he might be now.

LONDONIA

A voice singing a lone note makes me look up and the gosses turn from their game.

Dressed in swishing purple, a dame throws out her arms to the crowd.

'Friends—this darking let us praise the Lord that we been saved from the devil's tempest!' A group of five other mecs and dames join her on the stage, their voices filling the room with such intensity that my skin tingles from scalp to my feet. The crowd sway with the singers, hands shooting skywards, words echoed.

'What is this singing?' I ask an elderly mec who has pulled up a chair next to me.

He looks at me as if I have asked what breathing is for.

'Gospel, child!'

After what must be a cycle, I make my way around the joyous congregation to where Sardi stands cutting up a certain fruit I haven't seen for ages. I pick one of the pitted spheres and smell the skin.

'Oranges!'

'A gift from the Hampstedland's commune's glasshouse.'

She spoons some segments into a cup, passes it to me, and I devour them, savouring the acid sweetness.

'Benefits of hosting Saints' day,' she smiles, observing my expression of joy. 'We get enough leftovers for several days.'

'Who's taking the next turn?'

'Two Sundys time—the Pagan New Salvationists.'

'I might come along, take notes and start a Sureditch Press book on Londonia's many sects.'

'You joyed this one?'

'Inspirational, but I think I need to get home.'

She looks at me carefully as if guessing my thoughts.

'Tell me about it all, zaraz, eh?'

'I will, Sardi . . . very soon.'

LONDONIA

We hug and I walk slowly back downstairs. The singing sounds distant and unlikely as I reach the ground floor, as if I could hear saintly song from heaven itself.

The hallway is filled with two mecs heaving the butcher's block towards the back door, their voices raised in argument. I squeeze past them and out into the quiet street. The earlier crowds have left, now back indoors, the darking air having lost its tinge of warmth.

A few foxes and ownerless dogs roam, snuffing at rubbish piles, their forms flickering silhouettes under the few candle-lamps. As I reach Swanfield Street, a wild pig wobbles into a yard followed by a troupe of piglets jostling to suck on her long, pointed teats. An owl glides silently to land in the branches of a sycamore, a dangling rodent clasped in its beak.

A sudden spiral of wind whips the candlelamps, and the shadows of two approaching mecs loom grotesquely. I run the rest of the way home, glancing behind me and side to side, peering into the dim perspective lines of my road.

The church looms, its spire my sentinel. I slip into the gateway, slam the gate shut and put my arms around the writhing, warm dog-bodies waiting for me.

Inside, I feed Kafka and get the fire going. Slipping out of my clothes, I wrap myself up in ancient, comforting pyjamas and curl up with Zorro, Dickens and a shot of Sardi's eau de vie. Visions and sounds of this evening linger in my mind: gosses playing, the ecstatic voices singing of love, and Kitty's recollections of the past. As the lamp's flame starts to shudder, sucking up the last trace of oil, I lift the slumbering cat and enter the comfort of my bed knowing without doubt that I *will* find my missing gosse.

Waves of sleep are upon me as this day and eve dissolve into softness and warmth.

Capitula 7

The garden is slowly waking, the sound of birdsong from every tree-branch and roof. Blackbirds, thrushes, the *chip-chip* of sparrows and rasp of crows.

Sitting in a sheltered corner on this bright morn, I contemplate their voices; the joy in knowing a change of season has started. Nature just continues, adapts. It is us, some say, that have created the changes of landscape, flattened through wars, poisoned, flooded by our pollution and disrespect for this world. The birds know none of this. They sing when something in them says it's time to sing, or time to gather twigs, time to nurture and time to die.

Zorro stretches luxuriously in the early sun. How wonderful to be a cat: no decisions other than where to crap, which mouse to chase and where to sit in the sun.

Philosophy over, I go to find a woolly layer and commence the jobs until the routine is finished. This morn, I must start the Finds, and I'd rather get Bert out of the way in good daylight . . . he'll go for booze, porn—of course, and my trump card, an excellent pair of patent leather brogues. I still have two bottles of valuable Burgundy wine from 2036 found in The Lord's cellar, and a stack of zeitporn which I'm eking out in trade with Bert when the need arises—so to speak. . . . After writing the items in my trade book, I bag it all up, saddle Kafka and lead him out into the mayhem of the Londonia morn.

Taking a deep breath, I prepare myself for the visit to come. I'm not exactly scared of Bert; if it came to a fight, I'd probably win against his smallish, puffing form. It's just something about his proximity that makes me feel uncomfortable, a memory I can't quite clinch from some part of my past.

LONDONIA

It's a pleasure, however, to be out riding on this breezy, clear morn; seeing people attacking their plots of garden and pilched bits of land, earth being turned, saplings planted on what was rubbly nothing. The idea of making any spare potentially fertile ground into local food production is, and has been, increasing over these last few cycles thanks to the permafarm community benevolently spreading their words, *and* plants.

The strident sound of barge horns cause Kafka's ears to crank up; we are nearly at Black Lake and our destination. A few paces on and Bert's territory comes into view. Despite his stature, he manages to command eerie respect over would-be raiders of his patch. The legs of his black-planked stilt hut are no longer immersed in mud as the tide heights have gradually decreased again over the cycles. The building now stands like an angular crane fly some distance from the water's edge, the rest of Bert's domain behind it in the shape of a large metal hangar guarded by two bored heavies by day and roaming hounds during darking time.

At my approach one of the mecs stands up and squints at me. Then he recognises my top hat and Kafka's grey hide.

'Miss 'Oxton . . .' Striding over, he wrestles the gate lock with meaty hands. 'Ze Guv ees in ze small 'ouse—'e said to go up.'

This is not a good sign—*Bert in the small house . . .* anylane, I slip down from Kafka and hand over the reins. The mec leads Kafka over to Bert's horse-parking and I lift my long coat ends from the mud, step around the puddles and take the thin ladder up to Bert's abode.

I rap on the glass of the door and his oddly aristocratic voice answers.

'If it's *you*, Hoxton, come in. Anyone else can vertically saunter off again.'

Opening the door, I am greeted by the sight of the house-owner clad in a paisley silk dressing gown, tied worryingly loosely about his ample waist.

LONDONIA

'Goodly morn, Bert.'

'And to *you* too, beauty.'

'You got my pigeon message?'

'Indeed. Four fine ladies in need of antique communication devices . . . well, antique in age but a technology beyond our usage at this present time. Curious that, don't you think?'

Bert—a philosopher . . . and he's right. It is odd. Humans taking a step backwards. A technological descent.

'It is curious,' I agree. 'Do you think people in that era imagined technology actually going downhill?'

'They didn't,' he says, relighting the stub of a cigar, 'onward and forward with the next gadget. Take these phones for example —always bigger and brighter, more detail and *definition*.'

'But what were they for—these small screens? Why are my clients so fascinated? They already appear to have telephones to contact each other.'

'Ah, dear Hoxton. Have you not read up on the subject after I showed you these jewels on your last visit?'

'No. I don't have time, or light. Any I *do* manage currently are about improving soil and water capture.'

'Tsk. These things of metal, plastic and glass were quite extraordinary. Just with the brushing of one finger across the surface, you could find out, listen to, look at any article you desired to access.'

'Unlimited access?'

He nods, a manic look in his eyes. 'Virtually visit the interior of a world-famous site, watch amusing films of peoples' domestic creatures, find out any historical fact, learn how to make bread . . .'

'But books can tell me that, and I can make bread.'

'Ah, but there's *so* much more.' A slight film of sweat has appeared under Bert's sandy comb-over. He leans closer. 'Imagine an ocean of sexual acts available to you through that little screen—whatever your *persuasion*.'

LONDONIA

I step back and trip over a small embroidered footstool. He grabs my arm and pulls me back, face close to mine, whisky and tobacco breath wheezing through his overworked lungs.

I push him away and present my carpet bag.

'Well, while technology is rotting away in your barn over there, enjoy some paper substitutes.' He stops pawing me and looks hopefully at the bag as I pull out and splay three lurid works.

'Mm, quite titillating . . . but four devices you say, with their necessary cabling?'

'Four, yes.'

'And, no doubt, they will require pristine examples.'

I can see only too well which direction this is heading in. 'Within reason, yes. But you have many—I was given the tour, if you recall.'

'Yes, I have many but a large percentage of them are beyond any possible reconnection—their interiors leached away by rotting batteries, bodies dented, smashed, only useful for their components. I do, however, have a small collection which are completely mint—with their boxes . . .'

'I see. One question, Bert.'

'Seraph?'

'How do you come to have all these items?'

He smooths the strands of hair that have flopped loose and smiles, revealing an array of gold teeth that would impress a Vaux-haulers gang member.

'Because, my dear, I had a shop that sold these very things.'

'You *did*? In the Cincture?'

'This was long-cycles before the Cincture walls were built, when London was just London, made up of many boroughs. I left, with a lot of my stock, during the chaos of the Final Curtain and the Fashocom party took over, albeit for a short reign. I'd heard they were planning a scoop of all technological equipment, so for that, and other reasons I thought the largely ignored outer zones might be a better place to disappear to.'

LONDONIA

I wonder if other swaggers might have squirreled away such things from that time. He guesses my thoughts.

'I wouldn't bother, Hoxton. *They* come to me—I have the biggest collection of pre-Curtain communication. And I know the supply limitations in the Cincture. They may be starting up the internet, or inner-web as they are calling it but it's only for central computer usage—public *playing about* is a long way off.'

'How do you know all this?'

'I come from there, Seraph. Still have family in Mayfair, and the occasional letter communication.'

'So, if I take these *things* back they may not be able to use them?'

'Do you care?'

Do I? 'I suppose not.'

'And what do you get in return.'

'That's not really your business, is it?'

'It must be more than just straightforward trading. Perhaps I could assist you.'

I feel the day slipping away. 'It's fine. Thanks. Perhaps I could see the items?'

He gestures to a floral armchair. 'Certainly. Make yourself comfortable—whisky in the decanter there if you wish—and I will return tout de suite.'

I sit as invited and glance around his curiously feminine and fussy abode full of Victoriana objects, needlework cushions and twee paintings that sit uncomfortably with his taste in more *fleshy* activities. He reappears attired in a brown and black checked suit, fraying yellow shirt and odd shoes. Staring at them, I recall the brogues.

'Shame the shoes don't do the suit justice, Bert. However, I may be able to assist you.' I open my bag and hand him the cloth-wrapped beauties.

He gawps, checks the sizing, kicks off the odds and tries mine.

'Well played, mademoiselle.'

LONDONIA

'So, we're on the same page. Shoes and magazines for the four phones.'

He looks up from admiring the leather. 'Not quite.'

We begin the trade standoff—weighing up the other's will. I'm close to pushing him over onto his chintzy sofa, yanking the shoes from his feet and scrambling back down the ladder . . . but, to fail this Find? God's own phone, these dames will be paying.

'D'ac. Show me the articles. And *not* in those shoes.'

He grins, removes them and slips back on the tan mismatches.

'To the hangar then.'

After the warmth of Bert's fuggy stilt-house, it's vile outside. A greasy wind gyrates around the muddied compound, flicking up ash and bones. We hurry over to the hangar and the two guards leave their bin-fire to slide open the massive, wheeled door. Inside, Bert wrenches gruntily at the cord on an ancient generator and it reluctantly spits into life disgorging sooty fumes. Two suspended metal-shaded lights pop on and I gaze at the lines of shelving, their perspective lines disappearing into darkness at the back of this metal behemoth.

Bert waves a leather-gloved hand at each section.

'River mud finds—metal, wood and ceramic. Nails, screws, tools . . . there, wheels and vehicle parts. Over here, computers and associated paraphernalia, *and* what you are after.' I follow him to a compartmentalised section of metal containers. He draws one out, unlocks it and carefully takes out plastic-encased flattish white cardboard boxes. 'These were de rigueur in 2025 —the iPhone soft-screen Z and the Samsung Orgo. Note how exquisite they are, how smooth the glass is.'

I take the slippery object, hold it to my ear and nearly drop it.

'Why is it flat and not shaped like a . . . handle, or something ergonomic.'

LONDONIA

He smiles at me as if I am a very, very old person. 'I think it is impossible for someone of *now* to understand the design element and usefulness of such a thing.'

'I think you are probably utterly correct. Spades are useful, horses, wood-burning stoves, paper, ink pens, books and strong boots are useful, with or without a *design element*.'

He takes the object back from me, wraps it lovingly and places it back in its moulded nest.

'Four of these with their chargers will trade out at: the shoes, the three magazines, that bottle I saw in your bag—an excellent year—and five minutes of your time.'

'Doing what exactly,' I say, having a fairly clear idea.

A short while later, I gallop Kafka along the river edge, concentrating on the sound of his hooves drumming on the mudflats, shutting out the sounds of Bert the Swagger gasping in a shadowy corner of the warehouse. My hand still bears the imprint of his unpleasant member . . . at least he had been accurate in timing. A few turns of my pocket watch's hands and he was a happier Swagger and I was out of there with my trade accomplished including a *remote* for Mrs Caruso's television. I should go straight to Fred's and start hunting for garments but feeling utterly bone-chilled, a hot-water soak feels imperative.

I drop my valuable finds off at the church and continue to the Sureditch Bathhouse. Soaking time always produces solutions to problems as well as grime removal. Horse-boy engaged, I leave Kafka and enter the deco-fronted old cinema building. The most annoying of the bathhouse staff eyes me from behind her podium.

'Aye-eye, Hoxton. Been up to no good, 'ave yer.' I ignore this and ask for a full clockface, with tea. She examines a ledger. 'Owings on three sessions. Not sure if the guv'll go for more.'

'Oh, *come* on . . . four's not out of the way.'

She frowns and slaps the ledger down. 'Wait 'ere.'

A few moments later, Sabri-Ov-Tooting arrives from an anteroom, resplendent as ever in white robes and turban.

LONDONIA

'Hoxton. Always a pleasure to be seeing you, but I must ask what you will be offering in way of exchange if I allow you a further session.'

Easy. 'I'm sure you could manage a nice little side-line of brand new undergarments, fresh from the Cincture . . .'

He smiles and nods. 'Very good, *very* good. Take your time. Miley—send her in the best tea, and a macaroon.'

Miley scowls at me as she hands over a towel. 'Bath number six—tea'll be along in a quarter.'

The old cinema building now has rows of baths instead of the seats that once occupied its interior. There's talk of films being shown too if Sabri can get enough solar to run a projector. For the time being it's a dimly-lit and steamy oasis away from the clatter of Hackrovia. Number six is an ocean-going vessel of blue plastic, gradually filling with brackish, but hot, water. I light the candles of the candelabra, swish the curtain around on its rattling rings, peel off the many layers and step into paradise.

As I doze, two elegant pale brown hands pass a tray through the curtain gap. I open an eye and see one of Sabri's ado-gosses staring at my naked form—not that he can see a great deal through the now-deep, greyish water.

'Your tea, Miss Hoxton. And Father wanted to know if you require the massage service.'

I consider this. If it were to be anything like last time with Sabri's nephew, I'd end up sweatier and dirtier than before the bath.

'No. I'll just take the soak, grazie.'

I sip tea flavoured with rose petals and crunch the macaroon, while thinking for the millionth time of Marina's words. Maybe this next visit I'll be able to talk to Mrs Caruso in confidence—find out anything I can about hospitals, where I possibly would have given birth. But what are the chances of someone so fluff-headed being able to help. . . . Mentally slapping myself for this pessimism, I step out of the tepid water, dry off and shuffle back on the layers. I might keep some of this promised underwear for myself. When was the last time I pulled on a pair of un-patched knickers?

Feeling woolly-warm, I arrive outside the blackened brick edifice of Fred's Threads, descend from Kafka and bang on the door. Footsteps sound and the little hatch creaks open.

'Hox! Entrez.'

'I've got the horse with me.'

'Wants an outfit, does 'e?' Fred grins through the hole at my expression. 'Nah . . . bring 'im round the side—one of the pack'll open the yard. Water 'n straw there.'

A short time later, a metal gate grinds open revealing the yard, mostly filled with a large boat.

'What's that for?' I ask one of Fred's brood as he takes the reins for me.

He leads Kafka to the lean-to and turns back with a wry smile. 'Dad's ark—case the floods return.'

Entering the side door, I immediately start removing layers again such is the heat from their enormous wood-stove.

'Tropical,' I comment as Fred ambles over.

'Yeah. Gotta keep the mould off stuff, and Mimi seizes up if it's too cold.'

'We can't have that. In fact, I've a proposition that'll keep her rather busy. Is she about?'

'Just gone to 'ave a pizz. She'll be back soon enough. So, what's this job then?'

As I describe my meeting, Mimi returns.

'Aye up, Hox. So, was it as tha said last time? Fed up are they wi' last craze?'

I delve for the precious magazines. 'How's your fashion knowledge of the 2020s?'

LONDONIA

She turns and gives button, zip and ribbon sorting instructions to three of their younger brood then takes one of the *Vogues*. She flips through the pages with a small sigh.

'Me ma were bit of an authority on that era, working for the V and A like—'fore it all got done over. She always said fashion dribbled away after 'bout 1980, all got a bit samy—bit 'oh— animal prints is in again' . . . 'ere, look at this, see—ripped denim, blue leopard skin shirt, camouflage jacket, gold shoes . . . it's all stuff thrown together from previous long-cycles.'

Suddenly this Find seems relatively easy.

'So . . . with the right *labels* they wouldn't really know any more than I do.'

She shrugs. 'I've got a right nice little stash 'a tags—Gucci, Valentino, Guess, Pramino, Prada . . .'

'Mrs Caruso mentioned Beckham. Any of those?'

'Oh aye, and we've a couple 'a jackets of hers too—bit 'a moth in one, but dare say I could add a bit a somat t' cover it oup like.'

'It's not . . . green, is it? Like this.' I take the magazine, flip frantically to the page I had dog-eared and show Mimi the zipped tartan item.

She snorts a laugh. 'Jarvis always says tha's a magicked Finder. Follow me.'

At the wardrobe marked, *2000s jackets and coats*, she opens the door, rummages amongst hangers covered with sack and paper wrappings and triumphantly brings forth the very same jacket.

I put out a hand and feel the fine wool texture. *Christ in a suit-bag*. 'I don't believe it . . . suppose this is going to trade-cost a *lot*.'

Fred appears at the word, *trade*, and puts a boney arm around my shoulders.

'What's on offer, then?'

LONDONIA

'Well, it's rather open-ended as I wasn't sure how complicated all this would be—but how about a good batch of useful no-fuss underwear and some medical supplies.'

'Pants 'n stuff very useful—can't trade 'em quick enough. Tell yer what. Gather together what you want and discuss with Mi the add-ons and we'll make a slate.'

A clockface later, I've amassed a considerable pile of clothing: a few originals and others of which Mimi, having cut off the old labels, is busy machining in the required names. The Beckham moth problem has been solved by an inventive patch of sequins and similarly the damage to one of the bags has been covered by an adding of a red leather flower.

'You want Fred to make delivery?' says Mimi. 'S' bit complicated on't 'orse, int'it?'

Eyeing the pile, I agree. 'Might it be possible on the morrow?'

'Reckon, aye . . .' I follow her gaze to the front door where mecs are bringing in bolts of cloth and Fred is directing their destination.

'Where are those from,' I ask.

'Boat from long way away—Fred's brother's been down on't dockside waiting fr it t' come in. Only 'appens once a cycle and it's good strong cloth—makes for solid, long-lasting wear. Loggers unt' brickies'll be pleased.'

Glancing up at the skylights, I realise darking is approaching. I write the address for Mimi, thank them both profusely and go out to Kafka waiting next to the boat. The wind has lulled. An almost warm breeze brushes against my face. I gaze up at the stars and wonder if they are as visible within the Cincture.

Capitula 8

As the shaw drops me outside Mrs Caruso's house, I have a sudden fear that my message, or worse still, Fred and Mimi's carefully bagged-up stock might not have arrived, or been confiscated . . . destroyed. *Merda*.

The fears disperse, however, as I note my client's beaming face at the window. I expect Gubbins to open the door with all the usual brittle servant rigmarole but it's the dame herself.

'Hoxton! I'm just speechless!' But she isn't, nor the other reciprocates of my Findings who are obviously in the sitting room going through the clothes. The sound-wall of excited female yatterings reminds me of the starlings that occupy the biggest plane tree in my garden. The noise increases as she opens the door, stops, and then starts up again, now directed at me.

'These are just . . . fatablas!'

'Hoxton! How did you do this?'

'Fendi . . . *and* Gucci!'

I wave back the effusiveness and the noise decreases.

'I hope it's all in good order. Did the packages get opened?'

Mrs Nash, attired already in a gold skirt and denim jacket, enlightens me.

'They did. But it was done carefully, no damage—I would have got Nash onto it if there had been!'

I seize this opportunity to learn more.

'What does he do, Mr Nash?'

She stops fiddling with the clasp of a bag and looks at me with pride.

'He's *director* of Organisation and Order in the Cincture—the part that deals with the access points and external activity.'

Raids? 'Meaning the . . . control in Londonia?'

LONDONIA

'Crime control, yes. It must be reassuring to know the Cincturian forces will intervene in any trouble, hm?'

'Oh. Absolutely. Calm and assurance . . . so, everything arrived as I had expected.'

'For *sure*,' enthuses Miss Preen. 'And we need more! The factories are already wanting to meet us. Catwalk on Bond Street—me*ow*!'

Mrs Caruso stops admiring herself in the fireplace mirror and observes my grey bag.

'Might you have other *dee*lites in there?'

I had feared during the rigorous checking at the access point that my precious Finds would have been confiscated, but her family name appears to command serious leverage. Placing the bag on a table, I open it and take out the phone containers. A hush replaces the nattering.

'Before handing over these items,' I say firmly, 'I would like to talk of our trade.'

Mrs Caruso gestures to a stack of boxes by the door. 'Gubbins had them all prepped, ready, and transport has been ordered.' She claps her hands, face flushed. 'So! Show us then.'

Needing to check the goods first, I open the top cardboard box and find the glasses as promised, and a second larger box containing a vast number of size-sorted cotton briefs, vests and even a basic model of a bra—something I haven't seen for a while . . . I calculate roughly how much I'll have to give away to Fred and how much I'll need to replace the items and my *time* donated to Bert.

'For the clothing so far, this will be an equal trade but the phones cost me a great deal more, therefore I would like the same again in goods, and some information.'

'Information?' she enquires, an eyebrow raised.

'Yes. Of a personal nature. Perhaps we could talk later?'

'. . . If that's what you want.'

I deal with the slight atmosphere of suspicion by opening one of the flat white boxes.

LONDONIA

'This is a phone from 2025—unused, and with its charging device. These are similar models from the year before, also unused.'

I pass the boxes to eager hands and listen to the ensuing exchanges, which surpass the clothes excitement. As my earlier over-indulgence of tea has filtered through, I wonder if I could visit a Cincture bathroom.

'Mrs Caruso. Could I use your facilities?'

She glances up from caressing the shiny object. 'Gubbins will direct you.'

Out in the hallway, there's no sign of him. No harm in having a quick poke about. The cream-carpeted staircase beckons and I walk silently up to the first floor, admiring the series of gold-framed etchings of old London. The pictures continue along a wall: parks, monuments, churches . . . One of them causes me to stop my casual scanning: St Patrick's Soho Square. The exterior appears familiar. A ghost memory surfaces—organ music, crowds . . .

'Madame Hoxton?' Gubbins is staring at me from downstairs. 'Do you require something?'

'I was looking for the bathroom.'

'Two doors along on your right.' I almost expect him to add: *and don't touch anything* but he doesn't.

I enter the room and stare at the white porcelain—such beauty to crap in! And lie in. The bath could easily contain Kafka, such is its size. I run a hand over its smooth rolling edge, turn on a tap just to marvel at a clean, uninterrupted flow of water—no coughing and spurting like the plumbing at the bathhouse. I pizz, sniff the contents of various bottles of perfume and glance at my unusually pale face in the rococo-framed mirror above the sink. What would it be like to bathe in this bath, expect sumptuous towels to always be stacked ready, get slightly peeved with the house-keeper if the *right* soap wasn't provided.

I jump at a gentle knock on the door.

LONDONIA

'Oh . . . sorry, be out in a momento.'

I put back the wrapped bar of soap I had considered slipping into the allinone pouch and open the door. Mrs Hedgefund's pale blue eyes stare back at me.

She lays a hand on my arm.

'Quick. We don't have much time.'

I do occasionally use sex-exchange in more demanding trade situations—such as Bert, but lesigay is a new one for me.

'Here?'

I didn't expect it but she smiles—grins even, then harsh-whispers. 'No—not *that*! Did you read my note?'

'. . . Note?—oh, sorry. I lost it.'

'Never mind. Listen. I must see you without the others. Could you come back to my house after this?'

'I could do—except I told them at the access point I'd be leaving the horse for just a couple of clockfaces, I mean, hours.'

'I'll call them. Just say you'll come back with me, and I'll deal with everything else.'

I note her excited expression. Whatever it is she wants to say, presumably about some one-updameship over clothing or gadgetry, I can up the trade stakes.

'D'accord. I mean, certainly.'

'Good.'

I follow her back downstairs, let her enter the room and listen for a moment.

'I found her—she'd got frightened by the lav flush!'

'Suppose they don't have those out there.'

'I heard the *waste* is collected in buckets.'

'Dis-gus-t*ing*!'

'Moving on! So, who wants which phone? Actually—me for the gold one.'

'Aw—Bec . . .'

I gently open the door as the bog-chat has stopped, take my place on the sofa and wait for further Finding instruction. A little later when the initial fuss has died down and the subject turns to how these items are actually going to work, I decide it might be a good point to conclude the deal and leave.

'Mrs Caruso, I should be getting back to the access point. About my fee—when would you be able to procure my trade items?'

She yanks the servant cord and after a few moments Gubbins appears.

'Madame?'

'Gubbins. We want a re-order of the goods for Miss Hoxton. How long would it take?'

'The undergarments will not be a problem. However, I fear the spectacles may take a few days.'

'Why?'

'They were running short on the required glass. The ones I obtained last time were all they had left.'

'Well, get onto another company, Gubbins.'

She shakes her head as he closes the door. 'Such a inquensy thing to ask. Could we meet up again in say a week—for the next commissions too?'

I pick up my bag and wave a *no problem*. 'It'll give me time to research other clothing possibilities.'

'Don't forget to grab your stashies from the access point. Gubbins will have sent them.' As I walk to the door she calls back. 'You wanted to talk to me? You mentioned *information* earlier.'

'It's fine, another time.'

Mrs Hedgefund picks up her chosen phone and slips it into her bag.

'Have to go, crew—completely forgot. Matt wanted to meet me to look at wallpaper for his new bureau. I'll take a shaw and drop you off, Hoxton.'

'Back here tomorrow afternoon for Change planning?' suggests the host.

'Wouldn't miss it! Coda!'

LONDONIA

We leave the room, and walk down the street, her skirts bustling against her clicking shoes.

'*Christ alive.* I hate these garments.'

'Looking forward to the Change then,' I say brightly.

She looks at me wryly as we stride along. 'Oh—absolutely. *Any* cripping change.'

I realise with a start that Mrs Hedgefund is not quite who I thought she was.

'You don't care about fashion?'

'No, I don't. And you didn't either.'

'Sorry—*didn't?*'

She stops abruptly as we reach a small boutique at the corner of the street and pulls me gently to the glass. As we stare in at the artful displays of lingerie she continues in a low tone.

'Does the name Chantelle mean anything to you?'

'. . . No. Why? Should it?'

'It was your name. That's why.'

The silky garments in front of me seem to waver into a sea of pastel colour. I feel weak, sick.

'Is there a shaw there?'

She takes my arm more firmly and steers me towards the rank.

'Hanover Terrace, please.'

The young mec nods and she helps me in. I say nothing, just gaze out on the shining shop fronts and orderly pavement trees until the shaw stops at the beginning of a handsome line of buildings opposite a park.

I get out, clutching my bag with sweaty hands. These pilasters and railings . . . another memory twinges faintly.

The shaw pulls away and Mrs Hedgefund takes my arm again.

'Think you need something to eat. When did you last have a meal?'

I think back to the macaroon in the bath. Did I eat this morn? I can't recall much before Bert's. It all seems a confusion. She's

LONDONIA

unlocking a shining black door, talking to someone—Gubbins? I should get back to Kafka.

'Hoxton?' her voice seems streets away.

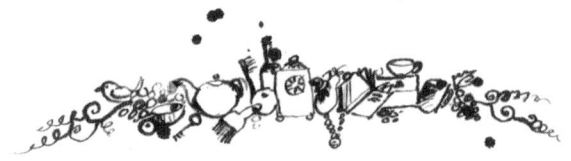

A lacy curtain wafts at a long elegant window before me. Trees beyond, a faint haze of green on bare branches. Someone sits at the other side of the room reading a book. She puts it down, walks over and sits on this very comfortable bed.

'Ah—you're not dead then.'

I sit up a bit, recognising friendly irony. 'Evidently not.'

'Bob's bringing you some soup.'

'Bob?'

'Well, his formal name is Fletcher but I prefer Bob.'

'Who are you—apart from, *Mrs Hedgefund*?'

'You really don't recall anything of here?'

'What do you mean, *here*?'

She waves an arm gesturing the room and beyond. 'This place, these streets, the Cincture . . .'

I consider her words. There have been odd moments. A chink of light on a memory I had imagined to be a dream—a certain building, this row of houses.

'Possibly—I don't know if I'd call it recollections.'

'To answer your question . . . my name is Iona.'

'Iona Hedgefund . . ?'

She smile's wryly at my expression.

'I know. Ridiculous, isn't it? Mackenzie was more lyrical—my maiden name.'

The door opens and, *Bob,* a smiling mec dressed in jeans and checked shirt, sets a tray down before me.

'My own tomato soup, bread and goats cheese.'

LONDONIA

I shuffle up from my semi-reclining position on the very comfortable sofa and beam at the food.

'Thank you *so much*!'

'Pleasure, miss.'

Iona calls out as he leaves the room. 'Bob, can you call the access and tell them Hoxton will be delayed, and, don't forget Mr Hedgefund will be back at eight—formal garb.'

'Gotcha.'

'He's from Londonia,' I say, surprised.

'A scoop truck refugee,' she says, '. . . anyway, back to the real issue—you. Your life here.'

I smear a large dollop of cheese on the bread and chew, words muffled.

'D'ac. Start . . . from fe beginning.'

She sighs. 'God . . . where *to* start. This might take some time. Right. You were at school with me—not junior, I didn't meet you until puberty college.'

'Puberty college?'

'When the sexes were separated.'

'But, wait. I still don't understand. I was *here* at school.'

'Boarding school to be precise—even though the parents were only within a five-mile radius of Buckingham College. The powers were looking for a new code of morality—strict discipline after the more ragged years following the Fasho downfall.'

'But who *are* my parents.'

'I only met them once, before they were about to make a voyage to Southern France—he was a French wine trader, and wealthy. She, an African—think they called them super-models.

I stretch out a hand, examine its pale brown skin. 'That would explain my colour.'

'And the fact you were top in French.'

'. . . What happened to them?'

'I'm afraid I don't know, Hoxton . . . can I call you Chantelle?'

She slaps me with this word.

LONDONIA

'No. My name is Hoxton.'

Iona looks apologetic. 'Sorry. That was clumsy.'

'Ça va—it's all a bit much to assimilate, but I know that name's meaning—tough like a stone.'

'How strange. It sounds so soft and musical. Are you tough like a stone?'

'I think you have to be to dodge through the Londonia life.'

She gets up and peruses a shelf of books. I hadn't really taken in these surroundings, and now I do while slurping the delicious soup. No angular furniture here—all softness and beautiful textiles, paintings, old things.

'Are you not following Mrs Caruso's 2020s trend in furnishings?'

She turns, a large book in hand. 'Plerk, no. Air-headed ideas.'

'So, why associate with them?'

Sitting down, she passes me the book. 'To blend in. Keep out of trouble. Have a look—you were trouble.'

Tentatively, I turn the first page and read a looping script—*mine*:

To my dear friend, Iona, on my WEDDING day! Life de facto.

The following pages are stuff of dreams. Me in an ivory gown, a sweeping train, lilies and white peacocks. Clutching my arm is a rotund, grinning man with a mat of ginger hair.

I point to him with a shaking index finger. '*Who is that?*'

Iona laughs at my tone. 'Your husband of course. The honourable Whitty Whiteman—gitcho of the first order but rich and after a knock 'em dead, gorgeous wife.'

'. . . But when was this, and where is he now?'

'This, my dear friend was after you were disgraced—'

I cut her short. 'Disgraced?'

She smiles. 'As I said. You were, and are, *very* beautiful and many thought so. Especially the one who managed to impregnate you.'

Her words cause me to falter. '. . . Who was he?'

LONDONIA

'That, I don't know. I just remember you were upset—he'd been brutal, that was for sure and you'd resisted. I saw the bruises . . . I know he'd become rather obsessed with you. But you were whisked away when the time was approaching and I only got to see you by making a huge fuss. Of course, everyone in *society* knew and your parents were horrified, so you were married off to the twat. He didn't care, just wanted something pretty on his arm and had enough money to live in his massive edifice with you and ignore any scandal.'

'And . . .'

'What happened to him? He was trying out a reconditioned Aston Martin with an early form of Methanerix and the condenser exploded.'

I stifle a laugh. 'Sorry! Suppose I should say, how dreadful.'

'Why? You obviously don't remember him and you certainly never loved him.'

I shut the book and pass it back to her. 'I was told by a mirror-dame—a fortune teller, to you, that I had a son. So, now I know that was true, but where is he?'

My new-old friend shakes her head. 'I only saw the baby for a few minutes when I was allowed to visit briefly.'

'So, you did see him!'

'I did. But you remember nothing?'

Delving into my innermost feelings and thoughts I try to recall the sensation of a tiny gosse in my arms.

She wipes away a single tear that has spilled out and rolled down my cheek.

'He was . . . lovely, really lovely.'

'There must be a way of finding out where he is?'

'Without a family involvement, I don't know. The unit you were in is no longer running, but maybe it would be possible through birth registers. I will try to find out for you.'

'It's so odd to feel I might pass him in the street here and not know. He must be a young mec now.'

'Mec?'

LONDONIA

'Man.'

'Oh. Mec . . .' She says the word a few times then turns to me. 'There is one way you would certainly know it was him.' She touches the skin at the base of her neck. 'Around here on his tiny neck I saw a birthmark which, unless it was later removed, would be instantly recognisable.'

'A red mark?'

'No. It was brown, dark brown and shaped a little like Italy. Very unusual.'

The slow ticking of a long-case clock almost booms in the silence that follows. I have a son. The greatest Finding mission . . .

Iona has stood up and is peering out into the now-dark street.

'There's so much more to talk about but you should leave—Matthew will be back any moment and it's possible he might recognise you.'

'That would be a problem?'

'He was part of the committee at the time who make decisions about mind-clearing.'

'*Mind clearing?* You married someone involved in such things?'

'Oh—crapit. Look, there's so much explaining to do, and believe me I didn't want to marry him, or anyone. Next time, I'll tell you more.'

Bob appears and picks up the tray. 'I 'ad a phone call from Mr Hedgefund's secretary to say he was on his way back.'

We all turn towards the window as a faint rumble vibrates the chandelier's glass droplets. A light pierces the gloom outside.

'That'll be him then,' I say, picking up my bag. 'How far is it to the access point?'

Bob stares at me. 'Shank's?'

'It can't be that far.'

'I can call you a shaw—no probs.'

'Think I need a walk . . .'

LONDONIA

'But you don't know where to go,' says Iona. 'I'll walk with you—it's about half an hour.'

Suddenly, I want very much to be on my own, to digest all this without further revelations.

'I'd rather go alone. Just tell me the direction.'

'You will come back, won't you? There's so much more to say.'

I open the sitting room door and glance back. 'I'll see you at Mrs Caruso's. Or if it's important to you—come out into Londonia! St Leonard's church, Hackrovia.'

'Londonia?'

I shut the door on her question and walk down the hallway.

The front door unlocks and a mec walks in, bowler hat specked with rain, coat pulled up high. He pulls off gloves, muttering. 'Hope that damned cook's made a good supper, Iona.' He looks up and starts as he sees not the blonde hair and pale skin of his wife but my black hair and coffee skin.

I back around him hurriedly without a word. He stares after me, his face quite white beneath the dark curve of his hat, eyes still fixed on me as the door closes. I reach the end of the crescent and instinctively turn right onto the wide road, feeling my section of Londonia to be that way. This is confirmed shortly by a group of evening-suited, lounging young mecs standing outside a drinking-house, wine glasses in hand.

'She's from the Pan.'

'Hey, beautiful. What are you doing in the Egg?'

'Fancy making a few guilds?'

I gesture a Londonia, *fuk off*, but one catches my arm, causing me to stop. He peers drunkenly at me with hooded eyes. 'They'ss only joking . . . you looking for the East Access?'

I soften at his smile and drink-fuzzy words. 'I am, yes.'

He points down the lamp-lit street. 'This is Grand-Euston Road. Just keeps walking and you'll gez to the old King's Cross station—'s access point.' He takes his jacket off and drapes it around my shoulders. 'S' a cold night.'

LONDONIA

'Are you sure—this is expensive cloth.'

'Got 'nother. Better gez going. They closes gates at nine tonight.'

One of his friends grabs him by the sleeve. 'You finished with the charity stuff, Fab? Squire's bought another birthday bottle. Cherbourg fizz!'

My saviour protests slightly. 'Goz trainin' tomorrow.'

'G's sake, Fab! Youz only eighteen once! *And* you got other training—*big* bash coming up, eh? Academy do—remember? This is juzt run-through!'

He glances once more at me and is hauled back into the drinking house.

I turn and pace quickly along the pavement, thinking of the young man and his ensuing thudding head on the morrow. I hardly notice the time passing or the few shaws and cars that share the street. If I could just now be at home, curled up with Zorro, a huge glass of *anything* in front of me.

As I approach the almost deserted access point, a mec appears from the main office.

'Eh—you there. Qu'est-ce que vous faites là? I 'ave to be back 'ere in six hours, vouz savez? And your 'orse 'e has made much merde.'

I'm obviously the last person to pass through this evening, and this is the remaining access point worker, keen to get home. He raises his shoulders in a Gallic shrug. 'C'est pas vrai!'

I quickly change clothes and locate Kafka in the last bay. He stops chewing hay from a rack and looks at me mournfully as I apologise. Feeling the tiredness of the mec waiting for me, I find a cigar from my bag and pass it to him.

'Desolé, monsieur.'

His smile emerges as he turns to crank the gate handle.

'C'est pas *trop* grave, mademoiselle.'

The massive doors swing open slowly. We pass through and they close again. The mec whistles as he turns locks and clanks chains, securing the walls for another darking.

LONDONIA

Quarter of a clockface later, I'm wearily opening my own gates. The padlock is undone. Could I have been careless enough not to take those few seconds, to hear the little metal curve click into place? However, the door is locked and undamaged. I walk Kafka in, fill his water trough and brush his grey flanks methodically, thoughts gradually untangling with the movement.

Task done, I head towards the garden to check the mess out there. The dogs will be mad by now. As I walk up the aisle, I hear a low rasping noise behind Kafka's straw pile. Grabbing a shovel, I pace carefully around and peer over. Jarvis lies in a foetal curl, black suit mussed and straw-covered. The two empty bottles by his feet suggest he must have had something to celebrate with me, and he had opted for finishing them both. I smile wryly at the thought of his head on the morrow, cover him with a horse blanket and continue outside.

It's worse than I thought. Tilly had managed to make a hole in the chicken enclosure and squeezed her slightly smaller form through. Three birds down, but at least she had shared them with Fagin. After soothing the hens as much as I can in their nocturnal confusion, I reinstate their roosting perch, block the hole and prepare to find that drink I had lusted after.

As I lock the back door, I remember Jarvis's comatose form in the hay and take over a flagon of water for when he wakes desperately thirsty after such a gnole-binge. The blanket has been thrown in a heap; no body, just an impression left in the straw. My ears catch a despairing wail issuing from the vestry. I run, push the door open then start back, shocked to see Jarvis hunched in the fireside chair, face creased and red, his hands twisting something: Parrot's woollen hat.

He lets out a heart-rending cry. 'Hoxton . . . they killed him.'

Captitula 9

It is a bleak, damp day. The hopeful spring sun, as if in mourning with Jarvis, has vanished, cloaking itself in seamless grey cloud.

Standing on a wooden jetty, we look out over the river. The remains of their barge drift gently with the current, tethered to a pole. Jarvis has wrapped Parrot's body in red silk, hiding the burned flesh. It now lies in the centre of the vessel, covered in flowers: a bright shape amongst singed wood and slate water.

The events of two days ago in the Cincture seem distant and muddied by this terrible happening. I've barely thought of Iona and her revelations, and those twittering dames in their soft, stupid lives . . . I'll do what I must, get the trades but the Cincture can sit there smugly surrounded by all this visceral, hot, bloody reality—where I really belong whatever my past was. But the gosse . . .

My thoughts are interrupted by a strident blare from a trombone. A mec stands on the river bank, the instrument a slice of silver against slate water. He projects a second note. It echoes around the buildings, smaller paler sounds shouting back from the bricks and concrete. People start to gather: friends and fellow workers, locals and folk I've never seen. They stand quietly. The barge will be set free into the flow when Jarvis says it is time.

Prophet-Jake acknowledges a nod from Jarvis, places his fiddle under his chin and draws the bow. Plaintive notes ring out across the water, mingling with the seagulls' cries.

As Jake lowers his violin, Jarvis speaks, the words cracked.

'Thank you, friends, for being 'ere. We live in a dangerous place with dangerous bods. I'd found one of the best bods, my

LONDONIA

best person . . . killed for no—' The tears start again and he stares up into the sky. After a short time of composure, he walks to the edge of the jetty, wrenches off the rope and tosses it into the water. The barge knocks gently at the edge of the wood for a moment then veers off slowly into the rolling water as more flowers rain down onto the corpse and into the vessel's wake.

Jarvis forgets his tears as furious words fill the quiet. 'I'll get you, putainfukkas! Kill you, I will!'

His last words quiver in the stillness; it seems as if the whole of Londonia is listening and absorbing each syllable.

Jarvis turns from the river and addresses the gathering.

'Now, friends, let's mark Parrot's name—to the Blue Pig.'

The crowd follows as we walk to the drinking house that sits glowering at the river's edge. There's a manic glint in Jarvis's eye as he walks up to the bar and I foresee a large headache on waking the next day.

The ancient landlord heaves a box onto the counter-top, his gnarled hands shaking.

'Saved this for important events,' he wheezes, lifting out dark bottles of wine. 'Can't think of a more fitting one. Tragic. Just get me some good bacco when you can.'

Jarvis squeezes back a tear. 'Thanks, Alf. It'll be goodly-apex.'

He pulls one of the crowd over to the battered piano lurking at the back of the room.

'Allez, Angelo—you can play this thing, can't yer?'

'Sure, just get me a drink.' He sits down on a stool, brushes back his tangled black hair and flexes his fingers. 'D'ac, request-sti? How about some old-time stuff? Lady Gaga?'

Running a finger down the keys and thumping a chord out on the bass notes he starts to play, singing raucously in a deep voice. I can feel the hairs rising on my arms as a memory ignites of my own fingers dancing over ivory keys. The image snaps into blackness again but I need to touch this piano's keys—memory or a daydream? Angelo crashes out a last chord and stands up to grab the glass that Jarvis is holding out as the room erupts with applause and whistles.

'Back in a momentito,' he grins. 'Just need a pisci.'

As he hops off outside, I sit on the stool, shut my eyes and place my hands above the keys wondering if some interior force will propel my fingers.

The notes are tentative at first, then more forceful. After a few moments, I realise that I am playing Bach; mistake-ridden, but Bach nonetheless. I turn around and see Jarvis looking as amazed as I feel.

'Kitten . . . whatthafuk!' He strides over and stares at my hands. 'Didn't know y' could whap the Joanna.'

'You're not the only one!'

I dart my hands away suddenly as if ghosts are toying with me. Angelo has returned and I leave the seat, glad for him to continue.

Shakily, I make my way to an unoccupied sofa near the fire, sinking down into its old upholstery. Someone passes me a glass and I swallow the wine, its warm, blackberry taste blurring the questions in my mind.

Gradually the evening dissolves into a comfortable blur of drink, food and music. The landlord's wife has made pies. I bite into one, wondering how she has made anything so sublimely delicious in that dusty kitchen: crumbly, buttery pastry, tender meat—lamb perhaps.

The wine has been replaced now by beer. Aware this is folly, I take a glass and raise it along with everyone else to the memory of Parrot.

As I leave the sofa and head towards the beckoning eve air, a mec with dreadlocked hair and the darkest of skins appears in the doorway.

Jarvis lunges forward and throws his arms about him. 'Sam! Merda, Sam . . . so fukkin' sorry.'

The mec returns the hug, dropping an instrument case to the floor.

LONDONIA

'I got news, but was in What-ford. Just got here—who did it? I gotta have retribution, you know that . . . no fukka kills my cousin and lives after.'

They stand in a silent embrace until Sam steps back, picks up the case and opens it. He lifts out a silver saxophone and yells towards the bar.

'Someone get me a drink. Need me some lubrication!'

Escaping the tobacco smoke-laden air, I stand in the courtyard swaying a little as I look out at the restless body of water. Where will the barge be now? Snagged somewhere on one of the raft-people's constructions or moving towards the open water of the sea. What would it be like to look at an ocean, not on a page: a real, vast, ocean, the horizon line between sky and water. Perhaps I could make a journey . . .

A hand lands on my shoulder, breaking the reverie. Turning, I see Jarvis's grey-blue eyes, rimmed in red.

'What you thinkin' about, H?'

'The massiveness of the sea, and where the barge might be now.'

'D'you think I did goodly. . . not to put 'im in the ground?'

'Yes, I do . . . was the best way.'

We are quiet for what seems like a very long time, just staring at the water and the moon's wavering reflection, broken by jumping fish.

'Jarvis?'

'Yeah?'

'You could move into the church . . . if you like—live, y'know, there, with me.'

'Really? You wouldn't mind?'

A blast of strident sax playing and a chorus of cheers spill from the doorway. I wait for the noise to die down.

'Really. Happy if you did, partner. Fact, stay tonight, if i' helps.'

My words feel messed up with gnole but I must have made sense as he grins, almost his old grin, just a little frayed.

LONDONIA

'Hadn't thought 'bout where to hang the old homburg. Don't think I could face going back to Mum's—she'll fuss me too much.'

'D'you lose *everything* in the fire?'

'Yeah, not that there was a lot. Main thing was I had Grandad's violin with me. I'd had a lesson with Jake, see.'

'Well, that's a goodly truc.'

'Vrai.' Jarvis yawns massively. 'Dunno about you, Hoxton, but I'm so dog tired, I'd be happy to be off.'

I nod, knowing I've already imbibed far too much.

'Suits me—s'long walk though. Didn't bring horse.'

'Taxi. No prob. Sam said he'd take me anywhere I want. Back in a mo.'

The chatter and song dwindle now, the last few notes from the piano spiralling into the night air as the landlord prepares to close.

'Sorry, folks. Time to go home.'

Jarvis and Sam appear at the door with various bags and instrument cases.

This way, gestures Sam and we follow him to a patch of grass on the bank where a black horse stands within the stays of a carriage. The moon breaks through the clouds for a moment, lighting up three golden words on the burgundy metal.

Sam's Hackrovia taxi.

'Merda!' exclaims Jarvis, 'Parrot said you was in the bod-delivering business, but I din' expect this.'

'What did y'envisage, man? A black motor cab?'

'No, course not, and this is right dandy.'

'Was Parrot's idea—weddings, funerals an' crud, for the eggers.'

The conversation stops as the name Parrot slips out from his words and hangs alone in the night.

'Alors,' says Sam, eventually. 'Where's it to be?'

'Sureditch,' says Jarvis in a decided tone.

LONDONIA

I climb in. Jarvis follows with his few belongings, jams on his hat and slumps into a corner, exhausted by the evening. Through the front window, I see Sam tying his dreads into a ribboned knot and donning a satin top hat. Shrugging on a great dark coat, he mounts the carriage seat, clicks his fingers and the horse moves off slowly, accustomed to a solemn walking pace.

I turn to look out of the side window at the silhouetted crowd leaving the drinking house, blue pipe smoke rising, voices just audible above the rumbling wheels. I sleep-wake-sleep, dizzied by gnole and the swaying carriage.

When we arrive at the church, I step out carefully and ask Sam for a card, pleased to now have a Cincture-working Londonia contact. He fumbles in a waistcoat pocket and hands me one: crinkle cut, black edges, his address and a pigeon station.

Jarvis emerges like a morose black-winged moth from the carriage's cocoon and squints up at Sam.

'Grazie, friend.'

Sam smiles sadly down at us. 'Least I could do. Has to go, J.' He takes up the reins and the horse moves off. He glances back once. 'Be safe.'

Jarvis stares for a while at the vanishing carriage then turns to open the gate. As I unlock the church door the dogs scoot out, bark-angry.

I stagger about trying to quieten them. 'Zut!—should have walked them earlier . . . do it now.'

Jarvis grabs their leads from the hook. 'Come wiv yer—could do with a stretch.'

We drop his bags, lock the church again and clatter down the steps. The dogs streak away, straining on their ropes.

'Let's run,' shouts Jarvis. 'Run and shake off these bastard blues.'

We stumble, pulled by hounds. Start to run.

'Love you, Parrot!' shouts Jarvis, his words filling the black sky.

Capitula 10

I open an eye and a stabbing pain runs from the back of my head to my eyebrows. I will *never* drink alcohol again. In any form.

Through the thumping of the blood in my brain, I hear unusual sounds: timber being nailed and a baritone voice projecting forth words that seem unlikely in a church:

'Gimme gimme, uh, uh, uh, I'll smack yo arse, come see my money, feel it feel it, feel this honey. Front, back, fuk—don't care, hold the phone, I'm almost there, uh, uh, uh, uh,'

I struggle from the covers, grope into my dressing gown and blearily step out from the vestry. The singing or rather, sing-song talking, issues from a half-built wooden structure in one of the transepts. I approach, the hammer's blows driving a second set of nails into my brain.

'Give me, give me, uh, uh . . . OW! Merda!' The hammering stops, and Jarvis looks up at me as I peer around the weathered planks.

'Kitten . . . Dieu, yer look like morte.'

'Not far off,' I groan, noticing he looks surprisingly normal, apart from the Hawaii shirt and pink flared trousers.

He follows my gaze. 'I know—lost a lot of clobs, in the fire.'

'I might be able to help you,' I yawn. 'There's a clothes swap before darking at the Angel exchange. Think we could spare a bit of stock to get you re-kitted.'

'Yeah? D'ac, I'll get up there . . . now, 'bout *this*.' He waves a bloodied hand at his work. 'Hope you don't mind. Just wanted to chuck myself into someink . . . solid, y' know.'

'Not at all . . . what is it?'

LONDONIA

'Thought I'd make myself a sort 'a living area, bit like you got the vestry. I'll get a stove and punch a chimney through that window.'

I cringe at the thought of what the stained glass-maker's spirit will think, but there's plenty more windows that have survived worse things.

'Whatever works for you,' I say, and hiss as another round of thudding starts up above my eyes. 'I'm going to make some very strong coffee. Join me?'

'Muchly. Be over in a gnat's.'

As I turn, the voice-noise starts again. I glance back around the structure. 'What *is* that?'

'Oh, some piece of crud from just 'fore the unknown's—a *rapper* called LI-ON. Mum says it was the last thing she ever heard on the computer and although she hates it, it's stuck in her 'ead—funny hearing the old bird stompin' round the house blurtin' out *Smack yo arse.*'

'Rapper?'

'Mecs mainly, singing, or rather proclaiming about stuff.'

'What, sex?'

'Mostly, an' cars an' how much money they had.'

'Wonder what they'd proclaim about now.'

'Probably trucs they should go on about, like scoop trucks, Sharks and stuff.'

I'm about to suggest we should try and rig up a record player other than the phonograph, when the bell jangles outside.

'I'll go, Kitten,' says Jarvis. 'Need a leak anyway.'

Shuffling back to the vestry, I return to my bed, unable to face a possible visitor. Jarvis pads along the flagstones, the song reduced to a whistle. The door opens and closes again and two sets of footsteps now approach: Jarvis's and female, lighter tappings. It won't be Sardi as she wears boots, in fact, who else around here, apart from a couple of local puties, wear heels? Jarvis peers around the vestry doorway and smiles at me and the cat all bundled up.

LONDONIA

'A dame to see yer. Just be over there doin' a bit more to the shack.'

Someone bundled up in a huge coat and scarf walks in and surveys the room.

'Yes . . . this is a little different to what you would have known.'

'Iona?' I sit up swiftly, then regret the brusque movement. 'Merda.' I squint at her. 'What are you doing here?'

'You invited me, albeit rather offhandedly.'

The brain-mist clears a little and I realise someone who professes to be from my past is now sitting here in my vestry after getting across Londonia, *and* I had been somewhat abrupt with her.

'. . . How did you get here?'

'Paid a shaw a lot extra.'

'And nothing happened—attempted robbery?'

'Not a thing, although I did ask for a very plain shaw. No bright colour, no fringes, music, or anything.'

'And it's gone back.'

'Yes. I rather hoped you might show me around a bit and then drop me at the gates.'

'In what?'

'On foot will do—or I could perch on your horse.'

Despite my hammering headache I smile at her faith in me, and lack of fear. I can see how we would have been friends.

'You were lucky, you know.'

She smiles back as she flops off her coat. 'It's so N to have exy in life for a change.'

'N? Exy?'

'Sorry—N is nice, exy, excitement. I'll try and minimise, and you'll have to help me with the colloquialisms of out here.'

'Have you been *out here* before?'

'Never. The Cincturian instructors make sure enough lurid stories circulate to make the idea of venturing out a *no-happing.*'

LONDONIA

I eye the plain brown trouser suit she is wearing. 'Just as well you didn't set out in one of those ridiculous dresses. Where did that come from?'

'Not everyone wears the stuff you've seen, or could afford it—that's just for the women who have little else to do. Workers generally wear the more simple clothing that's sold in shops out of the hyper-centre.'

'So, all this manic behaviour over fashion is only within a small sector.'

'It is. And you were part of it.'

I shake my head slowly. 'Still can't take it in, and you haven't explained the really big chunk yet.'

'Your disappearance.'

'That, yes. Why, if I was Mrs whatever-his-name-was, am I not installed in the enormous house you mentioned?'

'That's why I came out, to explain—and because I'm fascinated to see how you live. You're never too sure within the walls who might be listening or watching. Here, I assume you can do or say anything . . .'

'Go ahead, you'll only disturb the cat.'

'Really?' She takes a breath and shrieks out: 'Piss on the Custodian! Equal rights for all women!'

'Equal rights? About what?'

'Everything. It's like the titting 1950s in there—if you've recalled any history. Women should be pretty, sexual when required to be so, unquestioning. It's basically why you are out here.' I look at her quizzically and she continues. 'I said you were trouble . . . you devoured books, had theories, ideas, ran women's secret groups, and when the Twat got blown up, the *huge house* became a hotspot of alternative ideas. Not just about women's issues but about better conditions for the land-workers, militant rally-organising . . . you name it.'

'And someone had the idea about getting rid of me.'

'It wasn't just you. Several people were *removed*.'

'Removed as in . . .'

LONDONIA

'There are always stories of individualists being *recycled*. Especially if they are young, in good health and without any family background of note.'

'Sorry, recycled?'

'Oh, the burgeoning health and beauty service has many clamouring, wealthy clientele . . . and of course, there's always a possible choice from the policing vehicles when they return.'

'The scoop trucks?'

'Is that what they're called here?'

'A colloquialism for you,' I add, getting up slowly and filling the kettle from a bidon. 'Coffee?'

'Do you have it?'

'Dandelion root's the best I can offer for the moment. Perhaps you could get me some in exchange for some ludicrous bit of feltois.'

'Feltois?'

'Clothing. Feltys are boiled wool layers, sometimes called knappers. Feltois—something a bit more unusual. Posh, even.' I find two coffee bowls and invite her to sit at the table. 'You were saying about me being removed—not terminally, obviously.'

'The medical authorities were working at that time on a form of deep hypnotism that could be used to treat and rehabilitate reoffending criminals. As I said before Matthew was on the committee who made decisions and it was decided you would be a . . .'

'Guinea pig?'

'Better perhaps than prison, or worse, if the stories are true.'

'But, how did I end up in Londonia with a tag around my neck?'

'What tag?'

I explain briefly and she shrugs. 'Maybe an experiment that went wrong. Maybe there are other victims scattered about out here—dispersed in different places.'

'Can you find out from Matthew what happened?'

LONDONIA

'I tried at the time you disappeared but he said he knew nothing. He's not easy to talk to—at any time.'

The kettle is boiling. I pour water on the dried roots and put the pot on the table.

'I haven't asked you . . . do you have gosses—children?'

She smiles and reaches into her shoulder bag. 'Here.' I take the small leather book and turn to the pages inside. A brown-haired girl laughs back at me.

'. . . She is beautiful. How many cycles?—her age?'

'Maddy is five.'

I hand the book back. 'Will you help me find my child?'

To my surprise, she starts to cry. I lean forward and take her hand. She wipes the tears away with the cloth I'd picked the enamel coffee pot up with.

'S'all right . . . I just never thought I'd see you again. This is so odd, and . . . ugh, that cloth smells.'

I grin as I hunt about for a cleaner rag. 'Sorry. Washing stuff is a bit rudimentary here.'

She smiles back, tears gone. 'Of course, I'll help you.'

I pour the brew and we sip, looking at each other, she, presumably, remembering things of our joint pasts, me imagining what it would have been like.

'When do you have to get back?' I ask.

She glances at her watch. 'Mid-afternoon. I have to collect Maddy from school earlier today as she has a dance class.'

'No boarding for her?'

'Absolutely no way! Matthew wanted it but I was adamant.'

I look out of the window and guestimate the hour. 'Is it around midday by Cincture time?'

She glances around at my collection of battered clocks whose hands point randomly at their circumferences. 'Time doesn't exist here?'

'It does, but rather more vaguely—morn, midi, aft and darking . . . so, a small tour of a few Londonia sights and I'll take you back on Kafka. We have a double saddle.'

LONDONIA

'*Galore*!' Iona pulls her coat back on and watches me struggle into a sweatshirt, felty, jins and boots. 'Are you feeling all right?' she asks.

I explain about the inordinate amount of gnole consumed and why. She looks horrified.

'You mean *that* man's lover was killed, and the funeral was yesterday?'

'Correct. And *that mec* is Jarvis.'

'But he looks quite . . . happy.'

'He's shrivelled inside—it's just cheerful bravado. Life is probably a little more tenuous than *in there*.'

'. . . How dangerous is it, in fact?'

I pick up the old Glock and shove it into my waistband before filling the leather knapsack with small trade items. Her expression of interest morphs into one of worry at the sight of the gun.

'Ça va—I won't have to use it,' I assure her.

She pulls her bag to her and rummages for something. 'These are for you,' she says passing me a small, satin-padded box. 'In retrospect, I was stupid to come here with such things, but I wanted you to have them.'

I open the hinged lid and stare down on an intricate gold necklace, and a pair of ruby earrings.

'Is that—these . . . real?'

'All real, yes.'

'Why give them to me?'

'I don't need or want them. Matthew lavishes this stuff on me. Some guilt trip . . . I don't know. Anyway, I thought you could make some sparked-up trades!'

I think of the Vaux-hauler's dark, underground minting premises, the certainty of readies for many a cycle, *and* the arrogant patron of whom I have heard many a bad thing.

'Are you sure?'

'Totally.'

LONDONIA

I kiss her and feel the residual fondness in my heart from whenever we had been friends and I had been Chantelle.

Out in the street it's a good introduction to Londonia life.

As we pass the Rent-mec and Rotweiller the landlord throws a swearing figure into Kafka's path and returns to his doorway. The mec struggles to his feet, pulls out a gun and fires with a shaking hand. The shot lodges into the landlord's shoulder and he collapses.

'*Putain*!'

The regulars pour into the street and the dirt becomes clouds of dust as the interloper disappears under a blur of boots and fists. I kick twice at Kafka's belly; he launches forwards and we're out of the throng, Iona jolting and hanging on to me.

I slow the horse to a walk. 'Sorry. Not the best impression of Londonia life.'

'How can you live here?'

'I don't know, or at least don't recall any other way—it's just life.'

After passing several other fights, someone lying in a pool of vomit and avoiding a mec trying to grab Iona, I turn Kafka into Lincoln Inn Fields, hoping the flower market might be there so she can see that it's not all dirt and blood.

There might as well have been a sign planted in the grass: *Welcome to Paradise*. Several Romany caravans are parked. Horses graze and smoke curls from fires where dames in embroidered dresses prepare food. Daffodils and branches of catkins splay in a hotchpotch of containers. Someone has potted bulbs in buckets, the heads of crocus, snowdrops and hyacinth bright against tarnished metal.

'Can we get down?' asks my companion, a note of wonder in her voice.

We dismount and I tie Kafka to a tree, leaving him to enjoy the luxury of new grass shoots. People stare at Iona as we walk around, her clothes and carefully styled hair, things that set her apart. My fingers hover within reach of the hidden gun, but no need; the spring warmth has left a glow of benevolence on this place and the bods selling, buying or just wandering.

She tentatively picks up a bunch of blue hyacinths and breathes in their scent.

'How do you buy things? Is it always exchange?'

'It varies. I might offer tobacco, food, vegetables I've grown, or sometimes people accept silvers.'

'Money?'

'A coin system that's really only useful for small things.' I take the flowers and hold them out to the mec behind the stall. 'Silvers?'

'Five, or beer,' he says then looks at Iona, a grin forming on his weathered face. 'Or a couple 'a trices, m'be . . .'

I root around for the coins and hand them over. 'I don't think so.'

'What did he mean?' she whispers as we turn away.

'You could have got the flowers for a quick grope in his caravan.'

She pales.

'You mean people trade with . . . *sex*?'

'Yes. It's quite common.'

'Have you?'

I feel the heat rise in my face as I recall the visit to Bert's. 'If it's something I need badly enough and there's no alternative. Anylane, depends on the seller—sometimes, it might be a pleasure.' I smile at her expression. 'Can I ask you something?'

'Sure.'

'Have you had . . . *relations* other than with Matthew?'

Her mouth sets in a line for a moment before she answers.

'No. Well, a bit. But certainly not since we were married.'

We're approaching a temporary café of a few rush-seated chairs and oil drums.

'Let's sit and have a drink,' I suggest.

'Is it safe?' she says looking at the improvised tables.

'Utterly.'

LONDONIA

A skinny, dark-haired youth comes over with a hand-written menu.

'Voila, mesdames. Thé? Cafe?'

Iona gestures for me to decide.

'Deux thé . . . c'est du vrai?'

'Oui, de l'Inde.'

She sighs. 'Wish I'd paid more attention at school. You were so good at languages.'

The tea arrives. I pour, and offer her a cup.

'Milk? It's probably goat.'

'Err, no, thanks . . . Hoxton?'

'Yes?'

'If you don't mind me asking . . . why didn't you try to find out what happened before you woke up on that bench?'

Good question. 'I suppose I was just surviving. It's what you do in the Pan.'

'You didn't get married again?'

A brief image of me in a Fred's Threads wedding dress, Tom besuited in grey crosses my thoughts and I smile.

'No. I have been asked a few times though . . . a question for you now.'

She sips at the tea, eyebrows knitted at the taste. 'Carry on.'

'Do people in the Cincture talk about how the Final Curtain actually happened?'

'Not often. Although I did go to something masquerading as a women's cookery talk which turned out to be more of a history lecture. Most interesting, and the presiding theory seems to be that the entire internet system crashed in the summer of 2038 basically because of total overload—the final *straw* being someone uploading an hour-long film of their cat opening a refrigerator.'

While I try to understand this, Kafka, having exhausted the grass within range, is now snorting and braying.

'Think it's time to go.'

LONDONIA

We re-mount the horse, leave the bucolic scene and enter the crowded streets. Two roads away, a crowd of gosses play on the skeletons of two cars, planks running from one roof to another; a pirate ship conflict by the sound of it. The languages are mixed, but a rough English mainly prevails.

'Don't they go to school?' Iona asks.

'Sometimes schools start up.' I say. 'Nothing official. Mostly they just learn from their families . . . lucky for some if the parents are interested in passing on knowledge, less for others. Gosses take on the trade of the family, if there is one.'

'A little different to my Maddy. Talking of whom, I'd better get back. Can you drop me off?'

I turn the horse into Gray's Inn Road and risk a gentle canter with Iona hanging on. The access point is relatively quiet, just a small argument going on between someone with a pig on a lead, and a stubborn guard.

'I don't care if it's a rare, liver-spotted Dunstable. It's not coming in here!'

The ratty-haired dame is equally stubborn. 'I got trading rights! Get on that foitling phone and call the Hyde Park rare breeds office.'

Iona smiles at me as she adjusts her ruffled trouser suit jacket.

'So . . . I'll see you at the Caruso's for your payoff? Are you going to find more clothes?'

I think of the *womeny* hysteria. 'I'll have to try. It sounds as if their husbands might have useful contacts.'

'It'll keep our re-connection too.'

I study her face framed by blonde, now-windswept hair and feel a sudden rush of happiness.

'This is just *so* incredible.'

'Fate,' she smiles.

I hug her and stand back. 'Thanks again for the jewellery. Think of how much scran 'n drinks Jarvis and I will enjoy with the proceeds!'

LONDONIA

'I meant to ask,' she says as I turn back to Kafka, 'Is he your . . . mec?'

'No. Just someone incredibly important to me.'

When I get back home, half a clockface later, the *incredibly important* person is asleep within a pile of dogs on my bed. Tilly jumps off and greets me with a chorus of barks.

'Shhh!' Too late; he's awake.

'Kitten! Aw, desol. I got overcome with knackeredness—came in 'ere for a caf, never made it and fell asleep.'

'It's fine, really. I don't mind at all—good company for the hounds.'

'Who was that posh dame?'

'One of the group who wanted the phones and stuff. But, she turned out to be more than that.'

'Meanin'?'

'. . . She knew me when I was in the Cincture. *And* she saw the baby.' I brace myself for the incredulity.

'Wot? Could be pizzin' around wi'yer—what's she *after*?'

'Nothing. Look.' I find the jewel case and open it. 'People don't generally give you gold and rubies just like that—eh?'

He picks up the necklace and examines it closely in a shaft of daylight.

'God's own *tiara*! This is the fukkin' mana!'

'I know!'

'Why'd she give it yer?'

'I think she was just incredibly pleased to find me again. We were best friends.'

Jarvis grunts a bit. 'Yor not gonna go an' live there?'

'No! Even if I wanted to—which I don't—it would be impossible.'

'Yeah?'

'Seems as if I was a problem and was got rid of—hence the park, bench, tag and no memory.'

'My missis trouble, eh?'

'That's me.'

'Bit of a tasty 'ystoire that . . . d'you still not remember nuffin' after she told yer?'

'Only some faint impressions of being in certain streets and buildings.'

He twirls the necklace around on a finger. 'Wot about this and them red sparklers?'

'Well, I thought I'd hang onto the rubies as I'd like to wear them somelieu, someday, but that there? How about a *lot* of coinage? Like that I might cut back on the Finding, just for a while, and concentrate on . . . something else.'

'Wot something else—not the gosse trooving?'

'Yes. That. I've got to try, Jarvis. I'll never feel settled again unless I do.'

He shakes his head then looks at me with a faint smile.

'Yeah, well, ain't got no sprog, so I wouldn't really comprendo. Still, I'll be here now, so if you do go ahead with this diggin' about, the dog's'll get their scran at least.'

Suddenly I feel guilty at his words, as if I've profited from his loss.

'Jarvis?'

'Uh?'

'You know I didn't ask you to live here just for practical reasons, don't you? Dogs—garden and everything.'

'Eh?'

'I want you to be here . . . because, well, it feels right. We work well together and you're my partner.'

He grins the full grin. 'Never crossed my weary, foitlin' mind, H. Just happy to have a roof and to work with you. If I can help that's just part of it, innit? Parrot would agree, I'm sure.'

The grin fades again as the name hangs in the air. I wonder if he wants to talk about what happened.

'You know if you ever want to—'

He cuts my words with a wave of his hand.

'Ça va, ça va. Donecha always feel life to be so fragile, Hoxton? Out 'ere I mean. 'E 'ad a lot 'a near misses, and that

LONDONIA

one was just too near.' He stands up and fills the kettle, draining the last of a glass flagon as his voice wavers. 'Got any more?'

'The water cart hasn't been yet.'

'Hm. I'm gonna get on the roof morrow and sort this pizzin guttrin' out. We need proper facilities—easy water an' that.'

'If you feel like it . . . don't you still need some quiet time, thinking and . . .'

'Nah. Borin' sittin' about mopin' when there's fixes to be fixed.'

I realise this is his way of dealing with the grief—carry on, bury the sadness.

'D'ac. Great!'

Jarvis opens the coffee tin and sniffs at the dandelion grounds, brow creasing.

'Festering cat-head . . . back in a mo.' He nips out to his construction and comes back with a brown paper packet. '*This* . . . is the stuff'.

He makes the brew in my old, orange enamel pot and a while later clinks two cups down onto the table.

I pour, exulting in the rich aroma of something incredibly rare. 'Where did you find this?'

'Bert. 'E discovered an unopened bunker in the scrap yard down at Metropolitan wharf. No one else would go in . . . bit of a tomb—three bodies. Anylane, they hadn't got though all the supplies and he took a good haul.'

I push the images back to the blank areas of my mind and concentrate on the velvety, bitter contents of the cup.

'You must have traded something good,' I sigh, tilting the pot again.

'Zeitporn,' he grins, no other explanation necessary. 'So, when you goin' back in there?'

'I'm meeting the dames again next Twosdy. I've got to look for a few more bits of clothing and I think I'll do the Vaux-haul trip on the morrow.'

'Want me to come with yer?'

LONDONIA

'No. It's fine. Take some time off and make your home here.'

'D'ac. I'll do that. Wot you doin' now?'

'I might do some weeding before the light goes—need some thinking time.'

Jarvis gets up and stretches. 'Reckon I'll take the hounds out for a saunter. Abt, Kitten.'

He walks whistling to his wood-house and I'm glad he's here. My thoughts feel huge and unmanageable already. I almost wish I could wind time back—to change that first visit to the access point, Marina just someone I had passed briefly as she had left. Yet, it seems fate is pulling me inexorably along—that cabinet, the chances of finding it . . . Iona . . . *I need a drink.*

Remembering Sardi's bottle of eau de vie, I pour myself a measure and sit brooding for a while, eyes wandering over my nest of familiar belongings.

A black jacket lies draped over the back of the chaise longue. I'd forgotten about it—that young gosse in the Cincture and his chivalrous albeit drunken action. I retrieve the garment and inspect it for trade-worthyness. The cloth is fine: a wool and silk weave perhaps, the lining an unusual pattern of golden vines.

The pockets are empty apart from a dry disintegrating rosebud and a scrap of paper marked with a few plant names. I'm about to hang the garment in the wardrobe when I notice another pocket in the lining. Undoing its button, I delve a hand in to find a silver fob watch, its face pearlised, hands delicate. On the back the initials are only just legible such is their curly script. B. St V. The watch has the usual opening for inspecting the workings and another which is difficult to open. I persevere and the lid pings open to reveal a tiny photograph of a young dark-skinned dame. The writing on the back is smudged but I make out her name and the date: Zari. 2032.

Feeling voyeuristic and guilty, I close the watch and put in back in the jacket pocket. Its owner had been kind to me but he had also been pizzed enough to not know his actions. I should return the items to him somehow.

LONDONIA

Jarvis has left with the dogs, and the church feels suddenly empty. I need a more challenging task than weeding or clothes searching for Cincturian dames. Iona's padded jewellery case catches my eye and I think of the Vaux-hauler's famed but feared location South of the river. That would be certainly challenging *and* trade-lucrative. Maybe I'll take the watch too—just to get an idea of its date and value.

Without considering it further, I get Kafka ready, stash the jewellery carefully along with the pistol and leave, heading southwards along Bishgate.

Half a clockface later, I'm approaching the messianic metal entrance to the Vaux-hauler's domain, the old tube-train station of the cartier. It's one of the few that has been successfully broken into and used as premises, the others remaining impenetrable. As I halt Kafka and start to scan the crowds for a reliable-looking horse-guard a rumbling, grinding sound causes me and everyone else to turn towards the river. One of the remaining glass and steel edifices is leaning noticeably, glass bursting out from the higher floors. Its trajectory, if it goes, will be onto the green glass and beige-stoned cluster of buildings that line the river front, their own corpses semi-rotted after the last major flooding.

'Hope the buggers got out,' observes an elderly mec, looking up at me. 'Want 'orse minded? Good rates—long as tha likes.' He notes my hesitation, delves about in a waistcoat pocket and pulls out a crinkle-edged card that states.

Archi's-arches horse facilities. Short or long term. Good grazing.

'Just over there. I'll walk thee.'

He leads Kafka to one of the old railway arches and I note the straw, and contented-looking other steeds.

'Thing is,' I say, dismounting, 'I'm out of funds until I make a deal over there. Ça va?'

He smiles as he strokes Kafka's nose. 'Three silvers a clockface, and I got tha's collateral anyroad.'

LONDONIA

We shake hands and I walk back to the entrance to ask if it's possible to see someone now with a view to a deal. The spotty ado-gosse security bod at the top of the staircase mentally undresses me.

'I think Capo will see *you*—no problemo. Your name?'

'Hoxton.'

'Certo—come.'

The small crowd of people yakking and poring over small boxes and bags part as we descend into the dim and smoke-laden atmosphere of this underground place I have heard much about. The heat is intense as we walk further away from the stairs, the atmosphere heavy with the smell of metals and coal.

'Un momento,' says my guide and paces off into the smog. I must be in the concourse of where people once bought tickets to go on carriages that passed worm-like to different parts of old London town. Beneath the many hand-written posters advertising various sexual trade possibilities, boat passages, soup clubs and shared food-growing grounds I catch site of older paper layers of the past. Lifting the corner of a sheet of paper proposing painless tooth-removal, I scan the map of coloured spaghetti and the poetic names of the original tube stops: Baker Street, Mornington Crescent, Black Horse Road . . .

'Miss?' I turn to see the youth pointing down a gloomy tunnel. 'Il Capo dos clockface.' He nods for me to follow and takes the stairs again two at a time. I hear his voice raised amongst all the other clamourings up there. It's strangely quiet down here, just the distant clank and hiss of the procedure producing these ferrous smells.

As I stand alone, the cold of the tiles seeping through my boots, I wonder whether to abandon the idea—leave a message with the youth and return home. This was, after all, a stupid thing to be doing at the end of a day. *Merda*.

Another sound emanates from the tunnel: thumping bootsteps. El Capo strides from the fug, stripping off large stained leather gloves and shoving them at a minion just behind him.

LONDONIA

'Get these clean. *Pronto*.'

With his flowing, semi-grey hair, he could be a biblical character striding across some desert in search of enlightenment. He stops abruptly, pushes back a lock of hair and stares at me. A beguiling grin erupts on his scarred face.

'Hoxton. Dame-finder. Your reputation precedes you and visually it is *not* inaccura . .' He stops, wavers backwards for a brief moment and mutters something in Italian. 'Non pùo essere . . .'

'What?' I ask.

He regains his swagger, hesitation gone. 'Nothing, my dear. You resemble the wife . . . of a friend, that's all.'

His accent is unusual—a mixture of Italian with an overlying English elocution, as if the former had partially been beaten out from him at some point.

I hold out a hand anticipating a grasping shake but he takes it delicately, kisses the back and bows.

'Will you join me for supper?'

This is *not* what I had imagined. 'You ask all your clients to dine with you?'

He laughs, the sound booming about our ceramic and steel surroundings.

'Not usually but I've had it with t-dui and there's a pig stew waiting my attentions.'

Hunger obliterates any worries I might have about this proposition. 'What about the trade I came for?'

'We can discuss it over a glass or two.' He turns to the waiting minion and barks various orders ending with: 'Keep the fire in low. Who's on the last shift?'

The grubby gosse points at himself. 'Me an Pepito.'

'Bene. I'll send vitals. Buona Notte.'

He takes my arm and gestures to the stairs. 'Just a short walk.'

As we leave, I thankfully breathe in the darking air. 'How do you work down there?'

LONDONIA

He glances back at the slight greyish smog hanging over the entrance. 'It's not always so bad. We had a problem with rats in the flues. Here—my abode.'

I stare up at the bowed façade of the Vaux-haul tavern. 'Sublime . . . you live here alone?'

'Almost. My gosses stay sometimes, and my house-keeper.' I wonder what happened to Mrs El Capo but say nothing as he unlocks the door and then tackles two mastiffs. 'Mavis? *Mavis*!'

An oldish, hard-faced dame appears bearing a rifle. She pulls the hounds back. 'Sorry, sir. They's a bit overexcited this darking.' She peers out at me and then nods knowingly. 'She 'ere for the night then?'

My host pushes her back with a stubby index finger. 'This, Mavis, is Hoxton, and she has come for supper and to discuss *business*.'

'Oh, right . . . business. Anylane, hog's done and I've set you up in the salon.'

'Bene. Send some vitals for the lads, house-captain.'

We pass through a main room containing many chairs and tables and then up a carpeted staircase. He opens a door on the right.

'After you.'

In the centre of the room in front of a snappling fire sits a round table: two places laid, candles, a casserole pot in the middle on an iron trivet, two large bowls, wine glasses and a bottle of something deep and red.

'You were expecting someone?' I say, taking off my felty and glancing in the mirror above the fire. Having expected a quick gruff exchange in semi-darkness I am not dressed for dinner.

'Ah—no. It's just a ritual I observe after Mrs Straightfish passed away.'

'Oh—sorry. Your wife . . .'

'Yes.'

Curiosity prods at me. 'Straightfish . . . an unusual name.'

LONDONIA

'Actually, my name *was* Italian,' he says, carelessly. 'But I changed it on entering Londonia.'

'From Italy?'

'No . . . from the Cincture.'

'Oh. You were in *there* . . . Why did you decide on a name-change?'

'Let's say it didn't sit well with someone intent on building a large enterprise.' El Capo yawns impressively. 'Enough of the past. Let's do this stew justice.'

I'm still intrigued by the name-change business.

'So, what was so abhorrent about your family handle?'

He sighs gruffly. ' . . . It means, *shop-boy*.'

'Oh. Mr Ragazzo di Negozio?'

He smiles at this language-mangling. 'Nothing as complicated . . . Caruso.'

I start. 'Caruso? I have a client in the Cincture with the same name.'

A faint shadow seems to fall over his face as if I've delved into something unexpected. Then just as quickly he wrenches back the broad smile.

'You regard Straightfish an odd name. What about *Hoxton*?'

'It's a complicated story.'

'Tell me over supper.'

Eyeing the wine, I feel it might be prudent to sort out the deal now. 'I know we're now not at your premises, but could we sort the trade—why I came here.'

'Si si. Why not. Silver? Gold? *Diamonds*?'

'Gold.' I unearth the satin box, take out the necklace and pass it to him. He hoists up a small chain from his waistcoat pocket, retrieves a tubular magnifier and wedges it into an eye socket.

'Bene . . . nice piece. From the Cincture and recent.'

'It was a gift.'

He turns his gaze to me, his eye weirdly huge. 'From an admirer?'

'A friend.'

176

LONDONIA

'You must be of value to them to give this away.'

'It seems so. What will it mean in coins?'

He takes the necklace to a small pair of scales, weighs it and *hms* a bit.

'Are you wanting silvers, branz or glorys?'

'Perhaps some of each?'

'Some of . . . each.' El Capo takes a metal box from a shelf, unlocks it and counts out a quantity of copper, gold and silver coins. 'This is an accurate trade. If you are unsatisfied tell me now.' Placing the discs on a wooden platter he passes it to me. I stir them around thinking of the sudden ease of buying staple goods. I don't know if he's being totally truthful, but it seems fair to me. I hold out a hand, we shake, he tips the coins into a cloth bag and we exchange. I feel elated, the confusing day shrinking away. Then I remember the watch.

'There's one more item—but not to sell, just an idea of its age and where it might have come from.'

He holds out a plate-like hand. I find the pocket watch and drop it to his palm. He employs the eye-glass again and examines the face.

'This has age and is a valuable piece. The engraving on the inside . . . manifico.'

He turns the watch carefully and studies the back. After a moment he swings his head back and the eye-glass falls. He catches it. His expression is one of shock.

'Santa Mardre!'

'Is it that valuable?' I ask.

I have the notion that he is controlling an outburst. He closes his fingers over the timepiece.

'Are you sure you don't want to trade this?'

'Absolutely.'

'Where did you obtain it—if you don't mind me prying.'

'I was given it.'

'By the same benefactor as the necklace?'

'No. But believe me. I am *not* trading.'

LONDONIA

'Certo?'

'Hundred percent.'

Mr Straightfish's smile covers another emotion but he gestures I sit, and I do.

We eat succulent pork and potatoes, drink the very good red wine and talk of his business. I'm happy to listen and don't want to embark on my own story. The housekeeper appears and another bottle seems to be sitting uncorked on the table, along with cheese and dried fruit. This velvety room is a warm sanctum tucked away from the wind scudding about the building. He tips the new bottle towards my glass. I should put out a hand, insist that it's time I left, but the large, cushion-covered sofa lurking in a shadowy corner could be a distinct possibility for falling onto.

'Tell me,' he says, filling his own glass, 'why you have not been snaffled.'

I smile at this word. 'Like a last scone?'

'Well, if we're using food as a metaphor—mm . . . the gold-leaf, white-truffle chocolate ice-cream my father once described to me.'

I glance at my hands with their stubby nails, the crescents of dirt that never seem to quite go except after a bathhouse soak.

'That's probably a little outlandish.'

'I disagree. So my question?'

Tom. What degree of snafflement . . . I do miss him, a lot. Even though it was only the beginning of something.

'I have been. But he's away . . .'

'You seem unsure.'

Without really meaning to allow it, the story slips out. He listens, his face a ruddy oval in the darkening room.

The fire has become embers; their burnished remains blur a little. The table slopes as I stand up and try to recall where my feet are.

'Oh-oh.' His voice is soft in my ear, his arms strong about me. His mouth tastes of wine and apple. We appear to be walking to another room, the housekeeper just leaving it, a large enamel jug in one hand a candlestick in the other. 'It's ready, sir.'

These four walls—which are now gently turning—contain a lavishly large bed, many candles and a roll-top bath which is half-full of scented water, steam rising like mist from grass in the Parkplace on a dark-quarter morn. I stop the internal poetic observations and strip off.

He sits opposite me, our limbs entangled. I still can't imagine his age—forty-five, fifty cycles perhaps? His eyes roam over my body, a hand under the water, faint ripples on its now scummy surface.

Soaped, scrubbed, talked out and more than dizzy, I glance towards the bed.

'Shall we?'

Capitula 11

Unfamiliar street noise: boat sirens, carriage-wheels, seagulls.

Turning over, I see a waterfall of greying hair. Its owner grunts a little and eases himself onto his back. In the light of morn, I study his scabrous features and hair-covered chest. A craggy battleship to be sure, and certainly *not* my normal choice. But he was an exciting lover and it was a rich, warm and satisfying darking in all senses—but *not* something I wish to continue. Wealth and ease would come from such a union—as he had proposed—I seem to recall, but, like the proverbial iceberg, I suspect there's a lot hidden away in deeper, darker waters about Mr Straightfish . . . *Caruso*.

Satin cover pinched between thumb and forefinger, I lift its weight, slip out into a chill room and shiver back into the layers. He doesn't stir, even when I place the chinking coins into my carpet bag's buttoned pocket. Should I leave a note? It would be courteous perhaps. On a desk by the window I find sheets of paper and a fountain pen. I open the curtain to let in a dusty slice of light and write a short missive thanking him for the supper, wine, *etc*, leaving it under a paperweight of bubbled green glass. As my hand moves from the paper, I knock a small leather book from the edge of the desk. I swoop to catch it and as I do so my eyes take in the looping script racing across a page.

Bowens: Pending—last chance for goods Frydy
Mayclark: Finished unless pigeon news Wedsdy
Pinker: ~~*Finished*~~
(Remind F to get Winchester repaired)
Acid, rope

LONDONIA

I close the book, replace it, remove my note and stuff it into a pocket as I very quietly leave the room.

Downstairs the housekeeper is polishing the tables. I greet her amiably as I walk towards the main door. She returns the salutation gruffly.

'Morn. Is Mr Straightfish *up* yet?'

'I left him sleeping.'

She tuts. 'He's got a convention at midi—minters of all the cartiers. 'Ope he's remembered.'

I step out into a breezy morn, squinting at the sun-highlighted buildings. 'Ow.' What was that *thing* I said about never drinking alcohol ever again? I cross the street and head for the arches where Kafka stands nuzzling another horse. 'Enough of that,' I grin, and call out for the minder. The old gar appears from sitting in a deck chair on the grass.

'Aye-up, grand day, in't it?'

'Magnificent. Thanks for caring for him.'

'Aye—he's a nice'un.'

'How much do I owe in silvers?'

Pulling a small cardboard dial from a pocket he pushes a wire pointer around it. 'Sixteen, reckon.'

I retrieve the coins and a few extra, pass them over and avail myself of the step-ladder provided for horse-mounting.

His leathery old face beams as he looks up at me.

'Got what tha came fr?'

'I did, thanks, and a bit more . . .'

Kafka's morning energy thrills through the reins; he needs a flat-out gallop so I turn him in the direction of the Oval and a short while later we're belting around the patchy grass along with everyone else needing to exercise their various beasts—horses, great-hounds and wildy-cats. When he's had enough, we take the Kenny-town Park road, Oldish Kent Road and over Tower Bridge. The big feed last night has re-set my stomach for expecting something substantial, and by the time I'm unlocking the church door, a feast of eggs and bread is foremost in my mind.

Kafka dealt with, I visit the hens, find a clutch of eggs and remembering the wood-stove needs repair try to concoct an omelette on the guttering camp stove.

'*Merdic thing!*'

'Aye-aye,' Jarvis has come in and is staring at my attempts. 'Think I'm going to build us a range. Them gas bottles is almost impossible to find now.'

'Sounds complicated,' I say, swearing again as the flame shudders and dies.

'Not really—me an' Jake did one for the Brazilians. We'll take the cart to the scrappers and get some metal. Anystreet . . . where'd you go? Came back from Jake's—empty church.'

'Sorry. I should have left a note. And I did intend coming back after . . .'

'After wot?'

I sigh, scrape the egg onto a plate and sit down, eyes averted from him.

'You gonna eat that?' he says.

'I'd considered it.'

'Well, you'll need a fork—'ere.' He sits down too and waits for me to demolish the egg. 'So?'

'I decided to do the Vaux-hauler trip yesty aft—late.'

His eyebrows reach impressive new heights. 'You went there on your own, at *darking*?'

'Indeed.' I grab my bag and take out the cloth pouch. 'And it was worth it.'

He inspects the contents. 'Looks like it was—but no *bother* then?'

'No. It was . . . good. Interesting.'

His grin spreads as he sits back, arms folded. 'Let's 'ave it then.'

'What?'

'Who was it wot you stayed with?'

LONDONIA

'Bartholomew Straightfish.'
Silence.
'Jarvis?'
'. . . You *stayed over* with El Capo?'
'He invited me for supper.'
'*Christ* in a casserole.'
'It was fine—civilised, actually. Although I can't . . . remember it all.'

Jarvis leans over the table and glances about him, whispers.

'You know 'e enjoys finishing bods off—in overly crea-if ways.'

The words in that small book seem to hover in my mind. 'Well, I didn't know that at the time—rather found out this morn when I saw something he'd written.'

Jarvis sighs and rubs his face. 'Well, I just hope he hasn't formed an *attachment* to yer.'

'I doubt it. From what his housekeeper said, he's probably fairly *laisser faire*, when it comes to relationships.'

'. . . So, how big is 'e, this gar?'
'Jarvis!'
'Just idle curiosity.'
'Well, if you must know he was . . . well-favoured.'

'*Well-favoured*, eh?' he considers this for a while then his brow furrows. 'But why did you risk a jaunt last darking? Could 'ave gone t-dui.'

I nearly tell him about the watch but he'll bluster about why I didn't trade it and that I'm being too soft over a Cincturian.

'I don't know. Just one of those spur of the moment madnesses.'

'Uh-hu?' he says, knowingly. 'Anylane, d'you want t' go to the marshes and do a bit'v fishin?'

I consider this but feel too intrigued by the black jacket still folded over the chaise longue.

'Thanks, but think I'll go up to Fred's and see what's new.'

LONDONIA

At my knock on Fred's door, it grinds open and I'm welcomed in by Mimi.

'Salut, Hox. Tha after Fred?'

We kiss cheek to cheek over my box and I walk into the fabric-y chaos.

'Is he out?'

'Aye. Wi' pack at shoutin' house—there's word out on spools 'a thread. Will I do?'

'Certainly.' I put the box down on a free surface and open the lid. 'I've got a batch of sensible knickers from the Cincture—even a bra!'

'Beauteous!' she pipes, taking the thing from me. 'Can tha ge' more?'

'Could be a steady supply, I think.'

She nods happily. 'What tha needin' t-dui?'

'Well, the clothes you doctored were a total hit and I wondered if you'd had anything else of that era in.'

'Mm. 2020s weren't it . . . now't that I knows of. Oh—'cept there were a batch 'a shoes, like.'

'Yes?'

She puts the bra back and searches in a nearby chest bringing forth a cardboard box.

'Tha'll like these. Vivian Westwood!'

I open the box and find five pairs of tissue-wrapped, pristine red tartan wedges, all size five.

' . . . I can just hear their squeaks over these! I'll take a couple of pairs—I know they'll fit two of the group.'

She bags them up and I unearth the jacket from under the pants.

'I'd like your opinion on this.'

LONDONIA

Mimi takes it and nods, mouth pursed in admiration of something classy. 'Nice . . . let's see.' She finds the label and chuckles. 'Ay—it be one ouv ours like.'

'Yours?'

'Aye. See label—Gershwin's. S' arty coffee shop an' clothes boutique in't Cincture. They asks us t'find top stuff and put Gershwin's label in.'

'So why didn't my clients go there for their antique fashion stuff?'

'Coz they only do belle epoche, 'n the like—an' it's a tadly bit . . .'

'Arty? Boheme?'

'I were going t' say iconoclastic—but, aye, bit off the wall fr most Cincturians.'

Capitula 12

I put the jacket aside for a few days on my return and concentrated on garden-prep, outstanding trades to be finished and forays to shouting-houses. Jarvis's fishing-jaunt resulted in a fine catch of perch and trout which have now been pickled and stored away for next dark quarter. Further clothes searching resulted in nothing other than a Gucci bag which I think might have been a *knock-off* from around the required era but I'm hoping it and the shoes might excite my clients. T-dui, I'll find out . . . but scrote to that irrelevance! This is the day I will start my most vital Find ever!

By the time the sun is casting blue shapes from the central window, I'm ready as I can be. I close the vestry door behind me and follow the sound of swearing at the front doors where Jarvis is attaching Kafka's double saddle.

'You don't mind dropping me off?' I say, tentatively.

'Nah—course not. It's just this foitling leather's got manked in the last quarter.'

We lock up the church to encounter more than a hint of warmth in the outside air.

The month of Avi has finally arrived. Trees in the yard are tinged with fresh growth; new grass breaks through the torn road surfaces and birds flit, their song speaking of the brighter quarters to come.

The recent storm's damage is still visible: buildings without roofs, makeshift shelters being rebuilt, salvaged windows replacing broken ones, but today the air feels full of hope.

As Kafka pauses for a moment to lift his tail, someone scoots out from a small dwelling and scoops up his deposit with a well-worn spade. He salutes and returns to the building, hurling the merde into his garden.

Our steed's defecation has been added to a particularly fine example of urban husbandry, the mulched soil, storm-survived crops and various livestock presided over by a wolf that paces the enclosure.

'Where would a wolf have come from?' I ask, as the beast's howl causes Kafka to pick up his pace.

'The old zoo, reckon. Must 'ave been chaos during the Curtain. Course there's descendants of them all over the Pan—Jake's brother in Catford's got a water-buffalo in 'is garden.'

We fall silent again as the clop of Kafka's hooves rebound from the looming Cincturian walls.

Jarvis gestures back down the road as I slip from the saddle. 'Wot 'bout gettin' back?'

'I've got enough coinage to hitch a ride. See you later.'

'Abt, Kitten—and be wary, eh?'

I watch them leave, Kafka's dappled shiny arse swaying, Jarvis steady in his long tweed coat, just a hint of mint-green flares visible. Suddenly I want to laugh and cry and run after them but I turn, hoist the knapsack over my shoulder and walk to the scrum of bods by the gate.

There seems to be a holdup of the normal efficiency. I ask a young mec in front of me. He grins at me after a quick look up and down.

'Something wrong with the showers. You in the pleasuring bizz? Got a client waiting?'

I mentally slap him—a lot. 'NO. But I do have a meeting. What are you *doing* here?'

'Got a garden to finish—in Kensington.'

'Don't they have gardeners?'

'Not like me—it's all a bit staid in here—controlled, you know, lines of begonias and stuff. Anyway, the patroness, she likes a bit of Londonia dirt . . .'

'So, *you're* in the pleasuring game.'

LONDONIA

He grins again. 'Yeah—could say that, as a sideline.'

A mec appears and shouts over the crowd.

'The following names come forward. Everyone else disperse *now*. No further questions.'

A volley of raised voices greets the words. He picks up a megaphone and his voice booms distortedly. 'NOW, or there will be consequences.' The crowd volume drops to a murmur and people start to mooch away. 'Access granted to: Ov-Norwood, Stevenson and . . . Hoxton.'

The young mec nods as we walk to the gate. 'Looks like your clients have a certain say-so too.'

I think of the house, the trappings, the butler. 'Money, certainly.'

The gate grinds open and we are shown into a small windowless room. A dame appears and asks questions about our visit to come and inspects our baggage, after which allinones are handed to the two mecs and a brown trouser suit for me.

'Ov-Norwood—a car is coming for you,' she announces, 'Stevenson take a shaw from the rank. And, Hoxton, someone is meeting you . . . *on foot*. Change and wait in here.'

When re-attired, the mecs saunter off and I stand in the room studying the one picture that graces the otherwise featureless walls. A cart stands in a river, its wheels, part-submerged, horses waiting while the driver talks to someone. The sky is filled with immense cloud. The artist must have spent hours admiring and sketching their lofty forms. I wonder if it's an original; the paint is raised, brushstrokes visible. I could stand and look at the picture for a long time, just imagining this tranquil world of a long time ago that perhaps does exist somewhere beyond Londonia.

'Hoxton?'

I turn from the painting and see Iona, not attired in a simple trouser suit but a long flowing dress.

'Still in the 1900s?' I smile.

LONDONIA

'For the moment, and could be for some time. I don't think the factory owners are too excited about this change. Do you want to take a shaw?'

'No, walking's fine. Thanks for organising the outfit.'

'I thought you should start blending in a little more. And we have the authority.' She swishes along, heels entangling in the fabric every so often. 'Arg—bloody dress. I'd be happy just wearing the standard suits.'

We stop while she unwinds a band of lace from a spiked heel.

'Why don't you?' I suggest.

'I will when I leave *Matthew*.'

'You sound as if that's a definite plan.'

'It is—once Maddy is old enough.'

'What's so bad?'

'He's a philandering bastard, and a bore. Do you want some more jewellery?'

'Wouldn't say no . . .'

'He's given me an emerald necklace—a new woman, I assume . . . how's your very important person?'

'Ça va. He's fine—throwing himself into all sorts of practical projects around the church.'

'Useful. You didn't tell me, however, if you have an important person in the *other* sense.'

I flush slightly as I think of Tom and Mr Straightfish. She notices.

'Come on. Tell!'

'There is someone and then there's someone else who I probably shouldn't have got involved with . . . anylane, there's more urgent things I need to do.'

'Which are?'

'Start a search for my son, and something else I feel obliged to rectify.'

'Oh?'

LONDONIA

I describe the incident with the jacket and what I later discovered, by which time we have arrived outside the Caruso residency. Iona glances at the front door.

'We won't stay long—I'll make an excuse. I know where Gershwin's is.' The door opens and the dame of the house sashays down the steps past Gubbins.

'Hey, damsels. The others are here, and I have your stashies, Hoxton. To be delivered as before?'

'If that's possible.'

'Gubbins. Get the boxes sent this afternoon.' She turns to us, her grey pallor slightly flushed. 'This is going to kill you!' We go into the sitting room and find the other women examining a brochure. 'Mrs Nash had an incredidea after that beauty talk,' she continues. 'A nail boutique!' Images of shelves containing small cardboard boxes and racks of tools enter my mind.

'Nails?'

'Yes! It's *so* artistic what you can do—like they did before the Whiteout. There's hardly any salons and what they do is *dullstown*. Iona? You in? Matthew could put up some funds—we might buy a shop. Have a look at this agent's brochure. Shizz! This is IT.'

Iona takes the book from Miss Preen and studies the photographs, her expression unreadable.

'I'll have to talk it over with him. But I think I'm really going to be too busy with school. I've volunteered to help with the theatre group.'

Mrs Caruso turns to me and I know what she's going to ask.

'We'll need original colours from back then. I read that varnish can last forever if not opened. Imagine. Real nail polish by *Chanel* . . .'

'Can't it be made here?'

'There are a few basic colours but we want to offer a rainbow, and the real old Frenchy stuff.'

'I can certainly try. Did you want to look at the items I found, by the way?'

LONDONIA

'Oh . . . could do. Though we've changed our ideas to a sort of *mixy* look coz of the hold ups in design production. This whole 2020s thing's become a pain in the b-hind. In fact, I might be asking you to take this cabinet back, and the other furniture in exchange for something more *artisanal*. Peasant craft—that's the new phrase. Real wood, a bit rustic-y. You were thinking about commissioning someone, in . . . Hepping-forrist? Weren't you, Abby.'

'Correcto,' chips in Mrs Nash, 'D'you know him, Hoxton?—a person called Mange. He lives in a tree house but makes the most sensi furniture.'

To stop myself screaming: *shut the merde up,* I open my bag and take out the carefully wrapped, painstakingly searched-for shoes. 'Vivian Westwood. 2023?'

The women jointly stop looking at the brochure and glance over as I remove the paper layers.

'Oh. I don't care for those,' says Miss Preen.

A quarter clockface later, I'm storming down the street with Iona tripping along behind.

'Wait . . . wait, Hoxton!'

I cease outside a shop selling of-the-moment colour-statement guns and wait for her to catch up.

'This place is foitling mad—all of it. How can you stand it? And them!'

'I can't,' she says, catching her breath. 'As I said when the child's older, I'm off. Meeting you again has made me really think.'

I smile at her in her ridiculous outfit, hair a little dishevelled, and she giggles. Then we both laugh, raucously, at the stupidity of everything said back in that room full of nail-chat. People passing by stare at us: a cackling Londonian and a hiccupping Cincturian.

'Gershwin's?' she says.

LONDONIA

The café-shop is in an area called World's End. We walked most of the way and then took a shaw at Green Park as Iona's feet hurt—and I'm not surprised in those stupid heels. Now we stand outside, looking at the black and gold frontage which, for the Cincture, looks a little faded.

'Have you been in here before?' I ask.

'Once,' replies Iona. 'With you, actually . . .'

I try to recall this street, the building before me but nothing emerges. 'Why didn't you come back?'

'It has a certain reputation that Matthew wouldn't approve of but I do recall the tea being excellent.'

We enter and a waitress whom I think may be a mec, shows us to a table and produces an atlas of choice.

'Voila mesdames. I weel return in a short while. I can recommend ze lemon cake of cheese today.'

I'm so excited by the list of teas, scones, tarts and much more that it takes me ages to choose. Iona waves the young dame-mec away again.

'Another couple of minutes, thank you.'

The café's interior is very different to any Cincture shop I have seen so far—brocante furniture, old photos of 1920s and 30s London as it was; and the clientele definitely, as Mimi had mentioned, a little off any Cincture wall.

I nudge Iona. 'How is this place allowed.'

'It nearly hasn't been quite a few times—rumours of drugs, debauched behaviour and so on. Here's the nippy again—made up your mind?'

At last, I decide on the proposed cheesecake and ginger tea; the order is taken and I sit almost hugging myself at this rare pleasure. I turn to Iona with a slight smirk.

LONDONIA

'So, a *nail* shop, eh?'

'Not getting involved. Anyway, it'll be something else in a week's time. They're as fickle as cats.'

A tray edges gently onto the table and our waitress unloads two silver pots, delicate cups, sugar bowl, and the cakes. Iona pours the tea and I revel in this indulgence.

'Look at *my* nails,' I sigh as I fork up another sublime slice of cake.

'Start a shop out there,' she smiles, wryly.

'I don't think it would figure highly on bod's lists of weekly activities.'

'Going back to what I asked earlier—this Tom, would you marry him?'

I sip tea and consider. Would I?

'It's not really something I've thought about.'

'What about this other person you got *entangled* with?'

'Oh—he really was an accident. I went to trade your necklace at his premises and ended up in his bath and bed. I think he did ask me about marriage . . .'

'Chantelle! You are . . .'

'*Hoxton*. And yes, incorrigible, possibly.'

'Actually,' she says, pouring another cup of tea. 'I'm jealous. Matthew's out there rolling about in other beds, and I've only really *known* him.'

I point to a suited mec reading a newspaper. 'He looks comme il faut. Go and ask him if he'd like to see your etchings.'

'I couldn't, even if I did etching.'

The waitress returns and collects up our teacups. 'There is to be anything else, Mesdames?'

'Just the bill, please,' says my friend.

We gather our things and Iona nods at my bag.

'What will you do with those shoes?'

I shrug. 'Plant lettuces in them? No—ça va, I know several traders who'll take them, possibly for a better deal.'

'Will you look for nail-varnish?'

LONDONIA

We both grin at this madness.

'Why not? It'll get me back in here again. I'll send a message and let you know when and if I find anything. So, the shop part of Gershwin's. Care to investigate?'

Iona glances at her watch. 'I'd better not. I'll get a cab back and ask them to send you one too on the Hedgefund account. Half an hour do you?'

We kiss and she walks to the door while I make my way to the shop part of the establishment behind saloon-style doors. A grey-haired dame attired in a red silk robe looks up from behind a magazine. She tops up a glass of something from a decanter and gives me a mauve-lipsticked smile.

'Happy browsing, mademoiselle?'

'. . . I would be but I have a couple of questions, if you don't mind.'

She places the magazine down, re-gigs her pince-nez and peers at me.

'You are not from the tax depo are you?'

'No . . . not at all. I'm trying to find out about a young mec—man.'

She nods knowingly. 'You're from Londonia.'

I wonder if this matters but decide, judging by her cagey words regarding tax, that it won't. 'I am. In fact you must know Fred—Fred's Threads?'

'Dear Fred and Mimi. Yes, I do, indeed. Our most beautiful pre-curtain goods generally come from that source.'

'In that case, you might recall selling a black silk and wool jacket with an unusual lining.'

'We sell quite a lot of black jackets. What was so special about the lining?'

I describe it and she nods again. '*That* one I do recall . . . came from Fred's a couple of months back.'

I feel the usual Finder thrill of being on the right path. 'Do you recall the buyer of it?'

LONDONIA

She suddenly looks a little suspicious so I tell her the story after which she searches under the counter, pulls out a ledger and flicks through the pages. She stops and scans a section. 'Ah—this was the day. I remember because there was that incredible storm. I could hear the rain lashing the counterveils and we had a bad leak as they keep not repairing the two closest to us.'

I wait patiently as she rambles a bit then gently intervene. 'Do you recall the person who bought the jacket.'

'Hm . . . there were quite a few young men here as it was some ball or other—a flapper thing at one of the colleges. I'm afraid I don't recall which of them purchased the jacket but I know they all do frequent the café quite often. You could ask the manageress, Miss Holt, when she's in.'

'Did you notice if one of them had green eyes?'

'Oh . . . Actually, yes. Blond hair. In fact there was something else unusual about him. He was still buttoning up a shirt he'd tried on when he came to ask me the price and I noticed he had a mark on his neck.'

' . . . What sort of shape was it?'

'Oo. I know it was like a country . . . reminded me of . . .'

'What?'

'Mm. Africa? No . . . it was longer, I think . . .

She knocks back the glass of spirits and my own spirit sinks at the realisation that her recollections might not be very reliable. She's nattering again, The room seems to dim as all my thoughts converge on that one moment a few darkings ago when I had been given a jacket by possibly . . . my son?

'Taxi for Hoxton.'

'That's you, dear. I think,' says the dame, prodding me. 'Come back and talk to Miss Holt—most days in the morning.'

I thank her and walk out to the taxi, a mad mix of emotions crowding my mind.

LONDONIA

After my luxurious conveyance back to the access point, the lift on the other side had been a little different—an old dame with a cart and donkey. Still, I arrived unmolested and glad to be back, although a tinge of despair colours the aft.

No dogs leap, howling at my return; Jarvis must have taken them out. Kafka has been tethered in the yard, head down, lips snaffling the new grass. He sees me through the iron bars, horse-grins and stamps a foot. Unlocking the gate, I sway over and lean against his smooth bulk.

'It's good to be home, Kafka.'

As we stand silently, the sun tips over the edge of a cloud. The force of the rays hits my face and for the first time in eons I can imagine cold water being welcoming. I enter the church, grab a blanket and fresh clothing from the vestry and stuff them in a bag. The door re-locked, I scrabble up onto Kafka, swinging the bag onto my back and we're galloping up the Hackrovia Road towards the Parkplace, dust rising into the sun's glare.

The bright day has transformed this brambly space. Daffodils, crocus and daisies spot the grass; birds compete for nesting material and humans bask in the warmth along with their drying washing.

After tying the horse to a tree close to the pond, I knock on the door of Prophet-Jake's hut. It squeaks open and he squints into the light.

'Ah, Hoxton . . . back from the Cincture, eh?'

Nodding an affirmative, I ask if he could keep an eye on Kafka.

'Swimming?' he guesses.

'I know. Mad, but I have to.'

LONDONIA

'I went in this morning—foitelin' cold, but it shook me up right and properly. Go ahead, I'll fix us a brew.'

I scoot to the pond, throw off clothing and wade in rapidly, the leaf-mud squishing between my toes. A few women slapping clothes on a rock, point towards me and laugh, their squeaky voices ringing around the Parkplace.

God in a shed! It's *so* cold. My limbs seem to have parted from the rest of me, but I strike out, shoving the green water, hands caressed by soft weed.

Diving down, I open my eyes into the khaki murk, the sun's shards illuminating the hidden depths. A duck passes, a fish clamped in its bill, and then pops to the surface. I follow and we observe each other for a moment: he contented with his catch, me with my newly-clear mind.

Wading out from the water, I grab the blanket, dry roughly and stumble into my clothes, shivering.

Jake has placed two chairs outside the hut.

'Sit,' he invites, handing me a bowl of coffee. 'You're shaking! Just from the chill water? Or something else?'

Emotion chokes me and I say nothing.

Confusion fills my heart. He notices and moves away from the subject.

'Is it as they say, in there? You know, cars, shops, buildings looked after—like what it would have been here?'

I glance at Jake's briar-covered dwelling and think of the preened façades and manicured plants within those copper walls.

'It seems false to me. It's too perfect . . . as if it's all part of the scenery for a play—and the people! Jake, you should see the clothes, the hairstyles . . . the stupidity of it all. I was so glad to get back to—'

'The gritty reality of Londonia?' he suggests.

'It's where I belong, wherever I started out from.'

'But you've learned things now—about there . . .'

LONDONIA

I wonder whether to divulge the story, here sitting in the sun but he gestures towards the park gateway. 'Your church-mate.'

I look around and see Jarvis running, one hand holding on to his hat, the other grappling with the straining leads of the great-hounds who have scented me out. They leap and he skids to a halt.

'Woah, blimey, these beasts love you, H! Got any more coffee, Jake?'

'Can do,' he says rising. 'Refill, Hoxton?'

I nod a yes, and smile at Jarvis as he sits down.

'Thanks for taking these two out.'

'Not a problem, and it's good for me,' he pats his stomach. 'Gotta look after meself a bit more.' We sit quietly for a moment, the dogs calmer now, ears twitching at any sound in the undergrowth.'

The door creaks open and Jake reappears, handing over the coffee bowls. He pulls over a stool and sits down.

'How'd it go with the mad dames?' asks Jarvis. 'They got them phones working?' I groan at the thought of Mrs Caruso's sitting room gathering.

'They've gone off the whole 2020s thing—the furniture, clothes . . .'

'Why?'

'Oh, I don't know, some delay in making the copy-clothes they want. *And* she wants me to take the cabinet back and get other furniture called . . . peasant craft, I think it was.'

'Pampered git-esses,' he growls. 'Sounds like they all need to work the merde-cart fr' a moonful or two—get a bit 'a tangibul in their foitling lives.'

I laugh at the thought of Miss Preen hoisting buckets of crud onto the compo-land's soil.

'They do. Indeedly.'

Jarvis gets one of his clay pipes out and faffs about with bacco and old brass lighter. At last lit, he squints through the twirling smoke. 'Wot you up to, Jake?'

LONDONIA

He smiles serenely. 'Preparation.'
'Oh yeah? For wot?'
'A fete—Satdy darking.'
'Birthday?' enquires Jarvis, knowing nobody really bothers.
'Brighter quarter welcoming truc, and birthday, perhaps—why not. No idea when it is, so let's say, it's then, eh?'

Capitula 13

Prophet-Jake must have his hands on the weather. Satdy has dawned mild with torrents of bird song. I stand in the garden, my senses taking in the new quarter's delights. The air smells different, no longer raw; new vegetation and earth turned by the blackbirds. People are emerging from their near hibernation, windows open and cooking smells drifting.

The plane trees at the end of the garden creak in the soft wind, the ink-blue sky busy with crow silhouettes as they fidget from one branch to another, their rusty voices speaking of nesting rights.

In the chicken hut, I find two eggs and go back indoors to try Jarvis's new range—a wonderment of fused metal gleaned from many sources. I build a small fire inside it and wait nearby with a bucket of water in case he was over-optimistic. The flames ride upwards, smoke rattling the chimney, and in a short while the heavy metal plates are warm. Kettle on, I prepare scrambled eggs with rosemary and new spring onion. It works. The egg is cooking, kettle boiling: a triumph. I lay the table with more care than usual, adding a tiny vase of snowdrops then go to wake Jarvis.

The wooden construction rattles gently with his snores.

I creep away again, thinking perhaps it's unkind to wake him, but he hears me.

'H? You got the kettle on?'

'And more. It works.'

'Be there in a taddly.'

By the time tea is made, he appears at the door in an interesting ensemble of an undone striped shirt, revealing a T-shirt

LONDONIA

blazoned with the words: *kill them and eat them*; beige suede trousers, hiking boots and the usual homburg.

'Looking good, Jarvis!' I invite him to sit down.

His magnetic smile shines through the straggly beard as he looks at the table and the stove.

'Told you it would work, din'I. You notice the tap?' He points to the brass tap, low down on the black metal front. 'You put water in the cavity at the back, there, and voila, no longer cold!'

'That's incredible.'

'*And*, I got us a bath!'

'Vraiment?'

'Yep, Bert's got loads and nobody wants 'em. If you can help me get it in when the delivery mec comes, we could try out the heaty water.' He rubs a hand over his chin. 'Need to get rid of this mangy hair and look sharp, for later!'

I smile, realising that his period of mourning is possibly over.

'D' you think there will be a lot of people there at Jake's tonight?'

'He knows most of East Londonia, so reckon, yeah.'

'Think I'll try and make a chicken pie in this new contraption,' I suggest, folding an omelette onto a plate and passing it to Jarvis. 'If you could see your way to . . . terminating Queen Victoria. I think she's about to go anyway.'

He makes a twisting motion with his hands, nods and attacks the breakfast.

''S' good with the herbs, anymore nettle tea? Ta. Oh—forgot.' He scoots off and returns with a potted rose wrapped in a piece of red silk. He hands it to me with a knowing expression. 'Pritty innit?'

'Thanks, but why?'

'Not from me—Straightfish. The water-mec found it outside the gate.'

'Ah . . .'

'Told yer, wasn't a too brilli idea!'

LONDONIA

He watches while I unwind the silk and read the note. A slight foreboding hovers.

'Abandoned by an angel. Don't stay in the East. Think of what I offered you.'

I place the pot on the dresser, shut my mind to the note's words and start clearing the sink area to make way for Queen Victoria.

By late aft, the pie is constructed: wobbly and thinner than I would have liked, as our stock of flour has just about gone. The range works well but I realise we'll need to haul a lot more wood. As I throw on another wormy section of beam, the door-bell jangles.

Jarvis, looks up from sorting a box of runner beans. 'Bath's 'ere.'

Shoving on shoes, I skit down the aisle and into the courtyard. The bath, tied onto a donkey cart, is murky green plastic.

We wrestle it into the vestry where it sits like a mossy battle ship. I pay the donkey-mec, and run a cloth over the bath before Jarvis fills it with hot water, kettle on the stove for top ups.

'You go first,' he insists. 'Yor smaller and I'm dirtier.'

'How do we empty it?'

'Pots an' buckets for the mo, but I got an idea.' He goes back to sorting and leaves me to strip off. I step in and lie down, the water just reaching over my stomach.

I've never looked at my lodgings while lying in a warm water cocoon. My eyes scan the walls covered in old photos, pages from books and letters.

The kettle is boiling. Jarvis hears its plaintive whistle and whips it off the range.

'Mind yor feet.' He pours then refills. 'I'm gonna start serious on the roof water collection stuff morrow. Bonce-vide not to rammas the rain, eh?'

'I know,' I say, realising how reliant I've become on the water-mec's round. 'Don't go and get yourself attached elsewhere, you're *far* too useful.'

LONDONIA

'No danger. Meby just a bit of a laugh 'ere 'n there, but this works goodly.'

I stir the water around, the new heat infusing my limbs.

'Wonderful . . . just a little bit longer, then your turn.'

He sits on the couch and admires his find. 'Not bad that. Ugly as crud, but does the job.'

'I'll help you sort out a drainage system. I need to learn some more practical stuff.'

'Done ça va for a *dame*, H.'

He dodges my slap, passes me a piece of sheeting and I step out to dry myself, aware of his gaze.

'What?'

'You really are a looker, Kitten. Just as well, I'm gayster—don't rek this would work otherwise.'

I smile at the compliment, covering my slight embarrassment by taking the re-heated kettle off the stove and pouring the water.

'Your turn.'

He takes off his layers.

'Don't forget the hat,' I remind him

His eyes crinkle up in humour. 'Forget it's there sometimes.' He flips it off onto the bust of Mozart and his curls bounce.

'Who had the curly hair?'

'Grandad. Can just remember as a gosse watchin' 'im play the violin even when he was oldy, eyes shut, hair flyin' about.'

'I expect he'd be happy to know you'd continued the tradition.'

Jarvis smiles at the thought. 'Yeah—'e would.'

By early darking, we're dressed in our finery. Jarvis has been pressing a black suit under a pile of boxes. Worn with a white

LONDONIA

shirt, electric orange tie and the habitual hat he looks the desired *Sharp*. Much indecision later I have opted for a rustling, aqua silk gown, red shoes and matching bag, courtesy of Fred's some cycles back.

After proudly contemplating the pie sitting on the table, I pack it carefully into a straw lined box, locate a certain bottle of wine hidden for a special occasion and I'm ready.

Dogs and livestock fed, we lock up and walk arm in arm to the Parkplace feeling like royalty.

It seems as if most of Hackrovia is out on the streets this darking. Smoke drifts, not just from fires to keep warm, but fires for cooking, for relaxing around, sharing food, drink and stories; everyday problems laid aside for a few clockfaces.

A soft breeze plays around the buildings—no need to walk hurriedly, grasping a felty close to your chest, thinking only of being inside, somewhere safe.

Jarvis smiles at me. 'Good innit, sort a fundamental—warmth—freer.'

'Imagine if it was always like this,' I say.

'Ha, y'd miss it though, chilblains, colds, rat-baine, possible death.'

'We've been lucky. That last bout of Xtra-flu got so many.'

'Got to look after ourselves, Hoxton—protect the body, exercise, eat lots 'a cabbage.'

'What about tobacco, wine, beer, drugs?'

'In moderation,' he grins. 'Talking of which, got some great mushrooms—harvested on the heath by a fat moon. I dried 'em and kept a stash for just such a darking as this.' He rummages in his suit inner pocket and produces a paper bag.

I take it and look at the small shrivelled forms.

'What happens?'

'Colours, smells, touch . . . everyfing b'comes sort 'a heightened and changed.'

'In a good way?'

LONDONIA

'Mostly. Had a couple of jaunts wot was a bit scary, p'raps took too many.'

We reach the rusting gates of the Parkplace and slip inside to a dreamlike place. The lake shimmers with reflected lanterns and the moon's soft light. Small vessels constructed from sticks and thin paper float on the water; lit up inside by candles they resemble delicate amethysts. Incense drifts on the warm air mixed with the scent of hyacinths that Jake has planted over the cycles. Next to the lake on a temporary platform, a band plays: accordion, fiddle, double bass and some sort of drum kit made of boxes. People are dancing, best clothes on show, a whirl of different fabrics and stamping feet in shining shoes.

A long table set up on the grass holds a mass of different dishes, pots and bowls.

'Clock this scran,' says Jarvis, advancing hungrily. I take the pie from its box and place it next to a tray of cakes.

'Think we should hang onto that and share it with Jake,' I suggest, as Jarvis takes out the bottle of wine from his knapsack.

'Yeah—goodly idea.'

Jake is sitting outside his hut with a group of gosses, their smiling faces lit up by the flames of a small fire.

'Check the quails, Marcel,' he says, pointing to a metal contraption over the fire holding the speared bodies of tiny birds. A young boy dutifully turns the metal sticks, eyes fixed on the story reader. 'Good, good,' continues Jake, nodding. 'Now where were we.'

'The dragon that brought the storm,' chorus the small crowd.

'Oh, yes . . . So, the biggest storm of all was brought by the slithery water dragon. Yes, you think dragons only make fire . . . not this one.'

Jarvis smiles at me through the fire's smoke. 'Don't want to disturb this.'

He holds up the wine bottle and Jake grins, thumbs up. Wielding his knife, Jarvis dispatches the cork, goes into the hut and finds three cups. He hands one to Jake and we sit with the gosses listening to the tale of how the great floods came.

The wine is worthy of the price I paid for it: two pairs of immaculate leather brogues. We savour every mouthful of raspberry, chocolate and all the other particles that seem to exist within the dark liquid.

Not pausing from the story, Jake points to the roasting birds and gestures eating. Jarvis takes a stick and dislodges two small crispy carcasses. The meat is tender, flavoured with herbs and I think of adding some quail to our livestock.

'I'll get us some pie 'fore it all goes,' says Jarvis. He returns with two slices, sits again, and we try the first product of the range.

The pastry is firm, a little burned on one side, but not bad.

'So, d'you want to dance or wot?' Jarvis asks, brushing crumbs from his tie as he stands up.

I can't remember the last time I danced, apart from in the church when Tom put on a scratchy old record of Hungarian folk tunes. Tom: I haven't thought about him much since that morning he went, thunking the door in heated misunderstanding. I suppose my mind's just been so full of other complicated things.

'Well?'

'Oh, sorry . . . yes, I would.'

He holds out a hand, pulls me up and we leave the circle of glowing faces.

'Good chicken 'n mushroom pie,' he remarks.

'I didn't put mushrooms in it,' I frown.

'No, but I did.'

'What?'

'Just a few of my special'uns.'

'Jarvis!'

'Wot? Yor not *averse* to the odd spot of Snash.'

'Yes, but when *I* might choose to!'

'Relax, H. Not gonna trip you up, just intensify.'

'How long?'

'Till it kicks in? 'Bout 'arf a clockface.'

I glare at him until the manic twinkle in his eyes makes me laugh. We run to the dance floor and gyrate to the wild melody that's vibrating the planks. Across the crowd of bobbing heads, one stands out under its thatch of thick, fair hair. I signal to Jarvis that I'm moving on. He grins, already homing in on a gar.

Weaving through the crowd, I reach the spot and stand for a minute watching Tom dance in his patched jins. A discarded floral shirt stuffed into the waistband whips from side to side as he performs his eccentric dance moves. He might be with someone; a red-haired dame sways opposite him, eyes closed, a hooch-stick between her lips, arms snaking.

I move up behind him and place a hand on his glistening back. He spins around and his eyes widen.

'Well, Miss Hoxton. Looky at you, all dressed up.'

His eyes: that blue. As blue as the hydrangeas that crowd next to the church wall in summer; not moss green like the dream ones. I stumble a little, focusing too intently on the eyes.

'Hey, H. What you on?' he says, words fusing into the music.

I can't recall the name of the things in the bag now; something else escapes my mouth.

'Tiny birds.'

He smiles. 'I see. Jarvis gave you them, did he?'

'He didly-did.'

As I draw my hands gently over his arms and up to his shoulders, the other dame, her eyes open now, frowns slightly and moves away. He is mine: muscles, slippery skin and a perfect mouth shaped like an archer's bow. My lips are against his now: such a strange and wonderful thing, a kiss.

'I missed you,' he says as we stop and gaze at each other. I can't seem to find the words I want; other ones appear in my mind and spill out.

'It was wrong, what I did. Serpents we were, all gilded and secret.'

LONDONIA

He looks perplexed. 'Think we should go and sit somewhere quiet.'

Taking my hand, he guides me through the mass of bodies. I feel the hearts pounding, a mass thudding in time with the music. The swish of fabrics is watery and silken; colours flash: crimson, peacock, silver. The Parkplace has become a mystical moorland, filled with unknown beasts that lurk, eyes yellow-bright, pointy-teethed, flesh in mind.

Tom finds an empty space in the shadows near a wall and gently pushes me to the grass. I lie back and watch the stars dance between the branchy fingers of the giant plants.

'What are these herbages?' I hear my voice say.

'Blimey, Hoxton—those tiny birds must have been quite strong.'

An idea is forming in my head. I don't know if it's a good one, but it seems irresistible.

'Tom?'

'Mademoiselle?'

'Fuk me.'

'Here?'

'Yes. With earth and beetles. Like animals.'

I can see two expressions on his face: merging, separating, merging: lust and concern. Lust wins and his eyes narrow, a grin spreading.

'Why not?'

The party pulsates, a blur of colour set in a deep blueness of night, but we are alone with rustling unknown creatures and sweet grass blades. The silk of my dress has become a river. Tom sits back on his heels, pulls at his belt and pushes away the fabric.

Tom the outside-mec. My eyes roam over his body where no fat lives, each muscle defined from lifting earth and climbing trees, not like the other's indoors body of white, craggy skin and scars from darking fights. I register the ground's fragrant herbs, his delicious weight, my lungs tasting sweet darking air and his musk sweat.

A fantasy world of misplaced senses makes me cry out into the dark sky where shooting stars streak and scatter.

'Favourable was it?' Tom laughs as he scrabbles for his clothes, aware that the noise might tempt onlookers.

I think I say it was the most moving and profound sexual experience of my life. He looks suddenly serious, tears in his eyes, and I think my words must have been as I'd desired.

'We didn't use anything, Hoxton, and I didn't recule. You don't want to be in nipperin' do yer?'

I silence his angsty-ness with a kiss. 'Lie back, look at the great black arc and the ice points.'

He smiles again and obeys, lying back with a whump into the grass, and sighing.

'*Zoots*. That was just unbelievable. Now d'you want to get married?'

I giggle and stare into the sky where the stars still spark in rhythm with my thudding heart.

Sitting up, I shuffle back dizzily against the wall. Tom joins me, takes my hand and kisses it. We sit for a long time watching the bobbing crowd and the streaks of colour shooting into the night.

Capitula 14

A sound of metal on metal wakes me. I open my eyes expecting a vivid spectrum of colour; instead the greys and pale flaking blue of the vestry walls stare back. Turning groggily towards the sounds, I see Jarvis dressed in a fur coat, raking ashes in the range.

'Where's Tom?' I hear my grating voice say.

'Gone to Hepping. S'got logging work again . . . left you a note though.'

'Any chance of coffee?'

'Working on it. Why? You got a headache?'

'No, I only had one glass, but *someone* gave me some other stuff.'

'Sounds like you 'ad a right vig-rous time last eve.' I stare at him, confused. 'After wot you was saying, 'anging on to Tom and givin' us all the sexo details.'

The images seep back into my cloudy mind: soft grass, black sky and that one upward movement of Tom's body tensing, shuddering and releasing.

'Oh, yes . . . sorry.'

'I, or I should say, *we*, didn't mind. Quite an aphro—*not* that I needed one.' He nods in the direction of his abode and grins manically.

'Is he still here?'

'Mmm. Unfinished business. Coffee and fukin', great start to the day.'

Suddenly I feel the need to go for a long walk and a long think.

'What have we got on today? I can't seem to remember anything.'

LONDONIA

Jarvis reaches for the black book. 'Sundy, so nothing too pressing. Thought I might roast soming, 'cept we 'aven't got much *to* roast. You got cabbage written here.'

My mind clears a little. 'Ah, yes . . . I said to Sardi that I'd take the cabbages to hers and we'd try making sauerkraut.'

'Goodly for trading,' Jarvis says. 'The Russians'll go for it.'

Feeling in need of a plan I suggest the day's layout.

'I'll take a long walk with the hounds, see if I can get a rabbit, then, if I do, you can sort it while I go to Sardi's with the cabbage, and back here for lunch.'

'Sounds sound,' he smiles and hands me a folded piece of paper. ' 'Ere's the note, by the way.'

I take it, unfold it and read Tom's scrawly hand.

Sorry, had to go and I couldn't seem to wake you.
Be back in a few Sundys. YOUR Tom. X

Jarvis pours a cup of coffee and hands it to me. I sit for a while amongst the rumpled blankets with Zorro, absent-mindedly stroking his fur. Then, more awake, I get dressed, glancing at last night's gown and smiling at the memory. *Marry me.* I *could* settle down with Tom; have a family and ignore the nagging thoughts about my past and who might be in it.

The barking of Tilly and Fagin in the courtyard shakes me from my thoughts. I grab the rifle, pull on boots and leave Jarvis the whole church for a while.

The dogs twirl with excitement as I leash them and unlock the gate. We head off to the scrub ground near the railway tracks, me running in their wake, the morn breezes clearing my mind. The scrub looks different. A shimmer of yellow and pink flowers now cover the ground; very different to the last time I visited when ice-covered puddles reflected wintery clouds, the grass dead and crisped.

Any potential game has been recently disturbed by something; not a single rabbit is in sight. We cross the tracks and wait quietly within a clump of trees. I could stand here for a long time just listening to the yellow parakeets chatter in one of the oak trees. I think of the brighter quarters stretching out: swimming in the ponds, reading in the churchyard, maybe riding Kafka a little further away and exploring, perhaps even beyond Londonia.

Fagin suddenly looks up, a growly bark deep in his throat. I follow his gaze and see, standing amongst the bright flowers, a pheasant. A double gift: tasty meat and feathers to trade. Lifting the gun silently, I aim, squeeze the curve of metal and the bird falls. Tilly is more delicate than Fagin for collecting a bird. I release the lead's clasp and she streaks away, returning with the warm body held gently in her mouth.

On my return to the church, I find Jarvis playing his violin in the vestry. He smiles at the sight of me and the bird and lowers the instrument.

'You got lunch, then.'

'If you've got time to deal with it.' I notice his smile is only at about fifty percent. 'Has he gone—your visitor?'

'Yeah. Had to get going . . .'

'Sad?'

'Nah . . . not really,' he sighs. 'Like I said, bit of a laugh here and there. Anylane, you going to see Sardi?'

'Yep. She's probably got those repairs done by now too, so I'll pick the clothes up.'

'That'd be good. A couple of bods's been asking about their warmer weather stuff.'

I lay the bird down, its feathers shining in the sunlight.

'Actually, it might be best to leave this hanging for a few days. I wasn't expecting a pheasant.'

Jarvis looks at the soft heap. 'That's a real treat worth waiting for—yeah, I'll 'ang it in the chapel—still froidly in there.'

I find two sack-bags and go to the door.

'I'll probably eat something at Sardi's. See you later then.'

'Yeah . . . later.'

LONDONIA

'Ça va?'

'Goodly, it's just . . .'

'Parrot?'

He smiles wistfully. 'You should have been a head-doc, Kitten. Nah, I'm fine, really. I'll take Kafka fr' a pacer, make a couple of deliveries too.' He gets up abruptly as if shaking off the past and grabs the bird from the table. Feathers dance and drift. 'D'ac. I'll 'ang this, and get going on them deliveries. A plus, Kitten.' He clumps into the aisle, his voice echoing,

'You'd be so easy to luv . . .'

I leave the vestry and head to the garden where surprises are happening. Rocket and coriander sprout from last year's seeds; clumps of scented daffodils and vivid crocus break the winter mulch, and in neat lines, the first tentative leaves of the potatoes.

Most of the savoy cabbages were hail damaged but I cut the remaining good ones and load them in the sack-bags where their leaves grind and squeak as I walk to Sardi's house.

When I arrive, the door to the faded brick building is open, some of the residents sitting outside on a collection of ancient chairs. A serious air prevails over a card game, winnings carefully stowed next to each person: bacco, a net bag of potatoes and a live chicken in a cage.

Stepping into the hallway I'm startled by a blaze of voices, sharp contrast to the peaceful scene in the street. It appears to be a row over meat between two Ukrainians and an Italian mec. I slip past as the cleaver imbedded in the block on my last visit zings through the air to land in a doorpost.

'Figlio de putanna! Bastardio.' A third youth has appeared with a pistol. I race up to the next floor as a shot cracks the plaster: 'Ti amazzo!'

On the first floor the deranged bird dame seems to have added to her flock with a screeching parrot: *Come here, wanna kiss you, come here, wanna kiss you!'*

LONDONIA

Her door is open and I catch a glimpse of her living quarters: bird merde-stained furniture, several crows perched along the back of a couch and a herring gull staring back at me with a hypnotic yellow eye. On Sardi's floor, warmer chaos greets me. The long table is occupied by a dead pig; most of the family engaged in stripping it of entrails and arguing about the right way to dissect the animal. Sardi waves a bloodied hand.

'Salut, Hoxton. Sorry, din't s'pect this. Unc turned up with a present! Said he'd come back later and help—'ope he foitling does!'

I put the cabbage sack under the table and kiss her cheek. 'Maybe another day for the sauerkraut? Looks like you've enough going on.'

She wipes her hands on a cloth and pushes back an escaped twist of braided hair from its floral scarf.

'Morro?' she suggests. I nod but she must have read the unrest in my eyes. 'D'you know,' she sighs, 'I'd love a break from all this, and a chai. Take a perch on the roof and I'll join you in a quarter-cycle.'

I greet the gosses then make my way past the turmoil to the roof door.

The patched glass panel grinds open and I step out onto slate and tarpaulin. Sardi has made a new gazing area on a flat portion of roof: an old door serving as a floor, two chairs and a packing case table.

I install myself in a frayed cane armchair and admire this crows' eye view of Londonia speared by the copper walls. Somewhere within there, my son might be looking up at the walls wondering what is beyond . . .

The glass hatch opens and Sardi comes over with two cups.

'D'ac. Tell me all the happenings.'

'It might take a bit longer than you have now.'

'Might need a longer break—tell!'

I pick up the cup and start as I notice the worn gold lettering—*Chantelle*.

LONDONIA

'Where did this come from?'

She shrugs. 'Spitalfields free-for-all, I think. Why?'

'I'll start with the name on that cup then.' I do tell, all of it: Iona informing me I was once called Chantelle, Marina's revelation, the Cincture trips, the Findings, Mr Straightfish . . .

Sardi sits back, eyebrows raised. 'I like my life, even though it's tuffard—gosses, cooking, mending . . . but yours! S'like a foitling novel! Two mecs fervid for yer, mysterious friend . . .'

'D'you think I'm mad to delve into my Cincture past, if it's true—to try and find my offspring?'

She studies me with an even gaze, dark eyes a little tearful. 'All I know is that if there was chancey of a gosse of mine being out there somelieu, I'd do *anytruc* to find 'em.'

I smile back at her. 'I think that's what I needed to hear—from another mother.'

'Spotton, Hox—you'll deal it, like any other trade or prob. And what's the worstist that can happen, eh?'

'Thanks, Sardi. Good chai and even better advice.' I glance once more at the lettering on the cup.

'Take it,' she offers.

I pass it to her and stand up to leave. 'No . . . I don't think I want the reminder. D'ac, better leave you to the pig mayhem and get back to my own tasks.'

She follows me back into the house and sighs at the abandoned scene before her.

'Where's big Mo gone?' She asks one of her younger brood.

Missi points at the staircase. 'Fracas—he gone see.'

'Stay here with babe. I'll be back—deux seconds.'

We hurry down the stairs towards the hubbub of voices.

A seething crowd has converged, beyond which I see bright violet lights flashing, washing the walls of the buildings. An eerie strident noise rises above the crowd's noise.

Sardi clutches at my arm, her eyes strained.

I shout at her above the din. 'What is it?'

'Shark visitation. Can you see Mo?'

LONDONIA

Sharks—merda.

I shake off her hand and climb up onto the table that's still upright in the street. A V shape cuts into the crowd, filling with black-uniformed men. Behind them a silver vehicle moves slowly. A mec seated in a metal turret directs a tube, sending bursts of white dust over the crowd. As several bods lunge forward in protest a collective cry fills the street, even louder than the eerie siren.

'Waster smoke!'

The Shark brigade smash out at the people crazed enough to approach the vehicle. Steel batons crunch into faces. Guns fire, blood spatters.

People flee, fallen bodies trampled under the stampede of feet.

I jump down and grab Sardi's arm as a wave of the dusty smoke envelops us.

'Allez—back indoors—now!'

A young mec streaks past us and stops as Sardi pulls him back by his knapper.

'Zeeb—where's Mo.'

He turns, eyes wild. 'Dunno. They might'a took 'im.'

Sardi sways; I catch her and half drag her back upstairs as the strident wail diminishes outside.

Back in their place, I lay her on the daybed in the corner of the room. The pig's half-dismembered body lies as people had in the street. I turn from the sight feeling sick. We sit in silence for a moment listening to the few remaining shouts from outside. The gosses huddle in another corner, eyes round with fear. Covering Sardi with a blanket, I go over to the small brood.

'Where does Unc live, Missi?'

'Scriven Street.'

'Go to your ma and I'll be back vite, vite, d'ac?'

As I run back downstairs I almost smash into the blotting-out-of-everything form of Uncle. Breathlessly, I convey the news. He says nothing but marches up the stairs as I stare after him. I call up.

'Tell Sardi I'm at the church when she wants me.'

He jerks his hand in a brief wave and I wonder whether to follow him back upstairs.

Deciding I can do nothing for the moment I walk back into the street and stare dumbly at the stains on the road where rooks peck at fragments of flesh.

Back at the church the silence almost hurts after the turmoil. Jarvis has taken Kafka out, some of the trading bags we had prepared now gone.

Zorro uncurls from a spot of sunlight on the table in the vestry. He stretches and jumps down revealing a folded piece of paper marked with Jarvis's chaotic script.

*This ca*me *from an ac*cess *point* delivery-*mec*

I slip an envelope from the paper, my already strained nerves twitchy. Cincture authorities? Someone's realised *Chantelle* has re-appeared? I sit and open the thing, pictures of prisons and worse forming in my head—that television broadcast I had seen at Mrs Caruso's house—public executions . . .

The opened sheet of paper has flowers on it. The childish script reveals Mrs Caruso's continuing concerns.

> Hello, Queen Finder. I Had to get this to you as it's very, very important! The salon is going to happen! We need you to source varnishes now!—any era will be fine, but must be ace condition—preferably from expensive make-up houses.

I crush the letter into a ball and open the range door to obliterate this pathetic missive but then stop and unfurl the paper again. Pathetic or not, this dame is still going to be useful.

Flipping the letter aside, I concoct a soup with what's left in the vegetable basket while my mind returns to thoughts of the violence.

LONDONIA

I lose myself in sorting through books after lunch, unaware of time passing until the dogs' barks, signalling scran-time, pull me from the task. Leaving the pile of encyclopaedias, I go outside to silence the noise with a bowl of scraps.

Odd that Jarvis is still out. A faint shiver of fear passes through me at the thought of the Sharks—could he have been in that street too? There had been a delivery of jins to be made to the hostel in Grimsby Street, nearby . . .

A cycle later I'm jumpy and anxious, and there's still no sign of him. I'm about to leash the dogs and go back up to Sardi's road when the main door grinds open and a familiar stream of profanities reaches my ears.

'Merding-pizz-fuk! Hox? You in?'

Relieved, I run down the aisle and find Jarvis fuming, second-best suit ripped and dusty, hat missing and blood streaked across his face.

'Merda! What happened?'

'Got caught up, din' I—with the cruddin' Sharks.'

He's shaking despite the relative warmth, even in the church. I lead him towards the vestry and make him sit while I run off the range's stored hot water into the bath.

'Get in and I'll add to it.' He strips silently while I get the stove going to its maximum and put the kettle and various pans of water on the top.

He sits morosely in the inch of water splashing at various wounds.

'We got any whisky?'

I search about and find a third-full bottle of pastis.

'Not quite—this'll have to suffice.'

He nods: 'Mugful.'

I pass him the required vessel and sit down on a chair next to the bath. I don't dare ask about Kafka.

Jarvis drains the mug and hands it back. 'I know wot yor thinking—Kafka. Don't get excited but 'e was ruffed up a bit.'

'What!'

LONDONIA

'It's fine. 'E's at Maud's and she said it's only minor stuff. Anyway, I left him as 'is shoes needs doing.'

I think of the horse-dame's oddly calming, straw-filled yard and her gentle round face. The fear falls away.

'When can we get him back?'

'Morrow—said she'd take a basket of veg for the work.'

I sigh with relief. 'D'ac. I'll go.' The kettle is humming, I lift it off and hold it over the pinky-grey bath water. 'Attention aux pieds.'

He pulls his feet in and swirls the water about.

'Apex. Thanks, H.'

'So, where's the hat?' I ask.

He scowls. 'Bastard Shark took it as a trophy.'

'But why were you there?'

'Saw Sardi's boy, din' I.'

I draw in my breath. 'Was he taken?'

'Dunno.'

I sigh, head hanging. 'Merda.' Jarvis coughs harshly and I remember the waster smoke. 'You didn't inhale that dust did you?'

'Nah—just messed up my suit, din' it.'

I pour us both another measure of pastis and sit staring at nothing, just thinking of Sardi.

'When you next goin' to see them dames again?' says Jarvis after a while.

'Soon as I can—that letter you took in had a request.'

'Wot for?'

'Nail varnish.'

'. . . Fukkin' *wot*?'

'You know. Colours for finger nails.'

He shakes his head. 'Ain't these nags got anything *real* to be doin'?'

I sigh. 'It's real to them, but yes, it seems somewhat unimportant after what we've just seen.'

'Under-fukin-statement . . . we got any soap?'

LONDONIA

I pass him a tablet I'd removed from the café's washroom.
'You're in luck.'
Jarvis takes the pink soap and sniffs it.
'D'you think you can lift some more goods from in there?'
I smile at my friend and stand up to get the next vessel of hot water.
'I'm sure they collectively wouldn't miss a few things.'
As I lift a saucepan from the range the dogs start up barking outside. Jarvis growls a response and starts to stand up.
'Who the pizz . . .'
I add the water and put the pan back.
'I'll go. It might be Sardi.'
He sloshes back into the water and I scoot to the door. Outside, the great-hounds are in a frenzy of recognition but not for Sardi. The mirror reveals the squat form of Bert the Swagger. I open the gate and recoil slightly from the peculiar smell that always surrounds him.
'Bert . . .'
He takes off a battered straw hat and lunges towards me squishing a wet kiss on my cheek.
'Hoxton . . . ravishing, as always.'
His dark eyes rake me and I wonder which particular tome of zeitporn he's been reading in his stilt-hut this morn.
'A social visit?' I enquire.
He brushes back the few strands of hair remaining on his scalp, replaces the hat and grins. His collection of gold teeth gleam in the sunlight.
'Partly, my seraph. Just found myself wondering how your Cincture-connection is going these days.' He looks hopefully towards the church doorway. 'Shall we go in?'
Feeling relieved that Jarvis is in the vestry I nod and gesture towards the interior.
'You'll have to excuse Jarvis being in the bath.'
Bert follows me, my Finder brogues clopping on the flagstones.

LONDONIA

'It worked out for you then—the bath.'

'Brilli, thanks.'

Jarvis's baritone version of 'I did it my way' crescendos as I open the vestry door. The song cuts and he looks around.

'Bert, you old bedswerver. Come in, take the weight off. Drink?'

Bert looks about the room as he removes his decrepit safari jacket.

'I don't suppose you have a snifter of gin, do you?'

Jarvis heaves himself up and out of the bath, wrapping himself in a blanket.

' 'Scuse me, Bert, while I troove someing not covered in blud.' He picks up his stained clothes and disappears to his wood house.

I gesture towards the bottle.

'No gin, I'm afraid . . . pastis?'

He nods. 'If you have ice.'

I smile at the irony, pour out a measure and hand it to him.

'So, you've heard rumours then, Bert.'

'Only vague ones.'

'And you were hoping I might be able to Find something for you in there?'

He strokes his small mangy beard. 'Well, if the opportunity arose, shall we say.'

I sigh. 'Drugs?'

'That would be lovely . . . and as they are ahead in porn-inventiveness, *that* could be interesting. Who knows what a society that invests itself totally in pleasure might be capable of producing, don't you wonder?'

Suddenly his eerily polite voice talking of such irrelevancies infuriates me.

'Bert! There is more to life than drugs and sex.'

He smiles infuriatingly. 'Like what, my dear?'

'Like the fact that my friend's oldest gosse nearly got taken by the sharks.'

LONDONIA

'Ah . . . you saw the latest show of Cincturian Law firsthand, then?'

I sit down opposite him, pour myself a drink and glug it back, shaking my head as the fluid sears its way down my throat.

'. . .Yes. I went to see Sardi and when I came out there was a huge vehicle and smoke, and people being dragged up screaming . . .' Tears rise. My words shake. 'It was the first time I've actually seen a raid so close up.'

Bert's smile has disappeared. He straightens up in the chair with an air of someone relishing the prospect of delivering information.

'I've heard that younger people are in great demand for the food-plantations, and certain experimentation.'

'Experimentation?'

'It's a wealthy place, the Cincture, its occupants concerned with self-image . . . and longevity.'

'So, captives could be taken there depending on . . .'

'The demand, either way.'

The room suddenly feels suffocating. I stand up and pull the window cord. The top arched piece grates down a little and I see sparrows hopping about in the sycamore tree outside.

Bert appears silently next to me. He places a hand on my shoulder and I turn, noting the gleam in his eyes.

'Like I say,' he murmurs. 'You know they still practice drawing and quartering in there—without the hanging part . . .'

The door opens and Jarvis walks in, resplendent in a yellow and pink flowered shirt. He notes my expression and thumps Bert on the back.

'What fears you puttin' into H, Bert.'

'Just informing her of what I've heard about the Sharks, seeing as she—and you, apparently, had the misfortune to witness one of their missions . . . anyway, I'd better be going. I've a tooth to extract for someone in Brick Lane.'

'Poor bastards,' grimaces Jarvis. 'Ain't you found a better way of knocking persons out than gnole?'

222

LONDONIA

Bert smiles at me. 'Open to suggestions, and of course, goods, if you find a way in there, Hoxton.'

'You'll be the first to know, Bert,' I say, hastening his exit by stepping over and opening the door wider.

I sit down again, brooding over Bert's words while they walk to the main door, voices diminishing within the echoes of the church. Jarvis returns and notes my uneasiness.

'Big, foitling pinch 'a salt, H. You know what he's like, Bert.'

'Yes, but do you actually know anyone that's come back from being seized?'

He shakes his head slowly as he rounds up the empty vessels before sitting down next to me, his hand on mine.

'Can't say I do . . . no.'

Capitula 15

Three days have passed and my searching has procured nothing other than two gloopy bottles of varnish, both with scratches and the printing unreadable.

I now stand outside a strangely-pristine, 1920s semi-detached house in Leesbridge where, I have been told by a shouting-house contact, lives an eccentric dame with her fine collection of cosmetics from before the Curtain.

The garden is also immaculate, the privet hedge as it might have been in the early 2030s. A clipping sound emanates from behind it. I open the little wrought-iron gate and peer around the greenery. A bespectacled man with neatly combed hair and a checked shirt lowers a pair of shears and looks at me.

'Hello, love. Are you lost?'

In time, perhaps . . . 'I was looking for Mrs Myers?'

'Ah—my wife. She's in the house. Just knock.'

'Thanks.' I walk up the weed-free path and rap on a door which looks as if it's just been painted such is its gloss.

The door opens. 'Tea's nearly—oh, thought you were Colin . . .' She looks at me suspiciously. 'Are you selling something?'

Words seem to have run off. I just want to stand and stare at this extraordinary dame's cloud of brittle blonde hair, thick blue eyelid-colour and crows' feet lashes. Her clothes too—bright turquoise, orange swirling patterns. The *fashion through the ages* book back in the vestry would suggest her to be from the 1970s. A hundred years ago.

'Has the cat got your—'

'Sorry.' I cut her short, realising I haven't started this Find off too well. 'No. Not selling. I was hoping to buy, or rather trade something. I heard from a friend that you have the most extraordinary stock of pre-Curtain makeup products.'

Her heavily lipsticked mouth produces a slight smile.

'He or she is right. I might consider letting certain things go. It depends what you're after.'

'Nail varnish.' I mentally prepare for the smile to purse into an, *ah, if it was anything else . . .* but it doesn't.

'You'd better come in then.'

I follow her down a hallway where a line of shoes sits neatly paired, an assortment of hats hanging by colour order, and into a front room which is more of an art gallery—bottles and boxes of cosmetics as the paintings and sculptures. The decor echoes her clothes: geometric patterns of bright colour on the walls and a shaggy carpet of lurid green.

I stop gawping and start trading. 'This is . . . beautiful,'

She brushes a hand over a veneered sideboard and *tuts* at the result.

'It's so difficult to keep the dust off, don't you find?'

'Oh—yes. Absolutely. If you don't mind me asking . . . how has this all been so well preserved from the last century—the 70s?'

'Ah—no this was the revival. 2034. I loved it so much after all that terrible austere stuff.'

'But how did you manage to keep it like this during the unknown time and before that—the Final Curtain, the chaos?'

Mrs Myers picks up an orange plastic cat and rubs a small mark from its head.

'Guns, really.'

'Sorry?'

'Colin—it's what he collects. I don't know how many people he might have shot but we kept everything just as we wanted it here.'

Suddenly I want to be far away from this house; perhaps walking around the Parkplace, *without* a gun.

'I see . . . so, would you be able to trade some nail polish?'

LONDONIA

She gestures. I sit down in a violently floral chair. 'I'll see what I can offer you. And of course, it depends on what you might offer me. Right. Polish, polish—here we are.' She places a blue plastic box on the nest of tables next to me, lifts the lid and splays the various sections. 'These are L'Oréal, and these, Estée Lauder and Yves Saint Laurent. The black glass bottles are from a company called Orphic who made a limited range between 2029 and 31. I don't think I could let those go.'

I carefully pick up a couple of the first ones and inspect them for damage. They appear unopened and untouched.

'These are unused?'

'Yes. I have ones I do use, but most of them are mint. You see I used to work in Harvey Nic's and we got a discount. So, I just kept collecting . . .' She glances at my outfit that I'd actually thought about due to the nature of this visit—fairly clean jins, a cotton shirt and *not* gardening boots.

'Why do *you* want nail polish?'

'It's not for me. I'm sourcing certain things for a client in the Cincture.'

Her expression changes at the name. 'You've been in there?'

'Several times.'

'Is it as they say? Wonderful shops and everything—as it was before the Curtain?'

'I suppose it is, yes.'

'And this person wants *my* nail polish?'

'Yes.' I wonder whether it matters if I say more but decide she might like the idea. 'It's actually for a nail salon they are starting. She wants as much original stock as possible.'

'How marvellous! Maybe they'd like an assistant . . . Of course, I know so much about antique makeup.'

'Possibly yes, but for now, could we decide what I can take?'

'Absolutely. Have any of these—the peacock blue is rather special, and that yellow.'

I choose ten bottles, show her what I had brought for trading and we get down to the deal, deciding on two pairs of the reading glasses, a pot of Jarvis's mushroom caviar, a book on the history of *Vogue* magazine and five branz.

With a promise from me that I will ask if she might be able to recommence her career in cosmetics retail over the wall, I carefully pack the precious bottles, say a hasty goodbye to Colin and his shears and walk back home via the marshes.

Jarvis is scrabbling around with bits of old pipe under the bath in the vestry as I walk in. He looks up, hair wild, eyes wilder.

'Ah—apex timing. Hold this will yer.'

I drop my bag to a chair and go to assist. 'I didn't know you were going to do this t-dui.'

'Just 'ad the urge. Did you get the foitling nail stuff?'

'I did—and more than I thought. The dames'll have a big trade bill to pay back when I go in on the morrow.'

We fix the last bit of pipe and Jarvis shuffles out from under the bath.

'Job's goodly.' He wipes his hands on a rag and flumps into the armchair. 'Got great news, H.'

I place my bag on the table and sit down expectantly. 'So?'

'Sardi's lad's back. Two gosses found him down a snicket.'

'And he's d'ac?'

'Broke arm and bleus all over but yeah—fine.'

'Oh. The Guv be praised!'

Jarvis grins, head nodding, 'Yeah—s' brilli. Goodly great.' Then the grin flattens. 'Ah—morrow you said fr' goin' back in there?'

'Yes. Why? What's prevued?'

'Remember, there's them bods comin' 'ere mid-aft for the Snash?'

The remainder of this sevday forms in my mind. 'Oh—yes. Is that a problem?'

'Nah—'cept there's a apex shout on in Holborn. Need us both 'ere.'

LONDONIA

'It'll be a quick trip,' I assure him. 'Just got to deliver the goods and back out.'

Capitula 16

It's a warm, windy day, but no eddies of rubbish blow about in *these* streets.

As I wait, cleansed and brown-suited for a shaw, my confidence and hope both seem to be leaking away. Visions of the Shark incident and Bert's gleefully exaggerated tales of prison loom darkly in my mind. I focus on the Gershwin's shop-keeper's words: *I noticed he had a mark on his neck* . . .

I don't want to stand around. In fact, why not walk? I go back to the cleansing area and ask for directions. One of the now-familiar dames gives me an *A to Z* with a stern warning to bring it back. I lean against a wall for a moment and examine the pages compared to a pre-Curtain one back in the vestry. The streets, parks and important structures are beautifully marked out, the sprawl of Londonia an indifferent shading. I'd very much like to keep this; perhaps if bribery is as rife as I imagine it to be . . .

I set off in a Westerly direction, enjoying the sensation of pacing an evenly paved surface, mind not partially occupied with negotiating debris or possible lurking trouble. The bright-quarter has brought change to the Cincture. The shop windows I pass are full of displays echoing the warmer weather. People pass by in suits and dresses of lighter fabrics, the early twentieth-century styling still very much in evidence.

The Cincture streets seem to be undergoing a collective and unnecessary overhaul of railing-repainting, stone-scrubbing, tree-trimming by dark-green uniformed, I suspect, Londonians.

Quarter of a clockface or so I have reached Wigmore Street, where about halfway down splays a pile of wood, paint-pots and stepladders which I assume is to do with kitting out the nail salon. As I reach the shop, a mec in overalls appears from the interior and nods at me.

'Hoxton?'

'That's me.'

'They've gone to have coffee at Quixy's down the road there. Mrs Caruso said you could join them or wait here.'

'Any idea how long they will be?'

He looks at a paint-spattered watch. 'Said they'd be back by eleven. It's nearly that now.'

'D'ac, thanks.'

I wander down the street a little way taking in all the details of this calm and ordered place so different from the clatter and colour of just a couple of miles away. Further down the road a dame emerges from a shop and waits for a chauffeur to open the door of a bronze-coloured limousine. The shop assistant emerges with a small pyramid of wrapped boxes, placing them carefully in the car's boot. An elegant couple pass me, both with a clutch of stiff, glossy carrier bags. I catch his words: 'It'll mean a promotion to State House . . .'

'Hoxton!' I stop earwigging and turn to see the bulbous form of Mrs Caruso, her hand beckoning me back. I catch her up and she grips my arm. 'Come see the salon! The others are there—well, not Iona. She wasn't feeling so switched . . . did you find anything?'

I gesture to my bag. 'I did. But before we go in, can I ask you something.'

She glances back to the salon with a slight sigh of impatience. 'All right. Yes?'

I take a deep breath and hope she won't combust at what I'm about to say.

'If you want the contents of my bag, my trade this time will be for you to arrange a meeting for me with Dr Caruso.'

She cocks her head like a fluffy, surprised dog. 'Why?'

'I'd rather not say but I think he may be able to assist me.'

LONDONIA

'Oh. Well, I can ask him. He's *always* busy, but . . .' she glances at my bag, 'I can be persuasive.'

We are back by the pile of wood and a very clean shop front that bears the name: Blanchett's Nail Parlour painted in an aqua green swirling font.

'Incredible,' I say as we go inside to meet the others. 'You only had the idea a few days ago.'

'My husband had this space and was thinking of selling but *I* stepped in,' says Mrs Nash, overhearing my words. 'I've ordered all the kit and we've been on a crash course of nail-art. Open for business by the end of the week!'

'The publicity mentions,' adds Mrs Caruso, 'unusual colours, retro, exclusive, famous pre-Whiteout names. So . . . counting on you, Ms Finder.' She looks anxiously at me, and, as I open my bag to bring out the prized bottles, I recall Iona's joke regarding ear protection . . .

Needing to escape, I leave them to it, after another quiet word with Mrs Caruso to finalise the deal: a letter fixing a date for a meeting to be sent as soon as possible. I wonder whether to go straight to Gershwin's and hope—ridiculously—that fate might somehow procure a sighting of my son, or whether to call at Iona's house first to see if she really is ill. Deciding on the latter, I walk swiftly to Hanover Terrace praying *Bob* might take pity on me and produce a sandwich.

I arrive, stomach clamouring now as my imagined sandwich has mutated into a three-course meal featuring a large steak.

Iona opens the door a few moments after I've pressed the bell, and is evidently not ill judging by the fact she is obviously dressed to go out—in the brown trouser suit.

'Hoxton! She hugs me and I feel for the first time a real frisson of recollection and warmth for her. I hug her back, close to weeping. 'Hey, Lady Finder,' she murmurs, 'what's happened?'

'Can I come in and tell you—and possibly 'seech you for a bit of scran?'

LONDONIA

'Of course.' She ushers me in and yells up the staircase for Bob. He appears almost instantly, a suit in hand. 'Bob—could you make up a plate of something for Hoxton, please.'

'Certainly. Delighted.'

'Why no flouncy dress?' I ask her as we go into the lounge.

'Because I like this—unencumbered by layers of superfluous cloth. Mm, could be the title for my book.'

'You're writing one?'

'Oh—I'm dabbling but I want to, yes. It's you—and Londonia. I feel as if I've been trapped in aspic for years.'

'Most literary . . . by the way, talking of viscous substances, I've delivered ten time-untouched bottles of nail varnish to your cohorts.'

'Were they *moved*?'

'To the point of orgasm.'

Bob enters the room and raises a very neat eyebrow at my last word as he places a tray on the table. 'Can't promise that, Miss Hoxton, but I hope you find my soup satisfying.' He smiles as he leaves the room and I grasp in that instant his probable gayster-ness.

'I know someone who'd love to meet Bob,' I remark, sitting down in front of the bowl of beetroot soup.

Iona joins me at the table. 'Who?'

'Jarvis. He's still in mourning for his lover, but on the lookout.'

'You think Bob is . . . homosexual?'

'Undeniably.'

'Oh . . . really?'

'Why? Would that be a problem in the Cincture?'

Iona looks at me as if I've suggested he might be necrophiliac. 'I told you—in here, women are for looking at, etc, men are the money-hunters and anyone out of that mould . . . well, it's not easy. I mean even me wearing this is going to cause consternation amongst our social strata.' She stops as she probably notes my slight drifting from her words. 'Sorry. You have things to tell me?'

'One thing, and your advice.'

'Listening.'

I spoon up the last of the soup and place the bowl back on the tray. 'Bob is a marvel! So . . . it's *possible* that the woman in the Gershwin's shop might have met—briefly—my son.'

My friend's eyes shine. 'Hoxton—that's creddo!'

'It is only possible, like I said. But at least it's a small lead.'

'But how did she know?'

I mention the probably unreliable fact that she had noticed the strange mark. Iona nods slowly. 'I see . . . and the piece of advice?'

'I asked Mrs Caruso as to whether her husband might be able to help me—being in the medical area.'

Iona considers my words. '. . . Caruso is a complete shit but certainly knows everyone. He's another womaniser and I'm never too sure if Beccy knows or not—possibly doesn't care as long as he keeps providing the lifestyle. I think he'll honour your deal to keep his wife happy.'

'Could you remind her for me—in case in all the shop-excitement she forgets?'

'Of course. How did you get the stuff by the way?'

'A cosmetic aficionado who used to work in the old Harvey Nicholls store . . .

'Oh—I just remembered, Mrs Caruso said you were unwell.'

'I feigned a headache,' smiles Iona. 'I want to start distancing myself from them and re-connect with women who think and discuss things other than their appearance. Matthew won't like it but . . .'

'Scrote-bag to him?' I suggest.

'If that's what I think it is, yes. So, are you going back to Londonia now?'

I pause, thinking of my earlier words to Jarvis.

'. . . Should do, but I need to try Gershwin's again.'

LONDONIA

'Don't get too hopeful,' warns Iona. You're pinning a lot onto something I saw a very long time ago. Anything could have happened. The mark might have even been removed.'

The café is busy this aft. I decline the offer of a table and make my way to the shop where the grey-haired dame is engaged in sewing a button on something. She looks up.

'Ah. Our Londonian visitor. Did you ask Miss Holt about your quest?'

I recall what she had said about the café manageress's work times. 'I assumed she wouldn't be here as it's still the morning.'

'No dear—I said she's here in the afternoons.'

'Oh.' I turn and finger the velvet of an evening gown, feeling pizzed at her.

'However,' she continues, 'I might have some information for you.'

'. . . You might?'

'Possibly. Yesterday, one of the young men came in and took a liking to a pair of cricket trousers. The waist was too wide so I suggested a tuck. He agreed and asked if he could pay and they be sent to his address.'

'He of the green eyes, blond hair and the mark.'

'Well . . . I couldn't swear it was who you seek as he had a silk scarf about his neck, but I'm fairly sure it was the same lad as before.'

'And you have his name and address?' I feel a buzz of excitement zip through me. She must have noticed something as the eyes narrow a little behind the gold-framed spectacles.

'Can I ask why you wish to know about him?'

This is something I should have prepared for. Hunting for my son might sound a little too memorable.

LONDONIA

'Well . . . I've been told he may be my long-lost brother.'

The last word is tremulous and her expression softens. 'I see. Well, perhaps I can help you. I do have a favour to ask of you though.'

'Certainly—what is it?'

'Do you know a good Finder?'

A quarter clockface later, I'm walking up the King's Road, with the stub of a fucsia-coloured lipstick in my pocket having promised to Find a replacement of the exclusive pre-Curtain brand she has been eking out for the last few cycles. Repeating the given address as a sort of mantra against fear I turn into Markham Street and find number 6, a well-preserved Georgian house. A maid opens the door at my knock.

'Yes. Can I help you?'

'Is this the Cliveborn-Smith residence?' I ask, trying to look official.

'It is indeed.'

'Are they at home?'

'No, madame.'

Thank the Guv. 'It was actually their son Rupert I wished to see.'

'Please come in and I will enquire if he is available. What name is it?'

'My name is . . . Perth—Mary Perth.'

She shows me into a sumptuous sitting room and goes to enquire. A few moments later I hear feet thumping on the stairs and a cross youthful voice.

'You should have told them to go away, Braithwaite. I've cricket practice in a few minutes.'

The door opens and a young mec walks in frowning. He's struggling with a half inside-out jacket, hand searching for the arm-hole 'Can I help you? Or was it Mother or Father you wanted to speak with?'

The neck of his shirt splays open as he fights with the garment. I see the mark. It's the result of high-hormone biting from

LONDONIA

a young lover. Nothing more. The vague shape of Iceland, perhaps. And the angry eyes are grey. Not green.

Time to move on.

'Actually, I think it might be better to see all of you. It's with regard to a Census survey, and I can see you are busy.'

I slip past him, walk down the hall and out of the door feeling their incredulous stares.

Capitula 17

China on wood. Thunk.

'Tea, Hoxton. Oi! Wakey-fukin'-wakey.'

I wrench my weary head from the pillow to see the belligerent face of Jarvis.

I groan at his expression.

'So, wot in the rotting l'enfer of Croydonia happened?' he continues. 'We missed a good trade at the Holborn Shout coz I 'ad to be here to see them fukkas about the Snash.'

I wonder where to start, apart from, sorry. 'Is it darking?'

'Nah—it's the morn. I stayed over at Jake's last eve—just got in.'

I hand him a bar of chocolate Iona had given me and watch his expression ease a little.

'So, have you got half a clockface?' I ask.

He crosses his arms and looks at me expectantly. 'All yours. Let's 'ave it from the point I dropped y'off.'

I tell him most of it after which he flops onto the bed.

'Christ in a eel-bag, H. You don't exactly sit around knittin' do yer?'

'I'd get bored.'

'Well, I got someing else to add to the mixipie.'

'What?' I ask, apprehension creeping.

'Straightfish, that's wot.'

'So . . .'

'Had one of his henchies here—twice! Wiv more flowers 'n merde. He's serious, Hox. And someone saw you with Tom at Jake's bacchanal.'

'. . . Not as in *saw* us.'

'Nah—not in *the carnal* but he did get the drift.'

LONDONIA

'What should I do?'

'Go and see 'im? Tell him in no uncertain.'

I sigh, wishing for once we had phones like they did in there—a pigeon message won't suffice.

'D'ac. I'll do it later.'

Jarvis sits up and jams his hat back on. 'Anylane, enough of that gold-nabbing walrus. Back to important stuff 'ere. You got the diary?'

Shuffling off the bed I find the black book and flip through to t-dui. 'Nothing marked other than garden stuff.' I close the book and look at my friend. 'I haven't said thanks—*and* sorry for dealing with everything here, and the trade-loss.'

'Aw, ça va. P'raps it was cruddy, anylane.' He jerks a thumb towards the crypt. 'Fancy that pheasant all roastied-up?'

'Wonderful,' I enthuse.

Jarvis stands up and stretches.

'D'ac—I'll prep the beast.'

He's about to walk from the vestry but turns back, serious now. 'Just gotta ask. All that beauty stuff and Madame this 'n that in the Cincture—sure you wouldn't want to swap?'

'No.'

'Sure?'

'Jarvis! This is reality for me. Here, this building, these animals, you.'

'Last, behind the beasts, eh?' he grins as I hop over to hug him, breathing in his familiar scent of wool, tobacco and Londonia.

'D'ac,' I say, releasing him and looking for clothes. 'Think I'll get some of the garden jobs done while you put the roast on. The potatoes need work and I'd like to put in the onion seedlings.'

I leave the vestry and head to fresh air, physical activity and to re-charge my optimism batteries run down after meeting the wrong young mec.

LONDONIA

A clockface later, I put down the fork, stretch and look over the earthed-up ranks with pleasure. A couple more months and we should be able to lift some new, flaky-skinned potatoes. The remaining broad beans look good, almost recovered from the storm. As I pick the ripe pods, I wonder if Jake would trade some for a bit of his mysterious insight.

I harvest a few leeks, plant the onions and garlic, then sit in the sun for a while watching blackbirds and robins searching in the overturned black earth. Generations of Hackrovians, and my compost system have made this patch of soil so fertile that you only have to drop a seed in and it's off. Green fingers, Jarvis says, maybe that too. Who knows what rests in my genes?

Back in the church, I wash the earth off my hands, smiling a little as I imagine the nail boutique in Wigmore Street no doubt full of dames who have never made a furrow, added compost and planted onions, or had the satisfaction of seeing them grow. Beans packed, I go back to the vestry to see how the scran prep is going. Jarvis stands back from the slab of wood and I admire the plucked bird.

He unearths the large cast iron casserole from the dresser and clanks it down.

'Got some beef stock from that cow-mec in the Parkplace too.' He places the body inside the pot, pours on red wine and the jug of stock. After a search in his jacket pockets he finds a twig of bay leaves and a lemon. 'Gave me these too, he did.'

'Where in l'enfer did he get lemons?'

'The Walthamstow gardeners—that commune up there. Got a few citrus trees there now. Course the fruit's rare as a true apology, but it's a start,' He notes my packet of beans, 'You off somelieu?'

'Just nipping up to see Jake.'

'D'ac—late aft for the pheasant.'

LONDONIA

Today, the Parkplace could almost be one of those cheap oil paintings we trade sometimes. A gar in Muswell Mountain makes them: slick, quick and full of comforting images: cottages, rambling roses and slumbering cats. People love them, and we have scattered his work all over this grimy city for a goodly markup.

Jake's hut sits in a bower of lilac surrounded by a blur of early yellow butterflies. From it drifts a sweet melody; something I recognise. A hidden memory surfaces briefly: a panelled room, rows of red velvet chairs, a whispering voice—*You next, child*. I try to keep the images but they fade, and I return to the blossom's pungent scent and the rusted metal of Jake's hut.

The door grinds open and he looks out, violin in hand.

'Thought it was you—beans and trouble, eh? Come in and have some killer ale.'

I follow him in and sit down on one of his homemade constructions, a sort of pallet wood nod to a fireside wing chair.

'Why don't you play outside?' I ask.

He looks around the tin walls spotted with pictures. 'I like the resonance in here.'

'Ah . . .'

'You've been back in there Jarvis tells me,' he says, eyes bright in the gloom. I nod and he continues. 'So, you have decisions. Retreat back to the life you know, or delve further into one you don't?'

'I *think* I know what I have to do.'

He puts a hand on my shoulder and I feel that strange sensation his touch provokes—as if my blood itself was listening. 'The question would never be quieted, would it?' he says. '*My gosse* out there somewhere.' His hand rises again and he goes over to his little kitchen area to return with two mugs of frothing beer. I stare at the words printed on my vessel: *Keep Calm and Carry on Shopping*. He shrugs, smiles and points to his mug that has *I Love Cleethorpes* stamped across it.

'Jarvis gave me them after a shelf fell down and the old ones smashed.'

'Oh . . .'

'Sorry, bigger trucs in your mind. You must go with your instincts, Hoxton.'

I take a swig of ale and think on his words. He's right of course.

'This is good stuff. Who made it?'

'A mec in Old Street. He's just started up and is experimenting with fruit beer—this here, apple and raspberry.'

I suddenly realise that I have no idea how old Jake is, and if he had, or has a family. It's just one of those things like trees have leaves and the sky has clouds. Jake is Jake: woolly hat, large hooded eyes, long tapering fingers.

'Jake?'

'Uh?'

'Did you ever have gosses?'

He looks unusually grave for a moment. 'Yes, I had one, a dame too.' Silence falls, apart from a small chewing sound in the hut somewhere. 'Mice, I think,' he says, unconcernedly.

Perhaps I shouldn't ask more, but it's too intriguing. 'So . . . what happened?'

He shakes his head. 'I don't talk of it, Hoxton—stays locked in my heart.' The large eyes glisten. He passes a hand across his face and smiles again. 'More suds?'

'A little, thanks.'

He stands from his carved stool and fetches the jug.

'Beans for me?'

'Straight from the plants this morning.'

'Nickel. Think I need to do more with my own veg patch, Hoxton. Would you help me?'

LONDONIA

'Of course, easy with the pond here, and the soil's good.'

Jake slips a clay pipe from his shirt pocket, lifts the lid of a box and taking a large pinch of tobacco, stuffs the bowl. It's one I haven't seen before, unusual with an intricate moulding of what looks like the devil's head. The buffed clay is bright in the dim light, like the belly of a fish turning in dark water.

'It's a beauty, isn't it?' he says and draws up the first smoke.

'Where did you find it?' I ask

'Someone I helped gave me it. Taken from the mud of Lady Thames, it was.'

'Play me something, Jake.'

'Surely. What would be your pleasure?'

'The piece you were playing before I came in.'

'Reminds you of stuff, eh?'

'Perhaps.'

He tenderly lifts the violin from its velvet nest and nudges it under his chin. Pipe wedged in the corner of his mouth, he lifts the bow and the notes rise with the curl of smoke. No memory of red-seated chairs returns, no whispering voice, just a ghostly image of the young mec who had given me his jacket.

The piece finishes. Jake swings the instrument away from his chin and lovingly wipes the wood with a cloth.

'You'll find him, Hox. Have faith.'

'Thanks, Jake.'

As I sit with my friend, the name Straightfish enters my temporarily placid thoughts. Jake's radio-mind tunes in.

'Trouble elsewhere, H? . . . over the river?'

I sigh, wishing I'd never made that deal, however useful the coinage is.

'What do you know of the Vaux-hauler's skipper?'

'. . . Likely not nearly as much as you, dear friend. A dalliance you now regret?'

'Utterly. What should I do . . . write to him, see him?'

LONDONIA

'He has a certain notoriety for being . . . inflexible, obdurate even, a *straight* fish. You could try either but I imagine you may be stuck with his affections.'

Great 'Hm. Think I'll try face-to-face. This aft—in daylight!'

I rise, thank him again and walk back to St Leonard's hoping Jarvis's promised roast might be ready. On unlocking the church door, a sound of distant swearing greets my ears. Entering the vestry, I find Jarvis red-faced and a few broken plates on the floor.

'Sorry, H,' he grunts. 'Couldn't get the foitling range hot enough—ça va now, but it'll be a tad lateron.'

I decide the over-river trip might be imminent. 'Not to worry. I'll go and deal with the head Vaux-hauler now.'

'Had a good chat with Jake, did yer?'

'Very good. I asked him his advice about Straightfish . . .'

'Ha. Bet 'e said you'd dug yerself in good 'n legit, eh?'

'Yep . . . what happened to the plates, by the way? Bit of a fire-failure tantrum?'

He grins at me. 'Yeah, maybe. Don't get distracted, eh—this'll be ready by darking.'

'I won't miss it!'

A thudding of footsteps and a colourful argument precedes Bartholomew Straightfish.

'Putain de merda! Told Pepito not to let them go until we had the deal . . . Ah! The angel has flown back.' He dismisses the minion and strides up to me. 'Charmant—le look garçon. The topper suits you, my lovely.'

I step back from his overpowering nearness. 'Bartholomew. Is there somewhere we can talk quietly?'

'My bath?'

LONDONIA

'No. I mean a *serious* discussion.'

He slips a great hand around my waist. 'It could be serious—I've already made my proposal.'

I remove his hand and push him to an empty part of the concourse as I compose my words.

'I am flattered by your offer but I can't possibly accept.'

A thunder storm seems to build within this tiled interior.

'. . . How not?'

'The other person I spoke of—I love him.' The words stun me *and* Mr Straightfish. Once out there, I can see them hanging there all pulsating and glittery—the truth.

El Capo stares at me. 'So, what my associate saw at the Parkplace fete was true. You in the possession of a . . . logger?'

'He's not just a logger. He's a good mec, and I wasn't in his *possession*.'

'He has nothing.'

'Wealth is unimportant.'

'Scrote! I can give you everything—warmth, security, primo-scran, Italian silks . . .'

'I don't need anything you can give me. It was a remarkable encounter for one darking—leave it at that.'

I walk away and he calls after me. 'I know things about you, Angel. You might not want to forget that.'

This encounter was swifter than I had imagined, but my mind feels jumbled, unhinged. What things does he know about me?

If the sea was nearby I would have run to it, sat on the shore and gazed out on its great watery mass. But we have the river. Leaving the Vaux-hauler's premises, I scoot over to Nine Elms Rafts and find enough silvers to hire one of their planky vessels for a clockface. The earlier wind has dropped and for the month of Avi, it's hot on the water. I shrug off my coat, place the hat carefully under the rowing seat and set off, stroke left, stroke right, until the exercise clears all the jangling thoughts away. I pass fisher-mecs returning from the outer estuaries, bods just making crossings to the other side, and narrowly miss a larger,

LONDONIA

restored ship full of revellers: a wedding judging by the flowers and vines laced into the rigging. Gulls and cormorants dive, dogs swim, and swaggers comb the tidal muds. I love the *Pan*. Why would I ever want what exists on the other side of those burnished walls.

Hauling out my pocket watch and noting the long hand has almost completed its circle, I row back to collect Kafka, heart hammering, but with a more orderly mind.

A half clockface later, I'm unlocking the church door to be greeted by excited dogs and an enticing smell mixing with the usual scents of stone and ancient wood. Jarvis appears from the vestry as I walk up the aisle.

'Acme timing, Kitten. We got any wine anywhere—secret stash?'

'Sadly no,' I reply, entering the vestry, 'and to be truthful, my head would prefer water.' The bird sits in its pot surrounded by potatoes and carrots, spicy steam rising.

I double-take at the sight. 'Where did you get potatoes?'

'That mec at Londonia-fields—one with the pike-swamp wot used to be a swimming pool. You should see that garden now—manifico. Anylane, I swapped some cabbage as we've a load.' He gestures to the table. 'Sit, an' I'll make you an 'appy dame. Fact, you look quite beamy already. Wot 'appened?'

'I saw him, told him I love Tom and that there's no chance of me becoming Mrs Straightfish and then I took a Nine-Elms raft out and rowed a lot until I felt like me again.'

'. . . 'E didn't try and strangle you or anyfing?'

'I think the stories must be exaggerated. He seemed quite calm—a bit affronted perhaps.'

'You told El Capo you love someone else when 'e'd proposed to yer . . .'

'It's the truth. I only just realised.'

Jarvis shakes his head. 'Don't reckon he's gonna just say *yeah, whatever*. I'd keep all yer sensors on max. Anylane, fuk 'im. Let's eat!'

245

LONDONIA

Jarvis carves a great chunk of herby meat and puts it on my plate along with the vegetables. 'Gravy there in that pitcher.'

'Thanks. So, back to normality, at least until I can figure out a way to start my gosse-search again.'

Jarvis starts to say something about my utterance but waves a hand. 'D'ac. Normality. I was thinking 'bout taking some of them medical kits to the shout on at Holborn, or d'you reckon a spont-market?'

'Let's try a spont in the morn—we've got spare female chicks too, and I've got those stupid shoes to get rid of.'

Jarvis waves a loaded fork at me. 'Take 'em back to Fred's?'

I reply, words obscured by wonderfully greasy potato.

'. . . Will do.'

'D'ac. Bit more.'

'Go on then.'

Capitula 18

The morn sun streaks across the vestry table. Jarvis sits reading a trial two-page newspaper from the Sureditch press.

'Anything terrifying?' I ask, looking through our agenda.

He lowers it and shakes his head. 'Nah—s'just an experiment by Jake and the others—goat found on roof, landlord of the Cat 'n Lizard exposed himself to a party of fisher-dames . . . that sort 'a thing.'

'Ah. World-shattering.'

'S' start, innit, and it's good to get the old press whirrin' again.'

'Definitely. I want to get involved when things are a bit calmer.' As I bend to look at the diary again, the tail of a last eve dream suddenly re-emerges: Tom in a violent argument with Straightfish somelieu. *Tom.*

'No pigeon news yesdy, was there?' I ask.

Jarvis folds the paper. 'Nope. Why, expecting anytruc?'

'I was just wondering about Tom.'

'When's he s'posed to be back?'

'It was a bit vague—a few sevdays.' Thinking of breakfast now I'm more awake, I stand up and check the various possibilities.

'We got no bread,' Jarvis says as I look in the tin box. 'And the bread-mec's got a problem with the ovens.'

I feel a craving for fresh, doughy bread that's not going to go away.

'D'you think that gar with the donkey and cakes might be up at the Parkplace orjordui?'

'Reckon it'd be worth a scan. Jake said he's there quite oft.'

'I'll take the hounds out and see.'

'D'ac.'

LONDONIA

A quarter clockface later, we arrive, panting—all of us, outside the Parkplace gate where I am in luck. The cake-mec's donkey is there, standing patiently, tail swishing at a drone of bluebottles. The space is quiet so I unleash the trembling hounds. Fagin smiles at me and bounds away, Tilly following.

A scent of gingerbread rises from one of the many sacks and baskets attached to the donkey. I'm just wondering if I could possibly serve myself, when the mec returns wiping his mouth.

'Sorry, lady. Got to be taking coffee with Jake there.'

'It can be difficult to get away,' I smile.

'What would be your fancy on this sparkling morn?'

Almost expecting him to break into song and dance in his checked trousers, I point towards the ginger-smelling sack.

'Gingerbread, if it is that . . . and a loaf of white if you have one.'

Delving into a sack he pulls out a white, paper-wrapped cake.

'Fresh ginger and dark sugar, and . . . voila, the bread of your sainted request.'

'Silvers?' I suggest.

He shrugs. 'What else might you be carrying in your bag constructed of carpet?'

Placing the bag on a tree-stump, I take out the contents chosen for this purpose. He picks up a pair of sunglasses and puts them on.

'These shadowy glasses—would they be worthy of bread-swap?'

With his unruly black hair, sharp cheekbones and my sunglasses, this bread-vendor might have been a, *rock star*, from the days when bods played instruments connected to electricity.

'I think you should have them,' I say, knowing they are worth more than a cake and a loaf.

Taking them off he looks at the frames. 'Police? The officers of the law in the olden times wore such fanciful things with those tall blue hats?'

'I think it was the maker's name.'

LONDONIA

'It is, and has been a deal, mademoiselle.' He hands me the goods and turns back to his transport, delving for something else in a basket. 'Treacle cakes. My Irish mother taught me of their making.' He smiles, puts the glasses back on and mounts his donkey, heeling it into a slow walk.

I look in the bag at the round crumbly cakes and call after him.

'Will you be here again soon?'

He looks back and waves. 'About a sevday, I should say, fair damsel.'

I watch mec and beast walk away slowly then whistle for the dogs. They bound back, tongues and ears flapping. No need for leashing now; they are happy to accompany me home and beg for bits from one of these rustling bags.

When I arrive back, Jarvis is lopping wood in the garden.

'Toast?' I suggest.

Jarvis thunks the axe into a log, takes off his homburg and wipes away a line of sweat.

'He was there then.'

'In all his beauty and poetry.'

'Pretty is he?'

'Ravishing.'

'I'll go next time,' he grins, 'get the kettle on and I'll just tidy this lot up.'

I go in, lay the table with care in honour of the various stodges to be consumed, fire up the range and read the Sureditch Flyer until Jarvis returns with a batch of wood.

'There's that house in Commercial Road wot's collapsed. I'll take the horse 'n barrow round later and snag some beams 'fore they go.' He eyes the spread. 'Looks good—last of the butter though.'

I pass him a slice of lightly toasted bread on the fork. 'I'll trade some at the café. Doreen wants a new pair of specs.'

LONDONIA

'Christ in a vest! This is *good*,' he says after chewing, eyes closed. 'Think he'd like to join our little commune? I could offer a share of my woodhouse.'

'He must be already snaffled, Jarvis.

'Yeah, s'pose. So, what we got on, then?'

'D'you want to go through those jumpers for Fred?' I suggest. 'I'll do some darning and wash stuff up at the Parkplace. It's warm enough to get a good drying done.'

We make a list and I start sorting through woollen garments that had come from the bean and brassica trading Jarvis had done. Half a clockface later I've sorted them into a pile for recycling at the felty-co-op, a small pile of near-perfect items and a larger stack for darning which I have started on; the procedure lulling and oddly comforting.

The door's bell jangles, interrupting my placid state and I jump up calling out to Jarvis in his wood-house. 'I'll go—need to move about.'

The gate mirror reveals a mec, his face partially concealed behind a large bunch of spring blooms.

'Is you Miss Hoxton of St Leonard's?'

'I am.'

'Sign here, please.' He produces a small book and fountain pen and I duly scrawl my name.'

Without expression, he hands over the bouquet and returns to a bicycle and cart standing in the road, after shooing off some interested gosses.

I walk back into the church's cool interior, burying my nose in the deliciously fragrant lilac and narcissus.

Jarvis appears from his hut carrying a box. 'Scrote—not 'im again?'

'Who?' I start, 'I haven't looked to see if there's a note yet.'

'It'll be Straightfish. 'E sent flowers yesdy too.'

'Why didn't you tell me?'

'Thought you 'ad enuff goin' on in yer head.'

'Vrai . . . what should I do?'

LONDONIA

He puts the box down on the remaining pew and nods towards the vestry.

'Put them in a vase? and . . . dunno beyond that. Ignore 'im and 'ope nothing more 'appens.'

I find an old sweet jar and arrange the flowers as fastidiously as if I was one of Mrs Caruso's house-staff. They are truly beautiful blooms and I wonder where he got them. Had he plucked them himself early in the dewy morn from the parkland near the Vaux-haul Tavern? I smile at the thought of those great scarred hands selecting the stems, and sniffing the scents . . . probably not. More like that dame, Mavis, had been booted out with a pair of scissors, moaning that she had enough to do.

I feel oddly unworried by this gift, much bigger things occupying my mind. I can't stop thinking about the useless trip to Gershwin's so decide to distract myself by writing a letter to Mrs Caruso, reminding her of our bargain. I'll take it to the horse-letter-mec in Aggerston pastures and see if I can exchange reading glasses for a cockerel, as *Boris* has just shouted his last introduction to the morn

After carefully composing the missive, I continue the darning, leave Jarvis to go to Fred's with the good items, and walk to the pastures. The morn is clear, rubble and plants glistening after a downpour in the night. I pace, mind relatively clear, concentrating on the beauty of birdsong, and buzz of Londonia activity.

The horse-letter-mec occupies a small stone house in the corner of the pastures, the main building being the farm community who have worked the soil here for many cycles before the Curtain. After clanging the gate bell, one of the commune appears warily, crossbow raised. She lowers it at the sight of me.

'Hoxton! Apologies for this—Clasher's came to take animals in darking but we shot their arses!' She laughs uproariously then welcomes me through, chattering in Polish and English. 'What you want? We got goodly milkes . . . szpinak?'

LONDONIA

I point to the extensive chicken enclosure. 'Would you have a spare male? Ours hit the dirt.' Opening the carpet bag, I take out the glasses. 'Good trade?'

She takes the specs in crabbed fingers, puts them on and examines the back of her hand.

'. . . Oh—I see how old skin is. *Bzdury*! But, hey, I can read book on cow I have. It is fine trade. I find you boy hen.'

While she hauls one from the run, I inspect the abundant crops and take mental notes. This place is a perfect symbiosis of plants, pollinating insects, animal crud and human labour; I resolve to do much more in our own plot.

She returns, bird in box with a thoughtfully-attached string handle.

'If you get more glasses I take them, dobrze?'

I shake her hand and look into her bright eyes amongst their nest of wrinkles.

'D'ac. And thanks for the cock.'

'Nie ma problemu. You see letter-mec too?'

'Is he in?'

'He is to go soon—walk quicks, eh.'

I scoot through the lines of fruit trees and find said mec loading his horse with sacking bags. He turns at my footsteps and grins.

'Aye-aye, Hoxton. Just in time, lass. Where's it to?'

I hand him the letter. 'Only to the access point.'

'Och, yer could a' walked it . . .'

'I know but we needed a new cockerel and I didn't want to go back over there.'

'Come out 'a there recenttime, has thee?'

This horse-letter-mec is a genial gossip-spreader as well as excellent letter deliverer so I decline a response and congratulate him on his own garden plot.

'Aye—it's comin' along.'

'D'ac for silvers? And when will it be dropped?'

LONDONIA

'Fine—six, and . . .' he glances at the sackbags. 'I'd be lookin' at end of morrow.'

'Apex. Thanks.'

As I turn to walk back to the gate, he calls out. 'Saw Mr Straightfish yesty for a delivery—he's a jumpin' thing oonder 'is sporran for thee!'

I wave a hand in response and stride off home, the bird scuffling in its box.

Back at base, Jarvis has returned from Fred's with a fine pair of boots for me and a new suit for himself.

'Fred 'preciated the woollens,' he says, admiring his dark grey Find. 'What d'you reckon?'

'Very smart—are you going somewhere?'

'Thought I might just lope down to the Stripy Horse drinking-house. Fancy it after we've finished 'ere?'

I think of the fuggy, sawdusty, interior. 'Is anyone playing this darking?'

'Irish, Polish, Hindi fusion band called the Goracy Potatoes.'

'The *what*?'

'Hot potatoes—lots 'a violin, jigs n'stuff.'

'Sounds like what I need. D'ac. I'll introduce the new cockerel to his harem and finish that mending.' I pick up my new boots and inspect the leather. 'Thanks for getting these—the old ones have just about collapsed.'

'Yeah. I noticed they was a bit morte . . .' He looks around as the gate bell rings out. 'I'll get it this time.'

He returns a short while later and pokes his head around the door. 'Bert fr you—gis' the bird. I'll be in the garden.'

I pick up the box, pass it to Jarvis and gingerly welcome in Bert the Swagger.

He takes off his boater and kisses my reluctantly-proffered cheek.

'Hoxton. You are looking as beauteous as this shining day.'

'Thank you, Bert.'

'How did the Cincturian ladies find their telephonic devises?'

LONDONIA

I'd almost forgotten about all *that*. 'Oh—they were temporarily ecstatic until they realised they couldn't use them but by which time they'd moved onto some other fad.'

'Which was?'

'Nail varnish.'

He guffaws, which I would have done too. 'Did you procure what they desired in that line?'

'I did.'

'You really are an exemplary Finder, my dear.'

I wonder what he is after. 'Are you needing a Find, Bert?'

He rummages around in his pocket, produces a scrap of magazine page and gives it to me.

I peer at the photograph of a rectangular white box with a round window in it. 'What is it?'

'A machine that washes clothes—this one being from about ten cycles before the Curtain.

'And . . .'

'I've made one—well, it doesn't quite look as bright and white as this *examplaire* but it will wash clothes.'

'What did you make it out of?'

'Complex and dull to explain but mainly the alternator from a car, a wind turbine, lots of welded metal and a dustbin.'

'Is the Bert empire spreading into clothes care then?'

'It might be popular . . . care to try it?'

I consider the massive pile I was going to drag up to the Parkplace; wash on the lavoir rocks and dry in the trees. 'Can you dry it all too?'

He spreads his arms expansively. 'The *lad* I have working as an intern has rigged up a veritable spider's web of drying lines that can be used in or outside.'

'Payment?'

'A plucked chicken, and something from your more lurid literary stashes.'

Trying not to think of this combination in a sordid way I agree.

LONDONIA

'It's a deal. Here's the clothing, and when should one of us collect it and bring you the bird?'

'Frydy?'

'D'ac.' He replaces his hat, I load him and myself up with the bagged garments and see him out of the church. He looks back from stowing the stuff into his cart.

'Ah, Hoxton. I meant to say . . . Straightfish *won't* take no for an answer.'

What? 'How do you know about that?'

'We play chess and drink of his burgundy on a darking every so often. Pip pip.'

I stare at him sitting astride his fat brown horse as it clops off down the road then storm back inside and start darning furiously. The wool needle splices its way into my index finger.

'Ow! *Merda*!'

'Ça va, Kitten.' Jarvis steps into the vestry, now dressed in earth-covered jins and pink sweatshirt with *Selfie-Time* written across it in silver.

'. . . Better now I've seen you in *that*.'

'So, wot's the snarlin' about?'

'Fukin' Bert and bastard Straightfish.'

'Oof—steady, you'll implode, H. Wot about them?'

I explain, after which he looks at me less wryly than he might have done.

'You needs a drink an' a dance about. Let me get this weird kit off and we'll go out an' see the Potatoes, yeah?'

The Stripy Horse is as full as I've ever seen it; Bright quarter mood in abundance and ale flowing. Jarvis re-attired himself in the new suit, and I searched out a long crimson dress and wove roses into my hair. If anyone else says Straightfish is after me . . .

LONDONIA

well he might have reason this darking. I've *even* put on eye-liner.

We walk in arm in arm and are greeted affectionately by our fellow Hackrovians. What a wonderful place to live.

Jarvis is soon in depthy conversation with a mec who looks a little like Parrot. I order a couple of pear beers, pass him one and leave them to it. A murmur replaces the crowd's chatter and everyone looks over to the stage where the band-leader, a young dame with swishing black hair clips up the stairs in her heels. Everyone whistles including all the other dames.

She waves her fiddle bow for silence.

'Mr Peacock and I, and the other Goracy Potatoes would like to welcome you to the Stripy Horse. Please delve deep for your silvers and branz!'

A rousing cheer fills the room and the other band members crowd onto the small stage. A quick tune up and they're into a delirious jig, audience bouncing, arms flailing. Roses cascading and sweat staining my dress, I shove my way outside and stand looking up at the cloudless night sky. A latecomer is walking up the street, light footsteps echoing. Under the solitary candle-lamp of the Horse, I recognise her dark face as she approaches.

'Sardi!'

She smiles and spreads her hands in gesture of wonder. 'Hey, Miss Hoxton—you do mop up well!'

I note her sparkling robe and careful application of makeup —something I have never seen before.

'You too! Look at us both in our finery.'

'A change from jins and jumpers, eh.'

She sighs happily. 'Unc's staying with the brood, and I've me a free license to do *anytruc*!'

'Let's start with a drink then.'

We go back into the throng and the eve progresses memorably until Jarvis produces a small quantity of Snash and I recall little more than laughing raucously as he, Sardi and I dance on the bar top scattering bacco-sticks and toasted walnuts.

Capitula 19

'Wewll, wewll.' I open sticky eyes to see Jarvis, hands on dressing-gowned hips.

'. . . What?'

He laughs wickedly. 'If Bert was 'ere, he'd *come* just at the sight 'a you two.'

'Uh?' I sit up and realise I'm in bed with Sardi, her top half naked, big breasts, dark nipples pointing at me. 'Oh!'

'Didn't know you was ambi-wotsit.'

'I don't think I am—it was just convenient for her rather than trek back to Wilkes Street . . . what about you? Got a companion in there?'

He grins broadly. 'Have indeed. Just making us a cupatea 'cept the stove's out—can I?'

'Of course.'

'For you two?'

'Please . . . is it mid-morn?'

He looks out through the clear top window. 'Yeah, reckon.'

Kettle filled, he prods the fire back into life and stretches.

'Foitlingly goodly eve, eh?'

The thudding rhythm still seems to be within my bones. 'It was. I love the Potatoes. Next time we have a fete—they'll be the music, and you could guest.'

'Yeah . . . bit of a way t'go 'fore that, but—' He stops his sentence as the gate bell jangles. '*Now* foitlin' wot—already 'ad the water-mec, knife-sharpener, and that wench from the Come-Cleanse-with-Jesus, lot round while you was zzzing.'

'I'll go.'

'Nah, you stay *cosy* and I'll tell whoever it is to pizz off.' He stomps off, footsteps resounding. 'Better not be 'er again.'

LONDONIA

A few moments later he returns, beaming, eyebrows raised. 'Visitor for you, H.'

I sit up and pull the sheet about me.

'Hello?' I suddenly recognise those blue eyes. '. . . Tom?'

He is as scrawny as a hatchling. Under a wide-brimmed khaki hat, dirty hair streams, his archers-bow mouth obscured by a straggly beard.

He grins. 'Interrupting anything, am I?'

Now awake, Sardi slips off the bed and gathers up her clothes. 'Better scoot away to the gosse-pack. Welcome back, Tom.'

They kiss cheek to cheek and he smiles at me as she disappears through the vestry door.

'Fancy a fuk then?' he says looking at my semi-sheeted body.

'When you get that hair off, yes,' I smile.

He nods at the bath. 'Jarvis get that figured out?'

'He did. I'll heat some water.'

'D'ac. While you're doing that I'll feed Coal.'

'New dog?'

'Horse. I traded him for work time.'

I get up, throw on old clothes, stoke the fire and start filling pans with water.

A little time later Tom lies in the moss-coloured bath, steam rising, his arms resting on the sides and an expression of total joy on his face.

'Look in that canvas bag, H,' he says, sitting up a little. 'There's two important things in there—envelope and the oblong box.'

Finding the items, I look back at him questioningly.

He nods. 'Open the box.'

I prise off the lid and gaze down on a tiny silver pomegranate, its seeds of rubies, bright against white satin.

Lifting out the delicate chain, I stare at the swinging globe.

'So very beautiful . . . where did you find it?'

LONDONIA

'I traded it off Jarvis ages ago. It was his father's mother's. I wanted to wait till you might think about me being, you know—the one. Love you, Hoxton.'

Tom the non-romantic ducks down under the water, hair spreading out. I sit down and study the silver fruit, thinking of his words, never-before-uttered, and when he re-surfaces I tell him I love him too.

Time passes while we just look at each other, plans and questions forming.

'Put it on,' he suggests.

I do so, and look at my reflection in the wardrobe mirror.

'Now the other truc,' he says, nodding towards the envelope.

The texture of the envelope is thick and ridged, and the sheet of paper I draw out holds importance in its fibres.

I read the fanciful hand of curling inked letters.

This is to state that Tom-ov-Brixton is the rightful owner of The Dodger, moored thus in Eric's Boat Yard, Thames Spur.

'You have a boat?'

'Yep, traded everything I have. Decided fishing was going to replace logging . . . I could almost live on the boat—s' just the horse problem.'

'So . . .'

He passes the razor one more time across his chin and smiles broadly, the laugh lines newly revealed.

'Got room to lodge Coal here?'

'And you?'

'Yeah, and me—part-time.'

With water slopping like the Thames on a stormy day, Tom heaves himself suddenly up and out of the bath. I hand him a pillowcase.

'No towels?' he says, flipping the cloth over his torso.

'All worn out.'

'Not like me!' He grins and takes my hand.

LONDONIA

I sit wrapped in a sheet listening to the bees outside in the honeysuckle and gazing at Tom's smooth, beardless face. His eyes open and he yawns.

'. . . You been awake for a while?'

'A few clockfaces.'

We smile shyly at each other as the shadows from the sycamore tree dance on the wall. Beyond the garden sounds I hear the church door open and close then the clump of Jarvis's feet as he approaches the vestry. Tom slides off the bed and pulls on his jins

Jarvis stares at his bare torso as he enters the room.

'Merda, Tom! Not much scran in Hepping?'

Tom squints down his too-obvious ribs. 'Nope. Not after the storm—too many pro-trappers out and most 'a the beasts got wind of it.'

They hug and Jarvis steps back. 'Alors, 'ow about a beef sandwich?'

'Beef!'

'Easy with Hoxton's mega-trade medicos. Got some beautiful stuff at the Exchange.'

Jarvis constructs three rustic sandwiches of beef and onion while I make mint tea and Tom unpacks his few belongings. We take the scran into the garden and sit listening to Tom's tales of work in the forrist until he stretches and decides we've all heard enough of his old life.

'So, if I am going to take up residence here I need to pull my weight. What needs doin' on this old building?'

Jarvis grins and slaps him on the back.

'You *won't* get bored. Gutter repairs and bit 'a roofin'? We was gonna attack that on the morrow. Also we 'ad this idea 'bout

LONDONIA

makin' a sort 'a observation deck up there—part for the pleasure 'a star-gazing, part t' watch out for Clashers, an' the like.'

Tom beams at this. 'Peak! . . . yeah, an *observatory*. D'you reckon you could find one of them things bods used to look at the planets with, Hoxton?'

'Telescope?' I say, through my sandwich.

'That's the one.'

'Shouting-house at Bethy-Green would be the best place. They often have scientific stuff. We'd need a good trade though . . .'

'Something'll turn up. D'ac. Ready if you are? Jarvis?'

'Gis a mec time to digest, Tom. Just 'ave a snooze and we'll start in a half clockface.'

By late aft, we've hauled enough scrap wood up the stairs and out onto the roof to start the project. Despite Tom's skinniness he's as adept and tireless as . . . well . . . Tom. Jarvis and I take a break as he scales the roof without fear, re-jigging slates, patching holes with reclaimed plastic, and lashing ropes to make the platform's basic structure.

'Useful fukka,' observes Jarvis, removing his summer homburg and wiping the sweat away. 'Oi, d'you want us to start passing planks yet?'

Tom spreads horn-glue on a last bit of plastic, wedges it into a hole and stands up. 'Yup—them two long pine ones with the bark first.'

We work until dusk creeps, the sky morphing from grey cloud into a clear opal turquoise. The structure deemed to be *safe enough* we sit watching for the first darking star.

'There it is.' Jarvis points to the tiny glimmer. 'Think there's any bods on it looking back at us?'

'Unlikely,' I say, 'as it's not unlike l'enfer on there.'

'How d'you know . . . how's anyone know? Looks icy from here.'

'Have a look in the vestry—there's a massive tome on space in there.'

261

LONDONIA

'Yeah . . . but how'd *they* know, really.'

'Because back then *they* could send probes into space and find these things out.'

Jarvis shrugs. 'Scrote t' that. Could 'ave all been giant stories.'

Tom nods to the moon, now just visible.

'So, you don't believe mecs got out of a metal ship and walked about up there?'

'Nah . . . trick of the powers that was. Something to keep the masses in awe and wonderment.'

'You'll be stating the Earth is flat next,' I add.

'Could be. Who's to say it ain't.'

'Strange to think there used to be airplanes flying up there before the Curtain, and satellites zipping about.'

'Wot was they for?'

'Observing other countries . . . sending information about weather, even how to get somewhere.'

'What's wrong with a map?' says Tom.

'Nothing. It was just an advancement, like so many other inventions.'

As we all stare upwards into the deep neverness, a small white light moves silently above us.'

'Shooting star?' suggests Jarvis.

I think back to the space book. 'No . . . those would move a lot faster, I think.'

'P'raps bods still sending stuff up there somewhere.'

Our chatter stops, silenced by enormity of the world, everything we know nothing about beyond Londonia.

A light breeze ruffles the new leaves of the plane trees. An owl calls. I lay my head on Tom's shoulder and sigh at the darking beauty.

Capitula 20

The next morn, I awake with Tom next to me, Zorro above my head and Fagin on my feet.

Tom groans as he turns over.

'Think I did a bit too much yesdy . . . what's the dog doin' in here.'

I kiss his stubbly face. 'You have to remember he was here before you—at least Tilly's decided to sleep outside.'

'Yeah—love me, love my menagerie, eh?'

'Afraid so. Even the fleas.'

Tom slides out of the bed, straw clicking as he moves. 'That bath was good. Any chance of another?'

'Not 'til we heat a load of water up. It's a bit of an occasional thing. I can recommend the Sureditch bathhouse, they do mud-coating and everything.'

'I'd rather get the mud off—not on.'

'Honestly, it's apex good. Mud from the cleanest parts of the estuary—makes you feel all smooth and calm.'

'I feel calm, just achy—hot water's what I need. D'you want to go?'

'No. I'd better catch up with some trade-prep.'

'What's it cost?'

'A Bath? Six silvers, two branz or you can try a veg-barter. We've got spare kale and potatoes.'

'Sounds goodly. I'll go after p-dej. We got any supplies in?'

I sit up and re-position Zorro. 'Have a look in the bread-bin. Anything?'

'Nope.'

LONDONIA

'Alors. Go and look in the hen-house for eggs, and I'll take the dogs for a run up to the Bread-mec. He's not doing a round t-dui.'

Tom hauls on his jins and goes out to the garden. Jarvis must be up too as I hear their friendly banter. I find yesty's clothes, pull them on and round up the hounds.

'Back in a quarter.'

Jarvis answers from his woodhouse.

'Get some of those bent bun things if he has 'em.'

I leave the church smiling at Jarvis's description of the Bread-mec's attempts at croissants, and walk into an already busy street.

Up at bread-headquarters there's a queue, and then an announcement that there's no bread left—or bent buns. I decide to see if the cake-peddling-mec might possibly be in the Parkplace with his donkey and head off, dogs pulling me as if they know where we are headed. When we arrive, I let them go and pace the overgrown grounds looking for the mec. I'm just too late; he's leaving by the other gateway, a trail of gosses behind him, an occasional small cake being hurled into the pack.

Merda. 'No bread.'

'Hoxton?'

I turn to see a plump blonde dame staring at me with eyes that once read my very soul. 'Marina? It's a step from the Barbican to here.'

She nods and waves a hand to the other side of the Parkplace. 'I stay with friend while they do things to drinking house for few days.'

'Oh—what things?'

'There was fire in main room. But ça va now.' She touches my arm. 'You find gosse in the Cincture?'

'I still have to make contact, but you were correct! He is there.'

I detect a faint smile of satisfaction on her round, pale face as she replies: 'Is goodly nouvelle.'

LONDONIA

I suddenly recall that I still owe her. 'You never did call at the church for your fee.'

She shrugs. 'Is fine. You were interesting subject, and was good to stretch mind from just, *why I have no mec,* or, *will I make fortune next cycle*, you know?'

I'm starting to wonder if she might like to have another go at her *interesting subject* when a familiar voice calls my name.

'Hey-o.' Jake is walking towards me with an expression of resignation. 'You missed him too, eh?'

'Salut, Jake. Yes. No bread. Or at the Bread-mec's.'

He grins at Marina and points to the paper bags she carries, 'Your luck's in t-dui, then.' It's more than just a grin; I note interest in those hooded eyes.

She opens a bag and shows us one of the gar's delicious ginger cakes.

'Maybe I share, if you make good coffee?'

'Think I make a reasonable brew don't I, H?'

I smile at this ember of something happening. 'I've never complained.'

'D'ac. Let's get the kettle on.'

I sit outside with Marina while Jake busies about in his shack. She's not the chattiest of dames and I wonder what to say.

'Ça va, the dogs? No one got hurt in the fire?'

'Oni khoroshi,' she nods. 'Fine, fine.'

I wonder if she can quieten a question that has been hovering at the back of my mind.

'Marina? Could I ask you something?'

'Ya.'

'Would you know if I am in nippering?'

'Crimson Time is late?'

'A little.'

She takes my hand and clamps it between her two. Leaves rustle in the breeze. A large black beetle wanders over my boot. After what seems like a very long time, she places my hand back in my lap.

LONDONIA

'No. I see nothing. Perhaps there was damage when gosse-babe was taken from you in Cincture.'

This is something I have often wondered and it's an odd relief to hear Marina's frank words on the subject.

'Is problem?' she continues.

'No,' I say truthfully. 'But it makes Finding my son all the more important.'

She nods an understanding then starts. 'Ah. Something else . . . I see you in water.'

'A bath?' I say flippantly. She looks at me as if I am a gosse of five cycles.

'Głęboki . . . what is word . . . *deep* water.'

Jake appears. He places a battered enamel jug and three mugs down next to the bag of cakes and sits on a log near Marina. The old woolly hat has gone, replaced by a new one I gave him, and, if I'm not incorrect, he has shaved . . .

'What's all this about water?'

'Marina was just telling me that she feels I might be immersed in deep water.'

'The Parkplace lake? Hoxton does swim in there quite often.'

Marina glances over at the placid expanse. 'No. Not this. Water that has movement.'

'Lady Thames?'

'I don't know. Is not clear . . . but perhaps to be careful, Hoxton.'

After promising I will be, I accept a cake, down my coffee and leave them to have a, no doubt, in-depth mystical conversation.

The dogs appear at my whistle, Tilly sucking up the remnant of a rat's tail like a fat piece of spaghetti. At least *they've* had breakfast. My bread-search is, however, happily completed as I traverse Temple Street and see an elderly dame selling sourdough loaves from her doorway.

LONDONIA

'You got the last one, deary,' she smiles, revealing her one remaining tooth. 'My son says it's goodly chewy—shame I have to soak my slices these days.'

I thank her, remind myself to start our own sour-dough to alleviate the bread problem, if we can find flour, and head back to the church.

' 'Bout time,' grunts Jarvis as I walk into the vestry and see the table laid all spick with flowers and everything.'

'Sorry, I had to take a detour to the Parkplace.'

Jarvis brightens. 'That cake-peddler there, was he?'

'I only saw the back of him, but I got bread from a dame in Temple Street. We've really got to start doing our own.'

'Yeah . . . see Jake?'

'I did, and Marina. We had coffee and *conversation*.'

'Oh? Wot she tell you this time?'

'To be wary of deep water.'

'And she should be wary of filling bod's heads wiv scary-crud.'

'She was right about my son!'

'S'pose so. D'ac—eggs is done and tea.'

'Where's Tom?'

'Back on the roof, finishing the planky construction. I'll call 'im.'

He goes out into the transept and bawls, causing the ghosts to mutter; then returns and pours out a big mug of tea.

'Jake on goodly form?'

I sit down and slice the bread which is as the son had said, chewy. 'Very goodly. And possibly smitten.'

'By wot.'

'*Who* . . . Marina. When he came out with the coffee, he'd *shaved*.'

'. . . Nah . . . Jake?'

'What about Jake?' says Tom, stepping over the threshold and wiping his brow on his balled-up t-shirt.

I hand him a clean one and explain about my visit. He nods with a wry smile.

LONDONIA

'I need to call on him later. Got a certain delivery for him.'
'Wot's that, then,' asks Jarvis.
'Woodland mushrooms,' he grins, '. . . of a particular type.'
'Aye aye. Might come with you then—fancy a trip, Hox?'
'Do you mean A Trip, or a walk up the road?'
'I mean a 'vestigation into yor soul,' says Jarvis half closing his eyes and sucking on an imaginary hooch-stick.
'Hundred percent natural Hepping-forrist high,' adds Tom. 'Non-addictive, and usually harmless.'
'Usually?' I question.
'Bad times have been known, but I think you'd be fine. You in?'
'. . . Mm, no. Think I'll stay and read in the garden—spend enough time working in it.'

We finish p'dej and I clear up while they recommence the day's work. After a quick trip to the pigeon station to check for any Finding requests, I join them in the garden where we have planned a new fruit bush area.

It's mid aft. Jarvis sticks the spade into a pile of newly-mulched soil and yawns massively.

'E-*nuff*! Tom . . . feel like taking a mooch up to the Park-place?'

Tom stands up from bedding-in a gooseberry bush, stretches and grins. 'Why not? Think we've earned it. Sure you don't want to come—even to observe, H?'

I imagine the scene and shake my head. 'You lot wriggling about on the floor, screeching with laughter and me trying to read. No. You go and enjoy it. *Don't* take keys though—you'll probably lose them! I'll let you in again.'

LONDONIA

When they've left, I wander amongst the flowers that scent the warm air, thinking about my life, now with two mecs: very different, but easy together. Supposing one day there was to be a third?

I stop day-dreaming and get back to the tasks.

Hen-house cleared out, I dig up potatoes and sow lettuce seedlings. There's still a mass to be caught up on and I go back to the vestry to start a pile of clothes-mending but push the garments aside as my eyes start to close.

Enough—as Jarvis had said. Having abstained from the proposed drug-fest, I decide on a glass of elderflower wine. I peruse the book shelves stopping at a well-preserved copy of a tome entitled, *Last London*.

As I slip the hardback from the shelf I catch a small noise outside the vestry. Zorro seeking a mouse perhaps . . . nothing more.

Footsteps, not a cat.

'Hello . . . Jarvis?' I pad to the door and inch it back; a drug-fuelled blag perhaps? 'Jarvis, Tom? Is that you?'

Silence.

I call the cats. 'Zorro, Eccles.'

The ghost choir answers with a faint chorus from Mozart's *Requiem*, the soprano solo wavering in the still air.

Merda. I suddenly remember what I said to Jarvis and Tom about me locking the door. I run back to get the keys from their hook

Sweat is pricking my arms now. My senses tell me someone is in here. *Crud*—the dogs are still out in the garden. Stepping quietly back into the room, I pick up my pistol from the side table and slink back through the door out into the church, back against the panelling. I must have imagined the noise. So many odd sounds occur in this ancient place.

'Is someone there?'

I start to move towards the garden door to let the hounds in. A shadow slinks along the transept wall. I run. Footsteps follow.

LONDONIA

A hand reaches out and wrenches me back into a hard embrace. A soaking cloth is against my mouth . . . sweet smell.

My words garble behind the fabric: 'Fukker—off—kill y . . .'

I twist, bring the gun around behind me and crush the trigger awkwardly.

The pistol shot cracks, echoing around, splitting plaster somewhere. The gloved hands still hold me hard, no slumping body, my bullet lodged in plaster not flesh.

'Tom . . . help me.'

Dark now.

I have become a chrysalis: one of those brown shiny ones I often come across in the garden. I shake off the disturbing images to then focus, not on the vestry walls, but a plank floor, boxes and fish baskets. The chugging sound that featured in my dream is real. I *am* a prisoner—not encased in an insect's body, but sacking and rope.

'Hey!'

Wriggling about I manage to move a little towards a shaft of light. 'Oi! Up there! Where am I?'

A thump of feet and the wedge of light becomes a square. A bearded face looks in through the shape.

'You in the gantry. Shut up.'

The little door closes again, this time completely. Further wriggling produces nothing and gradually my fear subsides back into exhausted somnolence. Maybe cycles or maybe just minutes later the trap opens again and the bearded mec clatters down the steps, something black grasped in one hand. The chugging sound has stopped. I stare at him wild-eyed until I see no more, the black fabric now over my head.

'Get the fuk off! Get this off!' My wriggling turns into thrashing and he strikes me hard.

'Lady. Better for you if you is silent.'

Face aching, I opt for his suggestion and allow myself to become as limp as a dying bird as he hoists me effortlessly through the hatch. The muffled thunk of wood against something solid but giving suggests another boat is alongside. Someone else is here now, quiet instructions given as my bound body passes from one vessel to the other.

Down more steps and I am deposited on what feels like a bed. This is a very different craft; I can smell polished wood, flowers . . . wealth.

The heavy footsteps recede and then a short while later lighter ones tap-tap on the wooden floor; someone hums tunelessly as they arrange things in this room. The dame, I assume, stops in front of me.

'Miss Hoxton. Listen to me good. I'm going to undo you now then you'll dress in the garments provided. There's a basin with hot water, and I'll return to prepare you afterwards. Don't resist or there'll be *consequences*.'

'*Prepare* me?' My voice sounds peculiar under this stifling cloth. Realisation surfaces; I know I've spoken to her before. 'Who are you?'

She is silent as her hands are busy undoing rope. One binding must be knotted too tight as a sawing motion reveals she has a large knife. A knife that is rather too close to my stomach for comfort. I remain still as she hisses.

'Merda. Pepito why'd you tie this so foitling tight.' Pepito. I know this name—that darking at the Vaux-hauler's premises. I feel ill as I realise how stupidly complacent I had become.

She sits me up free of bindings, removes the hood and I'm looking at the wry features of Straightfish's house-keeper.

'Mavis, isn't it?'

She re-lights a bacco-stick and casually regards me through the small cumulous.

'S'right. And *you're* a pizzin' pain. I probably mentioned he won't give up. Got a ton to do back at the tavern and instead I'm out here on the fukkin' ocean making *you* respectable.'

'You could just let me go?'

LONDONIA

She laughs a tight little laugh, coughs and waves her cig to the porthole.

'Go where? And anylane, I'd cop the fallout, wouldn'I?' With her other hand, she draws a small pistol out from her housecoat pocket. 'I'm an apex cracks-mec, so don't do anything foolish, d'ac? Get dressed and I'll be back in a quarter-cycle.' As she turns to leave I pluck at her nylony sleeve.

'Wait—just something I need to know. Why me?'

She huffs. 'Donaskme. I'm not lesso . . . but I can tell you he's stuck on you as tough as barnacle on this boat's arse.'

When she's gone, I sit rubbing where the ropes had dug in while scanning the room for any possible makeshift weaponry. Soap, cushions, eiderdown? I almost laugh at a ridiculous image of me brandishing a bed cover with a view to suffocating my captors. There's nothing in here other than soft furnishings, and a couple of candle lamps firmly attached to these varnished plank walls.

The clothes laid out are not just clothes—the Italian silks of which he had spoken: a long scarlet dress embroidered with golden birds and flowers and a shawl of delicate cream wool.

Hey-ho. Live in the moment as Jake sometimes says. I peel off my sweat-damp old clothes, wash with the perfumed soap and dry off with a towel as lux as the ones I thought about lifting from Mrs Caruso's. *He*, or another Finder, has also searched out shoes that more-or-less fit me—red satin with golden bows. Standing in front of the mirror-glass I observe myself naked apart from the shoes—not bad, perhaps a tad too thin. The dress swished on, I pose as narcissistically as one of the Cincture broads. Then reality whaps me. I am on a boat with a potential maniac somewhere watery beyond everything I know. Stepping to the little window, I peer out on an expanse I've often longed to see but perhaps not in these circumstances. *You were right, Marina—deep water.*

The door unlocks and Mavis reappears humming casually as if about to do a spot of dusting, not deal with a trembling

LONDONIA

captive. She eyes me for a moment, bacco-stick smouldering. Did I catch a glimpse of surprise? If I did it vanishes again.

'D'ac. You'll do. Sit there and I'll complete his requirements.'

I sit on the gestured chair and she fusses about with my hair and face, applying lipstick, stuff on my eyelids, and finally jewellery, including the very gold necklace of Iona's I had traded for the coinage.

Mavis puts away her kit and points to the mirror. 'Have a squint.'

I do, and it is quite a transformation. I wonder how many times she might have done this before.

'Is this a habit of his—to dame-knap and employ you to mould them into what he desires? You seem to know what you're doing.'

She removes a strand of bacco from her tongue and examines it.

'Nope—you're a special case. I makeup the dames used for the poker eves—makes a change from cleaning. D'ac, let's get you up on deck.' I hesitate and she grabs my arm. 'C'mon—I've other stuff to be doing before we land on the morrow.'

'Land where?'

'Better let Mr Straightfish tell you about that.'

Reluctantly I get up and totter out of the room to walk up a flight of Mavis-polished mahogany stairs. *Above board* is utterly overwhelming. Used to seeing the familiar Thames and her borders, or the Parkplace lake this never-ness of placid water makes tears come to my eyes. I turn slowly, taking in the sight of golden-edged clouds that hover at the line between sky and ocean, the varying hues of green, blue and slate-grey. The point of land to our left is gradually diminishing. I stare at the green mass and its outline of white rock. 'Where is that?'

Mavis pushes me on. 'Allhallows. Watch the deck here, s'a bit slippy.' I pass by the cabin and see before me the unmistakable back of El Capo seated at a table. He turns, gets up and gruffly sighs, hands outstretched.

LONDONIA

'The angel returneth, and what a beauteous sight she is.'

I stand before him, gracelessly, hands on hips.

'Returneth under duress. How do you think *this* is going to ever win my affections?'

He pulls out a chair for me. 'Oh . . . I think you'll come around. Better to of your own volition rather than remain a prisoner, eh?'

Huffily, I sit. Despite my fury and fear, hunger wins at the sight of a sumptuous dinner. We eat in silence, him gazing at me in the dusky light, me furtively regarding the land mass sliding slowly to our right. He pours wine and I sip a little knowing I need to keep focused. Acting is possibly the only way out of this situation.

'Goodly chicken. Who made the dish?'

He waves his glass in the direction of the stairs. 'We have a chef on board—used to work at Rules in the Cincture but defected to Londonia. He'll remain with us on the island.'

'*What* Island?'

'Sheppy. No panico—it's not a thousand miles away, and if you accept what I'm offering I'll take you back to the city every now and again—not that you'll want to. More chicken?'

I shake my head, suddenly feeling nauseous, not from the gentle swell of the boat but his carefree words.'

'How long will it take to get there?'

'Oh—after supper, a couple of cycles . . . just time to,' he raises a glass and grin, 're-kindle what was there before.'

'There wasn't anything there before,' I protest.

The grin stretches into something dirty. '*I recall that darking rather differently.*'

'. . . D'ac. It was, and you were an exceptional fuk.'

'You can't say it was *only* that.'

'I just did.'

He stares out over the now tenebrous skyscape then back to me. His eyes appear as dark as the approaching night. 'Well, I'll have to convince you further.'

LONDONIA

A mec appears from the stairwell carrying a silver tray. He silently clears the main course after a nod from Straightfish, and places a stemmed platter of strawberries between us.

'Weel zat be all, monsieur?'

'Coffee and the Honfleur cognac.'

'A tout de suite. I will leave it on the side table, sir.'

The fruit is too enticing to sulk it away. I take a berry, dip it in the dish of sugar and eat, eyes closed.

'Mm. Where did these come from?'

He takes one and leans forward, pointing at it. 'D'ac. This will be a useful demonstration of my ardour, Angel. These were brought up by horse yestdy from the Cornish-wall. For you.'

'I wouldn't have asked for them. A last season's apple would have sufficed.'

'Why make do when you can have anything you want?'

'I have everything I want.'

'A life of second-hand underwear and potato soup?'

Finally, this wheedling talk infuriates me. I announce the one thing that might stop it.

'D'ac. I told you before—I love someone else and we're buckled.'

He looks at me as if I've shot him, the bullet shutting him down bit by bit.

'That *logger* . . . you're promised to him?'

'He's not a logger, and whatever he is, it's nothing to do with you.'

El Capo puts out a hand and strokes my arm.

'Remember I said I know things about you.

' . . . Yes.'

'That pocket watch you had—you still have it?'

'I do.'

He sits back in his chair and takes the last strawberry. 'Strange that . . . how things can make their way back to a family member.'

LONDONIA

The interlaced initials float into my mind. 'What do you mean?'

'You might recall I was slightly surprised to see the piece. The truc is, it belonged to your father and I knew him—both of your parents.' I say nothing, just sit staring out at the near-black sea. He's talking again. 'I've been told you don't have memories of your life in the Cincture—that you were removed to Londonia.'

'Who told you . . . Bert, I imagine.'

'We've known each other for long-cycles—left old London town centre at the same time. Saw the same opportunities you might say.'

I don't know if I believe any of what he says but the words slip out anyway.

'What happened to my parents?'

He doesn't answer, just stands up and snuffs the two candles on the table. 'Enough of the past. Bit of present now, I think.' He's approaching me, a certain look in his eyes. I get up and start to back away—to where? Straightfish reaches out, grips me to him.

My spare hand flaps behind me, searching. I feel a solid corner—the waiter's side-table. The cognac bottle greets my fingers and I curl them about it.

El Capo is breathing like a randy horse. He releases me a little as I kiss him. His grip relaxes and he sighs. 'Better, Angel.'

'You want something *really* memorable?' I whisper. 'Carnal perfection? A glass-sharp bang?'

'*Show* me.'

I windmill my arm, cracking the bottle over his head. He goes down, arms flailing on the deck. I stare at the remains of the bottle and its sharded glass. I could slice it into his neck... someone's running. The waiter. Twisting my gaze from one deck-side to the other, I choose the side where a small boat's light shimmers in the distance; clamber up, skirts lifted and jump.

Plunging oneself into water in undergarments is one thing; floundering in several pounds of billowing silk is another. Real-

LONDONIA

ising my fingers still grip the bottle neck, I slice and fight the fabric that rises jelly-fish-like. How in l'enfer did I get this foitling thing on . . . at last I leave silken wrappings and rise to the surface cautious of where El Capo's boat is now. It's there, feet before me, persons running about, shouting, glaring over the edge at the sea where I tread frantically, eyes just above the waterline.

'There!' Mavis's voice. My eyes blurry with water take in the sight of a gun being raised. I gasp in a lung of air, duck and push off in what I hope is the direction of land, or at least the other vessel. I've never swum so hard and so fast, not even aware of the chill seeping. After what seems like a whole cycle, I cease and risk a look back. El Capo's boat is chugging again, slowly moving off towards, I hope, the island.

The other boat is quite near now, the land behind a sleeping cat of a shape in the dusky light. My arms scream as I pull at the water. A strange warmth is enveloping me. Whoever is on this boat will be more welcome than the depths of the sea.

'Hey! On the boat!' Near silence. Just gulls and the clicking of waves against wood. 'Help! Au secours! Is anyone there?'

My mind starts to present me with comforting images of Jarvis, Tom, the hounds. *Merda*. Is this what they talk about—your life being shown to you—a last flickering film.

Voices. Dames chattering like rooks. I look up to see someone poised to dive. They do, the resulting backflow filling my eyes and mouth. Arms enfold me.

'Drink.'

Marina's voice? A gentle hand slips behind my back and sits me forward.

'Drink. Is good . . . nettle and elderberry.'

'Who are you?' My voice sounds as creaky as the vestry door.

'We are fisherdames, returning from mackerel catch. How you come to be in sea? Hey . . .'

I shiver before darkness enfolds me again.

LONDONIA

No sound of waves or smell of fish.

'Hoxton? Can you hear me?'

'Sardi?'

My eyelids crank open revealing my friend's concerned face. Her voice trembles.

'Oh—thank the Guv. We'd feared . . .'

'My . . . demise?' I groan.

'Jake did wonder—the fever was manky-bad.'

I sit up a little and look about me expecting the vestry walls. The buzz of young voices sounds from another room.

'Am I at your place?'

'Yes.' She passes me a cup. 'Beef tea.'

I sip and try to recall what happened. I remember odd snatches: Straightfish, the dinner, leaping from his boat . . . strong hands and a voice like Marina's.

'How am I here?'

'A strange and luckful coincidence,' she smiles. 'I was down at the fish-docks, seaweed-searching for iodine and one of the fisherdames shouted me over. They were coddling somebod with a grutty cut and wanted to see if I had any made-up.'

'. . . Me?' I start, suddenly realising how much my leg hurts.

'Yes—you. Under layers of blankets in the back of her shack, all boiling up and reed-shivery. They'd washed the wound but it was, well . . . not joli.'

'I must have done it while jumping Straightfish's boat.'

'Think you need to parler me why you was on his boat and then not on it.'

I nod slowly trying to piece together the bits of memory. 'I will, but why am I—not that I'm complaining—here and not at the church?'

'Jarvis 'n Tom thought it'd be better if you wasn't moved again for a while.'

'So, they know I'm here?'

LONDONIA

'Jarvis came round out-peeping for you . . . Tom's been here most-time over the last sevdays keeping watch, keeping the fever down.'

'A sevdays! *Crud*. What a pain I've been. I'm sure you have plenty to be worrying about without my woes.'

She shushes me kindly. 'So . . . why were you being on his boat?'

I tell her, after which she sits on the bed and takes my hands. I suddenly feel so utterly weary.

'Would you mind if I slept again for a while, Sardi?'

She stands up and strokes my hair. 'I'll be next door if you have need of me.'

I drift when she has gone from the room; a mad, half sleep where voices mingle and stretch until they become a single vibration that winks out, leaving a sound not unlike my ghost choir holding a long, high note. I awake at early dawn, knowing I am ready to go home.

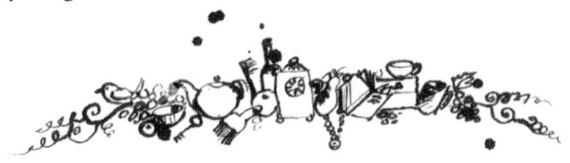

By the end of the morn I'm sitting outside the house with Sardi drinking elderflower cordial and waiting for Tom. It's seary hot and the memory of the chill sea seems impossible now. I should go back and see my rescuers, thank them, take them something useful.

'What can I take the fisherdames, Sardi?'

She frowns. 'Don't start worryment about that—get yourself righted first.'

'But I owe them so much . . . and you.'

'In time. Some Cincture medical stuff, be soundly 'preciated.'

'That's about all gone now . . . until I get back in there.'

LONDONIA

Before she can answer a shout echoes in the street. My heart jumps at the sight of Tom astride Coal. He stops the horse, jumps down and we embrace.

'Merda, Hoxton. You had us worried,' he whispers.

'I'd have had me worried about me if I'd known what was going on,' I sigh.

He smiles at this ridiculous statement. 'Home, then? I've got Jarvis's double saddle.'

I stand up unsteadily, kiss Sardi then climb onto Coal as carefully as an arthritic, ancient dame. Tom nudges the horse and we clop off steadily down the street.

'Beauteous day,' remarks my mec, throwing a few silvers to a saxophone-busking dame. It's true; even the straggly weeds glow this morning. The notes of the busker's melody stay with me as we turn a corner and I see the familiar and wonderful sight of my church. Jarvis is in the yard chopping wood. He helps me dismount and hugs me tight.

'Wot the fuk were you doin' in the sea?'

'It's a reasonably long story,' I reply.

'Make us a brew and fill us in, then. I'll finish up here.'

As I follow Tom into the church he grabs my hand.

'Come 'n see the vestry! We gold-quarter cleaned it.'

As I walk into my sanctuary, my heart fills with even more warmth. Wild flowers in jars line the cupboard tops; on the table, fruit spills from a glass cake stand and next to it, a pile of my clothes washed and flat-ironed. I sink down onto the bed and just look at this beautiful room until the colours become hazy through my tears.

Tom sits down next to me. 'That good, is it?'

I look up at him as I wipe them away. 'It's *wonderful*!' My joy seeps into slight angst, however, as I prepare to tell him why I was the object of El Capo's desire. '. . . Has Jarvis mentioned Bartholomew Straightfish?'

'Said you'd had stuff from him,' says Tom, cagily. 'An admirer, like.'

LONDONIA

'He didn't say more than that?'

'... Nope. Why, what?'

I sigh deeply. 'You know after we had that misunderstanding—before Jake's party and when we ...'

'Fukked.'

'Yes. Well, after the *misunderstanding* I was with someone else—him.'

'... I see.'

'It didn't mean anything.'

'But it did to him.'

'It seems so.'

'More like he became obsessed.'

'Enough that he dame-knapped me and took me away on his boat.' Tom nods, no words appearing. 'Say something!' I implore.

He sits up, all straight forward and *worse things happen in Croydonia*.

'What's to say? We wasn't welded and there *was* this drinking house-wench I had a bit of a darking with. But these things was before Jake's party—forgotten, done. Ça va.'

Jarvis clomps in and breaks the slightly stiff atmosphere.

'That tea done yet?'

I make to stand up, 'Oops, sorry ...'

He lays a hand on my shoulder, 'Na probs. I'll do it.'

Tom searches out a bacco pouch and rolls a clop.

'Hox's just been tellin' me what boat she fell out of.'

'I didn't fall out,' I protest. 'I jumped out to escape from ... Straightfish.'

Jarvis groans as he fills the kettle. 'Not that dung 'ead. Why'd you go on this little sea-jaunt?'

'It wasn't me who decided to go. He dame-knapped me.'

'So that's why the foitling church was unlocked ... lucky we came back when we did. *Not* that we was much in a state to attack any interlopers—merda, Tom! them mushies was strong.'

'So, you had no idea where I was until ...'

LONDONIA

'I went round to Sardi's the day after thinking p'raps you'd gone there for a damey chat or sumink, and there you were all bruised and fevery.'

'So, where's this Straightfish now?' says Tom, looking thundery.

I wave vaguely Eastwards. 'He was taking me to an island called Sheppy?'

'That's at the end of Lady Thames and round a bit,' says Jarvis. ' 'E got a place there?'

'A mansion house he was going to install me in, along with his ill-grabbed gains.'

'He was goin' to give up haulin' an' live on the proceeds—with you?'

'Seemed to be the idea. Hopefully he'll find a replacement and stay there.' I wonder whether to mention Straightfish's words about the pocket-watch but decide against it—for now. 'Anylane, enough about him. What's been happening here?'

'Worryin' 'bout you, mainly.'

'No, really. What else?'

'Err . . . got the clothes back from Bert the swagger and did the trade. Works well that weird washing contraption of 'is.'

'Apex. I've got more he can do.'

'Ah—it's broken, but 'e's workin' on it. Back to slappin' the rocks for the while . . . oh yeah, tell 'er about your pond idea, Tom. If the word *fish* ain't too distasteful.'

Tom relights his bacco stick, has a puff and waves it in the direction of the garden.

'Thought if we extended out into that rough land we could make a trout pond. Who owns the scrub, anyone?'

I think of the rubble-filled scrap-land where a row of buildings had collapsed some cycles ago. 'No one, as far as I know.'

'So, what d'you reckon. A goodly idea?'

'Brilli. We'd need a lot of help . . .'

'Easy,' says Jarvis. 'Invite a ton 'a bods for a pizz-up and get them to work first.'

LONDONIA

'Golden-quarter celebration fete?' I suggest.

'Apex. Music, dancing, scran and pond excavation—like it . . . s'that the bell?'

Tom hops up. 'I'll go.'

Jarvis clunks teapot and bowls onto the table. 'You two ça va?'

I think of Tom's last words about our *meanderings*. 'Yes. It's fine.'

'Christ in a vest, H. Why d'you ever fuk that jewellery-tic?'

'Has it ever stopped you after you've had too much gnole,' I retort. 'You know—nice body, but he's a bit of a scrote-bag so I'll refrain . . .'

Jarvis grins at my speech and slaps me gently on the cheek. 'Yeah—s'pose we none of us angels.'

Tom walks back in holding an envelope. 'For you, H. I had to sign a bit of paper as it's from the Cincture.'

Ripping open the flap, I find a reply from Mrs Caruso.

My dear Hoxton. You must think I am so rude to have not contacted you regarding our arrangement. We got busy with the salon. Caruso will be able to spare half an hour this Tuesday evening at 17.00 to speak with you.

If you are coming in, could find some more nail varnish for us? The salon is doing hyper-well and we are low on the unusual colours naimly, green, blue, silver and yellow—anything you could find would be divine. Hopefully see you on Tuesday in the salon at about 16.00.

Your friend Beccy.

'So, says Jarvis, 's'it from them dames?'

I hand him the letter. 'She's made the arrangement I asked for.'

Jarvis scans it with a grunt and passes it to Tom who looks up from the words, mystified. 'You mean there are dames in there who will give over good doctor stuff to get . . . what is it?

LONDONIA

Colour to put on nails? You're going to bang 'em into wood—why would you paint 'em?'

I laugh until tears squeeze from my eyes. '. . . Yes, why would you. Have a look at this.' I pass him a copy of *Vogue* 2016 from my fashion reference pile and he carefully turns the pages gawping at the various pictures.

'Foitling weirdi. Red finger nails . . . and this dame here, is she starved or what?'

I look at the sullen-faced girl draped over a tractor. 'No. Well, possibly—but from her own, or rather the industry's choosing. They all looked skeletal. It was the fashion.'

'Why's she in a field with rubber boots and a see-though dress on? She'd get foitlin' freezed—apart from her feet. And that feathery scarf thing—get all tangled up in the gears. Here, have a look Jarvis.'

He does for a couple of moments and flops it down with disgust.

'They could photo some of the dames round about here who's bags 'a bones—and not coz they want it . . . anylane, you got a passport to go back in.'

'What day is it,' I ask, replacing the magazine.

Jarvis checks the agenda book. 'Satdy.'

'D'ac. I'll go and see the dame about the varnish orjordui, and then get on with the rest of the trades in hand. Could you take me to the walls on Twosdy?'

'I'll take you,' suggests Tom. 'Coal needs shoeing and there's a good smithy near there.'

'Perfect. Shall we start the jobs?'

Tom pushes me gently back down to the bed. 'Have a day off, H. You still need to rest. Start again on the morrow, eh?'

I'm about to protest but certain aches suggest a day lounging in the vestry might be a better option, so I smile, round up some books and join Zorro for a relaxing aft on the bed.

Capitula 21

Twosdy has arrived and after a successful trip to relieve Mrs Myers of some of her varnish collection, I now stand in a gusting, gritty wind outside the walls with the usual knot of bods trying to gain access.

An official appears and reads out a short list.

'Three entries approved for this Tuesday afternoon: Felixston—portrait painter . . . Collins, what does this say?'

A guard approaches and stares at the paper. 'Beverly Black, therapist—I think.'

'Oh—thought it said Beddery Plack is pissed—whose *is* this writing?' He takes back the sheet of paper and reads out what I was hoping to hear. 'And, *Hoxton*? Finder.'

I step forward, wave to Tom standing with Coal some distance away, and proceed into the cleansing zone. Half a Cincture clockface later my shaw turns into Wigmore Street and Mrs Caruso, attired in a canary-yellow dress steps from the shop and kisses me—*mwe, mwe*, taking care to stand back from the cleansing's carbolic smell.

'Hoxton! Peeped you got my little missive! Come in and have a Valdivian-vodka ice-storm.'

Mrs Nash is sitting in a rococo armchair sipping something in a cone-shaped glass.

'Coo-coo, Madame Finder. You managed it then?'

I put the bag down and take out the pots. 'I did. She still has a good supply so if you want—'

She cuts me short.

'Actually, we wanted to talk to you about another project. Remember we mentioned the new furore for rustic-peasant?'

'Err . . .'

LONDONIA

'Did you go to see that person called Mange in the forest?'

My head is beginning to feel soft and full of air. Perhaps I could escape and walk over to Iona's house.

'No . . .'

'Oh—well, glad you didn't as we are thinking more pastels and florals now . . . stripped pine.'

Mrs Caruso picks up each bottle and examines it. 'Yes. In *fact*, we may be closing this salon and taking bigger premises to sell fabric and furniture of that era. Have you heard of a woman called Laura Ashley?'

I can see where this is heading: me scouring all the shouting-houses for pastel floral fabric and them changing their minds. But, I might have to keep this madness rolling if Dr Caruso is of no use to me.

'No. Sorry, I haven't, but I can certainly ask a few contacts of mine.' They yak on for some time, me nodding and adding a few encouraging words until a small interlude arrives allowing me to ask Mrs Caruso about my trade-fees. 'Are the medical kits here?'

She glances up from trying a lurid blue nail-polish. 'I left them with Gubbins as you'll be seeing Caruso as arranged.'

I thank her, down the peculiar iced drink I had been given, say my unacknowledged goodbyes and walk out to find a shaw to take me to the Caruso house. Fury burns in me at the wasted time searching for unwanted, stupid, useless things—*again*. Still, I have my meeting as traded and a way back in here if they are going to start yet another *hobby*.

The shaw drops me and Gubbins opens the door at my knock. He stands back to let me through.

'Dr Caruso is expecting you in his study. This way, please.'

He raps gently on a door further along the hallway and a deep, resonant voice answers. 'Is it the Londonia woman?' Gubbins replies in the affirmative. 'Let her come in, and fetch another bottle of whiskey.'

'Yes, Sir.'

LONDONIA

The door is opened for me and I walk into a blue-walled room where glass boxes containing animals in arrested states stare down at me with their black, shiny eyes. As the door closes behind me I see Caruso stretching to replace a book onto a bookcase's top shelf. He lowers his arm, readjusts his clothing and turns. His figure is tall and slim, encased in an expensive-looking grey suit, his angular face topped by slick-backed greying blond hair.

'So, you . . .' He stops and stares at me, his started sentence hanging in this shadowy room. I stare back at him wondering where I have seen his face before. It is as if time has disappeared. I notice every detail of this room and him in absolute clarity: the polished guns mounted on the wall behind his desk, a large glass paper-weight filled with bubbles. His green eyes behind severe black-framed glasses.

'Apologies,' he continues. 'I've just recalled something important I have to do . . . I don't have very long.' His voice is breathy, anxious. I have the impression that seeing me is probably the last thing he ever would have imagined.

'I won't take up your time, Dr Caruso but your wife did make this trade with me.'

He emits a sound like a cross between a grunt and a sigh.

'Was it for the damned furniture or the *beauty* accessories?'

'It stands from the furniture-finding, sir. You must understand it was a lot of work for me in Londonia.'

'You . . . yes. You are all right there—in Londonia, then . . .'

'Very well. Why?'

'I was just . . . interested to meet someone who survived—I mean survives out there.'

After searching for a cigarette in a silver box on the desk, Caruso lights it with a still-shaking hand. He throws the box of matches to the desk, inhales and blows out a stream of smoke. I feel the relief as the nicotine hits. Gubbins enters the room with the demanded whiskey.

LONDONIA

Caruso gestures to his empty glass on the sideboard. 'Fix me another, Gubbins, will you? Would you care for a drink, Miss Hoxton?'

'Please.'

The servant pours out two measures of amber fluid, adds a spritz of soda and passes us the glasses before quietly leaving again.

Caruso's breathing seems to have calmed. He perches on the desk, glancing at me. He hasn't offered me a chair; it's as if he wants to observe me in totality—head to foot.

'What is it that you require?'

I down the whisky in one and gasp slightly at its fire-descent.

'. . . I understand you work in the Cincture hospitals.'

He straightens up a little. 'I am *chief* surgeon in Cincture One hospital.'

I dig out an air of being impressed. 'Wonderful. Therefore perhaps you might have contacts in the births records department?'

He pours another drink and swigs half of it. 'Births . . .'

'Well, actually adoptions, or records of orphans.'

'And when would this have been?'

'Either the Cincture year of two-thousand and fifty-one or fifty-two. Also there was an important identifying feature of a birthmark on the child's neck.'

He turns from me and locates a metal tablet on the desk. His hands tremble a little but he's gained his starchy composure. He pushes the spectacles onto the bridge of his nose, runs a hand through a section of greased hair that has flopped forward and sits to consult the thing after pushing a few buttons.

As he looks back at me his eyes meet the glare from an anglepoise lamp, the green irises weirdly illuminated. I know I have seen eyes like this before—such a strange colour. *The dream.* He starts to speak stiffly.

'I do have the name of the correct contact for you but I think it would be better if I make the enquiries myself. I don't think you would get too far under your own efforts—there's a lot of red-tape, you understand.'

I put the glass down on the desk, it's small *click* loud in the silence.

'Will you be able to ask your contact soon? I have other requests from your wife and would like to have my trade paid up so far.'

His forehead furrows at this. I have the impression his wife is a niggling thorn, and not just in his side.

'Yes. I will look into it tomorrow and a letter will be sent to you if and when I have any information—although frankly, I think it may be unlikely. Now. If you can excuse me, I have a meeting to be getting to.'

'Certainly.' I hold out a hand and he takes it reluctantly, eyes averted, a brief shake.

I leave the room, its door's swish over the carpet not quite covering the whistling sigh I hear him exhale.

It's late now. Getting back out though the access point took longer than usual as a scoop truck had just returned, apparently from an incident near Old Street. The wind still flays the streets of Londonia as I walk, heavy bag of medical stuff over one shoulder and my stomach protesting at its alcoholic contents. I pass a late-eve café and although I want to get back, the spicy smell drifting from its doorway is too much.

I enter and take a seat near the smouldering fire. This golden-quarter seems to have retreated back somewhat in time and I'm rattly cold. A dame weaves her way towards me through the cluster of chess tables and lounging dogs. Her Portuguese-Spanish-Londonia mix is complex for my addled brain so I point

LONDONIA

to a bowl of something an old gar is hunched over on the next table and give her a thumbs-up.

'Vinho?' she smiles, gesturing to the bottle in her hand.

'Nao obrigado,' I manage.

The blue of these walls—apart from their stains and patches—is not unlike the colour of that study I had stood in and heard Caruso placate me, those odd eyes full of Cincture secrets I doubt I will ever access. A shout from a couple of tables away disrupts my recent memories. Chess pieces jump as one of the mecs palms the board hard.

'Merda—Stalemate!'

Stalemate. Is that where I am at with this most important Find ever?

My bowl arrives and I dig into a heap of salted fish and potato, wash it down with some brown-ish water, hand over a tube of antiseptic cream and aspirin in way of payment and leave the place with a wave.

Rain has now joined in with the wind. I pace furiously, fuelled by cod and patatas and arrive at the church to be greeted by over-excited hounds and indifferent cats. Jarvis, judging by the snores from the woodhouse has decided on an early night but Tom is still awake sitting by the stove reading a book on fungi. He uncurls from the armchair and jumps up.

'H. You look frozzed. Sit here and I'll rev the fire up a bit.' I take his warm chair and allow him to fuss about with blankets and wool-shoes. A short while later I'm happily bundled up with a cup of hot milk in hand, staring at the flames while he sorts the bed out.

'Could do with some more straw for the matrass. I've turned this but it's a bit pitted.'

I look over at the rumpled ticking and nod. 'They'll be doing a first cut at the Lees-bridge meadows soon. We'll get a load and re-do them . . . so, what have I missed here?'

Tom sits down opposite me and smiles. 'S'only been a day.'

'Feels like about three.'

LONDONIA

'We've done a lot in the garden . . . but what happened in there?'

'Mostly a foitling waste of time.' I explain about the dames and their new obsessions and then the meeting with Caruso. Tom gets up and replaces the book on a shelf. I feel the atmosphere change as he turns and glowers.

'You just can't leave it, can yer? Just coz that mirror-dame told you about a gosse don't mean it's true.'

I feel an argument brewing and I'm tired and frustrated enough to oblige.

'Tom. You can't understand what this feels like—and anyway, my friend Iona saw the babe. It is true!'

'Fuksake, H. We can make another! Leave the pizzin Cincture alone—it's dangerous and that bastard, Crusera . . . sounds shifty.'

'Caruso. And yes, maybe he was but it's a chance! *And* maybe I can't just *make another* as you put it.'

'Well, maybe we should try—unless you want t' have a go with that jewellery-gang merde-head.'

'Oh, fuk off, Tom.'

'I am—gonna spend a bit of time on the boat.'

He grabs his jacket from the back of the door and lunges out from the room, turning once.

'Forget the past, H.'

Capitula 22

The days pass as I wait for a letter back from Caruso. Maybe Tom was right, but right isn't necesarily easy. The thought of my offspring somewhere within those walls is never far away.

The wind and rain of a few eves ago also now seems unreal as I sit in the early morn sun planning the day's jobs. As I bend my head to write a list, Jarvis appears with breakfast.

He puts the tray down on a tree stump and flops into a chair. 'Eggs but no butter left.'

'We could get a cow,' I muse, thinking of regular butter supplies. 'Take it up to the Parkplace, or perhaps this new garden extension idea.'

'Hampsteadland's commune's got them brown cows—pale with big eyes. Owes me, he does—the main mec.'

I smile at the thought of the pastoral scene: a Guernsey cow and a few goats grazing, their bells tinkling; me dressed in white with a milking stool and a pail.

'Something drole?' he says.

I pour the tea. 'A bit, but also completely wonderful.'

Flicking a last bit of shell to the ground, Jarvis dips his egg in a pot of salt and munches.

'Veg, milk, rabbits, chickens . . . could be almost self-sufficient, us, this place.'

We eat and talk of the extension until Jarvis abruptly stands up and walks over to the shed. He returns holding a pickaxe, strips off his shirt and jerks his head towards the back wall.

'No time like the now, eh? Mind, could do with Tom's help. When you two gonna sort this stupid tif out?'

'When he apologises.'

LONDONIA

'He 'as a point, H.' Jarvis observes my expression and drops the axe, hands up in mock surrender. 'D'ac—d'ac, just sayin'. Keep yer felty on.'

He lopes off with the tool and I sit growly-minded while the sound of cracking brick and stone covers the birdsong. My mood subsides as interest takes over and I go to see what he has revealed.

Beyond the pile of old wall a rubble-filled field dozes undisturbed in the sun. Groups of scrawny saplings crowd amongst fallen dead trees, brambles and weeds everywhere.

Jarvis surveys the road beyond where a gang of ado-gosses languish by a wall smoking and talking. Two fingers in his mouth he emits a piercing whistle, then shouts.

'Oi, you lot . . . job. Good for silvers, beer and Zeitporn.' The effect is impressive. They rise and descend like a cloud of bees, clamouring at Jarvis. 'D'ac 'ere's the deal,' he continues. 'Shift this lot. Concrete an' rubble over there, wood 'ere, and general dechets . . . there.'

'Show us the stuff first,' pouts the obvious spokesperson, a skinny red-headed girl.

'Fair point,' says Jarvis. 'A mo, d'ac?'

The group stand looking into the newly-revealed garden.

'C'est quoi ça?' asks a small bulldog of a boy, pointing at some overgrown Brussels sprout plants. I tell him, the idea of a gardening school appearing in my thoughts.

They continue to stare, some with interest, some feigning indifference. Their collective appearance suggests a diet of streepeeza and scrounged bread. I hazard a question.

'How about growing stuff yourselves?'

They shrug, eyes wary, but I can feel the interest rippling through the small crowd.

Jarvis returns with a box and displays the goods.

'Sound,' says the girl. She splits the group into units and they follow her orders.

LONDONIA

A long clock-face later when I return with crypt-cooled water for them all, the ground is virtually stripped.

'Expert scavengers,' remarks Jarvis, looking at the pack as they turn over the pile of detritus to the left of the land. The girl signals and they follow her over, snatching up the cups and drinking noisily.

'Where do you live?' I ask the bulldog boy.

'Quoi, madame?' he scowls.

I try again in French and the answer doesn't surprise: in the scrap wood and cardboard warren of the old Royal London hospital.

'Tes parents . . . ils sont où?' I ask, the answer depressing: both parents murdered while he was out trying to find his sister.

Feeling reckless, I announce to the crowd that I'll be starting a gardening school before the end of autumn. Most of them shrug, a few snort disbelief, but a small element nod, eyes bright.

'What'll it cost, Miss?' asks a scrawny girl, legs like a sparrow and eyes of violet.

'Nothing. Just your help.' She grins and nods as the group moves off, following the ginger girl and the box.

Jarvis takes off his hat and scratches his head. 'Blimey, H, you sure about that?'

'Yes, I'm sure. Maybe I've lost my own gosse but I could help some others.'

'Vrai, yeah . . . why not? In fact, building school too?' He looks over at the gosses re-installed, pipe smoke drifting and voices raised over the spoils. He tramps over the scrub, talks to them and returns, a smile playing. 'Wall-building. Starts morrow. We've gotta get this place circled and claimed.'

I've just taken the tray back to the vestry when I hear the gate bell. Memories of Straightfish in my mind, I take Fagin to the door and grind it back. A horse-letter-mec stands there whistling. I open the gate and smile back at him as he hands over two envelopes.

'From the Cincture?'

LONDONIA

He nods. 'Aye—and they needs signing fr'. I's going back there now—last delivery.'

'Does that mean they'll get my response t-dui?'

'Reckon, aye, or the morrow.'

'Apex.' I take the pad he holds out and sign my name. 'Silvers or potatoes?'

He thinks for a moment, twiddling his beard-end. 'Tatee's be grand. Now me shift's done, I'll get wife t' fry 'em oup.'

'D'ac. Would you mind waiting a mo?'

I scoot back into the church, bag up the potatoes and breathe in deeply before investigating the letters. Neither has the appearance of being intervened with as both envelope flaps have been stuck down with dark green wax seals that bear the imprint of two different family names: Hedgefund and Caruso.

I open the first and read the few words from Iona.

Dearest friend. I was just wondering how you got on meeting the great Doctor. Do come and see me soon. Iona.
X

The second letter contains a bald missive from Caruso but the contents of which make my heart leap.

Your recent request has been fulfilled.

There were only three recorded male orphaned children during the years you mentioned. I have information regarding a man called Todd who fits your description currently working within the tunnels as a trainee manager. An arrangement has been made for you to meet him at fourteen hours Cincture time, this coming Tuesday. Take the tour and he will find you in concourse three as you leave.

I hastily scribble a note to Iona saying I will call at their house on the Twosdy morn and telling her of the meeting, and another to Caruso acknowledging the rendezvous. After stowing them carefully in his near-empty sack bag the letter-mec re-mounts his patient horse.

'I'll mek sure this gets seen tout-sweet.'

I watch him sway off down the street then return to the vestry.

'Who was it?' says Jarvis coming in with a trug of broad beans.

I take one of the pods, crack it and slide out a bean. 'These look amazing . . . must have been all that rain.'

'*So?*'

I munch the bean, still shock-struck.

'Was a horse-letter man.'

'Which one?'

'The gar with the Northern burr.'

'Should have invited 'im in—quite a laugh after a couple 'e is.'

'I didn't want to stop him from his return mission.'

'Eh?'

'He had two letters for me that both needed signing and taking back to the Cincture.'

Jarvis sits down and starts faffing with bacco and new clay pipe. 'Tell—*all.*'

I pass him Caruso's letter. 'The other's just a note from Iona.' He scans the words.

'Let panners in the tunnels, do they?' He lights the pipe, breathes in the fruity smoke and exhales. '. . . Who's this Cincturian mollusc? And wot've you agreed to?'

'I haven't agreed to anything. It's part of my trade with his wife.'

'You shouldn't have nufink to do with these fukkas—probably knows the very ones wot removed yer brain.'

Snatching the note back, I fume at him. 'Like I said, they didn't *remove* my brain!'

'Sorry—evi not, but he is a fukka, vrai?'

LONDONIA

'He probably is but he's got me a rendezvous.'

Jarvis re-lights the pipe from a twig poked into the fire and peers at me as he blows out the flame.

'Believe him, do yer?'

Capitula 23

The shaw-driver turns to me.

'Hanover Terrace was it, lady?'

I lean forward. 'Thanks, yes. Number fifty-eight.'

He continues along two more roads, turns a corner and stops outside Iona's house. She's out of the door as I alight. The shaw wizzes off and we embrace.

'I was afraid the letter might have gone astray,' she says as we walk into the hallway. 'I'm so glad to see you! How absolutely amazing that Caruso has found this . . . person. You are prepared that he might not want to talk to you—might not even be him.'

'Yes, I am.' I assure her. '*And* I realise it may take many visits to convince him of who I am.'

'Did Caruso mention a DNA test?'

'. . . No.'

'Well, maybe he's right—just an initial impression, hm?'

'Iona?'

'Yes?'

'What is in the tunnels?'

'Something you won't want to see. In fact I want to come with you, and I think we should attire you in something other than the allinone or the trouser suit.'

Half a Cincture hour later, I'm dressed in a long peacock-blue dress with matching handbag, other hand clutching a small white parasol.

'Why do I need this?' I ask, fiddling with the up-and-down mechanism as we wait for another shaw.

LONDONIA

She collapses her own miniature umbrella as our carriage arrives. 'You don't. It's just what women are carrying about here this summer.'

We climb in and sit silently. She seems nervous.

'Have you done this before?' I half-whisper a few streets on.

She looks back at me, eyes huge under her silk hat.

'Yes. And I said I'd never do it again.'

'Tell me what it is.'

'Where do you think most of the meat consumed in the Cincture comes from?'

'I don't know—farms outside the parimeter somewhere? Cincture owned lands?'

'The highest class stuff yes, but for the rest of the population—they've developed new ways. Box-beasts is one lightly used term.'

The shaw turns into a wider road and then stops outside a glass building, the pavement outside busy with shaws and cars. Our driver helps us out and we join a group of dames evidently waiting to enter the building. From the chatter, I have the impression this is a popular venue to visit in the Cincture with tastings afterwards and a gift shop. From a gateway a trickle of uniformed bods walk both ways—some having finished a shift, some just starting.

A mec appears from one of the glass doorways.

'We are ready for the next tour if you would like to follow me. Payment will be taken either by idi-carte or Squares.'

Iona takes my arm.

'I'll put you on my idi-carte. *Don't* say anything as we go down there. Just concentrate on the meeting afterwards.'

The spritely guide walks ahead and we descend into a warm brown nightmare of a place. The noise makes me want to scream—a low hum of frustrated animals, and a constant whirr of machinery. Down flights of stairs kept constantly clean by minions we pass on and on, the noise becoming ever louder. The guide keeps up a merry chatter of information as if he were describing the manufacture of paint, or wine; dames ask questions and I keep my eyes trained on the embroidered dresses of the dames in front of me.

Finally, we arrive at the destination. I grind my nails into my palms as I catch glimpses of the horror before me. Boxed beasts extend as far as I can see into the yawning tunnels, their heads swivelling, eyes bulging as they live out this captive hell. Workers sweep, sluice, shovel. Great machinery sucks the foul air into tubes to be blasted out into the sky above us.

Iona squeezes my arm and whispers. 'Keep looking. Don't think about this now.'

Even the dames are quiet within this theatre of slow-motion death. The guide keeps talking.

'These bovine forms are created to fill each box—no need of legs and easy for the production line . . . and over here—our latest development in milk production. Sanitised, safe and easy for the workers too. The udder of each animal descends here,' he gestures to the bottom of one of the metal boxes, 'and we have managed to create a new model with eight teats—faster, more efficient.'

The crowd have started to ask questions, a bit of giggling at the word teats. I wonder if I might be sick. Holding on to the railings I retch and cover it with a cough.

'Iona. I *have* to get out of here.'

'We're moving,' she says still holding my arm, fingers tight. 'Imagine something normal, the sun, plants, your hounds . . .'

I fill my mind with images of the garden, the cow with dark brown eyes that Jarvis said he would get for us. Tears start to fall. I wipe them away and stare into the tunnel at the unmoving, encased bodies. Thank God, our group is walking on, the guide talking of the trains that still run out to the plantations at somewhere called Rick-worth, the marvellous abundance of foodstuffs, the fishing factories and poultry corporations. At last after much slow advancing we arrive at a room full of charts where we are requested to sit and are shown a film of the

LONDONIA

Custodian: a porky, ginger-haired mec visiting the various factories and praising the falsely grinning workforce. After this, the guide announces we will be able to enjoy refreshment and purchase fine leather goods from the tunnel-shop.

We walk back up a flight of stairs, fresh air seeping from above. Despite my utter relief at leaving that place, I feel anxious now about the proposed meeting. Iona takes my hand as we walk towards two glass-walled rooms, one, a shop containing the by-products of death, the other, concourse three.

I stare at the cold-looking room, unnerved now by what I have seen. 'This is where I was told to meet . . . him.'

Iona squeezes my hand. 'Come on then.'

She opens the glass door and we sit on two metal chairs opposite posters depicting happy cows grazing on undulating meadows. After what seems like a whole cycle, a door opens and a mec comes in dressed in an orange allinone. My heart thuds madly until I see he is middle-aged, dark hair sprouting from under his orange cap.

'Miss Hoxton?'

I stand up, legs shaky. 'Yes.'

'You are to follow me.' He gestures to Iona. 'There was no mention of two people. I'm afraid you will have to join the main party leaving now.'

She looks doubtfully at me. 'Will you be all right.'

I think of the Clasher gang attacks I've survived, the bouts of Xtra-flu . . . 'Yes. I'll be fine. I'll bring the outfit back later.' She walks away, looks back once and I grin with a confidence that is already ebbing.

The mec is waiting. I note his glance at a watch. He starts to walk through the doorway again and I catch him up.

'Why does he—Todd—want to meet me here?'

The mec doesn't reply just speeds on, me following, tripping on the dress. I hitch the skirts up and start to run.

'Wait. Why the rush?'

LONDONIA

After many yards of corridor he stops abruptly, opens a door to his left and grabs me, pushing me inside. He shuts the door after us and clicks on a light revealing a small dim room containing a basic single bed. One wall of the room is missing apart from a small wall and railing. I glance fearfully into the darkness beyond. The low chorus of beasts is faintly audible. A musty, warm draft rocks the metal lampshade above us. I back away from the mec who is now smiling unpleasantly.

My voice is reedy against the rumbling and rushing sounds. 'What is this place . . . where is Todd?'

'Got taken in good there, didn't you, Miss Finder. This is an observation room and Todd . . . figment of the boss's imagination.'

Something troubling about Caruso. I should have listened to my quieter, rational self. *Crap.*

'So you're going to baden-poke me and fling me over that precipice?'

He's removed the cap and is advancing. His hair resembles a mangy cat camped out on his head. Despite everything I start to laugh.

He grabs me. 'Don't bloody laugh. Yeah—they didn't specify how I was to do it, or what I might do before but that might be a good plan.'

I push back from his mouth that smells as bad as the stench from out in the void. He's strong despite his small stature but my fury at this trap is at its max. He rips Iona's dress right down the front. Mother of pearl buttons ping against the bare walls. Lunging forward, I grasp his scrote-sack and twist hard. He gasps, doubles up hissing and I back away, dress fabric dragging.

As he unfurls, I see the glint of a knife in his hand. We circle. Stooped, hands outstretched, waiting for each other to make a move. The stupid parasol lies on the bed where I had dropped it. Grabbing it, I crack it down on his knife-hand. He yowls like Zorro and springs at me. The knife clatters on the concrete floor. I scoop it, cutting wildly into his arm that now encircles my throat. He's somehow ignoring the blood that geysers from his arm.

His legs kick mine into moving forwards. The abyss yawns. The railing digs into my thighs. How far is it to fall? The pressure is still on my throat, the light seeming to dim. The knife is slimy with his blood. My fingers start to lose their grip on its handle. It falls, its twisting small shape disappearing into the blackness. He tips me, head down into the void, the railing now crushing my stomach. The old scar bristles and my half-numb mind recalls why I am here. I twist back with a last blaze of anger. The sudden movement catches him and I grope for one of Iona's pointed shoes, rip it from my foot and hack it backwards. The heel catches his face and he releases me with a screech, hands groping wildly. He's staggering close to the railing, hits it like a pinball and I pitch forward, seizing his legs and bundling him over the edge.

His reedy cry ends with a muffled thud somewhere. Now the room is silent, just the distant whirr of machinery and hum of bovine misery. I have no idea where I am in this maze but to go back to the concourse with ripped clothes and his blood on me seems a bad idea. Opening the door fraction by fraction, I peer out into the tubular corridor, lit intermittently by flickering cold lights.

Turning left, I pace swiftly, bruised bits of me protesting. As if in a dream the passageway rolls away into the distance, dotted with small pools of light and the occasional door. At the sounds of voices behind one, I start to run, trip and fall over the dragging folds of the dress. Ripping it at the knee, the cloth gives way until I stand in a frayed, thigh-length garment. Better.

I walk for what seems like several miles, the floor seeming to gradually slope upwards. I pass through doors and around bends, rodents streaking away from me. The light ends and I now walk in fusty darkness, hands outstretched, fingers grazing on the uneven walls. The sounds change from the low hum to sudden bursts of voices from above, the clatter of street-noise,

LONDONIA

horses' hooves. Tiny patches of daylight leak down to this never-ending corridor; judging by the sounds, daylight from Londonia. Forcing away a claustrophobic urge to scream, I walk on. This must go *somewhere*.

As the word, somewhere, forms in my mind, I notice a slightly larger square of daylight a few yards on. I reach it and peer upwards into a narrow shaft of some kind. I start to climb a series of metal rungs piercing the wall and after reaching the height of an oak tree find my possible exit blocked by a rusting grid. *Fuk*. All this way to be trapped in the top of a brick tower. Then I let the scream out—all the frustration, and fear and fury at being beguiled into this foitling *cage*. The grid is solid despite the rusting. My pushing and yanking procure nothing. I call out and then stand on the last rung knowing I will have to go back and face whatever will be my fate in the cow-plant. I try one last yell, fingers gripping and shoving the metal. Rust flakes. My eyes squint through orange dust. I shut them and prepare to descend.

As I put a foot gingerly down to the next rung, something touches my fingers. I recoil and nearly fall.

'Miss? Wot you doin' in there?'

Focusing beyond the bars I see a pair of brown eyes under a mess of fair hair and a gawping mouth. Another young face appears.

'How'd she get in there?'

I step on the last rung and smile out at them. 'Get me out and I'll tell you.'

The sun is sinking over the rooftops as the cart-driver drops me outside the church. He gallantly gets down and helps me out from the back where I sit amongst stacks of recycled paper.

LONDONIA

He waves away my offer of finding him some gnole or bacco. 'Was goin' to the press, anylane. Get yerself a goodly sleep!'

Praying Jarvis is in, I jangle the gate bell. The dogs answer with a chorus of howls then I hear a rattle of keys and the joyous sound of my friend's swearing. The door grinds open and he peers out.

'Hox! Reckoned you'd opted for Cincture lux.'

I gesture to my ripped clothes. 'Hardly.'

He hops down the steps and unlocks the gate. 'Where the fuk you been—wass all that soot 'n merde? Did you see 'im?'

Suddenly it's all too much and I lean, howling muffeldly into his suit.

'Allez, H,' he says. 'Let's get a bath goin' and you can tell us all 'bout it.'

'Us?'

He grins and takes my arm. 'Yeah. Tom's 'ere—time to patch up, eh?'

The pathetic pride thing rises within me and slinks away just as quickly. I've missed him. He looks up from the chess board as I walk in. Whatever anger he had has long gone.

'Christ in a *bin-bag*. What the fuk . . .'

He's over in a second, hugging me. I wince as his arms press into my various bruises.

'Ow. Careful.'

'Who did this?'

'Wosn't that crud-'ead, Caruso, wos it?' adds Jarvis rounding up pans of water and clanging them on the wood-stove.

'No. It was someone who was supposed to be taking me to see . . .'

'Yor son?'

'Yes.' Neither of them say what I expect they are thinking so I say it for them.

'D'ac. Maybe you are right. Maybe I should forget this dream of finding my gosse—give up.'

LONDONIA

Tom pulls me over to the couch and puts an arm around me as we sit.

'It's only coz we love you—don't want to see you hurt.'

The thought of shutting out this urge seems impossible, but in some way, a depressing relief. Could I just shut my mind to it—get on with this life? Probably not. But I might have to.

Sometime later, I sit washed and revived outside in the dusky garden having recounted most of the story. Tom is creating something out of beans, potatoes and sheep cheese while Jarvis treats me to one of his foot rubs.

'So. Where wos this tower thing and how did the gosses get you out—*and* wot d'we owe 'em.'

I think back to scrambling down the edge of the odd square, brick thing, wondering if I was about to fall and finish myself off as others had planned.

'It was one of the old vent towers of the Victoria Tube-line. Apparently, the local ghost-tales stop bods going up to investigate but these two gosses heard me and decided to ignore the stories—luckily.'

'How'd they cut the grill?'

'Two long cycles and a lot of saw blades.'

'We do owe 'em, alors.'

'I said I'd take a big cart-load of clothing, veg and eggs.'

'And Coaka.'

'Bien sur.'

Jarvis removes my feet from his lap as Tom appears with a tray. He puts it down and unloads bowls, a pot of steaming something, a bottle of Jake's cider and three glasses. He serves us as we look on hungrily then pours the amber fluid and raises a glass.

'Here's to Londonia, and *scrote* to the Cincture.'

Capitula 24

It is two sevdays since I returned from nearly being pushed over a railing to meet my maker. I've almost managed to prison away the thoughts of my son, but t-dui have allowed myself a visit to see Marina—just in case she might have been wrong . . .

Iona has written to me—a letter full of angst, and I have apologised by return for not telling her what happened. I will go back in there. I want to keep our friendship at least even if nothing else good has come of these traversings.

I stare at Marina's black door as my hand rises to knock. I know she is there and not with anyone, as the landlady told me as much. My knuckles are just about to meet the door's scratched black surface when it swings open and I'm looking into the peculiar pale eyes.

'Hoxton. I thought I was to have visit. Come. Have glass of nettle vodka.'

I pause, wondering whether to kiss her, think better of it and walk into the dog-filled room.

She pours me a small tumbler of clear fluid and we sit near the window. She stares at me as if already absorbing my thoughts. I sip and splutter and a smile twitches on her lips.

'Is goodly strong. I make it with friend in High-gate.'

I take another larger gulp knowing it will release my thoughts.

'It certainly is. How is business?'

'*Blyad*! Busy, busy. Many bods. Too many.'

'I hope I haven't called at a bad time . . .'

'No. I make time for you. Perhaps you can find me new boots for amber-quarter.'

'Certainly.'

LONDONIA

'So.' She shuffles her chair nearer after removing a stretched-out hound. 'Let me see what troubles you.'

She takes my hand and closes hers around it. My mind drifts. Caruso's green eyes illuminated by his desk lamp. A silver pocket watch. A young man with fair hair. Time passes. I've no idea how much but then I'm fully awake, head throbbing, looking back at Marina.

She releases my hand and nods slowly as she sits back. 'You question if he exists—the gosse.'

'I had started to wonder.'

'What I say before is truth. He is in Cincture and mec with green eyes is father.'

Her words floor me. I pick up the glass and drain the last drop of fluid, hands shaking.

'. . . Did you see another mec with long greying hair?'

She thinks, eyes roaming the room to stop at me. 'Mm. He of name like . . . Bentfish?'

'Ah. Straightfish.'

'There is connection with green-eyed mec. Perhaps to be wary—you had incident with him? I said to be careful of water.'

'You did, and I did—have an incident . . . with him.'

'D'ac.'

'Marina. I don't know how to find my son. I've tried but have only found dead-ends.'

'Dead—ends? Ya. Herring rouges . . . I think you not try hard enough.' She waves away my protesting. 'The dame who run shop in Cincture—she ask for something you not honour.'

'The dame . . . in Gershwin's. But she gave me the wrong information.'

Marina yawns neatly as she gestures to the bed. 'Prosti. Time to sleep. Perhaps I see you at Jake's.'

She's already up and walking slowly to the pile of greyhounds. I call an unacknowledged thanks and promise of boot-Finding then close the door quietly and walk downstairs to find Kafka still tethered to a lamppost, the horse-boy slowly reading

LONDONIA

out loud from the book I had given him. He turns from the pages and grins.

'S'good this—makes yer think 'bout 'fore the Curtain.'

I hoist myself up onto Kafka and suggest he can always call and borrow more books. As we ride away, Marina's words float back into my rung-out mind. *Man of green eyes is father.* I think back to Caruso's reaction to me and wonder how this might change any future traversings.

Back at the church, I brush down Kafka and close my mind to beyond the walls. Jarvis will be returning with a load of goods from a new shouting house to sort through and there's fishing nets to darn after Tom snagged the big one out on the Thames estuary.

I go through into the vestry, change into thinner clothes, locate string and needle and sit in the cool room head bent over the mass of netting. A cycle later I've repaired the main holes and dump it all to one side to make a brew. As the kettle starts to whine towards a boil, Jarvis comes in and drops a large box onto the sofa.

'Goodly place?' I ask.

He shrugs and searches about his person for his bacco pouch. 'Ça va. Most of it merda but I did get a cache of stuff from a basement in some posh flats wot's crumbled. 'Ave a look. S'that a cuppa in the making?'

'Certainly is.' I open the box and take out shoes, unused hairbrushes, sealed toothpaste and a big bag of pepper corns. 'Oh—brillo. Well done, J. I've so been missing pepper.' At the bottom of the box is a small pink bag covered with sequins. I hold it up. 'What's this?'

Jarvis turns from pouring water into the teapot. 'Bit of makeup crud—just in case you feel like a scrub up anytime. Thought we might go out—Rent-mec 'n Rottweiler's got a talent eve on next week.'

'Thanks. I could do with dressing up and letting go a bit. Violin duet with Jake?'

LONDONIA

'Might do, yeah.'

Unzipping the bag I find an untouched purple eye-shadow, eyeliner and a lipstick still in its plastic wrapper, the little round label at the end stating: Fucsia Smile. *Fucsia*. The Gershwin's shop-dame. What pocket was that lipstick stub in? I wind back time in my mind to the point I had left the wrong mec's house. A bright-quarter day but not as warm as now. I recall transferring the thing from the trouser suit to . . . what. Then I remember, a linen jacket that now hangs behind the door.

'Tea,' announces Jarvis placing two bowls on the table. 'Wot you lookin' for?'

I reach into the jacket pockets and rummage. 'Just an old lipstick. I said I'd try and get a replacement for someone and I think *you've* found it!'

I find the battered old gold case and compare. Yves Saint Laurent. *Incredible*. It's the same one, and a good Finder always honours her trades. Maybe this will be a good time to see Iona and pay my trade—however small it is.

'Has a horse-letter-mec passed t-dui?'

Jarvis stops stirring his tea and waves the spoon towards the dresser. ' 'E did. Letter by that coffee pot. Why you got summink t'send?'

'I need to write to Iona.'

'Thought you'd buried all that Cincture stuff.'

'She's not *stuff*. I like her and she might well move out here.'

Jarvis guffaws into his tea. 'Yeah. Likely as Bert goin' to monk-school.'

I take a slurp of tea, ignore his sniggering and fetch the missive. As fate sometimes steps in it's from the very dame herself inviting me to stay as Matthew has gone away with various other elite mecs on a shooting foray in the Cincture-controlled New Woodlands. Assuming I can come she will be waiting for me at the access point on the morrow at eleven, Cincture time. She has also included a Hedgefund headed letter stating that I must be let through for Finding purposes.

LONDONIA

I fold the sheet of paper away into its envelope and soften my announcement by suggesting I will tap Iona for as much stuff as I can return with.

Jarvis grins and theatrically disowns me. 'Yeah. Go. Don't *mind* us in this filthy squalor out here. Enjoy yer pizzin self.'

Capitula 25

The next morn as I emerge soaped, rinsed and dried in a stiff and itchy allinone, a sour-faced dame I haven't seen before stops me.

'Come with me, please, Ms Hoxton.'

I start to protest, politely. 'But I've been allowed through.'

'I know that. And I'm not altogether sure why.' She shows me into a small room, gestures I sit on a beige plastic chair and reads Iona's letter again. 'What are the Finding purposes?'

Then I realise. She's a new staff-member looking to prove something and I just have to go along with it. I describe a few spurious Finding missions and show her the lipstick, hoping she won't confiscate it.

She takes the tube and inspects it, her mouth pursed cat's arse-like.

'Mrs Hedgefund has employed you to locate items such as these?'

'Yes.'

She reluctantly gives it back to me, locates my file and disappears from the room.

A boring but fear-inducing quarter-clockface passes while I study the hay-cart and river painting and then she returns looking mentally deflated.

'You are free to pass through.'

Smiling with relief, I saunter off outside to see Iona standing by a shaw attired in brown, her hair pony-tailed severely and no make-up. I let out a long breath as I reach her. '*That* was the worst access point crossing—or one of them certainly.'

She looks back to the building. 'My letter didn't work?'

LONDONIA

'It did but there was a new job-lust guard there with lots of already-answered questions.'

'So, there was no mention of the Caruso/tunnel incident?'

'No. And I was petrified that there would be.'

'I think I know why. He's been somewhat over-occupied with an operation he performed on the Custodian's brother. There were complications.'

'Good—I mean for him not the brother.'

'No—that's good too.'

'Why the grey couture?' asks Iona as we climb into the shaw.

I describe the steaming room and the argument that had been going on between two access point workers and a Londonian who had called the Custodian a pig-scrote. She smiles wryly. 'So where your trouser suit had gone was of small consequence.'

'Exactly.'

'Well, lucky I brought you another one! I suspected it would get lost in the system.'

As the shaw whizzes on I extricate myself from the grey garment and into the brown two-piece. When re-dressed I decide to tell Iona of Marina's revelation regarding Dr Caruso. After an initial gawping, she sits back, nodding slowly.

'He used to come to the school as the visiting doctor. A lot of the girls got all giggly as we didn't really see men that often.'

'Would there have been a point he might have seen me alone?' I ask.

' . . . You did have a broken ankle, or possibly twisted. In fact . . . yes. He did come back several times to check it. Alone? I can't remember.'

'So, Mrs Caruso will have no idea of this?'

'God, no. She's psychotically jealous of any women who work with him. I'm surprised she let him get away on this jaunt.'

'Hence it was a good idea to get me out of the way.'

'More than.'

I suddenly realise we are not heading in the direction of Iona's house.

LONDONIA

'Where are we going?'

She smiles serenely. 'As I said, Matthew's gone for three days of killing things, drinking and I can imagine what else so I can do what I like. First stop, another café he hates. Hungry?'

'Always.'

The shaw driver pulls into the road-side and Iona takes my hand.

'Good, because we're here.'

We get out and walk down a small side street.

'You'll like this,' continues Iona. 'It's where some of my women's groups meet. Women who want to change things like the beast-boxes in the tunnels.'

We enter the warm, woody room, take a table by the window and order things made of lentils and vegetables.

I down a glass of water and fill it again. 'I thought after the Curtain—the Whiteout, that all this intensive farming stuff would have changed.'

'Remember we have gone backwards here,' says Iona. 'People had started questioning the need to eat so much meat back in the early 20s and many had even become used to a vegetable-based diet. But after the walls went up the advancements diminished—back to meat as a necessity—a healthy diet. *Healthy* . . . have you seen some of the Cincturians? And the Custodian—not exactly an advert for good eating.'

I put it all out of my mind, feast on the food that has arrived.

'How much do you believe what that fortune-teller says?' asks Iona.

I swallow an overlarge mouthful of vegetable crumble. 'Mm. S-orry . . . all of it. You'll have to meet her. It's like being in the presence of well-meaning lightning.'

She smiles at my weird analogy. 'I still can't believe what she told you about Caruso—well, I can but . . . it's so odd, knowing them.'

'I thought you were distancing yourself from that circle?'

LONDONIA

'I am. But it's difficult with Matthew being so strongly part of it. Anyway. Enough of him and them. We need to try and think of other ways to track your son. You said you overheard him on that evening that he had training the next day?'

'. . . Yes. But that could be anything.'

'Well. We have use of a phone and a compi. We could contact every college and training school in the Cincture.'

'We could start this when we get back to your place?'

'After sixteen hours. I have to go to see one of Maddy's teachers. In fact, I'd better get going soon. You could go back and laze about—Bob's there.'

'Actually, I have a small mission to go back to Gershwin's—something for the shop-dame.'

'Can I leave you to fend for yourself then?' asks Iona. 'Here's a purse of Squares to pay with and my pocket-map. You can get a shaw—or walk it's not far.'

'I'll be fine,' I assure her. 'See you later.'

She leaves shortly after and I sit for a little longer thinking of how many phone calls we would have to make and how unlikely a positive response would be. Still, it's a chance.

After paying, I leave and walk Southwards down side streets before turning into a bigger road that I remember from the last Gershwin's visit. A few shops down, I see the café and its small cluster of tables and chairs outside. The smell of coffee inside is enticing but I indicate to the approaching waiter that I am visiting the shop and enter through the saloon doors. The old dame is there stitching something as before. She looks up as the doors squeak.

'Ah—you were in recently, I think.'

'I was,' I reply, searching in my bag. 'You gave me information for a small trade.'

'Oh, yes. The young man. Did you find him?'

'I did. But he wasn't who I was looking for.'

She looks genuinely sad. 'Aw . . . sorry, dear. No. I won't take anything. Can't as it wasn't any use to you.'

LONDONIA

I insist and hold out the little gold tube. 'It's the one you requested.'

She takes it and peels off the plastic cover.

'That's extraordinary . . . how did you find it?'

'It's my job and I'm good at it.'

I turn to leave and she calls out. 'Best of luck dear. Remember, you *never* know what's round the corner.'

A slight sadness returns. How confident I had been when I had left her before with that address. Tea might lift my mood and anyway, Iona won't be back for a while. I choose a faded velour seat and run my finger along the pattern of marble-grain on the round table before me. He could be anywhere. *Anywhere.* Maybe not even in the Cincture. Another country even. Do Cincturians go abroad?

A waiter arrives and takes my order for Earl Grey tea and I sit contemplating the 1920s photographs of dames in slinky black dresses, and jazz bands that had played in old London Town. How extraordinary it would be to time-travel back to those times and see the city as it was then. My tea arrives and I sit back in the comfortable chair. *Forget all the searching and wondering just for a while.* People come and go, and I almost fall asleep in these soothing surroundings.

The grey marble clock on one of the behind-counter glass shelves strikes four—Cincture time. The teapot is empty and I should get back to Iona's. As I prepare to leave this haven the door opens. A couple leave and a young mec walks in to be welcomed by one of the waitresses. She shows him to a corner table near mine and leaves a menu.

He sits down, takes off a felt hat revealing fair curls, and hoists a leather messenger bag over his head, placing it on the seat next to him. The movement pulls his shirt to one side, the collar gaping momentarily. A long thin brown mark is revealed.

I must have made a loud enough noise of surprise that he looks around. I wonder if he might start back, exclaim at the sight of me, but the young brow just furrows slightly over very unusual green eyes.

'Are you all right?'

'Yes . . . fine, thanks.'

He nods and starts to rummage in his bag while I surreptitiously regard him.

'A black coffee and white toast, just butter. Thank you,' he says at the waiter's return then stands up leaving his bag, the hat placed on top of it, to presumably go to the pizzer. Our slight encounter has obviously made him confident to leave his belongings, or maybe there is no notion of crime in the Cincture.

I glance around me, checking who might possibly witness what I'm about to do. Earnest conversation about a sculpture class seems to be occupying the dames on the table next to me, and a little further, a discussion over wallpaper. Me and my actions will be of no consequence.

Sliding over to the bench seat he had occupied, I push the hat away and carefully explore the bag. In a zipped compartment my fingers find a few small rectangular cards. I take one and hurriedly replace the hat as the squeak of the pizzer door becomes audible over the chatter.

His order arrives as he returns and he's then busy with toast and butter while I pretend to search in my own bag in order to read the script on the card: *Fabian Harris: Flat six, Block three, Custodian Towers, Zone Two.*

I dare to take a few glances at him and the more I look, the more he means something to me: his mouth, his nose. . . the words are forming, I'm about to reach out a hand.

'Egad, Fabian!'

My arm muscles stop their brief but possibly portentous activity as a shadow falls across the table. Another young mec is standing next to my son's table.

'Can I join you, old thing?' he continues, in his theatrical voice.

Fabian gestures to the opposite seat.

LONDONIA

'Please. Good to see you, Rusty, but why here? I thought you were out on the Northern plantations.'

'*Father* thought I was messing about rather—well perhaps I was. Wiltingly pretty females amongst the latest batch—after they'd been scrubbed up. Anyway, he's got me a job as manager at the food processing complex down in Battersea.'

'I thought there was a problem with the tunnels to that area?'

'Fixed. Attempted raid from the Pan but it was dealt with pronti! What the devil are you doing now, hm? I ran into your mater in New-Harrods and she didn't seem to be overly keen to spill.'

Fabian plops a cube of sugar into his coffee and stirs methodically. I so desperately want to stand up and shout something loud and angry at this confusing conversation involving a *mother*. Eventually he looks up at his companion.

'Well she wasn't *overly keen* that I decided not to go to Cincture One Academy. I've changed direction from medical studies and am working with a chef.'

I note the ill-covered surprise from the young mec.

'A *chef*?'

'He's not just an ordinary chef, more of a nutrition specialist—re-education in food.'

'So, you're doing a sort of apprentice thing, what?'

'I suppose so, yes. It's a fascinating subject to me.'

'Oh . . . well, I can understand why the old girl looked a bit grey at my mentioning it and all that.'

'We haven't really seen each other since I moved into the flat.'

'Property owner, eh?'

'Hardly. It's a rented garret, five floors up in a redstone block in the *wrong* area. But I'm a free bird in its eyrie. What about you?'

'The parents chopped me off a jolly old floor of the mansion block. Not bad at all.'

LONDONIA

I don't know Fabian, but I can tell he's keen to get away from this high-school acquaintance. He glances at his watch.

'Zut—got to get back to my place. The heating broke down and there's a technician coming to fix it. Great to run into you, Rusty.'

He gathers up his affairs and heads towards the door while I consider my options—run after him or try a calm approach at his residence. The latter. A quick, *excuse me, but*, in the street probably wouldn't be a good start.

After I leave the café, I shuffle through the pages of the map book and realise it's a fair distance on foot. Iona has given me enough Cincture change so I hail a shaw and give the address. After assuring I am well settled, the young mec cycles off Westwards while I mentally dance about with excitement.

After perhaps a quarter clockface we arrive in a street of uniform red bricked Art Deco buildings. The mec turns back to me. 'Number two block, was it, madame?'

I look out and note the metal number above a glazed doorway.

'Yes. This one. Thanks.'

He helps me out and cycles off while I stand gathering as much confidence as possible before taking the steps up into the entrance.

A uniformed mec sits at a simple curved counter watching something on a small television screen. He looks up at my approach.

'Madame?' I'm momentarily silenced by the images on the screen of what appears to be a hanging body surrounded by a cheering crowd. He notices my gaze. 'Yes. I was hoping to get to the rectangle this afternoon but I had to do my colleague's shift.'

My voice seems reluctant to form words.

'. . . R-ight. Unfortunate for you. Could you tell me if Fabian Harris is in, please?'

He pulls an open ledger to him. 'Mm . . . Mr Harris. I think he came in and then left again.'

LONDONIA

My heart thuds.

'Ah, no, that was Mr Welch. He is in. Fifth floor. The lift doesn't work I'm afraid—hasn't for some time. They're all complaining, *especially* people on the fifth.'

The mec's soft, brown eyes and bright smile are engaging, despite his choice of entertainment. I could happily stand and talk with him, gleaning information about the Cincture, but time is precious, and I hurry to the stairs.

Shaking with exertion and nerves, I reach the fifth floor and walk along the corridor checking the identical veneered doors until I reach number six.

Please God, gods, anyone listening, let him be friendly.

The door opens shortly after my knock, and the young mec stands back looking surprised.

'. . . You were in Gershwin's earlier. Can I . . . how do you know where I live?'

Taken aback that he remembers me, I stutter rubbish and then start again.

'I'm really sorry to bother you, but could you spare a little time to talk?'

For a moment, I think he's going to hold the door open wider and usher me through, an expectant expression on his face, but the door starts to close.

'Sorry. Now is not convenient.' He turns away and I hear him speak to someone else in the room. I wedge my foot in the doorway.

'Please—just a few moments. I'm sorry but it really is important.'

'I *can't*. Please leave or I'll have to call the concierge.'

His voice is cold. I know that pursuing this encounter will lead to nothing, at least this time. The door closes and the conversation continues inside—or rather argument. An urge rises within me to listen, make out the actual words but I turn away wondering if I should write a letter, slip back and pass it under his door. No paper . . . ask downstairs? I run down quickly and

LONDONIA

approach the desk. The mec has gone, a piece of paper announcing his absence for a short while. I wait but the short while becomes long. I could 'borrow' his note but there is no pen, pencil, anything. I check my bag—nothing. Pockets—nothing. Just the stub of lipstick, and I don't think a few scrawled words in *Fucsia Smile* would do much to convince him.

Reluctantly, I turn away and walk back down the steps. I'll write a letter at Iona's, bring it back, or ask Bob to post it.

I sit wrapped in a towelling robe on a wonderfully comfortable sofa after a long and luxurious bath. Iona is upstairs reading to Maddy and there has been promise of champagne to celebrate my sighting. Whether Matthew is a boggost or not I think Iona would miss this room if she were to move away. The long windows glint with the sun's last light, rays highlighting the gold-framed pictures, satin fabrics and the ceiling's moulded cornicing. For a moment I see us as young ados laughing over some occurrence at school. Somewhere here in the Cincture. Somewhen lost in time.

My mind-wanderings cease as she comes in and sits opposite me on the other sofa.

'Done. She's asleep after a full-on day. So! Describe him. What happened? Bob's bringing drinks.'

I get to the part when I had reached the concierge's desk when the door opens and Bob walks in with a bottle and two glasses.

'Abergavenny?'

I stare at the frosted bottle he is prising the cork from. 'Isn't that in Wales?'

'It is,' says Iona—'the new fizz zone. Oh—get yourself a glass Bob. You know the suit's away.'

LONDONIA

He nips out of the room, returns and sits next to Iona. I continue the story after a quick re-cap for Bob. He pours the wine, kicks his shoes off and puts his feet up on the low table between the sofas.

'Could get used to this, Iona . . . so, what you going to do next, Hoxton?'

'I'll go back on the morrow and just hope he's more welcoming. I suppose. Any other ideas?'

'Not really. No. I'm trying to imagine it from his point of view. Mind you, I'd've been glad to have been offered an alternative mother!'

'Tricky gossehood out in Londonia?'

'Could say that.'

'But do you miss other things?'

' . . . Sex.'

Iona protests. 'Bob—you know I don't mind you bringing someone back.'

'Yeah—but *he* does, and it's not exactly easy to find anyone anylane.'

'Is gaysterism really that secretive here?' I ask.

'Fuk—yes! S' like they've zipped back into the dark ages.'

'So . . . why not leave?'

'Weirdly enough, we was talkin' 'bout that yesdy eve. At first, after being scooped I was just glad to have got this job—believe me there's others you *wouldn't* want.'

'Vendition,' says Iona, pouring us more wine.

'Auction,' clarifies Bob, '—like a shouting-house only posh with little gold chairs and wine and stuff. Anylane, I was chosen by Mr Hedgefund. It could have been much worse . . . there was this foitling old bitchbag all in furs and pearls. Think she was eyeing me for a sexo-slave but luckily the guv got there. Yeah—s'pose it could be worse.'

'So, what were you discussing with Iona?'

'What it would be like to go back.'

LONDONIA

'Sounds like you're ready to go. Did you realise how you've flipped back into Londonia-speak?'

He laughs. 'I did, din' I? Apex!'

'What would you miss from here?'

'Hot water, clean clothes . . . mind, it's not really possible to go back. Once yer scooped, that's it. Cincture property.'

'What about Cincturians?'

'Oh—they can leave, 'cept none of them would want to—'cept Iona, one day.'

I turn to look at my friend. 'Would you really consider it?'

'I have,' she says. 'And do . . . anyway, I sometimes wonder how long these Cincture walls and rules really will last. Maybe we'll all be out in Londonia one day.'

Capitula 26

I don't think I've ever tried to write a more difficult letter. Sitting at this small writing desk, surrounded by balled up sheets of paper, I sigh and start again.

Dear Fabian . . .

It's so difficult to put my thoughts into words; and to imagine, as Bob had said, what it would be like for the person being approached.

Finally, having done the best I can, I attempt to tidy the bed and go downstairs where Iona is engaged in re-potting geraniums in their conservatory. I note the garden of lawn with a few tidy beds, the sight of such a fertile but veg-less piece of land peculiar to me.

'Why all the grass? You could have some fruit trees—raspberries would do well here, cabbage, leeks?'

She presses the earth around a pink geranium and smiles at me.

'This is as wild as Matthew could cope with. He'd probably pass out if I suggested planting onions.'

'What about you? I think I can imagine you earthing up potatoes and pruning trees.'

'You imagined right. In fact, I've joined the women's horticultural society of Regent's Park. I suspect a few members are quite subversive. There was talk of rogue storing and planting of seeds to stop the main farm-corps taking over everything.'

'Another reason to come into Londonia—grow what you want, anywhere.'

'Well, I'll make do with geraniums for now. So, you're ready?'

'As much as I can be.'

LONDONIA

'The shaw'll be here. Just tell me where you're going in case of . . . I don't know. Just in case.'

Half an hour—Cincture-time later, I'm walking up the steps of Fabian's building again, letter ready. A different concierge is behind the desk: an older gar with sparse ginger hair and a worn, shiny blue suit. I wonder if I can just walk past but he reluctantly pulls his gaze from the television screen.

'Can I assist you?'

'I have an appointment with Mr Harris on the fifth floor.'

He opens the ledger and runs a finger across a line. 'Are you sure you have the right time. He has someone up there with him now.'

'Yes. I am sure.'

'I'll call him to check.'

'It's fine. I know the person he's with and I only want to give him something.'

'You can leave it with me.'

'I'll only be a moment.'

'I really think I should let him know.'

He's enjoying this belligerent exchange. In my mind, I tip the roses from their vase on the counter top, crack it over his balding head and run for the stairs. But instead I lean forward on the counter and give him the big eyes and pouty lips.

'Please don't. You see, it's a surprise. I haven't seen my little brother for years and you wouldn't want to spoil it for him . . . would you?'

An added almost tearful sigh and he succumbs.

'It's over there . . . the staircase. Apologies for the broken lift.'

'It'll be good for my *thigh* muscles,' I breathe. 'Toodleoo.'

I arrive at the fifth floor with said muscles straining and walk confidently to Fabian's door, optimism almost covering the feelings of panic.

Standing there on a precipice between exaltation and chagrin, I waver: letter slipped silently under the door or a rap on its

LONDONIA

veneer? As I bend to execute the former, the door swings open and a young dame stares at me with tearful, red eyes before dashing down the corridor. I step back as Fabian bolts from the door, his voice strained. 'Wait! Felicity . . . come back.' But she's gone, heels clattering on the stairs. '*Shite.*' He thumps the wall then stands, palms outstretched on the shabby wallpaper, head hanging until he notices my presence. Straightening up, he paces towards his apartment glancing at me in the shadows.

'*You* again! Whatever it is you want, I *don't* want to talk.'

He's not going to listen to gentle reasoning so I burn the bridges—completely.

'I have to tell you something. I can see it's not a good time but I only have limited access to here.'

His sullen face becomes a furious face.

I just say it: 'I think I may be your mother.'

Not good.

'. . . Get out!' His shaking finger points to the staircase. 'Leave me alone!'

'Please. Five minutes . . .'

'I warned you.'

I feel furious now too. 'I'm *not* going until you speak with me.'

He's back in the flat and the door is in my face. I hear his voice monotone. Matter-a-fact.

I'm not sure how long I have been here in this room with no windows but constant light. I did sleep: odd sleep of tangled dreams and images, and I have been given food—surprisingly good food, assuming this is some sort of prison.

How I arrived here now seems a blur of images—the smug concierge exchanging his views on prostitutes with a stern

326

LONDONIA

police-mec, a darkened vehicle, an underground bleached-looking place; a series of corridors and two doors that had opened to reveal a metal box. The doors had closed after which the box had moved alarmingly swiftly upwards.

The enforcement mec had looked at me with a condescending expression.

'It's a lift.'

Now I wait in this room alone with thoughts of the Sharks and a memory of Mrs Caruso's television screen announcement. As I'm about to stand and knock on the door, careless of what might happen, it opens. A dame steps in, dressed in a grey uniform that tenuously echoes the present Cincture fashions.

'Madame Hoxton. Please come with me.'

I stand and follow her on feeble legs down several corridors and into a room with a large desk, files and a wonderful smell of coffee drifting from a sliver pot.

'Wait here.' She disappears with a curve of her wide skirt brushing the floor. I sit for some time wondering if they will offer me coffee before torture or prison. Eventually two mecs enter the room laughing as they discuss someone. One, attired in a sand-coloured suit with burgundy cravat sits opposite me. The other in slightly more sombre clothes stands as if guarding the room.

Sand-suit regards me through an eye-glass.

'Madame Hoxton. I am Detective Chief Dawston, my colleague here—Sergeant Willsmore-Brown. Would you like some coffee?'

Thankful that the tantalising scent will become reality, I nod.

'Very much, thank you.'

He pours coffee into a delicate cup. 'Sugar? Milk?'

'Milk, please.' This is surreal. I wonder if a slice of Victoria sponge cake might be suggested next.

He passes the cup over, appraising my person as he does.

LONDONIA

'So . . . you were *visiting* Mr Harris, against his wishes. Soliciting in a public domain—*tut*. And being asked to leave repeatedly . . . Mm.'

Anger rises in me but I control it. Impetuosity won't help. The coffee and polite questions might easily transform into something very different.

Dawson puts down his coffee cup and walks around the table to stand close to me. Reaching out a hand he takes a lock of my hair, smooths it between his fingers.

'There could be further questions, incriminations you understand . . . or perhaps we could decide that it *had* all been an unfortunate misapprehension.' The smoothing becomes a meaningful tug. I look up at him, completely understanding what he means. 'What exactly do you mean?'

Willsmore-Brown steps to the door, his hand clasping its locking mechanism. Just before it turns a sharp knock breaks the silence.

Dawson growls a response. 'Yes—who is it.'

The door opens a crack and a dame glances into the room. 'For you, sir—in your office.'

He drops his hand from my hair, grunts and walks over to the door.

'I won't be a moment, W-Brown.'

His colleague contents himself with staring at me while I wonder how I can extricate myself from a Cincture police duo sex experience.

Dawson is back within moments, his mouth a thin line of annoyance.

'Well, Ms Hoxton. It appears that you are free to go.'

Such is my surprise that words slip out. 'How . . . who said so?'

'I am not authorised to say. A car is waiting to take you. Go into the hall, the driver is there and will escort you.'

Standing up slowly, I edge towards the door as if he may suddenly grab me and laugh in my face, the message a hoax. I want to ask more but it's obvious that the subject is closed. I walk into the hall and follow the swaying coattails of the driver.

I've never been quite so glad to see the church's front door. As I'm about to search out the keys, it opens and Tom is standing there, knapsack over his shoulder, Coal's reins in hand.

'Hox! Merda—have to go. I've got a bod comin with a new rudder for the boat. Yer not goin' anylieu again?'

I kiss him and sigh heavily. 'No. Certainly here for the foreseeable.'

He hugs me and murmurs things that make me forget all the stupidities of t-dui.

I whisper a *see you later* and walk into the church's cool interior. The bass notes of Jarvis singing an old Blues song make me smile. I enter the vestry and the song stops, replaced by a craggy grin.

'Guv in a eel-barge! Was getting right fukin' jitty. Sit—have this tea and gi's the histoire.'

I gladly take up the offer and slurp down the tea and relay him the events.

'But who let you out a'there?' he says, searching in a pocket and bringing out a crumpled bacco-stick.

'Iona. They told me at the access point. She got worried after I didn't return to her place, tried the police department, found out what had happened and—well, suffice to say they have a certain *say so* in there.'

Jarvis sits down, lights the drooping cone and expels a long stream of smoke. 'So, you got to see the young mec but 'e wouldn't parler.'

'My son.'

LONDONIA

'D'ac, *yor* son, then.' Jarvis looks at me wryly. 'How in Guv's greenhouse could you know it to be 'im after a quick sighting in a dingy café.'

'It wasn't dingy—far from it. And it was him. I know!'

'Ça va, ça va—keep yer felty on.'

'Jarvis . . . How could I get back in there and try again, now the police know about me?'

He turns to me, groaning. 'Why didn't you leave *yor son* a note on his door—invite him for tea?'

'I did leave him a letter . . . but he probably ripped it up.'

Jarvis notes my sadness and smiles his most comforting smile. 'I'll think of summink. Finders ain't we? Always a solution, eh?'

Capitula 27

A sevday has passed since I returned from the Cincture. The hurt at being escorted away still burns in my heart and the hopelessness of this ultimate Find crushes my spirit. Mais! It's a beautiful gold-quarter time with strawberries ripe in the garden and frequent séjours to darking do's.

This morn, Tom, Jarvis and I are making St Leonard's ketchup with the pounds of spare tomatoes that the garden has put forth. The jars are running out and I'm wondering if Sardi might have some spare.

As I'm wondering whether to nip over there, a jangle of the gate bell sets the dogs barking.

'I'll go,' I say, imagining a possible message from Iona, or, by some divine intervention, Fabian, or, *God, please no*, Mr Straightfish or one of his heavies. Instead when I reach the door, I am greeted by the sight of Sam the taxi-mec: dreads tied up into a knot, and clothing I wouldn't have expected. I haven't seen him since the night of Parrot's funeral when he was attired all in black.

'I know,' he says, noting my stare. 'Everyone expect me dressed in me suit and topper—not practical is it? Horses to muck out, bodies to be dealing wid, and stuff.'

I wave him through. 'Jarvis and Tom are here. Come and have a coffee.'

'Why you got on a *shell suit*?' says Jarvis, scathingly as we enter the vestry.

Sam flicks Jarvis's hat off. 'Goodly to see you too, man. This my day wear, J. Washes and dries easy. Still going strong from my mate's Dad's 1990s wardrobe.'

'Cuppa,' suggests Tom.

LONDONIA

' 'Nother time. Just passing, vite. I've come for a Finding, H, if yous have the time.'

'What do you need?'

'Want something really special for my dame. Jewellery.'

'Jewellery . . .'

I vaguely recall the name of his lady—something to do with precious stones.

'What's her name, Sam?'

'Ruby,' he says, closing his eyes and smiling.

There—the reason why I hadn't traded those earrings from Iona.

'Ruby? I may have just the thing.'

After searching under the bed, I draw out a tattered box marked *tinned pears* and place it on the table.

The mecs exchange glances, and Sam points a finger at the script. 'She like pears but I was me thinkin' of someting a bit more *celebratory*, H.'

I look at him wryly while taking out the flat velvet case.

'Will these do?'

He opens it and smiles broadly.

'Ruby earrings for my Ruby.'

'Real, and with gold fastenings.'

He holds the red ovals to the window's light.

'I feel it's gonna cost me good this, girl. What your price?'

'Take me into the Cincture in your taxi and make sure I have no trouble getting through the walls and back again.'

'Pas problem—can get you some goodly papers made up too.' Searching in his pocket he finds a small red book and consults a page. 'You free this Thursdy?'

I look at Jarvis. He sighs then nods. 'Yeah, go. Never hear the end of this son stuff otherwise.'

'Sure?'

His grin surfaces. 'Sure.'

'What's the reason for the visit, Sam?' I ask.

'Funeral,' he says, pocketing the book.

LONDONIA

'Wot happens to the bodies?' asks Jarvis.

'Dunno. I just takes 'em to where they say.'

'Why don't they use a company in the Egg?'

He shrugs: 'Some sort of nostalgia I tink. Not many horses in dere—mostly car taxis. And they like me—bit of someting unusual—dreads, top hat . . .'

I hold out a hand. 'So, it's a deal then?'

'At your service, dear lady,' he smiles, clasping my hand and pocketing the velvet box. 'Pick you up early morning, then you'll have de time to do whatever it is 'fore I takes de corpse.'

'. . . Won't it be a tad whiffy by Thursdy?' observes Jarvis.

'Like I say, man, I just the ride,' shrugs Sam. 'All I know is it's a big deal—some important dame.'

The idea of seeing such an event is intriguing.

'If I've managed to do what I need to do, could I come with you?'

He grins. 'Yey, Sam's funeral taxi assistant—like it.'

Capitula 28

The day dawns clear, stars still visible in a peacock-coloured sky as I wait in the courtyard dressed in a moth-manked, but still respectable enough black trouser suit and wide brimmed black hat.

The streets are still quiet, but the trees full of song as the birds herald the start of this bright quarter day; a day perhaps when I will be able to persuade my son that he is just that: my son.

A sudden rush of starlings leaving the nearest plane tree announces the arrival of Sam's carriage. I open the gate and step into the street as Sam slows the pair of gleaming, black horses to a stop. He grins down at me.

'Yo, ready, girl?'

I smile a little uneasily. 'Lovely day for a funeral, and . . . well, ready as I can be,'

'Look goodly, Hoxton. Just the job,' he says, gesturing for me to climb up onto the padded seat in front of the carriage.

We set off and he concentrates on a particularly rough piece of road, the potholes lit up, just, by the taxi's two brass lamps. The flames flicker as the cartwheels clunk into each dip.

'Merda! Just got me new wheels too.'

'It's better once you get onto the City Road,' I say, observing his dark face, screwed up in angst.

We get onto the gravelly but more even route and he relaxes.

'So, you not been to a trad funeral, H?'

I think about the last time I had stood with tears in my eyes watching Parrot's body in the blackened barge.

'Not since Parrot—if you'd call that traditional.'

LONDONIA

'A ting of beauty that—art more than goodbye. No I means formal, hymns. That sort 'a merde.'

'Not that I know of.'

'You not sure?'

'Well not in this life—I mean in Londonia.'

'Ah, your past—that why you want to come wid me today?'

'It's a bit of my past that I *do* want to recover—an important bit.'

'Family?'

'My son.'

'You gotta son in dere?' I relay him the details of my last visit.

'S'pose I would 'a been me a tadly bit suspicious too,' he remarks. 'Maybe not to call dee Sharks, mind.'

As the horse takes a slow bend, I look in the circular mirror attached to our seat that gives a view of the road and the carriage's paintwork.

'Won't they be expecting the word "funeral" rather than taxi?'

'I's all ready,' he smiles, 'have these curtains that we roll from de windows—gold scribin' on black. Very tasty.'

The carriage turns left and then the Cincture walls are before us. I recall all the times of standing under showers and climbing into grey outfits.

'How are we going to get through the cleansing procedure—and what about the horses? I always had to leave Kafka there.'

'You must know they can do whatever dey likes. Anyway, I and the horses is checked thorough every few trips. Have to keep us shining clean.'

'What about me?'

'Look mighty proper to me.'

'They might check.'

'I'll blague them, no worries—got you the pass too, like I said.'

Sam detects my panic and pats my arm.

LONDONIA

'Cool, girl. You my assistant, that all. Nothing gon' happen. Hold dee reins.'

He hops down, unstraps the black curtains and climbs up again. 'D'ac. Here we go.'

Before the walls, Sam pulls the horses to a stop and waits. A pale beam of light from a panel sweeps over us then a mechanical voice orders Sam to walk forward and through into the opening doorway. Metal clangs behind us. Persons appear, ask questions, and snip samples from the horses' manes. I shrink back and bow my head while Sam addresses the mec stepping forward. He examines the passes and stares at Sam for a while. I feel my heartbeat must be audible in this chamber. Supposing they decide all is not as should be, ask me to get down, check a bit more thoroughly?

One mec dressed in a red uniform I remember from a previous visit nods towards me.

'She isn't usually with you. Name?'

Sam sighs. 'Man—we late. You don't want no repercussions from a important Cincture family, heh? It's Anne Beethway, she clean, and she my assistant. Now, can we's walk on?'

Sam's stern face and deliverance cause the mec to hesitate. After perhaps weighing up the various forms of *repercussions*, he waves to someone in the shadows and the next door opens into streets I recall from what suddenly seems a long time ago.

Relief floods through me.

'God in a *box*!'

Sam exhales loudly. 'Merda. Thought we was in for a spot of checking dere. He was peering bit too close to me dreads—don't want no hygiene unit threatening anyting.'

I give him a friendly poke. 'Anne Beethway?'

He shrugs, looking amused as he urges the horses to a trot. 'Told yous I'd blague 'em . . . give me the creeping Jesus, this place. Jarvis said you went in a house here—that right?'

'Two, actually. The first one certainly made me feel uneasy.'

LONDONIA

The slow pace of the carriage leaves me time to gaze while Sam concentrates on his horses.

Few bods are out yet, just an army of street-cleaners, bush-clippers and shaws making deliveries. We pass one of the old tube train stations and I'm surprised to see the contrast to the entrances in Londonia, other than the Vaux-haulers. This one appears to be functioning, overalled mecs busying up and down the stairs with boxes; no sludge of debris and foreboding metal doorway.

'Do the trains still run?' I ask Sam.

He glances back at the activity. 'This mec at de last buryin', he said some dem tunnels still used to reach de plantations.'

'Did he say any more?'

'Said dere's other uses of der tunnels—s'periments or someting . . . look dere, H. Pizzy little house, yeh?'

I think of a magazine I'd found when searching for Mrs Caruso's desires—*Hello!* Dated 2022.

'Buckingham Palace—the Royal Family?'

'S'der Custodian's now—thems in Scots-land—Hey!' He seizes the handbell next to him, shakes it furiously and we narrowly miss a shaw that had pulled out from the pavement. 'Bean-brain!'

I stop asking questions and leave him to concentrate until he asks: 'This address—Custodian Towers, weren' it?'

'Yes. Are we near there?'

'Take me 'nother half clockface, I reckons. How long you tink you be dere?'

Good question, Sam. 'I don't know . . . if he's there, he might just slam the door, or maybe not.'

He hauls out an ancient watch on a chain and hands it to me then points to an ornate clock hanging outside a building.

'Adjust this timepiece to that. When I'm here, has to know their time—St Luke's church by their one and a half this aft.'

I wind the little wheel on the top of the watch, set the hands and pass it back.

LONDONIA

'That gives me what, a clockface here?'

'Exact—you's lucky the death was on dis side a' town, H.'

Sometime later, Sam turns the horses into the street of red brick buildings. I feel a thrum of excitement. This could be a memorable day . . . or not. Fabian might be out doing whatever it is he does; quite likely he will be out, in fact. Hope wavers as we reach the brass door number. Sam stops the horses.

'Gods be with you,' he says.

I breathe out a thanks as I step down.

'A clockface only,' he warns. 'I's gotta grab dat stiff in goodly time, yey?'

'If I depasse it, go on without me.'

He nods, shuffles back in the seat and picks up the book I saw tucked away on a shelf before the horse baffle. I take a moment to calm myself then walk up the steps and in through the glass doors.

First hurdle: which concierge . . . thank God, it's the first one sitting behind the mahogany counter. He looks away from the television as I approach, and points a finger at me.

'You were here before—recently. To see Mr Harris.'

'That's right. Is he in now?'

'Sorry—you just missed him.' He smiles kindly at my miserable expression. 'I think I know where he might have been going though.'

'Really?'

'Well, I don't know about right now but it's the Academy Dinner this evening and he left here carrying a suit-bag.'

'So, he must be going to see a friend before, perhaps?'

The concierge shrugs amiably. 'Possibly.' Someone else swings open one of the glass doors and his attention is taken. Thanking him, I leave and walk back to Sam. He looks away from his book as I approach. 'Son not dere?'

I scramble up and flump next to him. 'Foitling *not*.'

'You want to come wid me?'

LONDONIA

I consider the options. 'If that's d'ac with you. Perhaps you could drop me at a Martindale rank. I'll get a shaw to Iona's—see if she's at home.'

So, half a clockface later I discover she wasn't, or isn't. Nor is Bob.

I'm just sitting on their steps wondering what to do next when I hear the clack of footsteps approaching. I leap up ready to walk swiftly away if it's Matthew but instead I am relieved to see the cheery face of Bob.

He re-groups the various bags he was carrying into one hand and holds out the other.

'Miss Hoxton!'

I clasp his hand with relief. 'Oh. *So* glad it's you.'

'Come in?'

'Please. Is Iona around?'

'No . . . she's gone to a dame's dinner—dunno where. Sorry.' I follow him in and he closes the door behind us, noting my fear. 'Don't look so anxty, Hoxton. Maître's out till eve.'

'Oh . . . good.'

We go into the kitchen and I perch on a stool while he faffs about with fruit and ice and makes two long glasses of something.

'Try this.'

I take the glass and sip at a myriad of perfumy tastes. 'Mmm. A*pex*.'

He raises his glass. 'There is *some* 'vantages to 'ere.' He drinks then puts the glass down with a satisfied sigh. 'So . . . what you doin' at the Hedgefund residency?'

I give him a shortish version of the events after which he sits nodding for a while.

'D'ac. You need to get into the academy truc . . . think I might know a way.'

LONDONIA

It wasn't exactly a fairy coach and horses that delivered me to the event—rather a rattling old bus that had kept to the outer perimeters of the walls, collecting various Ex-Londonians to clear up the debris after the obviously huge event to come. Bob had made phone calls and then had found me a pair of old overalls which he assured me would be the right garb. And they obviously were as I joined, without any fuss, a queue of hopefuls at a designated point and was ushered onto the vehicle along with everyone else grumbling about having to clear up after pizzin' Cincture gosses.

We arrive at the far end of what was Regent's Park according to a gruff mec swaying in the seat next to me. As I regard the magnificent red-brick building now looming before us, a vague memory surfaces. 'What was it called,' I ask him.

'The Orangy—or summink,' he grunts, 'but all that glass stuff weren't there 'fore the Curtain.'

As the bus rolls slowly up a gravel road towards the back of the main edifice I note the frantic movement of black-attired staff laying tables, moving chairs and arranging flowers within the building's elegant glass addition.

The bus stops with a shudder and we troop out to be inspected. A mean-faced dame holding a clip-board picks out bods.

'You, you and you—kitchen. You, you, you and you—garden. You . . .' She stops at me and flips back the cap Bob had jammed on. An icy feeling wanders around my entrails as her eyes do the tour. After a few sweat-producing moments she bends her head to her papers, ticks off something and glances back. 'Serving staff—they're short on numbers. Go and see Mr Grange at the waiting station.' I do as she says and walk to the

LONDONIA

back door, her next chorus of *you's* diminishing under the gravel's crunch.

Mr Grange is a red-faced, limping, leering bastard; the limp probably from drink-induced gout but he knows how to organise his team. I am given a black outfit, shiny black shoes and a white apron—which he ties around my waist himself, hands wandering and breath heavy in my ear.

'Do a good job this evening, my dear and I'll see what sort of *bonus* I can find you.'

Resisting an urge to copy what I did to Straightfish, I listen to instruction then join the Cincture waiting team to polish glasses and cutlery, fetch wine, arrange fruit on platters and tie white tulle bows around a sea of golden chairs.

At sometime late aft we stop and are given a meal sitting at a long table in the main building. I say little, eat a lot and listen to the nearby conversation about the Academy.

'Bella? Did you say it's only the ones who are attending Cincture academy one who go to this?'

'I believe so.'

'And the parents come too—siblings?'

'Just parents, I think. All I know is it'll go on for hours—thank God they've hauled in a load of ex-panners to do the dirt at the end!'

I stuff away a slice of cake and wonder morosely if Fabian is actually attending this foitling event as he seems to be pursuing a chef apprenticeship. A bell clangs; the staff around me finish coffee and drinks and stand up ready for the eve's social onslaught.

Three Cincture hours later, my feet are complaining in these pointed shoes, my hands ache from folding serviettes into elaborate shapes, and I've had to twice dodge Mr Grange's affections in the cellar. And I've *not* seen Fabian. The evening dressed crowd are beginning to sit for dinner in the vast conservatory. Hundreds of candles are lit, and thousands of petit-fours now placed on the silver stands gracing each table. I strain my eyes in the subtle lighting looking for Fabian as I move carefully around the guests offering refills as instructed.

They are all half-way through a cold soup or prawn entrée when I see three people on the other side of the room take their places. Even from here I can tell the body language is awkward, the young mec hanging behind. Picking up a new bottle of chilled white I weave my way over to the table. One of my real Cincture colleagues gets there first and starts to fawn over the latecomers.

'Wine, madame, monsieurs?'

There's obviously an argument still simmering. The older mec looks up from the menu.

'Have you got anything from the new Dorchester appellation?'

'Yes, sir. We do indeed. An excellent white containing notes of apple, and citrus on the nose.'

'Very well. Bring it.'

The waiter notices me hovering keenly, checks the bottle and nods me forward. I pour with trembling hands as I try to peer at the young mec's face behind the fair curly hair that has tumbled forwards as he reads the menu. Of course, I'm not, as far as I know, a wine waiter, especially an emotionally charged one. Moving the bottle too quickly, I knock the dame's full glass. It tips and the wine floods towards her. The head-waiter nudges me out of the way and soothes ingratiatingly, replacing cloth, flowers, etc with magical speed. As I back away I catch the startled expression of Fabian, his eyes fixed on me.

Luckily for me, the incident wasn't reported as the head-waiter had far more to worry about. I continue to carry plates, fetch fresh water, serve cheeses and desserts, while keeping an eye on Fabian's table in case he were to suddenly depart, such was the almost palpable atmosphere of tension around the three bods.

At some point during the time-blurry eve, people start to leave the tables and head towards the main building for—

according to a fellow waitress—a concert of last year's graduate band, awards and a talk on the curriculi for the incomers. I clear plates near Fabian's table and watch surreptitiously as they stand to leave the conservatory. The dame has a grip on Fabian's arm, her face tense, cheeks flushing under the beige powder layer; the mec looking around expressionlessly, checking perhaps who might be observing. The room is nearly empty now. Fabian suddenly pulls away and the mec shoves his chair crossly under the table.

'Leave him to cool off, Angela. I told you we shouldn't have come. Damned embarrassing.'

They walk off into the hall, the dame throwing a steely look after Fabian as he almost runs for the glass doors now folded back, the eve air streaming in. Checking the maitre's eye isn't on me, I pad swiftly to the doors and peer outside. Fabian is pacing furiously towards an oblong stretch of water, its placid surface silvery-grey under the fat moon. I run along the grass paths, feet now blistered in these pizzing shoes. He stops and stands on the stone edging of the water, swaying slightly.

Something *maternal*? causes me to call out. 'Fabian. Stop!'

He turns, steps down, nearly trips.

'YOU! That's *all* I need.' He regards my expression of fear. 'What? Did you think I was going to jump, kill myself in a foot of water?'

The maternal thing turns into a desire to relay an ironic truth.

'. . . You can drown in an inch. *Actually*!'

'Oh, yes? And I suppose there are killer carp in here too?'

'Could be.'

Shadows dapple his face but I think I see an impossible-to-suppress grin lurking. I move towards him.

'Thanks for calling the narks on my last attempt to see you.'

'The what?'

'Police.'

He hesitates, offguard. '. . . Sorry about that. I was having an argument with someone and it really was the worst moment.'

LONDONIA

'Girlfriend problem?

'Not the girlfriend herself.' He jerks his head towards the building. '*She* doesn't approve.'

'Your . . . mother?'

He glances at me, a frown forming. 'She's not . . . well, she is but not really . . .'

'Your mother.'

The silence is huge now. I picture it as a yawning cave, both of us standing at the edge wondering whether to shout inside, afraid of what might echo back.

At last I nudge him. 'Sit—on that bench. Just hear what I have to say then I'll go.'

He sighs, glances at the conservatory, gives me a perfunctory nod. 'Two minutes.'

We sit down and I start without knowing where to start. '. . . I was told by someone that I had a gosse in my past.'

He interrupts. 'A *what*?'

'Sorry—a child.'

'Told by who?'

Scrote. '. . . A fortune-teller.'

I expect him to sneer but he doesn't. 'Okay. But why me?'

I tell him about the birthmark, Iona, everything, more than aware that my two clockfaces is up. The story is sinking in but he's, understandably, suspicious.

'How did you find me?'

I think back to the night we had unknowingly met.

'Do you believe in fate?'

'. . . I don't know. Why?'

'You were kind enough, and drunk enough, to donate a rather good jacket to an unknown dame—woman, outside a drinking house a few weeks back.'

He sits up with a start. 'Yes. *And* I regretted it the morning after.'

'That woman was me.'

LONDONIA

Fabian says nothing, just sits totally still, eyes round, cheeks pale.

'It's true,' I continue, 'and to prove it, I found something in the pocket.'

He starts out of shock. 'What did you find.'

'What might you feel you had lost.'

It's the perfect test and he tries it out. 'You tell me.'

'A silver pocket watch.'

'Describe the initials engraved on it.'

'B St. V.'

He nods slowly '. . . So, you've been stalking me.'

'A bit, yes.'

'But how did you find out where I live?'

'In the café, when you went to the pizz chamber, I took one of your cards.'

'He looks amused. 'The pizz chamber?'

'Why, what do you call them?' I ask.

'Lavatories?'

We both snigger like gosses and the card thing seems to fade in importance. He stops abruptly and peers over towards the glass doors where a dame is striding as fast as her evening dress will allow. '*Fabian*!'

He jumps up and glances back at me. 'Go—now!'

I leave the bench but she's caught sight of me. I stop and wait for the onslaught but it's directed at him.

'*This* is what you are doing instead of listening to the next year planning.'

He draws himself up to his lanky full height. 'I told you. I'm *not* going to Academy one. I already have a training.'

'To be a *cook*!'

'An educator. It's important.'

'You could be a doctor, or a lawyer . . . it's not too late. They're holding a place for you. See sense, Fabian!' I pace slowly away, aware that this could go on for some time. She catches my movement and grabs his arm, points at my vanishing form. 'And

LONDONIA

another thing. You know we have wedding plans for you—don't mess that up too!'

He pulls away from her, runs back to the building. I catch him up just as he enters the doors and harsh-whisper: 'It's true. All of it. Come and get the watch back. St Leonard's Church, Hackrovia. Londonia.'

Capitula 29

'Jarvis?'

'Here.' He sits on the bed in the dim light and holds out something. 'Drink this.'

I sit up, legs cramping, and take the cup. 'Ow . . . what is it?'

'Nettle and raspberry leaf. Jake swears by it fr' flu 'n crud.'

'Have I got flu?'

'Nah . . . knackerdness, maybe the tail end a' someink.'

'What day is it?'

'Satdy.'

'I've been asleep a whole day and darking?'

'Like a pizzed dormouse.'

The recent past returns as my fuzzy mind awakens fully and replays the eve's end which had been exhausting and frightening but thanks to a silver cigarette case I had *borrowed* from the leering Mr Grange I had managed to bribe my way back into Londonia and limped home. Beyond that I recall nothing except complex and surreal dreams.

'So, what did I miss here?' I yawn.

Jarvis stands up and stretches. 'Not much. Usualness—spot 'a trading, took the last of the kits to Holborn shouting-house for a sale on the morrow. Had a violin lesson with Jake, fixed the guttrin' on the outhouse . . . anylane, wot about you, then? Did you see 'im?'

I precis the events to which Jarvis's eyebrows climb to their max.

'You reckon he might come out 'ere?'

'I hope so.'

'When?'

'. . . I don't know.'

LONDONIA

An unusual feeling creeps over me—depression? Supposing all of that effort had been a waste of time.

'Ça va, Kitten?' Jarvis's expression of kind concern knocks me over this emotional edge. Tears fall.

'Hey-o. Hox! S'unlike you . . .' He hugs me and I sob pathetically into his musty pin-stripe.

'Sorry . . . it's just having seen him, and knowing it is him.'

Jarvis releases me and searches for a handkerchief in his suit pocket. He dries my eyes.

'Reckon you need a solid, normal bit a' Londonia-tangible.'

I nod, sniff a bit then brighten. He's right. Garden, sorting stock, a good long dog-hike. After a squeeze of my hand, Jarvis stands up.

'Be outside. D'ac?'

I doze for a while, hearing distant voices from the garden then get up, curious to see what's happening. The church is silent except for the faint, spectral chorus, voices from many long-cycles past. A sudden fragment of familiar swearing cuts into the ghost-sound and I run to open the garden door. Past the rows of vegetables, mulch pens and the boggost I see a swinging lump hammer. Young voices chatter and older voices direct.

'Nah . . . that bit should go there. You—what's yer name?'

'Baahir, sir.'

'D'ac, Baahir . . . see how that rock there needs a little bit just shoved in there . . . apex. Now that brick. Tom, you got the morta?'

'Yup.'

'Crack this boulder will you, and then that'll do for the edging.'

I walk over and stand looking in admiration until one of the gosses sees me.

'Hey, miss. You come t' do walling?'

I pick up a rock and pass it to him. 'I certainly have.'

Tom turns around and love sparks in his eyes. 'H! Couldn't wake you. What happened?'

LONDONIA

'Make me some tea and I'll tell you it all.'

'Will do.'

As Tom walks away, Jarvis gestures to the semi-built wall. 'I'll wrap this up for t-dui.' He waves his arms about. 'D'ac, gang. More on the morrow.'

The bulldog boy I recognise from before gazes up at Jarvis. 'On peut commencer le bassin aussi?'

Jarvis ruffles his hair. 'Bien sur, Cal. Bon idée.'

He watches as they all leap the wall and disappear, laughing and squabbling.

'So, you're going to start the fish pool?'

'Got a willing band 'a workers an' plenty 'a debris.'

'Did you feed them all?'

'Done a load 'a patatas in a fire and a mongeous salad. Some of 'em never eaten green stuff. Reckon your gardening school might be a goer.'

I hug him hard. '*So* glad to be back.'

'Crudish was it?'

Standing back, I smile at my craggy friend. 'Apart from one or two goodly things, yes.'

'Tell us then.'

'Goodly or the merdic stuff first?'

'Merdic.'

Tom appears with the promised tea. 'What was merdic?'

We sit and he hands out the mugs. I sip mine. 'Mm. The vrai stuff.'

'Didn't you have none in there?' says Jarvis.

'Yes, but it doesn't taste as good as when it's served in a cracked china mug with the words, *Lifted from Buck House*, written on it.'

I tell them all about the journey in, finally talking to Fabian and the return trip's last few weary miles.

Tom drains the last of his tea and puts the mug down. 'So! Now you've found him, there's no need to go back in there?'

LONDONIA

His words infuse me with joy. Fabian knows where I am, and if fate is kind to us he will join us. Maybe Iona will too. I don't need to go back . . .

I refocus on the present to find Tom gazing at me intently. 'What?' I ask.

He leaps up then turns back. 'Don't go nowhere!'

Jarvis shrugs at his retreating form. ' 'E 'as been acting a bit weirdy while you been off.'

'Tom?'

'Yeah, I know—unlike Mr, *don't worry 'bout nuffink.*'

The garden door clangs shut and Tom scoots back scattering guinea fowl. He kneels in front of me and I know what he's about to do.

'Hoxton. 'Fore you fuk off somewhere else, or Straightfish reappears, *please* would you honour me with splice-up?'

Before I can reply, he takes my hand, slipping a silver ring onto my fourth finger. He laughs at my expression.

'I guessed the size then.'

Splaying my fingers, I admire the band etched with leaves.

'Where did you get it?'

'Hepping-forrist, when I did the logging. There was a mec in the village who was starting up making jewellery. I did some work for him and traded for the ring. Got one for me too . . . so?'

I note his ardent expression and smile. ' 'Twas a genial proposal and . . .'

'And?'

'Why not.'

'Not 'xactly romantic,' he huffs. 'But it'll do—so, when?'

'End of the golden quarter?'

'A big fete!'

I smile, the thought suddenly enticing. 'A mad one—fancy dress.'

'Apex,' grins Jarvis. 'A yuge feed, gnole, dancing, music and stuff . . .'

350

LONDONIA

Music. 'A piano? Could we get a piano?'

He thinks for a moment. 'Yeah . . . reckon. Remember that gar wot had that trio—piano, double bass and trumpet?'

'The group we saw in Isling-town? Tempus Fugit?'

'That's them, anylane, I saw the bass player in The Exchange trading his trumpet. Told me the piano player got mauled to mort by a panther.' I stare at him in disbelief as he continues. ' 'Ad been a pet, got out, wandered about, bit bleedin' hungry and fancied the piano mec—end of.'

'So, there's . . .'

'Yep, a piano going spare, stocked in a railway arch. 'E said it's good. It'll cost.'

I think of the Straightfish necklace that I thought I'd keep for an emergency trade. Is a piano an emergency?

'Can you send him a pigeon? I've got something that can cover it.'

'Wot you got thet I don't know about?' says Jarvis, sensing a trade above others.

'Gold.'

'From in there?'

'No. From out here—well, originally it was from in there.'

'Straightfish?' he grimaces.

'Yes. And what better use? So, can you contact him?'

'Sure, Kitten. I'll find the mec and we'll 'ave ourselves an eighty-eight on the premises in time for the do.'

Capitula 30

'Someone's at the door.'

I answer Jarvis irritably. 'Go see, then.' It's stinky hot today and I've just wasted a cycle on some bod moaning on about his delayed Find—not my fault that moths got into Fred's darkquarter stocks. Jarvis kindly stops his own task of rudimentary shoe-mending and goes to answer while I crossly strike things off in the list-book. He returns shortly and shows someone into the room.

'A visitor for yer.'

'What *now*.'

The person steps out from behind Jarvis. I stare, not comprehending what I see.

'I don't belie . . .'

My words trail away into silence until Jarvis lets a phrase loose.

'Fuk, you're him, ain't cha.'

The pigeons cooing on the ledge outside the window fill the silence. My lungs feel like soft dough, breath trapped in the gluey texture.

'Well?' says Jarvis, ' 'S bloody obvious to me.'

My breathing starts again in a great rush, the words all mixed. 'How did you, you get . . . why now?'

He glances around the room, eyes wide. 'Well, I do want my watch back. But it wasn't just that—natural curiosity I suppose.'

'So . . . you did believe what I said?'

'It's still sinking in.'

I say nothing, just stare.

'You asked me if I believed in fate,' he continues. 'Perhaps I do.'

LONDONIA

Fate. I stop staring and pull out a chair for him.

'Have a seat and let's consider it further . . . perhaps me taking over from The Lord, and meeting Mrs Caruso was truly fate. These events led me to be outside that drinking house at that particular time.'

'The Lord?'

'I'll explain—it all.'

'Over tea 'n toast?' suggests Jarvis, checking the kettle for water.

Fabian nods a thanks, sits down and looks around. 'I'm really here, in a room, in Londonia!'

'Actually, how *did* you get here?' I ask, still not believing he has just walked in and, that he survived all the possible dangers.

'A shaw to the access point and then I walked. He reaches into his messenger bag and pulls out a book. 'A guard at the gates lent me this.'

'A to Z,' murmurs Jarvis, taking it and flipping through the pages. 'These is rare as an undertaker's smile. Any chance we could keep it?'

'I think I could say it got stolen?'

Jarvis grins. 'Like your style, lad. ' 'Ere, Hoxton, 'ave a scan.'

I take the open book and we study the section showing the whole of central London, as was. In this copy all the area that is now the Cincture has been blanked out; only the dense matrix of roads surrounding shown.

'He said it's an old copy,' says Fabian. 'There are new maps of the interior areas, but nothing of Londonia.'

'Coz none of them come out *'ere*,' says Jarvis, ' 'less on a foitlin' Scoop mission.'

'A lot of this has changed,' I note, running a finger along Holborn High road. 'All those buildings collapsed there, and Lamb's Conduit Street is full of the rubble.'

'The main roads are still clear enough,' says Fabian, 'and people seemed happy to direct me.'

LONDONIA

'Lucky you picked the right'uns,' grunts Jarvis. 'S' lot of persons you wouldn't want to stop and ask anyfing. Anylane, you blend in goodly . . . not too posh.'

Fabian fingers the lapel of his tweed jacket. 'That was easy. I like clothes that have been lived in.'

The kettle starts to shrill. Jarvis makes tea, puts down two cups and walks out from the vestry.

'Just takin' this back to my den. See yers later.'

As he walks away, Fabian looks at me with a confused expression.

'So, Jarvis is your . . .'

'My Finder partner and dearest friend, not anything else.'

I wonder when he might ask *the* question I would be reluctant to answer. We sit for a moment studying each other. T-dui, I have no doubt of the genes mixed with mine. His mouth, chin, cheekbones are all mine, and the slightly almond shaped eyes. Except his are lake-green.

'Tell me about you—everything,' he says, suddenly.

In this room, time is measured by the sun first illuminating the picture of St Sebastian above the door, passing round and finally scattering rose-coloured spots on the flaking wall as the rays pass through the stained-glass window. The patches of pink are fading as I end the story with Tom's recent proposal.

Fabian stretches and drinks down his cold tea.

'That was quite a history for someone who has no memory before about three years ago.'

I smile, a little embarrassed at monopolising the conversation. 'You did ask . . .'

'I did. And it was truly extraordinary.'

Jarvis must have returned at some point and has been quietly moving around from range to sink. A tantalising smell in the air now speaks of his actions.

'Lunch,' he says, in mock Maître d'hôtel style, 'will be served.'

LONDONIA

Placing a board on the table, he brings over the casserole pot and thunks it down; then more delicately, our best glasses and china.

Fabian suddenly wakes from his reverie and picks up a glass, holding it to the light.

'These are beautiful,' he says twisting the vessel. 'Very old. Rummers?'

'You know more than me,' I say, 'Jarvis got them from the Holborn shouting-house.'

'Shouting-house?'

'Auction room . . . that's probably what you would know them as.'

I want his reaction to my tale, but as Jarvis fills our plates, the conversation turns to survival in Londonia.

'You're lucky to have a butcher that sells hare, assuming that's what it is,' says Fabian. 'An underrated meat, I think.'

Jarvis looks at me, stops chewing and snorts a laugh. 'Butcher? I terminated this lovely wiv the Winchester on the scrub.'

Fork poised mid-air, Fabian starts. 'You shot a hare? I mean they're just roaming around?'

'Rabbits is more common, but hare can nip inta yer path on occasion.'

'There aren't many shops out here, and certainly not for meat,' I add. 'We mainly eat pulses and vegetables, and the meat we hunt ourselves. When someone does have spare game, it's often hawked, on carts, horseback, or sometimes in the Spont Markets.'

His brow furrows. 'Spont Markets?'

'Spontaneous selling points that spring up. You might have a trader who decides to set a small stand up, anywhere. Other traders, or anyone who's got stuff to sell, join in—et voila, Spont Market.'

'Is it controlled at all?'

LONDONIA

Jarvis smiles at the thought. 'Nah. Sharks can come if it gets really outa hand. Sponts' been known to start a riot.'

'Sharks?'

'Police from the Cincture,' I explain. 'They make a pretence of extending law out here. It's rarely implemented and Londonia's mostly a free-for-all but the menace of scoop truck raids keep things under control.'

'Ah—peace-mission vehicles,' adds Fabian, wryly.

'Where d'you get meat from, then?' says Jarvis, changing the subject, and taking another chunk of hare.

'Shops,' says Fabian. 'No one goes hunting in the Cincture, apart from the elite. They have assigned jaunts out into certain forests to hunt game.'

'Are all the shops like the hyper-centre ones?' I ask.

'No. Those are for the elite class. People like me shop in one of the Combimarkets.'

'Where d'they get all the stuff?' says Jarvis.

As Fabian starts to tell him about various plantations, the dogs announce someone's entry into the church.

'Heyo!' calls a familiar voice. 'The door wasn't locked . . . any lunch still going?'

Footsteps echo in the aisle, and Jake's standing at the vestry doorway.

'Surely, old friend,' says Jarvis, standing up and pulling over another chair.

I begin the introductions, but Jake gently interrupts.

'Let me guess, Hoxton. Your son.'

My son stands up uncertainly and puts out a hand.

'Fabian . . .'

'Prophet-Jake. Pleased to make your acquaintance.' Jake continues to hold Fabian's hand for some time, finally letting go with a smile. 'So, I think it won't be too long before you leave that place.'

'Leave the Cincture?'

'You find it intriguing, Londonia.'

LONDONIA

'Yes, but . . .'

'Leave him be,' grins Jarvis, 'the mec's only just arrived.'

'Just conveying the truth,' says Jake, sitting down and filling a bowl. 'This looks good. Did you use the lemon I found you?'

'Certainly did . . . was thinking about building us a orangery. What d'you reckon, Hox?'

I imagine the strange assemblage of found windows that it would be, and nod in agreement.

'Let's save the seeds—a small start.'

'Can you just . . . do anything, make anything, out here,' asks Fabian. 'No planning, no meetings.'

'Anything,' smiles Jake. 'Come and see my dwelling later—right in the middle of a park, it is.'

'We could take the dogs up there,' I suggest.

He smiles, his face suddenly relaxed.

'Yes . . . why not. I don't have to get back straight away.'

'What d'you do in there?' asks Jarvis, taking an apple and sitting back, feet up on a crate.

'I'm a nutritionist, well, a trainee one.'

'A wot?'

'An advisor on food. I help people with diet and what to eat.'

'Wot's to advise,' smirks Jarvis. 'You find food an' eat it, no?'

'Maybe in Londonia, yes, but we're talking about the Cincture . . . all the problems that go along with too much choice of the wrong thing.'

'I read that bods were most healthy in the second great war,' I add.

'Apparently, yes,' agrees Fabian. 'Little processed stuff, and of course people grew as much food as they could, anywhere they could.'

Jarvis jerks his head towards the back of the church. 'Like here. Sling an eye over the ex-churchyard.'

'Love to.' Fabian stands up and starts clearing plates.

'Leave that,' says Jarvis. 'Me and Jake'll do it after a game 'a cards. Show him the estate.'

LONDONIA

'I will,' I say, 'but first . . . this.' Going over to the dresser, I locate the pocket watch and hand it to my son.

He takes it with a smile. 'Good to see this again.'

'Have you ever wondered about the photo inside?' I ask.

He opens the back now, studies the scrap of paper and then back to me with understanding in his eyes.

I verify his unspoken question. 'My mother, apparently. And those initials—my father's.'

He picks up the chain and the timepiece twirls, its time-buffed silver glinting. He clasps it again and gestures I take it back. 'I don't remember how I have this but I think it belongs to you.'

I shake my head. 'No. It belongs to you.'

Jarvis sighs theatrically as he reaches for the cards. 'Wotever —just get out there and show 'im some Londonia stuff.'

We leave them to their game and walk into the echoing space of the transept.

Fabian gazes around.

'No one has ever asked you to go, or explain why you have taken this place over?'

'People think I'm mad to live here,' I say, 'and some would fear the ghosts.'

'Are there ghosts?'

'Sometimes whole choirs, but it's never bothered me.' He shakes his head as he walks around examining the marble wall plaques.

'You are an unusual woman, Hoxton.'

'Do you think you might like me?'

'. . . I think it's quite likely.'

I smile to myself. This is so strange, but how should it be when you have first met your son after . . . well, forever.

'Show me this park, then,' he says, turning away from the decrepit picture of haloed Mary.

'With dogs, or horse?'

'You have a horse?'

LONDONIA

'He's tethered in the garden now, but lives with me in the dark-quarter. Come and meet him.'

I open the church doors, letting in a stream of light. Fabian stands on the step for a moment, eyes closed. 'The noise,' he murmurs.

Shutting my eyes too, I try to imagine what it must be like for him, hearing these layers of sound. My dogs whine, emitting an occasional excited bark. Beyond the gate: birdsong, gosses shouting, someone selling firewood. 'Birch, oak, all dry, guaranteed.' A further layer: a fight, a single gunshot, screaming; and further still, drumming—one of the gangs, a strident note from a manoeuvering barge on the river and a distant siren warning of a fire somewhere.

'Yes, perhaps a little different to your usual soundscape,' I say, trying to remember the sounds of the Cincture.

He follows me around to the garden and is immediately scooting up and down the rows of vegetables, exclaiming excitedly.

'These leeks—incredible, and the cabbage, better than vegetables I ever see.' He crumbles some earth and sniffs it. 'So loamy . . . what do you use?'

'Nothing . . . well, us and the horse residue, and kitchen compost.'

Dropping the soil and wiping his hands on a patch of grass, he smiles.

'As it should be. But really, this is quite incredible what you have here.'

'There should be much more than this but the storm made so much damage.'

'What storm?'

I describe the events of that day and eve and remember he would have seen little of the meteorological ferocity.

He's talking to himself now, wandering, planning, 'I think you could grow a peach tree against this south wall, yes, possibly *olives*!'

LONDONIA

Words form in my mind: *Why don't you come and see for yourself?* Supposing he did live here . . .

'Hoxton?'

'Oh, sorry, I'd wandered into a daydream, there.'

Fabian is standing next to Kafka, his face animated, almost like a gosse.

'Is it difficult to ride a horse?'

'Not really, just a lot of practice required, but he's a gentle animal. Have you never tried?'

'I've never even stood near a horse before. The only ones I've seen were at celebrations for the Custodian, the mounted guard.'

'You can ride up to the Parkplace. We'll take all the beasts. Stay there and I'll show you how to put on a saddle.'

A short while later, Fabian is sitting astride the horse as we walk up the high road. It's a good example of an average day in Londonia for someone who has lived somewhere so different.

Passing a handcart drawn by a skinny young mec, Fabian blanches at the smell.

'Merde-mec,' I explain. 'Shit-collectors. Some areas have horses and carts for the bigger collections . . . he's our local one, although we don't need to dispose of it that way, having the veg garden.'

He's silent for a while, possibly wondering what happens to all the merde back in the Cincture.

An excited crowd buzzes on the corner of Bacon Street. A bulky dame is unfolding a card table, her chunky arms flailing as she pushes hands away from two tartan cloth bags. People shrink back suddenly as she draws an ancient pistol from her cleavage.

'Bleedin' stand back, and one at a time. D'ac, I got cats and oranges.'

I slow Kafka to a stop and tell the dogs to be quiet. Oranges and cats have to be worth stopping for. The crowd waits more patiently as she hauls out a mewling kitten and starts her booming spiel.

LONDONIA

'Pure bred ratters. Guaranteed free from plague.' She kisses the mite to demonstrate and grins, teeth as grey as the few, part-submerged grave stones in our garden. 'Oranges sweet as yr best fuk *ever*.'

I hand the reins to Fabian. 'Hold them tight.' Searching in the carpetbag, I find a bag of tobacco and a bottle of gin then push through the scrum.

She spots the bottle. 'Wot's the gnole?'

'Gin, and I've got four ounces of bacco?'

'Verified?'

'On my death. Cat and ten oranges?'

'Five'

'Six.'

She nods, hands over the wriggling scrap and delves into the other bag. Reaching through the sea of arms, I grab the proffered fruit and go back to the horse.

Fabian appears astonished at this street transaction. 'Will that develop into a Spont Market?'

I note other bods approaching with tables and boxes.

'Looks like it.'

Fabian leans down to look at the kitten. 'There's a bit of Siamese in there. Why trade cats? Aren't they easy to find?'

I hand him the tiny beast. 'There was an epidemic of cat-plague about four cycles ago that wiped most of them out. People breed them now and the strong ones survive. My old mogs are more interested in sleeping than hunting now, so, *this* will become the new mouser.'

The kitten crawls up Fabian's front and snuggles into his neck as we continue up the road past small everyday scuffles, impromptu football games and a few deranged people, wandering and talking to themselves.

'We could stop for a coffee,' I suggest, noting a new café, built in the ruins of an old one. 'Just for the experience of comparing it to the one I first saw you in.'

LONDONIA

He looks dubiously at the collection of decrepit chairs assembled outside the window and the equally decrepit collection of people inside and out.

'Is it safe?'

I steer Kafka towards a convenient lamppost and tie him.

'As anything else.'

The new caféist is standing on a stepladder, hammering a nail into the corner of a hand-painted sign. He misses, hits the wood and the sign swings downwards, narrowly missing an elderly dame seated underneath.

'Oi, you young creature, watch my new hat!'

Fabian smiles at he slides off the horse. The red, wide brimmed hat, trimmed with a monstrous collection of plastic flowers is far from new. He looks up and reads out loud the now-revealed, old sign; its green plastic letters faded, one missing.

'S t a r b   c k s? Starbicks? Starbacks?'

I shrug and sit down. 'No idea.'

'Coffee or tea?' announces the mec, giving up on the sign for a moment. 'An' we got a special of 2020 tinned sponge cake, today.'

'What teas have you got?' asks Fabian, taking a seat on an old stool.

The mec stares at him. 'Wiv or wivout milk, quoi?'

I order. 'Two teas, with, and a cake, thanks.'

As we sit, the sun emerges from behind a cloud, illuminating the heaps of broken furniture and boxes cluttered outside the buildings. The red-hatted lady starts to sing, and a small fight breaks out over the road.

Fabian laughs and shakes his head. 'Strange, but despite the squalor, I like it out here. It's like watching a surreal play.'

The kitten has wandered down Fabian's arm towards the table. I scoop it up and stroke the dusty, pale fur. The café owner appears and puts down an Arsenal football mug and a teacup bearing the words: *Happy Mother's Day.*

'Oranges,' I suggest.

LONDONIA

'Three?' he proposes.

'Two?'

He nods and I delve into my bag for the fruit.

When he has gone, Fabian picks up the teacup and examines the faded writing, his face suddenly pale.

'You'll want to know about my parents, then.'

Not expecting this sudden change in the conversation, I turn my chair to face him.

'If you don't mind telling me.'

He starts a little tremulously. 'I was taken away from the first place to somewhere else. I must have been about six. It was very different, clinical, people moving quietly about dressed in white—they did tests on me, physical and mental.' He stops for a moment, possibly reliving something. 'Have you ever seen a pet shop?'

The flow of his story, interrupted, I shake my head.

'It was as if I was on display—a puppy, perhaps. People came, talked to the shopkeeper, in effect, watched me perform and then left. One day a couple came back, asked me questions, signed papers and removed me to a new life.'

'Was it a good life?' I whisper.

The green eyes stare back, wet now.

'I think you could say a privileged life, but I left as soon as I was able to.'

'Why?'

Our cake arrives and we goggle at the peculiar mass of beige crumbly substance in a chipped blue bowl.

I hand him a spoon. 'You were about to tell me why you left.'

He digs the spoon in and tries the stuff. 'Mm, unusual . . . yes, the main reason was my *mother*.'

'You didn't get on?'

'I realised fairly soon that she didn't like me. I always had the feeling she wanted a girl but that perhaps my father had insisted on me, or I was what was on offer at that time . . . I don't know.'

LONDONIA

'Did she hurt you?'

'Not physically, but she made me fear her. I never felt comfortable with her, couldn't regard her as my mother. Can't, actually.' He shakes his head slowly. 'You saw an example of our contact the other night.'

'Did you ever think of trying to trace your real parents?'

'At the home, we were told that could never be possible, so other than thinking about it, I never tried.' Fabian finishes the last bit of pudding and pushes the bowl back. 'Anyway, back to now—I ought to be working out how to return to the walls.'

'I can take you back on Kafka,' I suggest. 'As I said, you were lucky getting here.'

'Is it really that dangerous?'

'For the inexperienced, yes, and not just from Londonians.'

'From who else?'

'As I mentioned—scoop trucks. It's unlikely but after I saw a raid recently . . .'

'Was anyone you know taken?'

'No. But many were and will probably end up working for the likes of your adoptive parents.'

Fabian sips at his tea, one eyebrow raised at the taste. I wonder why he hasn't asked about his *other* parent. Perhaps *I* am enough to deal with for this encounter. I so wish him to turn to me and say something soppy but definitive like. 'Well, I've found my real mother now and,'—sigh—'it's time to come home'. But he doesn't and I wonder, with an ache deep inside me if I have expected too much.

Capitula 31

The peak of golden quarter-heat has truly arrived, the days long and stifling. These past few sevdays I've totally immersed myself back into my Londonia life: trading food we have grown and helping Tom and Jarvis with our trout pond. The wall has been finished with the help of the ado-gosses, many of who said they will return with their siblings on the eve of the fete to show what they had made.

The Straightfish necklace was put to goodly use and we now own a tuned piano, or will when it's delivered. I had caught a wink of light from the gold as the mec had greedily pocketed the thing. He probably got a ridiculously good trade but I turned my mind from it, happy to be no longer reminded of El Capo.

This morn the pond's still water reflects the blue of a cloudless day. Kafka has knocked part of the roof-tile rain-collecting chute and I'm patching it with new-found mortaring skills. Jarvis hops down from the, *him-and-Tom* old bicycle aeration system they've concocted.

'Reckon a couple a long-clockfaces a day'll keep enough oxy circulating—good fer the fish and fer us, eh?'

I dip a hand in and swirl the clear water. 'So, now we just need the trout . . .'

'Parkplace, I reckon. Trout, tench, dace . . . whatever's edible. But not too much. Don't want no fish-bickering in there.'

'D'you think this weather will last 'til the morrow?'

He looks up at the one solitary puff of a cloud drifting above the plane trees.

'Jake reckoned it would . . . so, the Joanna arrives this aft— better start working on yer set for the do, eh?'

LONDONIA

I give him a wry grin. 'Set? More like a catastrophic, crudic one tune. What about you? Going to play?'

'Yeah—me an' Jake got a few duo bits and the Goracy Potatoes said we could join in if we want for a jig 'n that.'

'Oh—can't wait to see them again!'

'Did a rough gestimate last darking . . . should be about a 'undred bods 'ere.'

'I hope they'll all bring stuff.'

'Think they will.' He catches my sudden change of spirit. 'Wot, H.'

'I was just thinking about the invites I sent out to Fabian and Iona.'

'You haven't heard nothin' back?'

'No. I didn't really expect to. But I had hoped to have heard something from Fabian about his situation and perhaps moving out here . . .'

'Aw—come 'ere, H.' He envelops me in a big brotherly hug and my happiness re-bounds.

'Lunch? Got some of that weird nettle pie Tom made . . .'

'Sounds sound. Where is 'e, anylane?'

'He went to see Bert about a telescope he said he'd got in.'

' 'S true one hasn't turned up in a shouting-house. Bert'll want sumink fer that!'

'Is he coming to the fete?'

'Corse 'e is. Imagine Mr-the-Swagger passin' on easy booze?'

'No . . . not really. I'll get the pie. Pick some tomatoes, would you—the yellow ones need eating first.'

I wander into the cool of the church thinking of Fabian. There's nothing else I can do. Going back in there is not an option, mainly as I don't want to, but who knows what information might be now at the access point. Better to stay a long way away . . .

Taking the pie from the icehouse in the crypt, I cut two slices and take them back with a jug of water. Jarvis is lounging like a suited-lizard in the sun.

LONDONIA

'Don't you want to put a pair of shorts and a thin shirt on?' I suggest

He sits up and squints at me from under his hat brim. 'Nah . . . might strip down t'me vest if it gets too much. Anylane the 'omburg keeps it off.'

We eat and discuss the fete until the gate-bell sounds.

Jarvis leaps up. 'That'll be the pi-ana. Could do with Tom bein' 'ere.'

We scoot to the door. The instrument has arrived, strapped down on top of a cart, a crowd of bods around it, all suggesting ways of getting it off. I open the gate and Jarvis starts adding to the cacophony with talk of planks and wheels and rope. Tom appears with a lumpy sack over his shoulder and a grin on his face.

'It's here then?'

'I'm glad you are too,' I say, eyeing the sack. 'I can't bear to watch the piano's descent. Can you help, and I'll take this up to the platform—assuming it is what I think it is.'

He swings the sack down and unfurls the top. 'It's a Celestron—Bert said they were good. Came all the way from Canada at some point.'

I take the bag and head back to the door, calling back: 'It's a clear sky . . . we could look this darking!'

'Apex. Should be almost a fat moon.'

I take the platform stairs slowly, careful not to thump this precious piece of technology against the wood. I push the door and it creaks open letting a blast of warm air into the musty stairwell.

Placing the sack under the lean-to roof, I gaze around at the city before me. I haven't been up here for some time and the view has changed from bare trees and distant humps of dark hills to a thousand different hues of green. Nearby roofs have been patched after the dark-quarter, chimneys repaired and similar platforms to ours constructed for the velvety nights that are now with us. A few glassy, sky-touching buildings have disappeared,

LONDONIA

leaving new vistas to gaze upon; new distant spires. Perhaps someone might be looking at St Leonard's now from some Southwards church, wondering who might be standing on that roof structure, looking out across Londonia. To my right, the vast copper walls of the Cincture glimmer in the late aft sun. Somewhere in there my son is working, or walking, perhaps planning his escape.

'Oi, Kitten!' Jarvis is down below, hat off, red-faced. 'We got it through the church. Just gotta get it on the stage.'

'Be right down,' I shout. 'Deux seconds.'

Downstairs, I round up any available drinking vessels and a big jug of water and go out to watch the heaving, sweaty action of pushing and lifting an iron-framed piano onto the small stage area. I sit in the shade of the pear tree and try not to imagine a splintering and creaking of wood as the instrument lurches and disappears Titanic-like. After an impressive burst of swearing the clapping starts. I stand up and dare to look.

Our black and once-shiny piano now sits on the rough boards.

'Gi' us a tune then, H,' grins Jarvis.

I climb up, sit on the stool and rub my sweating hands.

Will the music still be in them, and my mind? Limbering up with scales, I find my small personal library to be vaguely intact. Tom drains his mug of water and leaps up onto the stage to listen. I feel his amazement and decide to try the Ravel piece that appears in my mind. It's ropey as l'enfer but I know it'll come back. I hazily recall the process; the fingering, deciding where the nuances should lie; how I would interpret what the composer had written. After the last notes shimmer into the heat haze, I sit for a while, hunched, just staring at my blurry reflection in the wood. Jarvis returns with a palm tree in a large pot. Huffing, he drops it to the ground.

'Gift from Angelo. To go with the piano—cocktail bar feel, he said.'

'Is he going to come and play on the morrow?'

LONDONIA

'Yeah. And he's bringing others.' His expression morphs into serious as I take the music from the stand. 'You must 'a practised a lot—back somewhen.' He nudges me off the stool, sits and whaps out a manic improvisation, a caricature of the most flamboyant concert pianist.

Tom reappears grimacing at the fracas.

'Aw—stick to the strings, J.'

Jarvis stops after a flourish of chords and snaps the lid down. 'There, that'll drive out any woodworm wot's lurking.'

Capitula 32

The dusky sky is clear apart from a small pack of clouds chasing each other nose to tail behind the silhouetted plane trees. A Louis Armstrong melody starts up from the new garden area as Angelo tries out my piano, the notes vibrant in the still air.

Sardi and I are washing salad and spinach while her gosses play in the pond—I decided to get the fish *after* the fete. Excitement thrums within me and not just from the thought of the eve to come. Sardi has organised a priestess from the New World-Light Church to undertake Weldage for us.

'What time will she arrive—the honourable Madame Jabari?' I ask, with slight apprehension.

Sardi bundles up a bunch of leaves into the metal salad dryer and whirrs it around.

'Don't you be worryin', H. She'll be here—sometime. For *sure*.'

Someone taps me on the back. I turn, shaking droplets from my hands to see Jarvis grinning. A branch rests across his shoulders from which two ducks hang, their neck feathers iridescent blue in the warm light.

'Got these at the marshes. Tom's making a spit, so if I can get 'em plucked, along with the pig, there'll be enough meat.'

'Give me a moment to get jins on and I'll do it with you.'

Jarvis fetches and lights three hurricane lamps and we sit ripping feathers, listening to the jazz group practice. At last, with aching fingers, I fill hemp bags with the soft piles and label them for trading. It's dark now as Jarvis washes the ducks and takes them to Tom to spear onto his spit. Sardi and I bring out the pies and cakes, baskets of plums and apples and beer she has been making. We arrange it all on a long table near the new wall as people arrive with more scran.

'Where you want de vittles?' asks one of our ancient Jamaican neighbours, showing me the contents of a vast casserole pot. 'Me special goat curry.'

My stomach growls at the sight of such spicy-looking food. 'Wonderful—over there, please.'

I follow him and gaze at the array of foods that people have managed to produce with their limited resources—bean stews, treacly-topped cakes, real pizza loaded with summer vegetables, onion tarts, skewers of roasted and glistening . . . somethings.

'Thems not rats, is they?' says Sardi staring at the twisted forms.

I pick one up and study the head. 'Hope it's not mole . . .'

Jarvis runs up. 'Leave *that* an' come an' see this!'

I follow him back to the church where a small crowd of gosses have gathered.

'Coaka, over there,' he shouts. They all turn and disappear into the garden at the suggestion of the sacred drink. Jake is crouched on the floor placing paper wrapped objects back into a large, flat box.

'What are they?' I ask, picking up a red one attached to a stick.

'Fireworks,' he raises his arms, spreading his hands. 'You know—woosh, bang, sparks and colour?'

I recall an image of black sky filled with blossoming silver stabs of light . . . from a book? No, a smell lingers in my mind too.

'So, you saw a display, sometime, eh?'

I shrug. 'Maybe I did. Maybe not . . .' The Cincture seems planets away—inconsequential this darking.

'And it doesn't matter, does it?'

'No—not at all.'

He pats me on the cheek. 'Let's get these set up, then.'

'Where'd you find 'em?' asks Jarvis picking up the box.

LONDONIA

Jake grins, hooded eyes even more hooded than usual. 'I helped a mec . . . big help. He couldn't . . . perform.'

'Musician, was he?'

'No, not like that. You know . . .' Jake thrusts his hips suggestively. 'He was so ecstatic that he gave me these—said they were representative of what he felt like when he . . . Oh, hello.'

We follow his gaze that now rests on a plump, blonde-haired dame standing in the doorway. She stares at Jake's movements, her expression unreadable.

'Salut, Marina,' I say, 'Glad you could come.'

She observes me with her pale eyes. 'I have present for you. Come.'

Leaving the two men with the fireworks, I follow her out into the garden to where she has placed a box on a bench.

I suddenly realise that we never agreed a trade for her first delvings into my mind.

'Marina . . .'

She stops me.

'Ça va, Hoxton. I was to ask you for new coat, but client gave me good one. There is no debt to pay. Open box.'

Untying the string, I fold back the cardboard flaps. In the bottom, asleep, is curled one of her tiny greyhounds. She lifts it out and into my arms.

I thank her profusely for such a special gift and she acknowledges my pleasure with a small nod before turning to walk away. She stops and looks back at me. 'Be guarded this darking.'

I stare back at her. 'Why?'

'I don't know—is just feeling. I wish now to see man called Jake.'

I smile at her retreating form and feel glad that Jake may be once again with a dame. Glancing down at the nestling puppy, I wonder if Zorro might share his bed.

The vestry is calm, the excited rumble of the party reduced to distant laughter and music. Zorro opens his amber eye at my approach and stretches a paw lazily.

LONDONIA

'Hey, old feline,' I say, testing his mood. 'Fancy a bit of fathering?'

Placing the tiny form in the folds of the blanket, I step back to observe.

Zorro sniffs the invader, shuts his eyes and repositions himself for further sleep. Assured, I sit for a while on the couch, reflecting on the cycles I have spent within these walls and elsewhere: peaceful now, the past no longer a half-submerged question. A slight apprehension haunts me this darking, however: Marina's words perhaps. The dream of green eyes seems to have melted away recently to be replaced by a raging voice and thundering waves. I push these thoughts away and think of dancing, eating and celebrating our Londonia lives.

A duck feather drifting down from my hair reminds me I am still in jins and shirt, and that my *merger* gown awaits.

Standing up, I cross the room and study the dress draped over the brass eagle lectern. I brush my fingertips over the cream silk and wonder about the gown's original owner. Had she been excited by the prospect of a ball or her own splice-up, waiting impatiently while the maid fussed with pearls and hairpins?

As I step out of my jins, the vestry door opens. My prickling apprehension leaps into fear.

'Hey, H,' laughs Tom, striding over. 'Those eyes—as big as a barn owl's. What you so fearful of?'

'Nothing,' I murmur, hugging him.

The new dog sits up in his box and growls like a tiny storm at Tom.

'Where's that rat-headed truc come from?' he laughs.

'That,' I say, 'is an Italian greyhound called Satie. Marina gave him to me.'

Tom frowns a little. 'Petrified you with stories, has she—bad stuff to come?'

'She's extraordinary, Tom. Not someone to take too lightly.'

'So, what she tell you then?'

'She just warned me to be on guard.'

LONDONIA

'We always have to be *on guard*.'

'Oh—I don't know what she meant . . . anylane, let's enjoy this eve.'

The door opens and Jarvis stands there, resplendent in a black pin-striped suit, trilby and dark glasses.

'What you two goin' as?'

'City business-mec,' says Tom, locating his suit hanging behind the door and showing it to Jarvis.

'Sharp,' remarks Jarvis. 'Got a hat then? One of them round, black ones.'

Tom reaches up on top of the wardrobe, takes down a cloth bag and pulls out a bowler.

'Mec's didn't really wear them much,' says Jarvis. 'Not like these.' He lifts off his trilby and brushes some dust from it.

'But then no one wore *them* much after the 1950s,' I add.

'Why though,' asks Tom.

'Fashion, I suppose—like they still observe in the Cincture.'

Jarvis shrugs. 'You wearing that beige number, H?'

I lift the dress down and step into it carefully. 'It's not *beige*!'

He leans forward and fingers the fabric. 'Holy creeping beetle! That's fine stuff—where d'you find it?'

'That sale in the costume house in Actonia.'

'Wonder who wore it,' muses Tom. 'Someone with meg-splosh, for sure.'

Reaching for the feathered headpiece sitting atop the bust of Beethoven, I smile at the two mecs.

'Well, let's go then.'

Our reclaimed land is filled with people dressed in a fantastical collection of fabrics and clothes from across the past: flapper girls, firefighters, ballet dancers, lion-tamers and silver cloth for imagined space voyagers.

'Well, looky over there,' grins Jarvis, pointing at the red cape of Bat-mec-Jake, which is now partially draped over Marina, her hair bright against the bark of the apple tree.

LONDONIA

Up on stage, the early darking jazz has ceased. The band descend the steps in search of refreshment and the Goracy Potatoes take their place. After a tune up, the black haired-dame waves her arms, gesturing to the dancing area. 'Allez—tous!' She looks over at the accordionist and he outlines the melody; their drummer clicks: 1-2-3-4 and a wild jig erupts, bringing gosses ado-gosses, the young and the ancient onto the sunbaked earth.

I circulate, catching up with old and new friends, admiring their costumes, laughing at the more bizarre: Bert as a dame of ill-repute in corseted dress and false mamos; the bread-mec as a vampire with slick-backed hair and red-lined cloak. Sardi comes to join me in her hand-constructed leopard outfit. I stare at her. 'Me-*ow*. Seen any prey that might *interest* you?'

She points at the lovely Able, for once not covered in flour and this eve disguised as a rock-star from the glitzy age sometime back in the late twentieth century. 'Wouldn't mind him unzipping those golden boots in my sleeping quarters.'

'Excellent choice, Sardi. I'd grab him . . . I'm sure Jerome would understand.'

She smiles cheekily and sashays off towards Bread-mec junior.

The eve must be the hottest yet this grand-cycle, our pond now a mire of muddy water, full of bods dancing and splashing. Just as I'm thinking of something to drink, someone nudges me and I turn to find Jarvis holding two glasses of fizzing wine.

'Champagne? Well, nearly—cava. Bert found it. Dated 1998 and still downable!'

I take a sip. It tastes of gooseberries and the raspberry sorbet I had tasted on Straightfish's boat on that now-distant eve.

'Wot, Kitten?' asks Jarvis, noting the slight shiver passing through me.

'Oh . . . nothing.'

Suddenly I wish to be away from the crowds, to see the expanse of the sky.

'Would you like to sit on the roof platform for a while?' I suggest, knowing it must sound mad.

LONDONIA

He runs a hand over his pin-striped chest. 'Don't want to get my suit all messed up.'

'You won't. Remember, Tom re-did the top stairs. It's all clean up there now.'

'Could do then, just for a tadly. Got my eye on a certain mec . . .'

'I don't want to hold anything up.'

'He'll keep, and you're more important. Nothing like acting a bit nonchalant, eh?' He takes my glass. 'Just get us a refill—catch y' up.'

Leaving the throng, I walk back into the silent cavern of the church and check on the animals. Fagin and Tilly are curled up in a pile of eiderdowns. Kafka and Coal brought in from the garden for the evening, stand chewing hay. The rustling stalks and the dogs' breathing are the only sounds in the church: no ghosts this darking.

As I enter the vestry, Zorro leaves his bed and bumps his head against me in greeting.

'Nothing edible in here,' I say, scratching his head. 'Plenty of mice though.'

The new dog is still asleep in the box. 'Satie,' I murmur, looking down at the fine, grey fur. The small head rises at the word. 'He only wore grey velvet—Satie.' The head drops again and Satie sighs as he regains the cat's warm spot.

Taking the hurricane lamp, I walk over to the dark mouth of the stairway. Made cycles ago, the wood of the staircase has moved and reformed, choosing its own settling place. The stairs groan as I climb upwards, the silk of my dress catching on splinters.

'Merde!' *Jins would have been a good idea.*

Halfway up, I stop: footsteps? 'Jarvis?' He doesn't reply. I shrug and smile at my imaginings as I continue up the stairs.

At the top, I push open the door and step out onto the platform. A rumble of thunder faintly vibrates the planks. The absolute beauty of the night catches my breath. Never was the

LONDONIA

sky so densely black. Stars hover in an arc. I stand transfixed, imagining people from other times wondering what the unmoving sparks were. The magnitude of the world touches my heart.

Lifting the silken folds of my dress, I sit and drink in the sights before me: the neverness of the sky, the tiny lights of a warmer colour that dot the slumbering city—candle-lamps, fires, other gold-quarter fetes; the ice-white lights dotted atop the Cincture walls and the dull glow of burnished metal beneath them. And here, the light and colour of our own celebration of warmth; troubles cast aside for one darking. The crowd bobs, hands wave, sound drifts. I see Jarvis, two glasses held high, nodding and joking as he weaves a path back towards the church. I can also just make out Tom's lanky form by the wall in front of the pond, its dark water dimly illuminated as a haze of green at one end. He's in animated discussion with someone—no, not one, more people. I strain to see, catching a flash of red on one face. They could be Clashers. The crowd turns as one shoal of fish. Jarvis has disappeared.

A small sound from the doorway causes me to turn and clumsily stand. A figure is framed in the doorway cloaked in a highwayman's costume, perfect in every detail down to the tricornered hat. Thunder growls, a prologue to the coming storm.

'Hello?' My voice quakes unnecessarily. This is just a friend with a good access to clothing . . . Fred, of course. 'Salut, Fred. Enjoying the soiree?'

'Absolutely. But not Fred.' The voice is familiar but not one of a friend. For a moment, I think it could be Caruso advancing towards me. My speech flounders. 'Who . . ?' Then I know the voice as he continues.

'Straightfish the highwayman. Has a certain ring, eh? Heard about your little fete and thought I'd call in. Sorry not to have brought anything . . . Oh, but I have.' From the folds of his coat he draws out a flintlock pistol.

I back away, glancing behind me. *Nowhere to run.*

LONDONIA

'No one's coming,' he adds. My lads are down there making sure and the gangster has been . . . *waylaid*, you could say.'

'Jarvis! *What* waylaying?'

'Nothing terminal, I assure you. He was distracted by one of my assistants—a handsome lad.'

Relief surges momentarily within me, making me careless.

'Why are you here. Surely I made myself clear with that bottle?'

'To simply offer you a choice, Angel—*and* you're wearing the right outfit for it.'

'. . . I don't understand.'

I scan the roof, snatching at ideas of escape but he holds the gun and I stand at the edge of a platform with a drop that would end my life. The silk of my dress billows from a sudden gust of wind. I feel dizzy.

El Capo smiles. 'Sit. Let's look at the stars.' He waves the gun towards the planks. 'SIT.' I obey and he follows, arranging himself cross-legged, the gun tantalizing, close. He feels my intentions. 'Ah-ah. Forget that.'

'So. What's this choice?' My voice sounds so tiny up here, lost within the thundery atmosphere.

'Truth is, Angel, I have someone in the Cincture who tells me that a certain plan *didn't* go to plan.'

'*Caruso?*'

'Yes,' he says casually. 'My brother. We don't see a lot of each other but keep in touch—he's a useful contact for trade in there.'

There's no time to assimilate this bizarre information. I manage a, '*So?*'

'He wants me to finish the job—so to speak.'

'I see. And the choice?'

'Back to my own plan that you intervened in with that bottle of very good cognac. To put it bluntly. Weld-up with me instead of the logger, or I'll just have to carry out big brother's wishes.'

LONDONIA

I start to shuffle away wondering what I might land on if I were to just roll off the edge. He pulls me back.

'You won't do it, Angel. You're hoping I'll just change my mind. I've seen it . . . hm, maybe a thousand times—"you wouldn't really do that, Mr Straightfish, would you?" *Wouldn't I?*'

'They'll hear the gun.'

'Who said anything about shooting.'

With his free hand, he reaches into a pocket, draws something out and holds it up: a syringe, its contents glowing gold-green in the moonlight. The needle is long and sharp. I imagine the brief pain if it were to enter my skin.

A groan of thunder sounds, nearer now. The moon's light winks out as a monster cloud devours the dappled sphere.

I hardly hear the noise of the crowd below. All my senses concentrate on that glass vial. I need time. Someone will come.

'What is that?' I ask, politely as if at a lecture on chemistry.

'Could be time to find out,' he smiles. 'Don't worry, it's pronto—although a tadly agonising at first. So. This, or Sheppy Isle, hm?'

Booming thunder now surrounds us. Lightning snakes from the clouds as they cover the stars. Voices from the crowd below rise in apprehension.

Amongst the tangle of sound, I hear something else. A crow, jostled by the wind flaps across the platform whipping my attacker's face. He starts, raises his hand in fear, drops the vial. He swears and twists to reclaim it. I turn hearing another sound behind us. A figure stands next to the spire. The next blaze of lightning reveals it to be Jarvis.

The moon appears briefly, its light glinting on the two glasses he holds. On seeing me, he casts them away; a tinkling sound lost in the theatre of the encroaching storm.

He's summed it up. His hand reaches into an inside pocket. The light folds up. I am in blackness again, praying that Straightfish won't sense him in the shadows.

LONDONIA

Surrounded by darkness, Jarvis bumps into the telescope. It keels over, metal crunching into wood.

El Capo springs up from me, spins around and lunges, grasping at the watcher. As I scrabble for the dropped syringe, a flash as bright as daylight reveals the cylinder rolling towards the edge. I stretch out, fingers splaying madly as the two figures crunch down on the floorboards, fists flailing. I can't see who to strike out at, where either gun might be.

Then one mec is standing as the other's cry is lost in the crowds below. In the next burst of light, Straightfish glowers down at me, his mask gone.

I am alone: Jarvis, gone? Thunder cracks. Voices shout. Then the rain starts.

'Jarvis? JARVIS!'

Straightfish grins: 'Dead. Now *you*.'

I flounder in wet silk. He moves towards me through a waterfall of rain, the gun a silver streak. All else is blackness and creaking trees. Then a vibration thrills through me, a sound of four paws thudding. My assailant yells as he is knocked sideways. In a lightning flash, I see white fangs and the mottled coat of Tilly. El Capo raises his pistol.

I shriek into the blackness. 'TILLY!'

He fires into her chest. Blood, steam and smoke choke the air.

Wrenching myself up in the clinging fabric, I hit out at the Vaux-hauler as he struggles out from under her limp form. He grabs my hands and twists them until I scream. I call for Fagin as Straightfish closes the gun to my forehead and presses the soaking metal hard.

'Goodbye, Angel.'

As I squeeze my eyes shut, waiting for the brief agony, another shot pierces the rain's hiss. A bullet clips Straightfish on his extended arm. His fingers unfurl and the pistol drops. He staggers backwards, breath creaking, arms outstretched. His blood spatters my face. I taste it and retch. Tripping forwards, I

LONDONIA

push him hard. He tips-regains-tips and I shove him again with every atom of my strength against the church spire. He mouths silent words as his gaze drops to his chest where the ragged tip of a green metal spike has now emerged. He slumps, caught, arms twitching. His eyes are still bright; a twisted smile sits on his face as he looks back at me.

I stride to him, grab a clump of his hair, pulling his head back. 'Why didn't you just take the fukkin' message?'

A last broken few words emanate from his drooping head. '... Credimi ... I tried.'

His words have ceased. I say nothing more, just watch the rain trickling from his hair.

The planks vibrate again, now with human footsteps. Jake, his ridiculous red cape flapping runs over to me.

I seize his shoulders, and cry into his face.

'Jarvis ...'

He pulls me wordlessly to the platform's edge and I look over.

A circle of hissing lanterns reveals a semi-flattened yew tree, a large gathering of bods and the belligerent form of Jarvis cussing and stamping while someone assesses the damage. Even above the clatter of voices I hear his, strident in anger.

'Kill the fukka, kill him I will!'

I scream through cupped hands. 'NO NEED!'

My legs quake as I move back from the edge. Jake takes my arm and leads me away to the door. I pull back, wanting to see that Straightfish really is *gone*. We stand together looking down at the body. I feel numb, unable to move. The rain is ceasing; clouds drift and the moon's light reveals the redness of El Capo's blood against the coppery green metal.

'What is that?' I ask, abstractly.

'Lightning conductor, I think,' says Jake. 'Must have broken —should be longer.'

Something so monumental has occurred yet we talk as if we are discussing a small change in the garden: a stunted tree, a bird's nest. We stand for perhaps the length of a song, watching as the corpse slips further, flesh giving way to metal.

I turn away, suddenly terribly cold. Jake leads me away speaking softly.

'Practical clothes, a bath if we can heat the water.' I stare blankly at the dark hulk of Tilly. 'Don't look,' he says, gently. 'We'll fetch her down.'

'What about *that*?' I say, jerking my head towards the figure slumped against the spire.

'Mutapigeons—they'll do the job. Allez.'

My dress drags wetly on the stairs, and I tremble uncontrollably, legs not cooperating.

'Ça va?' asks Jake, following behind.

'Just,' I whisper. 'Jake? Where's Tom?'

'. . . I don't know, Hoxton.' His voice is odd, distant.

'I saw him fighting, earlier.'

Jake says nothing and I continue down the steps, almost tripping over the fabric, tiredness filling my limbs. We reach the vestry and I stop, realising the hum of voices and music has ceased.

'The fete?'

'Over. Rain saw to that—*and* we had visitors. Vaux-haulers and a few Clashers.'

A clunking sound issues from the room. Jarvis is crouched by the range, raking ashes.

'Hox!' He stands up with difficulty.

I stare at his tattered suit. 'Anything else damaged?'

'No, just a fukin' load of bruises. Yew tree saved me.' His expression twists into something grim. 'Is 'e really dead?'

'Dy*ing* in certain agony,' says Jake, handing me a felty from the wardrobe.

Dragging off the wet silk, I wrap myself in the woollen garment. Its ginger colour reminds me of my faithful hound, now no longer. I slump down into a chair.

'Jake, could you bring Tilly down?'

LONDONIA

'Surely,' he says, draining a glass of wine. 'She, unlike some, deserve more than mutapigeons.'

A howl from the depths of the church resounds: Fagin, looking for Tilly. I whistle and he lopes in, ears down. Somehow, he knows. Picking up the new dog, I introduce them, hoping the great-hound won't regard the tiny form as a passing meal.

Jarvis spreads a blanket on the floor. 'Here, Fagin.' The dog obeys, collapsing with a grunt. The newcomer follows, tail like a metronome. He leans in close and there seems to be no objection.

The rain is heavy again and I suddenly remember the piano. 'Jarvis. The piano.'

'Sorted,' he says, throwing a clutch of sticks onto the new flames. 'Angelo got it covered before the storm.'

'Jarvis?'

'Kitten?'

'Why didn't Jake know about Straightfish?'

Jarvis grins as he gets up. 'Bit overloaded, his mind was.'

I recall his cape wrapped around Marina.

'Love?'

'Sure as the Thames has pike in it.' He shuts the fire door. 'In fact, can I kip on your sofa?'

'Your place is occupied, then?'

'Well, bad night to 'ave to walk back to his hut, or The Barbican, eh.' As if in answer, thunder vibrates the loose glass in the vestry windows and rain lashes again. 'If Tom don't mind?' he continues.

'Of course not . . . where is he, anylane?'

Jarvis looks towards the door. 'Dunno—thought he was clearin' up with Sardi 'n the others. I'll go and bring 'im in—could do with a game 'a chess after all this crud. Yeah—beer 'n chess.'

LONDONIA

He limps off, and I pour myself a small glass of eau de vie from the nearly empty bottle on the table, knocking it back with a gasp at its eye-watering strength.

For no particular reason, I stand up and leave the room, the steady rain replaced by the ghost choir's voices. I stand in the transept looking around its shadowy walls. The rumbling bass chords of the organ crescendo suddenly, threatening to shake the roof and dislodge its unwanted guest.

Going to the side door, I peer out into the night. The thunder is rolling off elsewhere, rain ceasing. A whisper of real autumn has infused the air. The remaining lit lanterns gleam through the pear tree's branches, the last fruits clinging bat-like.

Tomorrow I will pick them and make a trade for a new tree to watch over a dog's grave.

Closing the door, I return to the vestry and sit by the fire watching the twigs whiten and collapse in the heat. Straightfish's last words already haunt me. I wish so much I'd never taken that necklace to him.

I'm almost drifting off when I hear voices in the transept.

'Yeah—that's it. D'ac, few more paces.'

The door opens and Jarvis staggers in supporting Tom. I leap up and help half-carry him to the bed.

'Where the pizz have you been?'

He groans as he collapses onto the mattress. 'Inna fukin' ditch!'

'What ditch?'

'One next to the pond. Bastard Clasher clobbered me and I was out like a babe.'

I sigh with huge relief. '... *Merda*, Tom. Could have been so much worse.'

He sits up a bit and grins his familiar grin, mud flaking from his face. 'Yeah, right—and he'll have a headache himself on the morrow—wacked 'im good and hard.' He looks at my dress that has been stained with Tilly's blood. 'So sorry 'bout the weldage, H.'

LONDONIA

'We'll do it—soon,' I say.

'If you haven't changed yer mind.'

'I'll need Mimi for a few dress-repairs. Otherwise, ready when you are.'

Capitula 33

'*Chantelle? Chantelle! I have called you three times now. The governess will be arriving soon and the servants need to clear the dining room.*'

'Coming, Mother.'

I sit up, wrenched from sleep, and gaze on peeling blue walls. Not lilac wallpaper. Jarvis stands at the sink. He turns around, eyes wide, mouth open.

'Hox?'

I blink blearily and recall the odd sound of my voice still playing in my ears. He waits for me to answer, but I am momentarily distracted by the fact that he is nude apart from a pink mohair cardigan and holding a large bouquet of white roses.

He follows my gaze. 'Yeah. Couldn't find my robe . . . You called out—weird, it was.'

The dream is still intact, unlike most that on waking disappear, leaving only faded remnants.

'I was . . . Chantelle, sitting in bed, reading, in a lilac-coloured room.'

'Vrai?'

'Mm-hm.' I focus sleepily on the flowers. 'Where did they come from? NOT . . .'

'Nah—course not '*im*! Messenger this morn—and 'ere's a note wot came with it.'

He passes it to me and I open the little envelope to read Iona's now-familiar writing.

LONDONIA

Dearest Hoxton. So sorry not to be able to come to the wedding. I'm sure it would have been far more original than your other one! I think of you very often and will get out there again—one day perhaps permanently. I assume your Cincture Finding activities have ceased at least for the moment—I don't know about Beccy et al as I have broken communication with them. Feels good!

Your loving friend, Iona.

'Hox?'

I glance up from the letter. 'Hm?'

'There's sometruc I need to tell you.' Jarvis looks at me, apprehension in his eyes. 'When we went up to fetch the dog . . . Straightfish was gone.'

'Gone? But he was dead.' The daylight seems to flicker and dull, my words as loud as gunshot.

'Couldn't na been mutapigeons, or king-rats. They'd 'a left bones at least. And it would 'a taken a nib a' time.'

I shake my head, unable to absorb any more strangeness. 'Where is Tilly?'

'In the garden. We's dug her a grave.'

My sleepiness falls away. I pull on clothes and join Jarvis to walk outside to the back of the garden. The hole they have dug has made a perfect oval in the turned soil. Marina hands me a bowl of roses and I approach the grave. Tilly has been placed as if running, the wound carefully covered. Fagin lies amongst the red currant bushes with the new tiny dog. He watches, ears down, a low, moaning growl creeping from his massive frame.

I say some words of love for my dog, scatter the roses, then walk away as Tom lifts the spade to shovel the first earth onto her body. Marina takes my arm.

'Come, sit here. You should eat.' She has placed the left-over foods from last eve on the long table. I sit down wearily, staring at the slices of pie and summer fruits, not able to imagine feeling hungry ever again. She fills a glass of wine and puts a slice of

LONDONIA

mixibeast pie before me. I fork it miserably, knowing normally I would have happily devoured the whole thing.

'Eat. You must,' she reiterates and I obey her matriarchal tone.

When I have finished, and pushed the plate away, she puts a hand on mine. I expect her to mention the mysterious vanishing of Straightfish but she surprises me.

'There are new rooms open in your mind.'

'I don't know if I saw something from before,' I muse. 'Or if it was an imagining.'

'I think you make new memory. Perhaps chink that opens in mind-clearing process. Did you see her?'

'My mother?'

'Ya.'

'No, but I heard her voice and the noises of a house that I think I recall.'

'Perhaps later when all is . . . settled you may wish to search more answers.'

I sigh, the weight of the day too heavy. 'I don't know. It seems unimportant now . . . only Fabian and Iona concern me from in there.'

'Konechno,' she says. 'I thought you should know.' I lean over and kiss her expecting a slight cringe but she kisses me back. 'I think you need *big* expanse, ya?'

And she's so right. Sea or a mountain or a deep gorge—but Lady Thames will more than suffice.

I saddle up Kafka and slip out from the church unobserved. We gallop down to Billy's-gate, sun on our backs, rain an odd memory from last darking. After tying Kafka up on a marshy weed-patch, I roll up my jins and sit on a rock, toes wriggling in the squishy mud, watching Londonia bridge's usual slow traffic of mules, bicycles, camels and bods traversing this great grey-brown, never-ceasing water.

I turn and glimpse the curving edge of the Cincture's copper walls and think of Fabian. I smile, recalling our shared laughter and stories of our separate pasts. How very strange that our two lives had been just a few miles apart all that time.

Maybe a cycle passes, or more. The sunlight now reflects from the Pointy-Thing's vicious knife-like top floors—part destroyed and sheared away after the dark-quarter's hardest storm. The thought of my beloved, solid church fills my mind and I stand up to return home.

The vestry has been tidied, all the fete stuff cleared away and the chores dealt with. Jarvis welcomes me in and makes me eat fried eggs while he mends his suit ripped from last night. After a short while he growls at the tangle of thread.

'Scrote to this.'

'I'll do it later,' I suggest. 'You did everything else!'

His craggy face beams. 'Apex. Hate fukkin' sewin' . . . aside —d'you know Bert left you a note?'

'Last night?'

'Yeah. 'E was pizzed as a dog-fart but kept on at me to give it yer.'

'Oh. Where is it?'

'Beyond the stuffed squirrel.'

I leave the egg-remains and find the note. He was indeed gnole-wrecked but it's just about legible.

'Seraph. *Need* to ~~watch~~ see *you*. Come on morrow or *approx*. Amour. *Bert*.'

'You goin' there now?' asks Jarvis lighting a battered cigar.

'Think I will. There's Findings to be done with him, so I might as well . . .'

I pack my carpet-bag, get Kafka ready and lead him out into the street. As I'm about to climb up, my blurry-party mind recalls I haven't stashed a trade for Bert. The street's quiet. A

LONDONIA

mo won't matter. I go back in, find eggs, tomatoes and beans and then bump into Sardi as I leave the vestry. She smiles happily, makeup smudged.

'Never did get back.'

'Unzipped those boots, did you?'

She nods. 'In your veg shed. Hope you don't mind!'

'Is he still here?'

'Able . . . nah. Bread called. But think we might be doin' it 'gain soontime.'

I hug my friend. 'Goodly for you, Sardi.'

She hugs back then steps away looking at me with a serious eye.

'No sign of Fabian then?'

'I suppose I'd hoped he might turn up at the fete with a suitcase, plonk it down with a beamy grin—"*Mother. Here I am for good!*" But that was more than naive. He needs time to think it over. And he knows where I am.'

Sardi smiles and strokes my face. 'He does and I reckon he knows where he'll fit in best . . . d'ac, better rizzel back to Unc and th' brood. Where you ofta, H?'

'Bert's.' I smile at her expression. 'I know—has to be done.'

'That ol fragter. Be wary, eh.'

'I can handle him and his persuasions!' Then I recall the abandoned Splice-up. 'Oh . . . Sardi. I wanted to ask if you think the priestess would come back soon with the Gospelers? We want to do the Weldage before the weather turns.'

'If you can vital-em all . . . reckon anytime would be goodly. Just a tadly bit of notice.'

I recall my horse out in the street. 'Merda. Got t' go—thanks —see you soon.'

Downstairs, Kafka is still safe, in fact more than safe. He seems to have become the subject of a small group of gosses all clutching pencil and roughly hewn notebook. Their teacher nods at me. 'Just a quarter cycle?'

'Nosudor. Take your time.'

LONDONIA

I sit on a doorstep and watch them scribbling away, little faces tense with concentration. I wonder if Fabian ever sat in the street and drew a horse. Probably not. When they've finished, one of the boys presents me with a picture of a surrealist sausage with four stick legs. I thank him, promise I'll stick it on my wall (which I will) and ride off down Brick Lane towards Black-Lake.

Within a quarter clockface I'm facing the gates of Bert the Swagger feeling the usual creeping apprehension. Charged with Finding a certain bit of a rotavator speedily, Bert is the best option. *Unfortunately* . . . Then I smile, recalling his costume of the fete eve, the heavy rouged cheeks teamed with his mangy beard. *Aw—he's d'ac, is Bert,* Jarvis always says. But then Jarvis isn't a dame.

The heavies aren't at their post but the Doberman-wolves strike up a howling that causes Kafka to rear. After calming him, I reach for the metal rod hanging from the gate top and hit the bell. One of the mecs appears from the back of the hangar faffing with his belt. He notes me and waves after shooing off the hounds.

'Deux seconds. 'Ad to take a pizz.' He slopes over and unlocks the gate. 'Monsieur Swagger ees in ze back section—là bas.' He points to the hangar.

I nod, reluctantly and slide off Kafka.

'Oui. Tiens . . . I take ze horse.'

'Merci.'

I unstrap the carpet bag and walk into the gloom recalling the sordid transaction for those foitling phones; hopefully fresh eggs and vegetables will be sufficient for what I need this time. He must eat after all.

I follow the whistling to the recesses of the building and find tweed-attired Bert engaged in sorting through a cupboard of metal bits and obviously not feeling the effects of last darking's booze. He turns at my footsteps and gives me the whole gold smile.

'Seraph!'

LONDONIA

'Salut, Bert.'

'You look . . . ravishing. As ever.'

'Hardly, in these clothes.'

'Indeed—the silk was a little more elegant but lumberjack shirt and patched jins have a certain . . . *allure*, n'est-ce pas?'

'If you say so. D'ac . . . have you got the part I was looking for? I have to be getting back.'

He advances, wiping his hands on a cloth. 'Would you not wish to stay and sample a very good gin?'

'Not t-dui, thanks, Bert.'

'As you wish. Alors, I do have what you require here.' I wait for the following *but you must know that these are rare,* but it doesn't happen. Instead he hands me the cleaned chunk of metal. 'Voila. I think you'll find your client will be *ravi* to acquire this.'

'. . . Wonderful. Thanks. So . . .'

'The trade? This time—nothing.'

I stare at him as he smooths his strands of hair.

'*Nothing*? Why?'

'Just a small gesture of goodwill.' He gestures to an area of tweed above his heart. 'I do have organs other than the one I misguidedly asked you to make an acquaintance with, you know. It was such an unfortunate end to that formidable fete last darking. I'd like to offer some small mote of comfort for the hound-loss—no trade required and please accept these. He delves within the cupboard again and brings out a paper bag. I look inside.

'What are they? Onions?'

'Tsk, my dear. Semper Augustas—or near enough. Magnificent striped tulips brought in on a barge. I exchanged them for eight feet of heavy chain link.'

'But don't you want them?'

He gestures in the direction of his stilt hut. 'Not much of a garden. I thought you could plant them at Tilly's grave . . .'

Then it clicks; he's saved these specifically—for me and in memory of Tilly. This is so out of character. Or is it? Maybe I

LONDONIA

was always too busy worrying about where his wandering hands might go.

'... I'm not sure what to say.'

'The pleasure is all mine,' he says, bowing, his carefully flattened hair flopping. 'And now, someone is coming to have a tooth *evicted* so, I'd better say pip-pip.'

He kisses my hand and I curtsey absurdly in my jins before leaving the hangar. I wonder at the surreal event that has just occurred. Thanks to it, or Bert, or the sun, my mood has lifted completely to one hundred percent *me*.

I smile to myself, stow the metal whatever-it-is onto Kafka and scramble up shouting out a last thank you. He waves as he leaves the building and heads towards his stilt-hut, dentist-hat about to be worn.

We pass through the back streets where bods have started the serious business of protecting their dwellings for the approaching dark quarter—neighbours holding ladders, re-cut slates and planks being lifted onto the patched roofs. Remaining crops of tomatoes, peppers and aubergine are being harvested from communal patches and the talk I overhear is of storing vegetables, sauces, the new best location of firewood; mending feltys and acquiring new ones. The amber quarter is still to be enjoyed but just as the other Londonian animals do, Londonian humans must start the hivernal preparation.

Back at the church, I lead Kafka into the garden and find a sunny day's laziness pervades, jobs put aside and dark days still a long way off. Jake, Tom and Marina have joined Jarvis in playing cards and the sounds emanating from the pond suggest Sardi and brood have decided to come back.

As I brush down Kafka, I mention the industrious activity in the nearby streets. Jarvis groans. 'Morrow—we'll start. T-dui ... s'too foitling ...'

'Paradisiac?' I suggest, sitting down.

'Yeah—that. How di't go with the old bedswerver?'

'Weirdly, wonderfully good.'

LONDONIA

'Eh?'

I describe the meeting and he scratches his head. 'Tad too much sun?'

'No, I think he was genuinely moved by Tilly's demise. And perhaps some guilt about knowing Straightfish . . .'

'Ah—seen the rare flip-side 'a Bert,' he grins, 'Told yer. 'E's not *just* a walkin' tallywacker. '

Jake fans his cards and slaps them down. 'How's *that*!'

Jarvis throws his to the table. 'Merda—playing pokes with you is scrotey—got all the moves in yer 'ead.'

Marina quietly slides her cards together. 'Who wish to have scran?'

As everyone choruses a yes, she stands, summoning Jake to help.

'Lost mec,' notes Jarvis with a smile as they walk over to the door.

'Found mec,' I say.

'Yeah—p'raps more accurate.'

Food is being brought out. I pass plates, then go to tell Sardi that it's filling the brood time. She smiles up at me from her seat on the warm stones of the pond-surround.

'Be along in a tadly—just getting the littley used to water.'

I return to the table, take a plate and we sit discussing the turning year, the goodly trucs and the grim; the happiness that has passed and the happiness to come.

As I lift my glass of wine the aft sun glints on the ring Tom gave me a few sevdays back. I put my arm about his shoulder. 'Thought I might scoot up to Fred's later—see Mimi about the dress.'

He gulps a mouthful of blackberry wine and turns smiling.

'Impec . . . Jake? D'you reckon this weather'll be with us for the foreseeable?'

Prophet-Jake stops discussing pickling whelks with Jarvis and Marina and listens to the garden sounds. 'Blackbirds might say to get shuft-on with your weldage plans.'

LONDONIA

'Satdy, two sevdays time, Tom?' I suggest.

He takes my hand and kisses it. 'Deal, Madame Finder.'

A silence settles as we pass bread, fruit, cheese and slices of glorypye. The sun warms my back and my thoughts drift unintentionally towards the roof and what happened up there in the storm.

Jake refills my glass with pale apple wine and squints at me through a beam of sunlight.

'D'you believe in spirits, Hoxton?'

Pausing, I think of my ghost choir. 'I have no reason not to believe. Why?'

He says nothing but glances up to the church spire then back to the table.

'Time for a little music, I think.' He picks up the violin that rests in its case and Jarvis passes him the bow. The first sweet notes are lost in a sudden gust of wind. Crows flap and disperse from the plane trees. Leaves spiral down. I feel a shiver pass over my skin as I remember the dark-quarter's long eves, and perhaps the arrival of a new ghost in my church.

Jarvis leans over and strokes my cheek. 'Wot's the grim face for?'

I smile back, and the thought vanishes as quick as the wind's ceasing.

Glossary

Some words and terms for readers who might pick this book up in another time (or not Londonians)

A plus—see you later (French)
Abt—shortened from à bientôt (French)
Allez—let's go (French)
Alors—so/right (French)
Anytruc—anything
Babriana—mess (Polish)
Baden-poked—rape, (Londonian origin)
Bedswerver—from Shakespeare, meaning unfaithful
Branz—more value than silvers
Ça va?—is it going/you okay? / Ça va—it's okay/I'm okay (French)
Chaudy—warm and cosy (French-ish, from chaude)
Clashers—Londonia's most feared gang
Clockface—minute/hour
Coaka—brown drink of varying contents
Cycle—element of time, approximate to the old hour/year depending on the situation
D'accord/D'ac—Okay/all right (French)
Darking—anytime during and after dusk
Death-cart—Large wooden horse or man-pulled cart (depending on collection) for bodies
Dechet—(to take a) crap/poo
Felty—cloak-like recycled woollen garment

LONDONIA

Foiteling/Foitling—general Londonian swearword, origins not known
Fragter—one who creeps up on persons
Freeforall—occasional and spontaneous giving away-events held by benevolent, richer members of Londonian society.
Froidly—cold (from Froid—French)
Genial—brilliant, wonderful, great, nice (French)
Glorypye—fruit tart of anything available
Glorys—coins with an element of gold
Gosses—kids (French)
Great-hound—mixture breed (possibly London zoo input) but BIG with overriding greyhound genes
Hepping-forrist—large area of woodland known for supplies of brilloak (best firewood)
Homono—homosexual (also, gay-way/gayster)
Hooch-stick—tobacco mixed with any sort of found drug
Jins—jeans
Jubberknowls—oldy English for bastards, twats, idiots, etc . . .
Knapper—generic term for garment made of boiled down wool
L'enfer—Hell (French)
Mec/Gar—man, guy, bloke (French)
Merda—shit (Italian)
Mirror-Dame—Fortune teller
Mixibeast—rabbit/squirrel/hedgehog pie with potato crumble top
Moonfull—month
Mutapigeon—result of the common pigeon feeding on streetpeeza for cycles
Nippering—to be pregnant (to be in nippering)
Nosudor—no sweat
Orjordui/t-dui—today (French-ish)
Parler—to talk (French)

LONDONIA

Pepedi—Italian-ish swear word
Psubraty—bastard (Polish)
Putainfuker—'coagulation' of French and English
Rammaas—collect/pick up (French-ish)
Recule—to go back from something (French) but mainly used as 'withdrawing' in a male sexual context
Saaffend—island off the south coast
Salut—Hi there/hello/bye (French)
Sevday—week
Shouting-house—auction rooms
Silvers—ancient money system useful for very small trades: drinks, etc
Snash—rare and sought-after oblivion drug concocted from marsh weed and absinthe
Somelieu—somewhere
Sometruc—something
Streepeeza—dubious peddled food, often circular breads containing food and non-food
Swagger—someone who combs the Thames mud for objects to trade
Toot-sweet—straight away (French-ish)
Troove—find (French-ish)
Truc—thing (French)
Tue—kill (French)
Tuffard—tough and hard
Va—go (from French)
Vrai—true (French)
Weld-up/weldage/splice-up/spliceage—marriage
Zaraz—soon (Polish)
Zeitporn—any type of pornographic written/illustrated material causing more than a sharp intake of breath